Geraldine Jewsbury (1812–1880) was born in Measham, Derbyshire and moved with her family six years later to Manchester. The mother's death in 1818 caused Geraldine's older sister, Maria (later and better known as the novelist 'Mrs Fletcher'), to manage the household until her marriage in 1832, when Geraldine was left to look after her father and brother. Geraldine was educated partly at boarding school in Tamworth and later in London, where she learned drawing and became proficient in Italian and French.

Despite her domestic life, Geraldine Jewsbury found her way into the heart of Manchester's cultural scene, forging friendships with the Carlyles, W. E. Forster, G. H. Lewes, Lady Morgan and the novelist and actress Charlotte Cushman. She was known amongst her circle for her outrageous and 'unladylike' behaviour—smoking, cursing and wearing men's clothing; perhaps modelling herself after her literary idol George Sand. The novel *Zoe: The History of Two Lives* began in the early 1840s as a collaboration between Jewsbury, Jane Carlyle and a mutual friend, Elizabeth Paulet. Joint production was discarded when Jane Carlyle expressed her misgivings over the 'indecency' of the novel; Jewsbury went on to complete the manuscript alone, and it was published in 1845. A year later she began contributing to *Douglas Jerrold's Shilling Magazine* and then went on to review for the *Athenaeum*, and to read for Bentley publishers. *Zoe* was followed by *The Half Sisters* (1848) and *Marian Withers* (1851).

After her brother's marriage in 1853 (her father had died thirteen years earlier) Geraldine Jewsbury finally felt free to move to London—partly to be near her good friend Jane Carlyle—and to attempt an independent life. *The Sorrows of Gentility* appeared in 1856, and *Right or Wrong*, her final novel, was published in 1859. In addition she wrote two children's tales, contributed to two biographical memoirs, and was invited by Dickens to contribute to *Household Words*.

Geraldine Jewsbury moved to Sevenoaks, Kent, in 1866; in 1880, finding that she had cancer, she returned to a private hospital in London, where she died.

The *Half Sisters* is forthcoming from Virago.

GERALDINE JEWSBURY

ZOE

THE HISTORY OF TWO LIVES

Published by VIRAGO PRESS Limited 1989
20–23 Mandela Street, Camden Town, London NW1 0HQ

First published in Great Britain in three volumes by Chapman and Hall 1845
Virago edition offset from Chapman and Hall first edition

Introduction copyright © Shirley Foster 1989

A CIP Catalogue record for this book
is available from the British Library

Printed in Great Britain by Cox & Wyman Ltd, Reading, Berks

INTRODUCTION

"It is a wonderful book!—Decidedly the *cleverest* Englishwoman's book I ever remember to have read." So wrote Jane Carlyle in February 1844, having just read the manuscript of *Zoe*. Enthusiastically revoking her earlier opinion that the book seemed "an extraordinary jumble of sense and nonsense, insight beyond the stars, and blindness", she hurried with it to the publishers Chapman & Hall, who with similar enthusiasm immediately accepted it. The author of this work, which was to achieve such a *succès de scandale*, was the stormy and unpredictable young woman whose vagaries caused Jane so much concern and exasperation during the twenty-five years of their now famous and much-documented friendship, and whose writing embodies many of the tensions of her age, which she herself experienced both personally and professionally. Geraldine Jewsbury's own life, like her fiction, is a mixture of the conventional and the unconventional. She was born in Measham, Derbyshire, in 1812; six years later the family moved to Manchester, where her father set up as a merchant and insurance agent. After her mother's death the same year, Jewsbury's older sister Maria, herself a writer of some talent, managed the household until her marriage in 1832, at which point the younger girl took over, keeping house for her father and her youngest brother, Frank; when Mr Jewsbury died in 1840 she continued to act as Frank's housekeeper, and only in 1853, having seen him settled in marriage, did she feel free to move to London and set up her own independent establishment.

It would be wrong, however, to suggest that Jewsbury's spirit, like that of so many unmarried women of the time, was crushed by her early dedication to domestic duties and to the well-being of male relatives. She possessed both the determination and the vigour of personality to challenge, if not wholly to escape, many of the limitations of contemporary female lifestyles. After a somewhat piecemeal education, partly at a boarding-school near Tamworth and partly in London, where she learnt drawing, French and Italian (in which she became proficient enough to be recommended as the translator of an article by Mazzini), she found her way into the heart of Manchester's cultural scene; as her friendship with the Carlyles developed, and she made frequent visits to London, she became acquainted with other well-known artistic figures of the day, including W. E. Forster, G. H. Lewes, the novelist Lady Morgan (whose memoirs she later edited), and the actress Charlotte Cushman. She never allowed herself to become submerged by domesticity, either: in 1846 she began her own career in the world of letters by contributing to *Douglas Jerrold's Shilling Magazine*, going on to become a reviewer for the *Athenaeum* and a publisher's reader for Bentley, and probably also for Hurst & Blackett. On her own account, she produced six full-length novels and two tales for children, as well as helping to bring out two biographical memoirs. She made her mark among her contemporaries, too: on first meeting her, Carlyle considered her one of the most interesting young women he had ever encountered (though on further acquaintance he was to dismiss her contemptuously as "a flimsy tatter of a creature"), and Dickens was impressed enough with her talents to invite her to write for *Household Words*.

If the ease with which Jewsbury took her place in the essentially male-dominated literary and cultural sphere of her time was unusual for a woman, she certainly took no pains to cultivate a protective image of traditional female womanhood. On the contrary, she deliberately sought the outrageous, smoking cigarillos, indulging in "profane talk" and adopting men's clothes, in all these perhaps modelling herself on her literary idol George Sand, whose work had a considerable influence on her own writing. Jane Carlyle was probably right to suggest something of wilful perversity in such behaviour; interestingly, too, she argued that Jewsbury's tendency to see herself and others in melodramatic roles, fuelled by her "desire of feeling and producing violent emotions", was aggravated by "her trade of Novelist". Underneath this overt rebelliousness and rejection of "propriety" (a word which Jewsbury loathed), however, lay a sensitive and genuinely inquiring personality. Jewsbury was troubled by many of the dichotomies and paradoxes of the age; if she seemed to be defying femininity, she was also torn by the conflicting pulls of public life and personal needs; if she appeared a social and moral iconoclast, she also suffered much inner agony about the ultimate questions of existence.

Zoe, Jewsbury's first novel, begun in collaboration with Jane and a mutual friend, Elizabeth Paulet (though the joint project was soon abandoned), examines several significant contemporary issues in the context of the romantic tale, and in so doing breaks much new ground. Its two most important aspects are encapsulated in the subtitle, "The History of Two Lives". Fictionally, these lives are those of the eponymous heroine, Zoe Gifford, and Everhard Burrows, the Roman Catholic priest with whom she becomes acquainted when he is appointed head of her husband's sectarian college. However, the characters also represent the author herself, analysing problems which she had experienced personally—the predicament of a gifted and aspiring woman in a society which dictates gender roles, and the mental agonies of a conscientious thinker who can no longer accept orthodox creeds. Her novel is thus both autobiographical and representative of its time; it also unites two fictional genres which were to become popular in the period—the "novel of doubt", a form adopted by writers as diverse as J. A. Froude, Charlotte Yonge, Cardinal Newman and Mrs Humphry Ward, and what may be called the "female novel", a psychological study of womanhood in which Jewsbury's successors include the Brontës, Mrs Gaskell and George Eliot. That Jewsbury was a literary pioneer in both these areas was indeed recognised by her contemporaries: in 1893 the critic Francis Espinasse wrote: "So far as my acquaintance with modern fiction extends, *Zoe* was the first novel in which the hero's career is made dependent upon the victory of modern scepticism over ancient belief", while the *Manchester Examiner*, in 1848, commented on the novel's originality as "a strange and striking tale, the vehement protest of a young, clever, susceptible Englishwoman against the thousandfold dullness of her narrow sphere of provincial life".

7

Everhard's story, albeit one of priestly apostasy, is to a large extent a retelling of Jewsbury's own troubled spiritual experiences. Like so many others of her period she suffered a crisis of faith in her early twenties, which she attributed partly to reaction to her Calvinist upbringing and partly to the "paralysing influence of Materialism". In 1840, deep in gloom, she wrote a series of letters to Carlyle, seeking his help with what she recognised as spiritual dilemmas similar to his own, and expressing her gratitude for the solutions his writings suggested to her. Following Carlyle's example, Jewsbury was finally able to obtain relief in an essentially non-doctrinal code of morality, having briefly but temporarily turned to Roman Catholicism; her novel focuses particularly on the sufferings involved in the slow and uncertain journey from scepticism to a new kind of enlightenment.

Zoe herself undergoes a "dark night of the soul" during which all religious belief seems a mockery, while Everhard, undergoing a much more prolonged and agonising period of doubt, is, by Jewsbury's own admission, a partial self-portrait, into whom she "put my own religious botherations". His crisis of faith, which stems from his recognition of the weak external evidence on which the foundations of the Church rest, and from his accompanying realisation that he can no longer honestly fulfil his priestly functions, echoes Jewsbury's own anxieties, expressed so passionately to Jane:

> What are we sent into this world at all for? What ought we to do with our life? . . . My God! I would give the rest of the years of my life to be able to know why it is that Life is given us.

Everhard's crisis is far more representative of Jewsbury's own age, rocked by the revelations of German biblical criticism, than of the previous century of Voltaire and the Encyclopaedists, in which the novel is set. Like his creator and many other Victorian doubters, Everhard finds some relief in active altruism, though his final refuge in scholastic meditation is not presented as a wholly triumphant solution to his difficulties. Indeed, Jewsbury's whole treatment of religious issues in this novel shows not only her awareness that there are no easy answers, but also her fairmindedness towards a variety of beliefs—she is, for example, much more tolerant of Roman Catholic practices than many of her contemporaries, and

8

sees deficiencies in both Popish and Protestant clerics, as she shows by her treatment of Everhard's religious superiors as well as of the slippery O'Brian.

Zoe's "her-story" similarly treats an issue of deep concern to Jewsbury and many like her, though, as has already been suggested, the author is careful to maintain the novel's unity by paralleling the representative functions of her two main protagonists: both Zoe and Everhard suffer lonely and loveless childhoods, both go through crises of identity, both feel that their particular roles cannot satisfy their passionate yearnings for self-fulfilment, and for both their mutual involvement leads them to question traditional assumptions and their own attitudes towards these.

Zoe's dilemma is especially closely documented. As Jewsbury's letters indicate, she herself felt considerable ambivalence about women's roles, recognising the many contradictions in her own female nature. She saw restrictive images of womanhood as the creation of male fantasy, and looked to a better future "when women will have a genuine, normal life of their own to lead", yet she also regarded romantic love as central to women's lives and was, according to the somewhat exasperated Jane, "never happy unless she has a *grande passion* on hand". She demanded more social and financial freedoms for women, and signed Barbara Bodichon's 1857 petition for a Married Women's Property Act, yet she claimed not to understand "the emancipation of women" and dissociated herself from active political involvement. Her heroine embodies many of these dichotomies. Naturally unconventional and rebellious, educated like a boy, with her need for self-dependence strengthened by the knowledge of her illegitimacy and her vital energies untainted by the petty proprieties of feminine orthodoxies, Zoe longs "to know the world as women seldom have an opportunity of knowing it". Marriage to the elderly Gifford, to which she is forced to resort as the only possible "career" for her, merely stultifies her, and unlike Everhard—who, as a man, can at least find an active alternative to the orthodoxies he has overthrown— she is driven into extra-marital romantic involvement as her only source of fulfilment.

Jewsbury, then, would seem to be protesting at the narrow limits permitted to women (though in her next novel, *The Half Sisters*, she

9

does suggest a more positive outlet for female energies), a protest heightened by the O'Brian/Clotilde/Lady Clara subplot, which not only contrasts genuine and false love, but particularly criticises masculine callousness towards women. As she remarks in one of her more cynical authorial pronouncements, "it is no matter what wealth of love is lavished on a man—unless it can do somewhat towards realising whatever object it may be that he desires in life, it is worthless and importunate in his eyes". Yet ultimately the novel argues for the supremacy of love in a woman's life, and voices Jewsbury's conviction that because women are "without any strong tie to the world except through their affections, the most exalted female nature requires some visible manifestation to cling to". So Zoe's growing love for Everhard not only fulfils the passionate side of her nature, but strengthens and disciplines her; she becomes humbler, "pure womanly instincts" gush up in her heart, and she is surrounded by "a halo of moral beauty", thus enacting her creator's conviction (echoing George Sand) that "True love and high morality are the same". Even her love for Mirabeau, which lacks the elevated and elevating qualities of her feeling for Everhard, is presented as a valuable emotional experience, though this somewhat unconvincing figure (whose sexual exploits clearly fascinated Jewsbury more than his historically political significance) seems a rather lame addendum to the main plot.

Men, too, gain from the experience of genuine romantic love: both Everhard and Mirabeau claim that Zoe—who thus becomes an early example of the Victorian redeeming angel—has a truly purifying influence on them. This emphasis on the ultimate supremacy of emotional commitment is not, however, a mere capitulation to Victorian literary and social conventions. It is, rather, the expression of Jewsbury's ambivalence. Love offers fulfilment of a kind, but it is not the complete answer to women's needs; her heroine, like herself and Jane, represents "a development of womanhood which as yet is not recognised [and which] . . . has, so far, no ready-made channels to run in", but will continue to look to a future of new outlets and alternatives.

Today *Zoe* hardly seems iconoclastic, either sexually or spiritually. Of course the depiction of declared love between a married woman and a Roman Catholic priest, not to mention the introduction of a

French lover, is hardly the stuff of moral tracts, but the care with which Jewsbury stresses the triumph of will over temptation in both hero and heroine should guarantee the novel's ultimate respectability. But its contemporary success depended as much on what was regarded as its sensationalism as on the fact that it had influential friends to help promote it. It was widely viewed as outrageous (Manchester Public Library withdrew it lest it should corrupt young men); even its admirers—including Erasmus Darwin, Mazzini and Bulwer Lytton—who acclaimed its honesty and outspokenness, thought it was a not wholly suitable production from a female pen.

Jane Carlyle had grave misgivings about the novel's "indecency" and "want of reserve . . . which no respectable public could stand— which even the freest spirits among us would call 'coming it too strong'!", though she was astute enough to realise that this very indecency made both it and its author highly alluring to many people. The scene which especially worried her and others was, not unnaturally, the one where Zoe falls into Everhard's arms and they embrace in the chapel—a scene which not only drew attention to the book's questionable religious element, but depended for its dramatic effect on emotionally and sexually charged language. We may be amused by the overblown frenzy of the writing—"He crushed her into his arms with ferocious love. He pressed burning kisses upon her face, her lips, and her bosom . . . beads of sweat stood thick on his forehead, and his breath came in gasps"—but many Victorian readers would have been uncomfortable, if not downright horrified. In addition, although Jewsbury introduces into the story the gentle, dutiful wife Marian and the irreproachably virtuous Clotilde as salutary contrasts to her erring heroine, it is clear that her sympathies are far more with Zoe who, tamed and chastened though she becomes, is scarcely a model of female submissiveness.

Jewsbury herself, much to Jane's distress, was unmoved by these adverse reactions to her work. Laughingly confessing to her friend that she had tried in vain to make the novel "proper-behaved", she points out that there is hardly any temptation for her to be a "moral" writer, since the dreadfully "questionable" chapter has become a bait for the whole book and anyway, the "craft" of "respectability" is merely an acknowledgement of public morality. As she perhaps foresaw, the literary scandal she had created was, like all such scandals, relatively short-lived, and it is hard today to see what all the fuss was about. Few twentieth-century readers have even heard of *Zoe*, but its retrieval from comparative obscurity shows that its merits and interest rest on elements quite other than its sexual and religious melodrama. Above all it speaks passionately, if sometimes clumsily, for the needs of women and for their right to independent selfhood. Zoe's story exists partly in the wish-fulfilment world of passionate affairs and vows of eternal love, but the paradoxes and tensions she faces are still with us today. Even if loss of faith can no longer deeply disturb us, questions about women's roles have certainly not been definitively answered.

Shirley Foster, Sheffield, 1989

ZOE

VOLUME I

CHAPTER I

— · —

On the fourteenth of June, 17—, the little town of Sutton, in Warwickshire, was thrown into a state of violent excitement by the news, that the son of the old squire who "used to belong to the old Manor House, was to have his own again", that he had married in foreign parts some grand lady,—a princess at the very least according to some versions,—that the king had written him a letter with his own hand begging him to come to England, and making him welcome to the old house, and all the land, that had been in the family for generations and generations!

This astounding report was set forth on the market-day by old Peter Brocclehurst, the tailor, who had heard it read with his own ears out of a newspaper, in a public-house at Birmingham, where he had been the day before to lay in a supply of West of England broadcloths, and "superfine narrow", for the exigencies of his profession for the next six months. Old Brocclehurst was not an authority to be lightly called in question, for from the sanctuary where he sat enthroned on his shop-board, stitching at the tough corduroys of all the ploughboys and farmers for six miles round, issued also the news, scandal, marvellous occurrences, useful information of all sorts, that went to enlighten the ignorance, and refresh the united intellect of all Sutton. If his *on dits* were not all exactly true, any news, as he said, was better than none at all.

This report about the squire and the Manor House, however, far exceeded in interest the general run of his facts; and on the day in question the little miscellaneous shop over which the full-blown Mrs Brocclehurst presided, with her matronly charms shrouded in a Brobdingnagian pinafore, was, to use her own words, "thronged like a fair", with people eager, by becoming customers for "a yard of check", or an "ounce of worsted", to learn the mystery of this wonderful history.

Mrs Brocclehurst was a gossip to the very marrow of her soul, but like Mrs Gilpin, "she had a prudent mind", and measured out her information according to the importance of the customer:—a few, a select few, were allowed to penetrate to the little back kitchen where Peter sat in all his glory, gravely coquetting with the important news he had brought, by seeming more taciturn and intent on his work than he had been in the memory of man.

"Well, patience—patience and time will show, but there *are* such lies going about in the world," said Peter, virtuously, shaking his head, and looking to the ceiling, "an honest man does not know what to believe and what to let alone. But sure enough I heard that the son of the old squire—him who went into hiding on account of the Jacobin troubles—had been sent for back by the king, who said that bygones should be bygones, and that he would forgive and forget; and that he might come to the old place; which was very handsome, considering!"

The next market-day, Peter, whose zeal for collecting information was great enough to make him worthy of being a correspondent of the "Times", was able, from sources best known to himself, to inform his customers, that workmen were to come over from Birmingham next week, to repair the old house and put all things in order;—for the credit of Peter's veracity, all this came actually to pass.

The Manor House, like all old houses that have been long uninhabited, and stand in the midst of a garden that has become a wilderness, had the reputation of being haunted; no one cared to go near it even in broad daylight; as to going within half a mile of the park-gate after dark, it was a thing not to be contemplated if there were any other path open, and not all the charms of nutting and bird-nesting could tempt the most venturous urchin that ever played truant, beyond the park-palings.

Now, however, all was changed. The presence of the workmen dispelled the idea of ghosts as if by magic. All Sutton rushed to see what the mysteries were that had been so long concealed;—though when they approached the stately avenue of chestnut and lime trees, at the end of which stood the long, deep, red-coloured brick building, with its four castellated gable ends in front, its immense stacks of heavy chimneys overgrown with ivy, and its narrow windows carefully darkened by curious balconies of carved stone— a shudder came over the more timid, as if some evil spirit had taken shape in brick and stone; but not even the boldest had courage to venture through the winding passages and secret places which were brought to light by the masons and upholsterers.

The moat, which was filled with stagnant water, covered all over with duck-weed, was to be filled up and converted into a flower garden, with a pond for gold fish in the centre, which some of the rustic visitors imagined were to be, bona fide, made of guineas.

There is something ghostlike in the appearance of a garden in decay, one feels to sympathise with it under its weight of desolation, as if it were a living thing. One passed through the great entrance hall of the Manor House, out by a glass door on the opposite side, opening on a lawn of green moss like grass that sloped down to the edge of a terrace, to which one descended by a broken flight of broad low steps that had once been ornamented with stone vases, after the Italian fashion—but they too had long been broken, and the fragments lay covered with the tangles of creeping plants, which had also overgrown the balustrade on each side. It made one sad to see a place which had so evidently been once of stately beauty, turned to ruin.

A raised walk, shaded by a row of stately cedar trees, divided the flower-beds from the fruit-garden, and gave a still more mysterious, weird-like aspect to the place; for every thing, when tending to decay, has a mystery it did not possess in its bloom. The broken statue of a naiad lay on the ground at the end of the cedar walk, but the clear fountain still fell with a pleasant noise into the rivulet which wound through the whole domain.

The workmen's voices, the tinkling noise of hammers and saws, which went busily on for several weeks, soon brought back an aspect of life to the old place. The winding passages and hiding-places were all blocked up; certain distant rooms were also closed, and those needed for the daily use of a moderate-sized family were beautified and made habitable; and the arrival of a quantity of modern furniture completed the exorcism of the "ghosts" that for so long had enjoyed undisturbed sway.

Whilst repairs at the Manor House progressed, there were many debates in the village as to how the old family ought to be received amongst them. As none of the present inhabitants of Sutton had ever seen any of the family who owned the Manor House, it is not wonderful that curiosity was the only sentiment aroused—but that was intense. Every body remembered to have heard their fathers and grandfathers talk of the ancient glories of the Manor House in the days of the old Squire Burrows, and many were the traditions about the riches, liberality, and virtues of the real gentlefolks who once belonged to the Manor, and every body hoped for some vague benefit to themselves from the return of these good old times.

Every man, woman, and child in Sutton had been for weeks past in the highest excitement of which they were capable; looking forward to the arrival of the family, and each one dreaming dreams after his own fashion; the older ones, of an ox, or at the very least a sheep, roasted whole,—the younger ones, of cakes and ale, with a dance in the park.

Never were mortals so consigned to disappointment! On the day fixed for the entrance of the squire and his family, the inhabitants of Sutton were on the *qui vive* from early in the morning—but nothing came to pass; the most strenuous watchers had retired in despair to the tap-room, where Peter Brocclehurst explained in his most oracular manner, that nothing was more impossible, than for people coming from foreign parts to arrive on the day they fix,—because they are dependent on the winds and the waves which are not under the control of any body: when, unluckily for Peter's theory, on the appointed evening—but when it was quite dark, two travelling-carriages drove rapidly through the town, and turned up the avenue leading to the Manor House. They contained Arthur Burrows, son to the old squire, his family, and two domestics who had accompanied them from France.

"Welcome to the home of my fathers!" said he, turning with a grave and stately courtesy to his wife, a tall imperious-looking woman, who seemed slightly impatient of their delay in the chilly old hall.

"Is this to be our house, papa?" cried two boys at once, who might be respectively seven and eight years old.

"Yes, my children," replied he, "and I hope you will be both good and happy in it."

"Oh, what fun it will be," cried they both; "is there a garden?"

"Don't make such a noise, nor ask silly questions," replied their mamma, peevishly. "La Noix, give them some bread and milk, and take them off to bed." This was spoken to a lean, austere-looking female, whose age it was hopeless to attempt to guess.

"Now, young gentlemen," cried she, with a shrill, prim tone. "You hear what your mamma says;—wish your papa good night, and come along."

The two children looked timidly at their papa, who said, with a slight hesitation, "I think Adèle, this first night they might sit up to supper. I should like to have all my family about me."

"Indeed, they will be much better in bed," replied the lady, drily; "and there will be plenty of time to have them with you to-morrow; there," added she, kissing them impatiently, "Good night; you shall look about you when it is daylight. La Noix, see that their beds are warmed, and that they have plenty of clothes on, for I am sure this house must be damp."

Arthur Burrows looked as much mortified as the children, but he never contradicted his wife; so he kissed them fervently and followed his wife into the parlour, where a cheerful wood fire was blazing, and the table stood laid for supper. A small Turkey carpet covered the middle of the floor, and the shining oak boards appeared at the sides. English ideas of comfort have changed since those days, and the reader, entering the room, would hardly exclaim, as Madame Burrows did, "Well, this room is charming, it must be confessed!"

"I hope you will find every thing in the house equally so, my dear Adèle. I trust we are brought back to my father's mansion for good ends, and that we may be honoured as instruments to raise up the persecuted church in this apostate country."

"Ah, here comes supper!" said his wife in reply.

As soon as the meal was over, Madame Burrows retired to see whether the children had been properly attended to—and in wife-like terms desired her husband not to fall asleep over the fire, but to come up stairs without delay, which order, as he had endured a ten years' training to conjugal obedience, he immediately complied with, and the whole house was shortly wrapped in repose.

The father of Arthur Burrows had been obliged to leave the kingdom in the troubles of 1715; he was then a rash, fiery-hearted young man, full of ultra-loyalty and the divine right of legitimacy. His enthusiastic notions, however, were tolerably calmed down by a few years' exile, and some real or imaginary slights which he received from the court of St Germains. At first he destined his only son, Arthur, to the Church, as he had no desire to see his ancient family perpetuated in poverty and obscurity; but an excellent alliance unexpectedly presenting itself, when his son had nearly finished his studies for the priesthood, he did not scruple to change his destination, and the match was concluded, his son being consulted as little in the second instance as in the first. Arthur, however, felt strong scruples after a time, as to the step he had taken; but the overbearing and imperious temper of the clever woman to whom his father had married him, might have some share in raising them.

A short time before our tale begins, the indefatigable exertions of his father to make his peace with the English government were successful, though he could no longer profit by his success, for he had been dead more than a year; but Arthur, who, with his wife's dowry, was able to pay the fines and bribes according to his father's last instructions, was reinstated into a good portion of the family estate, and arrived to take possession, full of the idea that he was selected by Providence, to raise up the Catholic body in England from the ruined condition into which it had fallen.

He destined his youngest son, Everhard, for holy orders, and though he had been so signally fortunate in a worldly point of view, he could not help sighing when he looked back to the peaceful days when he was himself preparing for the priesthood.

The next morning all was bustle at the Manor House; the children were up by daybreak exploring every nook and corner of the old house. Madame Burrows was an early riser, on principle, and therefore, never allowed any of her establishment to be anything else.

As soon as breakfast was despatched she sent her husband and the children out of the house to visit the garden and park, or whatever they chose, so that they did not themselves return till dinner-time, in order that she might be able to lay the foundations of her domestic throne in peace and quietness.

It was market-day in Sutton, and a very full market it was, for every body hoped to catch a glimpse of some of the new comers.

Sutton was a genuine specimen of a small English market town in an agricultural district. It consisted of one long straggling street, which contained a few spacious houses of dark red brick, with ample gardens behind them. These belonged to professional men connected with the neighbouring county gentry. The rest of the street consisted of smaller houses with their high roofs of red tiles become green with age and moss, shops, such as flourish nowhere but in country towns, and abounding in most miscellaneous productions. There was no library, nor indeed, any place where a book could be bought nearer than Birmingham. A few articles of stationery were sometimes kept by the druggist, who was also the tea-dealer and grocer of the place. Nearly all the inhabitants were either farmers, or farm labourers, and a new house had not been built in Sutton for many years.

The whole place might have belonged to the dominions of the Sleeping Beauty, so little change passed over it from year's end to year's end.

The church was a fine old building, containing many curious effigies and monuments of families that had been of distinction in the time of the Crusaders, but they had all been more or less mutilated, partly by time, and partly by the zeal of the Reformers and the soldiers of Oliver Cromwell, who all seem to have been a prey to a mania for breaking down "carved work with axes and hammers".

The Rectory, which had been erected in the time of Charles I, was at a little distance from the church, and was a favourable specimen of the comforts provided for some of her favoured sons by the dominant establishment.

The whole place seemed to sleep peacefully in the bosom of the richest and most finely wooded district in England. The masses of fine old trees with which that part of the country is studded like one vast park, seemed as if it were beyond the power of a tempest to move them from their majestic repose. Several families of wealth and distinction resided in the neighbourhood, but they seldom visited Sutton, except when they changed horses as they passed through on their way to London or Birmingham. The Manor House was the only residence of any distinction within several miles of the town.

After rambling through the Park, Arthur Burrows and his two children, Louis and Everhard, stood at the gate which led to the town. "Oh, papa, do let us go into the town, it is market day, and we shall see such beautiful things!" cried both the children at once.

"Very well, with all my heart," said their papa, "but we must not be late for dinner; your mamma desired us to be back by a certain time."

The children were wild with spirits at the sight of the beautiful green of the meadows and hedgerows, so different from any they had seen before. When they drew near the town the market was nearly over, and the country people were gathering up their baskets; some had assembled round the steps of the market-cross for their weekly gossip. "The new squire and the children!" was soon buzzed on all sides, and every eye was eagerly turned on them.

Arthur courteously saluted them, and began to enter into conversation with a respectable farmer who stood near; but the two children, seeing the cross, reverently took off their caps and crossed themselves, as they had been taught to do; which excited no little astonishment from the bystanders. "Why!" cried a dozen voices, when they were out of hearing, "they will be Papists, or idolators, or something outlandish!" "Ay," said Peter, in a decided tone, "the old family were all Papists; but they were a good family for all that. This place was all Catholic once." "Nay, ye don't say so," cried another. "I thought the parson told us that Papists were Anti-Christ, and had the mark of a beast on them, as we read in the Revelation; and I remember hearing my grandfather say, that when King William came in, he delivered us from Papists and wooden shoes, which they wanted to put on all England, instead of Christian-like nails and leather."

At this moment an elderly serving man, in a dark livery, came up, followed by a lad bearing a large basket. He came to make purchases for the Manor; and the little crowd were disappointed to see how much like an ordinary mortal he transacted his business. No one dared to ask him questions, for he was very grave and austere looking; but the Protestant sympathies of the inhabitants were roused, and they made it a point of conscience to charge double for all articles bought for the Manor House.

Of course all the neighbouring families who went to church on the Sunday following, in the hopes of catching a glimpse of the new comers, were disappointed. The rector called, as in duty bound, but he told his wife on his return, "That he did not think he could lawfully visit people who were heathens and idolators, and who had actually fitted up a chapel within their own house."

All the neighbouring gentry made an early visit to the Manor House. The ladies, after they had been edified with the fashion of Madame Burrows' velvet gown, and the new pattern of her sleeves and head-dress, found themselves awed by her stately manners, and the look of surprised contempt with which she listened to the detail of the small interests and events that seemed to fill their whole souls.

The gentlemen on their side did not get on much better; they found Arthur absolutely insensible to all their topics of interest. The only point he seemed anxious about, was to learn the statistics of Catholicism in the county, and where the different places of worship stood. This was bad enough, for his visitors were all ultra-Protestant church and king men;—but when he declined to join the hunt, and declared that he never tasted any thing stronger than water, their indignation was high. They decided unanimously that Arthur was a fool—a Jacobin, a Jesuit in disguise—and that, as loyal Englishmen, they would have nothing to do with a milksop, who ought to be hunted from the country, if England was ever to prosper.

Arthur Burrows, however, was not destined to be long an offence to his neighbours, for he fell ill of a pleurisy before he had been two months settled in the home of his fathers. He was only ill two days, and then died, in spite of the best efforts of the Sutton doctor to prevent him.

There was no priest within many miles of the place to give him the last sacraments. He was buried in the chancel of the parish church, the prayers of the establishment were read over him, and there was an end to all his dreams of becoming the apostle of Catholicism.

CHAPTER II

— · —

Madame Adèle Burrows found herself a widow in a foreign country, at the age of eight-and-twenty. For the first few weeks she was very unhappy indeed; she was surprised to find how much more she had cared for her husband than she ever suspected. She had petted him sometimes, governed and hen-pecked him always, and now she found herself suddenly without employment. To be sure, after a while she recollected that she had been left sole guardian of the two children, with complete control over the property until the eldest attained his majority, and a handsome jointure of her own besides. This was all very consolatory; she dried her tears, and set herself strenuously to her dearly beloved task of making every thing go on in her own way. She had a natural aptitude for business, and an inexhaustible activity, which would never suffer her to delegate her power into the hands of another. Louis, the elder boy, had always been his mother's favourite, and to secure him as brilliant a fortune as possible, was the end she assigned to herself in all her actions.

So soon as the bustle of the funeral and the necessary affairs it entailed had, in some degree, subsided, the whole establishment at the Manor House was placed under the most rigid system of economy, to which, however, her own comforts were quite as much sacrificed as those of any other member of the household. She rose every morning at five, and, wrapped in a large riding-coat like a man's, she accompanied her bailiff to the most distant part of the various farms, and personally inspected all that was going on. She had the rare merit of never meddling in what she did not understand; but, with her quick, penetrating black eyes, she soon saw whether those who had the work in hand were doing their business properly.

The country gentlemen in the neighbourhood made her many kindly intentioned offers of service, but "she could bear no brothers near the throne", and declined them all. At first, they laughed at her notion of managing for herself, and declared that she would come to ruin in a twelvemonth; but, as she did not, and the property went on improving, they declared she was a clever woman, with a fine spirit of her own. She had the policy to keep on good terms with them, though their lady wives and daughters could not endure her, declaring that she was an unkind mother, and neglected her children.

The fact was, that Madame Burrows had all her energies so absorbed by the management of her large property, that she never troubled herself with the minor details of her domestic establishment, except to see that the weekly expenses did not exceed the specified sum she had laid down for herself. She was too much of a French woman to bestow much attention on her toilet, when there was nobody to see her, and it was hardly to be expected that she would take more trouble about the dress of her children. La Noix, the *bonne*, who had accompanied the family from France, was nominally responsible for them, but she was a great *dévote*, and not too fond of children, so she was generally saying her rosary when she ought to have been mending their stockings; besides, she did not consider that her surveillance extended beyond putting on their clothes in the morning and putting them to bed at night. During the intermediate period the two boys were allowed to run wild about the grounds, and to associate with the servants; they saw their mother once a day for about a quarter of an hour, whilst she was taking her chocolate in the morning, when they were enjoined to sit very still and make no noise; their own meals they always took in the servants' hall, though there was an obsolete standing order, never complied with, that they were to eat with La Noix in her own sitting-room.

Everhard, the younger boy, had never been a favourite with his mother, perhaps his being destined for holy orders, which put him beyond the need of having his worldly prosperity schemed for, had also removed him beyond the sphere of her sympathies; certain it is, that she never showed him any tenderness, nor any of the caresses so prodigally lavished by mothers on their children. She invariably treated him with a dry and distant coldness, amounting often to harshness; his most trifling faults were vigorously punished, and the natural gaiety of childhood was repressed as levity. His brother, on the other hand, was allowed much more liberty; even for him his mother seldom made many demonstrations of affection, but she did not chide and repulse him, as was the case with poor Everhard.

The servants did not fail to perceive this, and to aggravate the effects in a way Madame Burrows little suspected. They were always telling him that his mother hated him, and in a thousand mortifying ways made the distinction between him and his brother more galling. Everhard was a gentle, timid, affectionate child, to whom kind looks and words were more than his daily food, he willingly yielded to his brother in all things, who tyrannised as boys do, when they can with impunity. If Everhard ever ventured to resent a grievance, he was beaten for being quarrelsome; and once when he ventured to complain to his mother of some more than usually afflicting dispensation from his brother, his mother summarily disposed of the case, by subjecting both himself and Louis to the same punishment: to teach them, as she said, "not to tell tales, and to be better friends for the future". The next day the servants all taunted him as a "tell-tale, like a little deceitful thing as he was". Servants and low people are all very fond of affixing the epithet "deceitful" on every body who does not happen to please them.

From constantly hearing himself called "deceitful", "naughty", and "troublesome", poor Everhard grew up to have a vague sense of being always wrong; the gay recklessness of childhood was crushed under the embarrassment of living under unloving eyes; the natural affectionateness of his disposition was thrown back upon himself; and he became shy, sullen, and very unhappy. That he really would have been an affectionate child, if they would have let him, the following incident will show.

It was the first anniversary of his father's death; prayers had been said in the little chapel which Madame Burrows had fitted up in the house; her feelings had been softened by the service, and she kept the two children to breakfast with her. She talked to them about their father, and was particularly kind to Everhard;—his little heart was quite melted, and when they were dismissed to play, he began to think what he could do to show his mother how much he loved her.

He pondered for a long time; at length he recollected having heard her say that she liked early mushrooms, and he determined to gather some for her supper. He and Louis were that day to have gone on a secret expedition with the gardener's boy and a friend of his from the village to see a badger hunted;—this he magnanimously gave up, in spite of the threats and entreaties of Louis. Arming himself with his basket and a small knife, he left Louis to pursue his scheme in peace, and began a vigorous search for mushrooms. There were none in the park, but he recollected that in a certain field beyond, there were always a great many. This field happened just then to be full of cows, of a peculiar breed, very wild, and uncertain in their temper. At first, Everhard felt inclined to be frightened, but then he thought of his mamma and her supper, and mustered courage. He found abundance of mushrooms—but in his eagerness to fill his basket, he got, without perceiving it, into the very midst of the herd. Somewhat startled, on raising his head, to perceive this, he began to make the best of his way to the gate. The cows, which had hitherto paid no attention to him, now tossed their heads and began to pursue him;—luckily a man working in the next field perceived his danger, and ran to his help, otherwise it would have fared badly with him;—however, he had kept the lid of his basket safely shut down, in the midst of all his fright, and on his way home he gathered a large nosegay of wild flowers to present along with his other prize.

Arrived at home, despite of the standing orders to the contrary, he made his way to his mother's apartment. Out of breath, looking very flushed and heated, his clothes none the cleaner for his excursion, he opened the door with trembling eagerness, and stood in the presence of his mother. All the effusion of the tender feelings of the morning had long since subsided, and Madame Burrows sat at a small table entirely absorbed in settling some complicated accounts. At the noise of Everhard's entrance she looked up impatiently. "What are you here for?" she asked. "You know you

27

are not allowed to come here unless I send for you. Go to La Noix, if you want any thing; and what is that dirty basket in your hand?"

Poor Everhard had never thought of what he should say; and this address completed his confusion, so he looked down at the carpet and did not speak. "Well, what do you want? Either speak or go away," said his mother.

"I have brought these for your supper," said he, at last, pulling the lid off the basket so awkwardly, that some of the mushrooms fell on the floor. "I thought you liked them; and I gathered these flowers for you too."

"You know I never allow flowers to be brought into the house," said she. "And as for those mushrooms, go and throw them away directly; they are poisonous for what you know; and I desire you will never meddle with those sort of things again. Here, La Noix," cried she, as she passed the door, "why don't you keep these children out of mischief? It is all you have to do."

"Indeed, it is no fault of mine, madame; but Master Everhard is just the naughtiest and most worritting boy I ever saw. See, now, if he has not tore those trousers I mended for him only last night."

"Well, well," replied his mother, impatiently, "take him away and don't let him come here again with his dirty feet."

Madame Burrows only wanted to be delivered from the interruption; but La Noix, to revenge herself for the reprimand she had received, sent the unfortunate Everhard off to bed, "to teach him to take care of his clothes". When his mother heard of it, she did not interfere, because, as she said, she must keep up La Noix's authority in the eyes of the house. Madame Burrows, in her dread of encountering the ill-humour of a favourite domestic, magnanimously ran the risk of alienating the affections of her youngest son; but, to be sure, one annoyance would have fallen upon her immediately, whilst she would suffer no inconvenience from the other for some time to come.

In after life, Everhard was once with some friends who were speaking in the usual *banal* terms of childhood, calling it the "golden age of life", and all that. Everhard listened for some time with silent impatience; at length he broke out into an indignant recapitulation of his own childhood as the type of many others. "Childhood", said he, in conclusion, "is not, in its own right, a state of happiness; no one can tell the misery of an unloved and lonely child. In after life, a degree of hardness comes with years, and the man is not susceptible of pain like the child. A child is so tender, that no grown person can calculate the keen pain that penetrates to its little heart, from one cold or harsh word; it is so utterly defenceless, that it needs to be surrounded with gentleness, and kept warm in a nest of love; it can hardly be said to be fully born, for though put forth into the world, it has not yet an existence of its own; it is only dependent on all around it, instead of on one alone; kind looks and words are the nourishment on which it must gain strength, no less than from its daily food; and if it be deprived of these, the after consequences are not to be told. It may grow up to be strong in body, and like other children of men in outward appearance, but the human soul, will have been warped and stunted in its growth; the foundations of a cruel, artificial character will have been laid for life; the glad animal instincts, the bounding sensations, which the mere fact of being alive imparts to a healthy child, and which are bestowed to carry it over the first stage of existence—that fresh first stage which has been feigned by common consent to be the fading away of the glorious beauty of that world from which we are called forth; that one portion of life, that has been given to man at the outset of his journey, in order that when, hereafter, 'wearied by the greatness of his way', he may recollect it, and not be tempted to say 'there is no hope!'—all this, when a child is made unhappy, is blotted out from his book of life; he is defrauded of that which, for a long time, would have 'kept his eyes from the seeing of evil'; his first lessons in life have been of suffering, taught before he has strength to receive them; what wonder, then, if in after life he belong to the number of those 'who pass through the land hardly bested and hungry, and curse their King and their God, and look upward?' For he has no recollection in after life upon which to stay himself,—the dawn of his day was turned into darkness; others, too, in their turn, will suffer by him; the scale of his sympathies has been rendered imperfect; he, in his turn, will become harsh and reckless about giving pain; he will become either unmindful or unconscious of the bitter pain that may be inflicted by indifference and harshness; he will have imbibed a scorn for the soft, sympathising amenities which disguise the ills of life, and for those also who need or value them!"

"Why, Everhard, I never heard you so eloquently indignant before," said his friend.

"Possibly not," replied Everhard, "for I learned in suffering."

Everhard was saved from the above fate by an event that occurred when he was ten years old. Madame Burrows began to think it time that the two boys should have better instruction than Madame La Noix and the parish clerk could impart, which amounted to reading, not very fluently, and writing, in something between mysterious "pot-hooks" and large joining hand, words of four letters. Accordingly she engaged an old priest, named Father Martin, to come and be confessor to the household, and to undertake the education of the children. In due time he arrived, to the great joy of Louis and Everhard, to whom any change was welcome. Father Martin was a good, kind-hearted, chirping old man, without much talent or learning, but endowed with great singleness and simplicity of heart; his religion was a real *croyance*, and supplied the place to him of father, mother, wife, children, in fact, of all humanities. The saints in the calendar were to him as real friends; the ceremonies of the church filled his heart, and took him back to the days of the apostles and martyrs; all his faculties were absorbed in religion, which gave a genial beauty to his whole character. Let a common-place person once be imbued with a real genuine feeling for religion, and it redeems them from all coarseness of feeling, gives them graces of intellect, and an elevation of character far beyond their natural standard.

From the arrival of Father Martin, Everhard dated his happiness.

The old man had a fund of affection in his heart, and hitherto he had met with no object on which to exercise it. He soon found himself especially drawn to poor Everhard; he was very sorry for the harshness and neglect with which he was treated, for Madame Burrows used to excuse her coldness to others, and perhaps to herself, by saying, "that as he was destined to holy orders; it was far better that he should be accustomed betimes to the privations and mortifications which would hereafter make up the staple of his life."

Father Martin taught Everhard his own love for religion. Before he came, Everhard knew nothing except from the formal mass, without music, in a cold, dark chapel, and the long Latin prayers which he had been taught without explanation, and often as a punishment for some trifling offence. But when Father Martin talked to him about the saints and martyrs as though they had been his near and familiar friends,—then, the dry Litanies became touched by a quickening spirit. They were to him a "power and presence"; they were really men, women, and children, who had once lived and believed as he was now doing. The mysterious sacrifice of the mass, had been offered up before their eyes, as it now was before his; they had taken part in the very words he now repeated; he was destined to fill the same holy office which many of them had filled; and in time his name might become associated with theirs in the Litanies, for the comforting and strengthening of some yet unborn worshipper, who might be as lonely and unhappy as he had so long been.

All this opened a new world to him. The prayers which had hitherto been penances, became the grand enjoyment of his life so soon as he was aware that he might ask boldly and without fear for every thing he wanted. For a long time he could scarcely believe that so great a favour was indeed his. "And may I really talk to the saints, and will they listen to me, and not get tired of me as mamma always does?" asked he one day, when Father Martin had been talking to him upon the subject.

"No, my child," replied the good old man; "the more you pray, and the more you occupy yourself about them, the more rejoicing there is among their holy company."

Everhard lived henceforth in the world of his darling saints and martyrs. On any childish emergency he applied to them as naturally and undoubtingly as another child would have gone to its mother. Father Martin to him, was one of the saints not yet dead, and for that reason alone not put in the calendar.

No event worth recording happened during the first six months of Father Martin's residence. But about that time it happened that Madame Burrows had some business about which a lawyer's advice was needed. Many household wants had accumulated which could not be supplied in Sutton, a journey to Coventry was therefore solemnly agreed upon. She promised the two boys to take them with her, and as there was much to see as well as to do, they were to stay all night at an inn, and not to return till the next day.

This was the first treat of any sort that had been promised to the boys, and their delight knew no bounds. They had never been beyond a few miles round Sutton since they came there; and besides, Coventry had been invested to their imagination with a mysterious charm, ever since they had read the history of Lady Godiva; and now they were actually to see the streets she had passed along, and the very likeness of Peeping Tom himself! It is no wonder they could neither eat nor sleep for thinking of it. As to Everhard, the first thing he did was to inform his darling friends, the saints, and to entreat them to send a fine day for the journey.

And a beautiful day it was. Everhard and his brother both dressed in their new clothes, which had come home from Peter Brocclehurst the night before, stood watching the process of harnessing the four horses to the large lumbering family vehicle, which they had never beheld brought from its resting-place except on rare and grand occasions. But, alas! for the hopes of either men or children. At the moment when Madame Burrows, followed by La Noix, appeared in the courtyard ready equipped for the journey, a dashing-looking gentleman rode up, followed by a servant on horseback. Madame Burrows, with some surprise, recognised her brother.

"Why, when did you arrive?" exclaimed she, embracing him, "I did not even know you were intending to come to England."

"It was quite unexpected," replied he, "I transacted all my business in London last week, and I intended to take you by surprise; but you are going out it seems,—that I should have been so unfortunate!"

"Come in and refresh yourself," replied his sister, "and then perhaps you will join us; you should see as much as you can of England whilst you are in it."

"Oh, no refreshment for me, but I will join your party, and welcome; we can talk as well in your carriage as in your parlour, if you have room for me."

"Of course there is," replied Madame Burrows; "then we need not delay any longer."

She proceeded with her brother to the coach, where La Noix and the two boys were already seated. "Here," said she, "one of you must give up his place,—not you, La Noix, for I shall want you. Everhard, you are the youngest, and besides, you must learn self-denial betimes, do you get out and give your place to your uncle."

"Cannot we find room for all?" said the good-natured Frenchman.

"Oh dear no, for the coach will be quite full of things when we come back, and besides, what does it signify, he can go another time." Then, without waiting to cast a look on poor Everhard's face of astonished disappointment, she ordered the carriage to drive off.

At first Everhard could hardly believe in the reality of his disappointment; but when the carriage was fairly out of sight, he sat down and cried with all the bitterness of childish indignation and helplessness: the perfect indifference with which an affair so important to him had been dismissed was the worst part of all. In a little while Father Martin passed across the court, and was surprised to find him there, thinking, of course, he had gone with the rest. When he heard the story, the good old man could hardly help crying too for sympathy.

"My brother is never punished," said Everhard, sobbing, "he has every thing he wishes for, and every body loves him. What have I done to be left at home?"

Father Martin could hardly find in his heart to rebuke this natural burst of passion; at length he said, "Come, come, my child, you know anger is sinful, recollect the saints were all tried a great deal more than you are, and yet they never gave way to temper, and you most not envy your brother; you are told to love him better than yourself; and besides, if you don't love your own brother, how can you pretend to love the saints and Jesus Christ whom you never saw?"

"Well, but they do not vex me; they are never spiteful to me as he is," sobbed Everhard.

"Well, well, my child," said the old man, half-smiling, "you must learn to be patient; but now let us take a walk in the fields; I want to show you where those curious flowers grow, and we will bring home some of the roots with us to set in your garden."

The kind-hearted old man, full of his desire to console poor Everhard for his disappointment, went back to the house, and begging a few cakes and some slices of cold meat from the cook, he filled a bottle with cowslip wine, and did not forget the little silver cup which belonged to himself. He packed every thing neatly and rejoined Everhard, who had now dried up his tears, and found his spade and basket.

They set off together into the wood, and when they were tired of rambling about, they dined under a large tree, where they rested during the heat of the day, and the old man told Everhard many tales, whilst the pleasant sunlight came through the transparent green leaves, and played and flickered as they moved about upon the moss and tree trunks beneath.

"Now," cried Father Martin, at last, "I think we will go and look for the flowers, they grow beside the trout stream."

It was a part of the wood where Everhard had never been, for Madame Burrows seldom allowed them to go beyond the park gates. Everhard was enchanted. The flowers were quite white, and so transparent that the green leaves could almost be seen shining through them; a poor little quail had fallen out of its nest and hurt its wing; Everhard carried it home in great triumph to nurse. Coming home they had to pass through a village where there was a fair, and they met a club walking with blue staves, with the accompaniment of a band of music and gay flags; so, on the whole, Everhard had not once time to think of his disappointment. As soon as they reached home, the first business was to put the bird in a cage, and then to set the flower roots.

"I think", said he, "I will put some of these into Louis' garden; he likes pretty flowers as much as I do."

When he went to bed at night Father Martin sat beside him till he fell asleep, in order that he might not think of the troubles and unkindness of the morning.

Who can calculate the amount of perversity, misanthropy, and all sorts of evil feeling which was averted from Everhard by the opportune kindness of this one day! Not averted only, but changed into wholesome human affection, which, in after life, kept him from the evil of the world, and abided by him in his days of darkness, when all the imposing array of creeds and precepts broke under him like reeds, as he leaned on them for help. A day, an hour, often contains the vital principle of what is elaborated into the conduct of years.

The next day all the party returned home. Louis was full of the wonders he had seen, and the coach was laden with purchases. Madame Burrows, to make some amends to Everhard for his disappointment, had brought him a beautiful new knife and a large kite, which his uncle good-naturedly undertook to teach him to fly.

CHAPTER III

— . —

After the departure of M. du Pont, the brother of Madame Burrows, every thing at the Manor went on in its usual course, and nothing worth recording happened for the next twelve months.

One fine morning, in harvest time, Madame Burrows said, at breakfast, "I wish, Father Martin, if you are not engaged, you would go with the doctor to visit a poor Irishman who lies ill in one of the barns; he has come over every harvest for many years past, and now, I fear, he is very ill. See what things are needed, and they shall be sent."

Father Martin did not fail to do as he was directed. The poor man had been ill some days, but had struggled on with his work till that morning, when he fainted in attempting to rise from his straw. The doctor pronounced it a bad case of typhus fever, and recommended that the rest of the labourers should be lodged elsewhere. But the precaution came too late. Ten other of the unfortunate creatures sickened shortly, and five died notwithstanding every assistance that medical skill and kind nursing could bestow.

Madame Burrows, who, in spite of her imperious nature, had a genuinely kind heart, and a great deal of good sense, took such judicious steps, that the dreadful disease was confined entirely to the spot where it first showed itself, and did not spread either to the labourers on other farms, nor into the town itself. Madame Burrows and Father Martin were indefatigable in their attentions and kindness to the sufferers. When the excitement caused by this calamity had somewhat subsided, and things began to fall into their accustomed course, Father Martin complained of being ill. At first he only felt languid, which he attributed to the anxiety and fatigue he had recently undergone, but the next day he grew worse, and could not leave his bed. He had a presentiment that he should not recover. The only distress this gave him was, that he must leave his dear child, Everhard. He did not know how long they might be left together, so he lost no time in calling him to his bedside to give him what strength and comfort he could.

"My dear child," said he, taking his hand, "if it should be the will of Almighty God that I should die and leave you, you must not lament after me; recollect that I am going to see Jesus Christ and the saints, whom you love to hear about; and I shall never know pain or sorrow more. I shall not be very far from you, though you will not be able to see me. Will you think of this, and try not to be very unhappy when I am gone?"

At first Everhard's surprise and grief were too great to allow him to speak.

"My dear child, do not break my heart by letting me see you so miserable. We shall not be long separated. You will come to me at the end of a few years. If we lived in this world, you would have to go away and leave me to follow your studies; and how much better it is that I should go into the safe keeping of God and his saints. The dead never change; and when you come to me I shall love you as much as I do now."

"Will you be a saint, and watch over me?" asked Everhard, sobbing.

"I will pray to God for you when I shall be purified; and then I shall be able to love you, and serve you far better than I can as a sinful mortal. Nay, nay, my child," continued he, perceiving that poor Everhard's grief was uncontrollable, "you must not rebel against the Divine will in this manner. Come, let us say the Litany of Jesus together; it will compose us both."

This was the last conversation Everhard ever had with his old friend, for shortly afterwards he sank into a stupor, from which he never roused till a few minutes before he breathed his last, three days afterwards.

Everhard was removed from the chamber almost by force, and he saw his dear friend no more. He assembled with the rest of the household in the chapel, where the coffin was laid on a bier surrounded with wax tapers, a solemn service was performed, and

37

then the remains of the good old man were conveyed to the vault, and laid beside those of Everhard's father.

At first, Everhard's grief was not so violent as might have been expected, it was rather a stunned astonishment, for it seemed to him quite impossible that so great an affliction could have been laid in earnest upon any one. Father Martin had given him his missal, and he would sit for hours, with it upon his knees, not reading, but gazing vacantly at it.

He sat at table when he was summoned, and ate mechanically what was put upon his plate, but he spoke to no one, nor did he seem to notice any thing.

Those round him, albeit little accustomed to notice his ways, became alarmed, his mother endeavoured by kind words and even caresses to rouse him, but he paid no attention to her, and escaped the first moment to his old station where he had left his missal.

A priest from a distance who had administered the last sacraments to Father Martin, offered mass in the chapel the following Sunday. As the service proceeded, the conviction that his dear old friend was really gone, and that his place must evermore be supplied by a stranger, flashed on Everhard as for the first time. He screamed aloud, and was removed from the chapel in hysterical convulsions; a violent passion of tears followed, after which he was put to bed and a composing draught administered. He did not again relapse into his former stupor, but it was very long before he regained his usual cheerfulness.

Some time after Father Martin's death, Everhard and his brother were sent to Bruges to be educated at a seminary, which was of great repute in those days. English Catholics of the higher classes were obliged to send their children from home if they wished them to receive a liberal education, Catholic schools not being at that time permitted in England.

The remainder of Everhard's childhood passed without any thing to be recorded. He and his brother outgrew their childish bickerings, and became the friends that brothers ought to be. When Everhard was seventeen and his brother eighteen they returned home, Louis to take his place as the head of the family, and Everhard to have a little relaxation previous to proceeding to Rome, to study for the priesthood at the English College there.

Madame Burrows felt a mother's pride at seeing the fine looking young men her sons had become, and all her ambition was more than gratified when she beheld them cordially received into the ranks of the country gentlemen, amongst whom their frankness, good humour, and keen sportmanship, soon rendered them great favourites.

A letter from M. du Pont, the brother of Madame Burrows, arrived after they had been a short time at home, inviting Everhard to visit him on his way to Rome. After some demur, Madame Burrows gave her consent; she exhorted him to be very steady, and on no consideration to exceed his allowance, assuring him that she would not advance one single farthing beyond. She then embraced him, and saw him depart with great composure.

Louis showed much more feeling on the occasion, for though his new importance had all the flush of novelty with it, yet it did not reconcile him to the loss of Everhard's society, and it would be doing him a great injustice were we to omit to inform the reader that, unknown to his mother, he added a hundred a year to Everhard's allowance out of the income allowed to himself during his minority, and that his first act on coming of age was to double the amount.

Everhard accomplished his journey to Paris without accident or adventure, and a new era in life began for him.

CHAPTER IV

— · —

It is very troublesome to have to deal with a hero of seventeen! A girl of seventeen, fortune favouring, may be made into a very interesting heroine; people will believe all that can be said of her beauty, wit, and wisdom, and will patiently read through three or even six volumes full of her adventures, and find themselves much edified with the perusal. But a lad of seventeen! merciful heaven! to make a hero of him would require a suspension of the laws of nature! All his graces of childhood have run to seed, and the victims of manhood have not yet replaced them; he is no longer the chubby darling, of the red shoes and coral; nor yet the interesting child in a picturesque hat and tunic; but an unfinished, uneasy biped, a plague to every body within his reach, and with whose doings and sufferings, nobody, not absolutely obliged, wishes to have the least concern. The gentle reader will easily sympathise with the dismay in which Madame du Pont was thrown, when her husband informed her that he had invited his nephew to pay them a visit on his way to Rome.

Madame du Pont was a woman of quality of a certain age. She felt a motherly vocation for forming the minds and manners of interesting young men, but then they must be—no matter stopping to define what. But she knew when she saw them, who would be likely to profit by her lessons, and she was quite sure beforehand that Everhard would be utterly destitute of all the qualities of an interesting young man,—that he would be awkward, that he would be a caricature, that, in short, he would be altogether unbearable. So she made up her mind that he should be satisfied with a very short visit, and be quite as anxious to proceed to Rome as she could be to see him depart.

Madame du Pont was one morning sitting in a ravishing dishabille, half reclined on a large fauteuil; a graceful middle-aged man, in the dress of an abbé, stood leaning on the side of her chair. He was her confessor, for she was a great *dévote* in her way, and took much pleasure in the abbé's society. They were interrupted in their conversation, whatever it might be, by the entrance of Monsieur du Pont, who led Everhard by the hand.

"Allow me", said he, "to present my nephew to you, and to entreat your favour for him whilst he remains with us."

"Have I the pleasure of seeing the M. Everhard you have so often mentioned?" said she, in a silvery voice, and a smile of satisfaction at seeing something so much better than she expected. "I am rejoiced to see you," continued she, stretching out her little white hand to Everhard, who was almost too abashed to raise it to his lips; but his naïve want of confidence had nothing awkward, and it completed the favourable impression his first appearance had made.

"Allow me to present my husband's nephew to you," said she, turning to the abbé; "he is intended for the church; *n'est ce pas?*" added she, glancing at Everhard with a smile of that peculiar fascination which can only be had in perfection by women who have passed their *première jeunesse*. The smile of a young beauty loses in meaning what it has in brilliancy, it is the mere expression of personal pleasure or coquettish display; it wants the penetrating sweetness that makes the object feel it as a peculiar favour, not bestowed lightly or without intention.

M. du Pont was delighted to see his lady treat his *protégé* so graciously, and after a little unimportant conversation prepared like a wise man to retire before she grew weary of her condescension; he would have carried Everhard off with him, but as the visiting hour was at hand, Madame du Pont desired he might remain that she might present him to her friends. M. du Pont thanked his wife for her amiability, kissed her hand and withdrew, leaving Everhard, divided between admiration and embarrassment.

Madame continued to ask him questions about England, until the entrance of visitors interrupted her. Everhard was introduced to every one, but as the conversation fell on topics of which he was utterly ignorant, he would have been wearied if the Abbé du Pré had not devoted himself with great good nature to entertain him. The abbé was neither very wise, nor very learned, but he had the genius of tact and good breeding, which upon those immediately under their influence, supply the place of beauty and goodness and wisdom by blinding the eyes to their absence.

When the visitors had departed, Madame du Pont began to consider whether it might be possible to make her handsome nephew presentable in good company on so short a notice. She was going to supper that evening at Madame d'Aligré's, and she wished to take him with her. Though *dévote*, she was still too young and handsome to remain contented with merely spiritual diversions, and she had a great taste for the society of the *esprits forts* of that day, though she had no ambition to be considered an *esprit* herself. As one of the set once said of her, "She contrived to be on respectful terms with God, whilst she kept up an agreeable acquaintance with the Devil."

She called Everhard to her, and turning him round as if he were a child, she said, with the smile that had so much enchanted him before, "You must be my cavalier tonight; I am going out to supper, but you must let me dress you as we dress in Paris. What beautiful hair!" exclaimed she, passing her delicate hand through his thick, silky, auburn locks; "but you wear it like a wild man of the woods! And then your clothes, oh, Heavens! are there tailors in England? or does every one make his own? However, there is no fear for your success in society; every thing English is the rage just now; you will soon become *un jeune homme charmant*, with the advantages you have. Now ring the bell for Gaspard; we must lose no more time in talking."

Everhard did as she desired; he felt at once both pleased and ashamed at being the object of such a scrutiny.

"Gaspard," said his aunt to her page, as he entered, "go to Fleurion, and tell him that he must have a dress proper for a young clerical student ready for my nephew this evening; then call at Henriot's, and give orders for all that will be necessary in the way of ruffles, lace, and all that. Tell La Force to be here early, that he may dress monsieur's hair; in short, you will go to M. du Pont's people, and order all that monsieur may require for his toilette, and you will consider yourself as his attendant whilst he remains here."

Everhard, who heard these sweeping orders given with some dismay, took out his pocket-book instinctively; his aunt stopped his hand hastily, saying, "What folly! Go, Gaspard, say the things are for M. du Pont." The page made a reverence and left the room. When he was gone, his aunt gave Everhard a long lecture on the extravagance of paying tradespeople, and the necessity of taking care of his money for things that were indispensable; then she dismissed him to his own apartment to take some rest and refreshment.

When he was alone, Everhard could hardly help smiling at the two lectures on economy he had recently received. His mother and his aunt both spoke on the same subject, and there the resemblance ended.

He was tolerably fatigued, and in no mood to quarrel with either the rest or refreshment prepared for him; still he sat down and wrote a letter to his mother, informing her of his safe arrival; and a longer one to Louis, telling him all that had happened since they parted.

The "ministers of grace" did their spiriting to admiration. Everhard could hardly recognise himself when he saw his reflection in a full-length mirror, even his aunt was hardly prepared for the improvement in his appearance.

She expressed all the delight at his transformation of a child over a new doll, and allowed him to lead her to the carriage with a feeling of infinite complacency.

"We must have you taught to fence," said she, when they were seated; "you only want that to make you perfect. Your French accent is admirable. We are going this evening," said she, after a pause, "to Madame d'Aligré's, who gives charming *petits soupers*, though they are rather *maigres*, but that does not signify, for she assembles the best and wealthiest people in Paris to eat them. The other day she gave a dinner that was very scanty, and the conversation became very scandalous.

"M. de Lauregais, who was present, said, 'it seems to me that in this house we should die of hunger if we did not eat up our neighbours with our bread'; but for all that, she is a very good woman, and exceedingly prudent, or of course I should not go there; what reward indeed would remain for virtue if we visited, and invited to our parties, the good and bad without distinction? The Abbé du Pré does not much approve of my going, because all the philosophers assemble there; but really it is too pleasant to be given up for the sake of a little danger to one's soul."

The carriage now stopped at Madame d'Aligré's *porte cochère*, and in due time they were ushered into the *salon*, which was about half full of guests.

Tables for play were set out, at some of which parties were already seated.

The hostess was sitting at the upper end of the room, talking to a group of men who stood round her.

Madame du Pont after paying her compliments, and presenting her nephew, glided to a sofa, where she perceived several of her acquaintances. Everhard stood beside her.

He saw men whose names have become historical; men who gave the first impulse to that movement which was destined to convulse society to its centre; but as yet, all was imprisoned in a chaos of theories and disputations, the surface of society was not yet broken, and all that was uttered that evening seemed to have no higher aim than to make brilliant conversation.

After a while Madame du Pont sat down to ombre, and left Everhard to make his way for himself. Madame d'Aligré, perceiving his bashful and painful look of strangership, beckoned him to come beside her. She nodded graciously as he came up, but did not interrupt her conversation. "Your *hommage aux dames*", said she, to a courtly smiling man who stood by, "is all very fine, but it is fictitious. You do not yourself believe one word of all you have been saying about woman's genius and equality. Out of the million of women who are flattered by being told they possess genius, not one ever achieves a work that endures, or that obtains higher praise than of being something very wonderful for a woman. Scarce one has ever achieved any thing that, in a man, would be considered first rate. I do not belong to the sisterhood of 'women of genius' myself, so my testimony is disinterested. Look at history, which is a tolerable criterion. If ever, by an extraordinary combination of circumstances, a woman has, from her position, influenced her age and country, her name speedily becomes a historical doubt, and her actions fabulous. The name of a woman has never authentically descended to posterity, unless preserved in the memory of some transcendent crime.

"Whenever a woman attempts to throw herself into the *mêlée* of action, and to contend with men on a footing of equality, she is always seen in the end, to commit either some grave fault, or some signal folly. No woman has ever succeeded in gaining lasting fame, but many have lost their reputation in the attempt."

"Because", said Duclos, who just then came up, "women are never engrossed by any object sufficiently to forget to display themselves; unless indeed, the object be a lover, and then they can be sublime. When a woman's affections are engaged, all her littleness disappears; women have been grand, almost superhuman, through the strength of love, but the moment they desire to distinguish themselves, they become stripped of the 'divinity that doth hedge' a woman. To be distinguished, seems a very grand thing, but to earn a name, is no holiday task; women are destitute both of patience and persistence, so no wonder that they fail, and their works appear ineffectual when measured beside those of really GREAT MEN who have laid out their lives in their work."

"How is it", asked Madame de Verset, "that society so bitterly resents all singularity, whether real or affected? It is tolerant of crimes, and long suffering with dullness, but it shows no mercy to those who are different from other people."

"It is desirable", said one of the company, "that the individuals composing a society should be in keeping with each other, lest if one be much better, or different in any way from the rest, he should play the part of a piece of new cloth in an old garment, and cause a rent wherever he goes."

"That is true," said M. Grimm, "men have a natural instinct against incongruities; and that may explain the dislike and persecution, with which those men are received who come to it as prophets and teachers. All that stands apart from the mass surrounding it, ought either to have a class of its own to fall back upon, or else to carry the germ of a new order of things within itself; otherwise, it is an ineffectual singularity, without any significance to atone for its bad taste."

"It is the instinct of self-preservation", said d'Holback, "that makes men look with distrust on all that tends to break through the train of things which have got themselves established. There is a sense of insecurity in the beginning of all change; we dread movement until we are fairly roused, and then we seem as if we could never know rest again."

"This mixture of restlessness and indolence is the key to many of the contradictions of human life. It is a pity we cannot calculate their action with precision, for then we might work miracles," said one who had not yet spoken.

"Till the secret became known, and then the miracle would become the ordinary course of nature, and we should have to fight and struggle as we do now," replied M. Grimm.

"Is it because we and our works endure for so short a time, that we attach so much veneration to all that has strength to resist change, and even for a little while to assume the aspect of permanency?" asked the gentle Madame d'E——.

"Possibly," replied M. Grimm, "ideas of permanence and endurance beguile the imagination of men because they do not seem to be impossibilities; we could never have the heart to labour if we did not hope that our works would live after us; in our heart, we each expect to attain immortality, though 'ready to vanish away' is the device inscribed by destiny upon us and all we do. The hope of achieving works which shall endure for ever, glimmers upon the horizon of things possible, like the elixir of life and the philosopher's stone, but none have arrived at the spot over which the star rests."

"What you say about permanence", said St Lambert, "applies in a peculiar manner to systems of government; there, all things seem to have attained the most unchangeable fixity, on the eve of a final breaking up of all forms."

"Ay," said Duclos, "the mechanism of society is then worn smooth with use, all goes on quietly, but it is the ease of that which is worn out. The system holds together in this state till some trifle jars upon it, and then like other moulds which have become effaced, it is broken up for fresh combinations."

"The energy of nature," said d'Holback, "lends itself to the form of our social institutions so long as they are adequate to some want within us, and have a latent meaning that is felt by all; but when

46

what once was religion, degenerates into worn-out traditions, and ceremonies emblematic of no truth—when what was in the beginning benevolence and human love, becomes the mere etiquette of polite society, when the structure of society, from one end to the other, becomes a mere tissue of legal fictions, and men stickle for forms and customs, (which are always the last things that pass away)—there is no life to oppose dissolution, all relapses into the elements, and the life by which they were supplied takes a new form. This is the secret priests fable unknowingly in their dreams of a 'new heaven and a new earth'; man reduces to chaos, and out of chaos God creates fresh worlds."

"Well, and what becomes of the poor inhabitants in all the confusion?" asked Madame d'Aligré.

"Why, madame," replied a pompous member of the academy, "minute investigation has showed us that the rocks which make the primeval foundation of the earth, are composed of bodies which were once organised living animals, and that proves—"

"Ay," said some one, interrupting him, "that the dust we tread upon has been alive and wretched."

But now supper was announced, and Everhard had the privilege of handing his aunt to table. When the supper was over, or rather when the guests had ceased eating, for they still continued at table, music was proposed, and Madame d'Aligré turned with a petitioning air to Madame du Pont, who had a splendid voice.

"You know," said Madame du Pont, "I am a Gluckist whilst you are all wild after Piccini. I wish the lot had fallen to some one better able to convert you than I am," and rising from her place she allowed herself to be led across the room to the harpsichord, when she played and sang the recitative and air of "In vano alcun", from the "Armida". After the expressions of admiration had somewhat subsided—

M. Grimm said, "We shall have some difficulty, to maintain the supremacy of Piccini after such singing as that, however, we must support the honour of our friend as well as we can."

Madame d'Aligré then joined one of the guests in the duet "Ne giorni tuoi felice", from the "Olimpiade", which was very successful. Another and another song succeeded, and the party broke up at a late hour.

During their drive home Everhard was quite unable to converse with his aunt; but as he kissed her hand, on parting from her for the night, she perceived that he looked handsomer than ever, so she was quite satisfied—much as she would have been with the success of some new point of costume on which she might have ventured.

Everhard found his way to his own room. All night he was in a vague reverie, rather than sleep; and the scene he had quitted, the lights, the music, the conversation, flitted in confusion through his brain, like scenes in a phantasmagoria.

"Well," said Emilie, the elder of Madame du Pont's waiting-women, to her companion, after they had been dismissed from their attendance on her, "what do you think of madame's nephew?"

"Why," replied the other, "for one thing, I think we shall have a very good time, for madame is in a good humour, and at such times she is always generous. To-night, to begin with, she gave me a worked apron."

"Bah! I was not thinking of her. What do you think of him, the nephew?"

"Oh, qui'il est beau comme l'amour, et gentil comme un ange," replied Flora. "When he passed me in madame's dressing-room he made a reverence, as if I had been a court lady. But he is very shy, and does not know the value of his beauty; for all the softness of his eyes, he looks out of them as if they were given for nothing else but to see with. Still there is something piquant in so much innocence."

"In the hope of spoiling it, I suppose you mean," replied Emilie, laughing. "Well, so there is, for it is a work one generally finds ready made to one's hand. That delicate bloom will not last long upon his cheeks in Paris."

"He will be handsome when it is gone," replied the other. "Did you remark him to-night after he came home? His face seemed to have gained meaning even in that short time."

"It is to be hoped he can take care of himself, poor youth," said Emilie, compassionately.

"Malheur à lui, if he cannot," replied Flora, as she smiled at her own pretty reflection in the glass, and arranged her hair under a most coquettish cap.

"Nous verrons, ma mie", said Emilie, yawning. "But now, in heaven's name, let us cease talking. You could live without sleep altogether, I think."

A few moments afterwards the whole household was buried in repose.

CHAPTER V

_ . _

Everhard felt on awakening the next morning, much as one of the seven sleepers might be imagined to have done; but he soon became accustomed to his new way of life, for one day only led to another, brighter and pleasanter than the last.

His aunt, quite satisfied with the impression he produced, made him accompany her wherever she went, and he had to share both her amusements and devotions. She was at an age when women find infinitely more interest in a fresh unsophisticated youth, than in the polished, hackneyed, successful man of society; and Madame du Pont found a fund of gentle _délassement_ in forming the manners of her handsome nephew. So Everhard's days passed on pleasantly enough. He was introduced to a perfumed, brilliant, luxurious version, of that hard, mysterious reality called LIFE. He mixed in female society for the first time; hitherto he had seen no women but his mother and her attendants.

His exceeding inexperience kept him from perceiving the licentiousness and immorality that lay under the graceful amenities of the society in which he was moving; though, it must be owned, it was a critical experiment.

He felt within himself the movement of passions which were beginning to make him sensible of their existence; and the host of undefined tumultuous sensations which filled his soul without pointing to any definite aim, gave him a sense of life and power, an intoxicating sense of joy, in the mere fact of existence. He was entering on the "heritage of HIMSELF", and felt endowed with new gifts and perceptions, a passionate desire after the beautiful in all things; all his faculties seemed bathed in an atmosphere of warm light; the crust of reserve and awkwardness, which had shielded him from himself, dropped off like scales; he had not been stimulated into precocious maturity, and there was no danger of his adding to the melancholy band of those "whose unripe blessedness has dropped away from the young tree of life", before it has fulfilled its beautiful promise.

The brief period between childhood and maturity is indeed the golden age of life! A fairy dust is thrown over all persons and all things, making that lovely which is not so; like eastern monarchs, who caused beauty and fertility to spring up for the moment, when they had to journey through desert and unlovely places, making all look rich and glad as they passed along.

Everhard remained four months in Paris; at the end of that time, a letter came from his mother, desiring him to fix an early day for his departure to Rome.

This announcement came on Everhard like a thunderbolt. Going to Rome had become a vague abstraction which was to occur at an indefinite period, and, until this moment, he was not aware of all the disinclination to his profession that had grown upon him. To be a priest, under a "vow of obedience", was a very different thing to being one of his old saints travelling about from country to country, on errands of benevolence: as different as a soldier in a marching regiment is from being one of the seven champions.

The *prestige* of church dignities had vanished before the bishops and abbés he had met in society, and his ambition to attain them had been crushed almost before it had sprung up. He panted for some occupation that would call forth the energy which he felt pent up within him. Alas! he did not know that he was grappling with the grand difficulty, the aforesaid mystery of life.

Thinking that possibly the Abbé du Pré might help him in his perplexity, he put on his hat, and went to call upon him.

Everhard entered a small, luxuriously furnished apartment, and found the abbé sitting in a flowered damask silk dressing-gown over the breakfast table; he was sipping his chocolate, and reading "La Reine de Golconde", which he quietly placed under the sofa pillow when Everhard came in. "I fear I am an untimely visitor," said he, "but the truth is, I wanted to find you alone; I am come to throw myself upon you for a little counsel."

"Oh fie! have you been getting into a scrape?" said the abbé, in a bland tone, with an arch smile; "but before you confess, sit down and do penance on a cup of chocolate"; at the same time pushing towards him the silver filigree stand; "you will find these rusks as delicate as those that regaled Vert Vert. Try this *pâté*, it is capital, and if you knew the fair hands it came from, it would seem still more exquisite."

Everhard felt very little inclination to do justice to the good things round him, but he saw the abbé was in a different mood, and he had the prudence to offer no interruption until the breakfast was finished. It came to an end, like all other things. "And now," said the abbé, wiping his lips after swallowing a petit verre, "what is it you want me to do?"

Everhard handed him the letter he had that morning received, and when the abbé had read it, he confided to him the dislike he felt to the path prepared for him; "and besides," said he, in conclusion, "I feel as if I could never perform the duties which the priesthood entails; there is something horrible in the suppressed energy, the still life endurance it requires. Nothing to do—nothing to hope for—no danger—no enterprise—no variety. I shall die, if I am made a priest; can you tell me no way to get out of it?"

The Abbé du Pré looked down and played with his snuff-box whilst Everhard was speaking, to hide the smile he could not suppress. "Well," said he, soothingly, when he ceased, "it is all very natural that at your age you should not feel tempted to renounce the world; but where, in Heaven's name, did you get your notion of what a priest's life requires? Poor boy! it is no wonder you should desire to escape from such an imagination! I fear there is no other career open to you; your lady mother would give neither help nor sanction to any change in your destination; besides, why should you wish for one? you have good prospects in the church; your uncle has interest to push you on; between ourselves, I shall be a bishop long before you are in orders, and shall be able to help you forward; you may depend upon it that I shall do so, for you will be a credit to us. There is no need for you to be either a saint or a martyr, you will come and live in Paris; the women here, who are as fanciful about their confessors as they are about their doctors and lovers, will adjust the balance between you and their devotions; only think

52

of the opportunity you will have of making a sensation when you come to preach! Eloquence (and you have it) opens the way to every heart, to every thing to be desired in this world; it can cover a whole decalogue of sins; it is a regular enchanter's wand! You may have a glorious life; you may be a politician, a statesman; and, though vowed to celibacy, you may enjoy the devoted friendship of the loveliest women; any thing, every thing is open to you; there is no career like it for a man who knows how to run therein. Be discreet, be prudent; that is the true secret of leading an exemplary life. So cheer up, and have no more foolish fancies. And now," said he, after a pause, "will you remain here whilst I dress? and then we will walk back together. Madame du Pont had a *migraine* yesterday, and requested me to come early."

So saying, the graceful priest glided out of the room, leaving Everhard plunged in a painful reverie. They walked silently towards the Hôtel du Pont, for Everhard was quite unequal to the lively conversation in which the other sought to engage him.

Everhard hastened to his own room, where he remained alone with his own heart. He looked helplessly round for some one who might speak words of strong counsel to him; but there was no one. The complacent wily abbé was about the best among his present acquaintance.

At length, with a start of surprise that he should not have thought of it before, he betook himself to his old resource in times of childish difficulty; he flung himself on his knees beside the bed, and with sobs and inarticulate words poured forth all his grief and perplexity. He did not as heretofore, go to any of his favourite saints; it was from the service of God he shrank, and it was to that God Himself he went now in his agony of weakness.

The only instant when man has any thing sublime about him, is, when prostrate before the invisible, he makes an offering of his own will and his own wisdom, desiring to be guided only to that which is best and wisest. Prayer is the appeal from the fluctuating incomprehensible aspect of this life, to Him who changes not. None but they who are sinking under some of the infinitely varied forms of human need and human weakness, can tell the strong consolation of taking refuge from their perplexities with one, "who knoweth all things, and to whom all hearts are open".

53

The remainder of that day passed as usual, but it seemed to Everhard that the beauty and delight which had fascinated him in this life of society had suddenly departed.

The next morning, as he was preparing to pay some visits, he received a summons from his uncle.

"Well, Everhard, my boy," said he, "you are become so *répandu*, that one must send for you early to get a word with you. Your mother has just sent me this letter, and desires me to advise you what course to take on the strength of it; but I think you are quite of an age to have a voice in the disposal of yourself. Your father bequeathed you to the Church, but you don't seem to me to have much vocation for it, at least you have shown none since you came here. Did you ever hear of a distant relation, who is a prosperous India merchant, and making an income of more livres than I possess francs? I suppose you never saw him; he has started up like the good uncle or father at the last act of a comedy. There is a letter from him to your mother; read it, and see if you are disposed to close with the offer. You had better take till to-morrow to consider."

Everhard received the large, heavy looking letter, and retired to read it at leisure.

The letter was from the only surviving member of a distant branch of the family, which, eschewing the politics which had well nigh caused the ruin of the elder branch, had given all their energies to making money, and had succeeded amazingly: but there had been no intercourse between the owners of Sutton Manor and the merchants of London for at least two generations. The first part of the letter in question was taken up with explaining to Madame Burrows the genealogy of the two branches, in a most prolix and herald-like fashion. The conclusion was more to the purpose; it was an offer to adopt the younger son, to initiate him in all the mysteries of trade, and finally to make him his successor in the old and wealthy firm of "Burrows and Co.".

"I am a widower without children," said the letter in conclusion, "therefore all my fortune will go to my nephew, if he takes kindly to the business; but a merchant like myself he must be, before he comes in for one farthing. I am rich enough to do what I like, and I am as desirous to continue a line of British merchants, as other people can be to found a family. I make no mention of your elder son, because he has already enough, and more than enough, and I will have nothing to do with gentlemen.

"I hear you have intended Everhard for a priest. If he does not choose to accept my offer, I shall bequeath my money to a hospital, and break up the concern. It has been carried on for more than a hundred years, from father to son, and I will not have a stranger for successor. Everhard is a name that has been in the family for generations, so I shall not so much mind his not being my son, but I expect he will bind himself to marry, that there may be no danger of the business going to a still more distant connexion.

"With all sorts of good wishes for you, though I never had the honour of seeing you,

"I am, Madam,
"Your obedient, humble servant,
"EVERHARD BURROWS."

Everhard read the last part of the letter through twice; here was the chance of an escape from the priesthood which he had so earnestly wished for the day before. Our wishes never seem so little desirable as when on the verge of accomplishment; we draw back instinctively, they look so different from what we expected.

Everhard was not at all smitten by the prospect held out to him; he had at the bottom a prejudice against trade, which he had imbibed from his mother; he thought it degrading; added to which, all his natural tastes lay in a directly contrary direction.

By a natural reaction of feeling, the way of life which so lately had looked hard and uninviting, seemed clothed with calm and mild dignity. Now that he was free to choose, all desire for a secular life seemed dead within him. Accordingly, when he met his uncle next day, it was to intimate his fixed intention to follow the profession to which he had always been destined.

A grateful letter was accordingly written to Everhard Burrows senior, declining his offer; and Everhard made preparations to depart to Rome. He went to his aunt's dressing-room to take leave of her the morning of his departure. He found her amid a chaos of silks, feathers, and tissues of every conceivable variety, and so engrossed in a privy council for deciding on a presentation dress for the next court day, that she could not spare a moment to show any sensibility, which rather annoyed him. She embraced him, however, very gracefully, saying, "Well, we shall have you back when you are a priest, and then you shall be my confessor! I wish you would send me some relics from Rome; I cannot meet with any here; if there are any pretty things worked in Lava, get them for me; they will be quite new. Are you a judge of Cameos? I am told you can get those sort of things for nothing there. I wish you were going with me to the ball to-morrow."

Everhard tried to express his sense of all his aunt's attentions, but the gallantly turned phrase died on his lip; his eyes filled with tears, he raised her hand to his lips, and hastened out of the room.

"Quelle sensibilité," said the pretty Flora.

"Oui; mais la sensibilité me pèse", replied Madame du Pont, and returned to the occupation which had been for a moment interrupted.

M. du Pont accompanied his nephew for a few miles on horseback. "Well, boy," said he, as he was about to turn homewards, "we shall have you amongst us again. I shall look out, and solicit the minister for a good thing in the way of a benefice for you. Be discreet, and you will be sure to become a great man."

CHAPTER VI

— . —

When Everhard arrived at the English College in Rome, he was ushered at once before the Superior, who had been prepared to expect him, and was sitting in the library, where new comers were always received. The walls were hung round with portraits of great men, in the different costumes of cardinals, judges, warriors, who had all in their time been inmates of the college, and there was a *prestige*, in thus sitting surrounded as it were by the halo of their glory, very calculated to impress the ardent imagination of a young aspirant.

But Everhard was not imaginative, and besides, he had no time to pause to gaze round. He advanced at once to the chair of the Superior, and, bending his knee, kissed the hand that was extended to him. The Superior, a man somewhat advanced in life, with a keen eye and a stern aspect, uttered a few words of encouragement and welcome; then summoning an attendant, desired him to conduct Everhard to the refectory, where supper was already served.

Everhard, following his guide in silence, entered the hall where all the inmates of the college were seated at supper, and took the seat indicated to him. At first, he felt somewhat confused at the idea of encountering the gaze of so many, but not an eye was turned towards him, all continued their supper with the silence and abstraction of Brahmins. A young man at a desk at the upper end of the hall, read aloud out of the works of Cardinal Bellarmine; lay servants passed to and fro with trays on which the dishes were ready carved, and placed them before each; whilst a stately professor paced up and down between the tables to enforce silence and regularity. The hall was vast and lofty; a carved walnut-wood wainscot ran round the wall with seats for more than a hundred persons; massive tables, raised a step all round, were fixed to the floor. Supper lasted about twenty minutes, when all rose and noiselessly retired to their own rooms; none of them approached Everhard, or seemed any way conscious of his presence. The attendant he had before seen, came up as he was standing in perplexity, not knowing whether to remain or follow, and conducted him to the apartment prepared for him, but all in perfect silence.

Everhard, chilled and depressed by every thing round him, sat down listlessly in the window-seat, more disposed to weep than he had been since childhood. He felt very miserable indeed. The strong passions of adolescence which were rapidly developing, had no aim; he desired, he knew not what; the very gifts of intellect that were in him worked like passions; there was no one in the world to whom he could address himself; the brilliant life of society he had been leading for the last four months, had given him a hold on no one; he had entered a stranger, and departed the same:—all he thought and felt, was pent up in his own heart, and ever must be. He had renounced the world, he had cut for ever the ties that bind men to men, the step he had taken was irrevocable, and he felt crushed down under the conviction.

A knock at the door at length roused him, and a robust, handsome young man entered, dressed in the close black gown and white linen band which was the usual in-door costume of the inmates of the college. He had withal, a dashing, jaunty air, which was not precisely the ideal of what a young priest should be.

"Welcome! thrice welcome! holy Saint Everhard!" said he, "to our pious and most intensely stupid abode! Saint Magdalen forgive me! but if Paradise be akin to it, I don't care how long I tarry in purgatory!"

The tone and manner recalled to Everhard's memory an old school-fellow, who had been expelled for some unpardonable transgression of rules. With a start of pleasure he grasped his hand. "Why, John Paul Marston, can it be you? Why, what brings you in such a place?"

"Yes, it is I indeed. I suppose I was pre-destined to the shepherd's crook, and the work of training up a nice little flock of lambs to the credit of the church's pasturage, and to gain to myself a bright reversion in the celestial city. God! I would give it all to be free to wander for a year through this eternal city. I have not much faith in the heavenly beauties; those glorious Roman women are worth the whole calendar of saints. I am so glad you are come; I can talk to you without needing to make believe to be better than I am. The discipline here is bad enough to endure, but the cursed hypocritical face one is obliged to put on is far worse. Dante's leaden cowls for hypocrites is no fable, but a Christian verity."

Everhard could not help feeling glad to see John Paul again, but he was somewhat scandalised nevertheless, at his freedom of speech. As soon as he could get in a word, he said, "Well, now, John Paul, sit down and tell me all you have been doing since you left Bruges."

"Since I was turned out, you mean; no need to mince facts. Well, I have leave to stay an hour with you, as you are a new man, and an old friend, or else it is not according to law."

John Paul trimmed the lamp he had brought with him, and set it down. It was quite night now, and they both seated themselves at the open window. A faint fragrance from flowers came in on the fresh, cool air; bats flitted to and fro like unclean spirits, and occasionally a large moth fluttered in, attracted by the light. The stars came out bright and many, but the moon had not yet risen.

"Well!" exclaimed John Paul, after a pause, "there is not another man in the world I would have been so pleased to see. I really like you, Everhard; I always did, and it is a comfort to have a natural inclination one can own to *à haute voix*, in this cursed place. Now tell me, how did you go on after I left you? was I soon forgotten? or do I still live among the school traditions as a beacon, pointing to innocent youths the way in which they ought not to go?"

Everhard could not help smiling. "You are as mad as ever, John Paul; what do they do with you here?"

"Oh, you will see fast enough; but now tell me something."

"It is little I can tell you," replied Everhard; "we soon recovered the quiet you had disturbed, and went on just as usual; Louis and I left school last Christmas; he remains at home to support family honours, and I have been on a visit for the last four months to my uncle in Paris. One of my father's English connexions sent the other day, wanting to adopt me, and make me a merchant, promising to leave me a fortune if I would follow his business; but I have no genius for trade, so I declined his proposal, and am now come here to study for the priesthood. You know I have been destined for holy orders from childhood."

"What!" exclaimed John Paul, vehemently, "and you really had an opening, a way of escape from this horrible bondage, and you did not avail yourself of it! No matter if your uncle had wanted to make you a chimney-sweep, any thing would have been better than the choice you have made; and yet, perhaps, no; you are peaceful by nature; you have a natural turn for goodness; above all, you believe; you are very different to me; and yet, I too might have made an honourable man, might have achieved something worth doing; I feel I have power in me; but here, here, all my strength is consumed within me, and for what? to enable me to keep myself within bounds, to make myself in appearance something like the cold-blooded clay around me. Oh, if they could but take the blood out of my veins, and fill them with new milk, I might be a happy man! The curse be on those who bind men by irrevocable vows!"

John Paul started to his feet in an uncontrollable frenzy, and began to stride up and down the room; the veins stood out on his forehead; his small, cruel grey eye glittered with ferocity, and his breath came in thick pants. Everhard attempted to calm him, but John Paul took no notice. After a while he recovered himself, and said, "You see what comes over me at times; if it did not break out in this way, I should go mad. I am right now for a while, and shall be able to go on in the mill round of prayers and fastings. Now I will tell you how I came here.

"My cousin, in whose hands I was placed after the row at school, took me home with him; my mother had been informed of the whole thing. To tell the truth, I was not sorry to be spared facing her for a while; every body said I required stronger management than a woman's hand, and my cousin undertook to break me in. You know that my father on his death-bed desired that the child my mother was then expecting should be dedicated to the service of the church; it was the dearest wish of my mother's heart: the family considered it settled; as for myself, I had got into the habit of looking on it as an evil day at an indefinite distance. It was a large town where my cousin lived, not very far from London. I did

60

not choose to be cooped up in the house, so I scraped acquaintance with several youths of my own age, or rather older. I had nothing to do; my cousin might have found me employment, but he did not, so I got into mischief. He called me to account, and, as I did not admire his method, I ran away to London. My good mother, who had the wise habit of supplying me plentifully with pocket money, had sent me a remittance only the day before, so there had been no time to spend it, which was lucky. When I found myself in London, I felt happy, for I was my own master. I had vague dreams of working my way in the world, and making myself famous; I felt energy enough in me for any thing; the sight of so many new and wonderful objects made me seem to be in a new world, and I felt proud of walking up and down the streets. I took a small room in a lodging-house in Holborn, dirty and comfortless enough in all conscicnce, but it was cheap, and I wanted to make my money last as long as possible. The third night after I was in London I went to Drury-lane Theatre. I had never seen a play; it was enchantment; I doubted whether such delight could be intended for mortals. I went again and again. By day I haunted the private door of a small theatre near my lodging, thinking it would be blessed to be even a candle snuffer, and looking with respect on the little boys who distributed the handbills. I contrived, by a lucky accident, to scrape acquaintance with one of the actresses, a pretty creature, and a great favourite with the manager; she spoke a good word for me, and I made my *début* as a s'lent page; but I had talents, and was soon promoted to talking parts. I was a great favourite with the women of our company, and I enjoyed the way of life amazingly. True, we were rogues and vagabonds in the eyes of respectable people, but really I don't think we were much worse than our neighbours, and we thought no small things of ourselves, I can assure you. As drinking was not one of my faults, I managed to keep my chin above water, and to live very gaily for a couple of months. I was better worth then than I am now, though nobody, perhaps, will believe it. After all, I have only left one stage to come on another; for what is saying mass, I should like to know, but acting a solemn charade? And in the sermons, which are a sort of programme, is it not asserted that the whole affair will finally be wound up by a magnificent *tableau* of a 'Last Judgment', a grand display of 'Lakes of Fire', 'Devils', 'Ministers of deathless Wrath', who will sweep away some into everlasting destruction; whilst a fair city of gold and precious stones, full of light, music, and rejoicing, will appear for the reception of the rest? I would not wish for a more theatrical *dénouement*. To all this, is to be added the terrible excitement for these blessed ónes of seeing 'the smoke of the burning rising up for ever and ever'. I hardly know which fate would make one shudder the most, if one believed it. But to go on with my story.

"It was not two months since I had run away. My poor mother, who had in the first instance been pacified by my cousin, with assurances that I should return of my own accord, became too anxious to remain passive any longer. At her entreaty my cousin employed a man, who had formerly been in the police, to ferret me out. They guessed I was somewhere in London. It was not long before I was traced, and intelligence despatched to my relatives.

"My mother, though in a feeble state of health, set off instantly to London; she repaired straight to the obscure place where I lodged. I was not within, and it was early dawn when I returned, for there was a farewell supper given to one of the company, who was leaving us. I was flushed with wine and excess of all sorts, but the sight of my mother sobered me at once. She had fallen asleep in her chair, and there was a painful look of infirmity in her countenance, as if mind and body were both tending together to dissolution. I can never forget the impression her face made on me. The misery my thoughtlessness had caused seemed heaped upon my own heart at that moment. I was terrified to think what I had done.

"My mother awoke as I stood gazing upon her. She rose before I could utter a word, and throwing her arms round me, she said, 'My son, come back with me; I am come to fetch you from this horrible place.' Her embrace relaxed, and her form became heavier—she had fainted. I placed her on the bed, but it was long before she recovered her consciousness. I sent for a physician, who adminis- tered cordials, but told me frankly, that the system was too much exhausted to rally, and that he could do nothing for her. She lay all the day in a sort of stupor, with my hand locked in hers.

"I cannot tell you all the horrible remorse I felt, for I really loved

62

my mother; but I had never realised all the pain I occasioned her till now.

"About the middle of the night she seemed to rally; her voice was clear and strong. 'John Paul,' she said, 'my own John Paul, promise me to quit this way of life. You know that in your cradle you were dedicated to the Church. All my life long it has been my joy to picture you ministering at the altar, and myself receiving from your hand the last sacrament at the hour of my death. Oh, my son! I have suffered much for you; what the grief of my heart has been since you left us all, God, who sent the affliction, alone knows. You have broken my heart, will you do nothing for me in this my last agony? Oh, my son, if you would have your gifts—a blessing, and not a curse, ratify my vow, dedicate yourself to the service of the altar.' I was silent. 'If,' she continued, more passionately, 'you would have my last blessing—if you would not have my blood upon your head—grant my request. Speak to me—you have been the anxiety of my life, will you not let me die in peace?'

"I began to answer her, to soothe her; I entreated her not to exact such a promise; that I could not be a priest; I told her that it would be sacrilege in me to become one. 'All devices of the evil one to slay your soul,' exclaimed she, interrupting me. 'I, your mother, entreat you.' And before I could understand her intention, she had sprung out of bed and thrown herself on her knees at my feet. 'No, no,' cried she, passionately resisting my attempts to raise her, 'you may trample on me, but I will not quit this place till you say you will fulfil my desire.' She sank exhausted on the floor as she spoke these words, but still kept her eyes fixed on mine. Everhard, there are men of a strong, firm nature, who can keep their determination, who can be shaken from their purpose by nothing. I have not one of those iron wills. At that moment I could not think of myself, it seemed of no consequence whether I had to suffer or not. I raised her from the ground, where she lay fainting, and solemnly promised to do all she desired. Her countenance gleamed with joy, she blessed me in a broken voice. I laid her again on the bed, and placed a cordial to her lips; but a sudden shiver passed through her, a slight spasm contracted her features for a moment, the breathing came at distant intervals, the whole expression of her face changed into something strange and different to herself; but she was quite sensible. She tried to speak, but the organs had lost their power; her eyes became fixed on one corner of the room; she lay motionless for some time, then she turned her head on one side, and drew a deep breath. It was her last—I had never seen death before. I kept my word to her," continued he, after a pause. "As soon as possible after her interment, I arranged my affairs and came here.

"I have property enough to support me handsomely, so at least I shall not do the work of the Church for lucre's sake, and that is some comfort.

"I am glad I have told you this, I feel as if I did not despise myself, and loathe my condition so much at least as when I began. But, Everhard," said he, abruptly, "seeing a person die is not the best way to convince one of immortality. What better is my mother NOW, for the horrible lot I have undertaken? and that thought is the hardest of all."

John Paul was silent, and Everhard was so too, he knew not what to say; at length he rose, and grasping Everhard's hand, said, "I must leave you now, good night; I will call for you to-morrow on my way to the chapel."

After the departure of John Paul, Everhard remained for some time in a profound reverie. The narrative he had just heard made a deep impression upon him. He saw, as in a glass, what might become his own case, that of a man divided against himself, without the self-control to conform to his lot, or the energy to emancipate himself from it, and all his strength consumed in idle chafing under the yoke.

It is only at times, and for a few brief moments, that the secret of our own hearts is laid bare to us; those are not the periods when we feel disposed to enter the revelation in "Diaries"; we see for an instant, then the veil which shrouds us from ourselves is again drawn, and we know not what we are; but the insight of that moment works within us, like an instinct, leavening our character and actions for years to come.

All have known such seasons, and can testify how widely they differ from the common run of "self-examinations", and the spasmodic ejaculations called "good resolutions". All can call to mind some period of life when there was a halt, a right course and a wrong lying equally open; as the decision is made then, the character takes its caste; it gives a start and bursts like a flower from the confining calyx; a crisis not at the time looking different from other incidents occurring every day. Such a crisis had this night been to Everhard.

The next morning he was dressed when John Paul entered his room, the emotion of the previous night had passed away, and he was the rattling, witty, amusing companion that Everhard remembered in old days.

After chapel the prefect invited Everhard to breakfast with him; when they were seated he said, with a forced smile, "You had a visitor last night—John Paul Marston?"

"Yes," replied Everhard, "we were school-fellows."

"Ah, he is a wild one," rejoined the prefect, "and the less intimate you are with him the better; he is always in scrapes of one sort or other; one cannot help liking him, but do not let him beguile you. Come, if you have finished your breakfast, I will show you the building, and tell you the regulations as we go along."

He led Everhard along several corridors in the dark, monastic building. The bright morning sun, shining through the deep embrasures, could not make the narrow windows look cheerful, but it did all that was possible towards making them so. A few lamps were fixed at intervals in the walls, and over the low doors that opened into the corridors, which were all closed. There was perfect stillness, except when the silence was broken by the tread of some of the inmates, or the shutting of a distant door. There was in the middle of the corridor a large open space, in the form of a cross, where the youths of that division met for recreation.

"You will find all things comfortable and regular here," said the prefect, "and you may be very happy if you choose; one piece of advice only will I give you, be very careful with whom you associate, and above all, let nothing tempt you to evade the rules. Obedience is our corner-stone. Now," said he, after they had seen all the place, "those are the apartments of the superior, who will appoint your line of studies. I will leave you here."

Everhard felt some trepidation at the ordeal he was about to encounter; but the superior was not one who understood nervousness, and he proceeded to examine him without any compunction, and as example has a magnetic influence, his composure tranquillised Everhard, who went through his examination with great credit. The superior said a few words of course, pointed to the portraits that hung on the walls, begged he would emulate those great men, be obedient to the regulations, and dismissed him. How very little other people can teach any one, and how much good advice is barren seed!

John Paul stood Everhard's friend, and introduced him to the rest and exerted himself with strenuous good will to avert the awkwardness and annoyance a stranger among a multitude always feels. John Paul had obtained the same sort of ascendency here that he had over the boys at school, and he was proud to let it be seen by Everhard.

The general aspect of college life offers nothing to record; all went on in the regular routine, till one might have thought it exempt from the common vicissitudes of humanity.

One day, however, when Everhard had been an inmate of the college about eight months, an event occurred, which caused an unprecedented commotion.

All were seated at dinner that day, when a letter was brought to the superior, which had just come by express; he opened it eagerly, and had no sooner read it than his agitation became obvious; turning to two elderly professors who sat near, he exclaimed, "Who would have thought it! at his age, and with his apparent zeal for the church! Francis Matthew Gifford has not only given up all thoughts of entering the priesthood, but has just gone and married again, a girl hardly older than his daughter, a heretic too, which makes the matter more flagrant."

The worthy superior's eyes flashed, and his face crimsoned to the top of his forehead, he could scarcely articulate for the very unorthodox passion into which such unexpected tidings had thrown him.

Such a breach of decorous discipline had never been known before in the refectory; the reading of Cardinal Bellarmine came to a sudden pause; the students looked at each other and whispered; the superior exchanged some hurried words with the professors, and, rising abruptly from their places, they all withdrew from the hall in manifest disorder. The students retired to recreation devoured by curiosity, but nothing transpired to enlighten it; all was calm and dignified as usual when they next assembled at their studies.

Everhard was far from dreaming that his future fate was involved in the news he had just heard, and yet, for him, it was the most important affair that had ever been transacted in the world. Gifford and his heretic wife will have a great deal to do with our history; we must give the reader some account of them.

CHAPTER VII

— · —

Zoe Gifford, the "heretic wife", whose marriage caused such a commotion in the college, spoiling the dinner of so many grave and respectable signors, was the daughter of Frederick Cleveland, an English officer, and a beautiful Greek girl, whom he had rescued from the hands of some pirates as they were bearing her off to their boats. Though captivated by her extreme beauty and gentleness, he honourably offered her means to reach her home in one of the small islands of the Archipelago; but her father and only brother had been murdered by the pirates, she had no near relations left, and she had no desire to quit her handsome and gallant deliverer. Her wild attachment and gratitude to him, were only equalled by his passionate love to her. She followed his wanderings for three years, and was to him all that the most faithful and devoted wife would have been; he owed his life more than once to her skilful and careful attendance. They had lived together little more than a year when Zoe, our heroine, was born, who formed a new tie between her parents.

Two years after this happy event Captain Cleveland was severely wounded, and his recovery was made very dubious by low intermitting fever and fits of ague. He was ordered home to England as his only chance of life; he, however, preferred going to France. On landing at Marseilles, his first step was to marry his beautiful Greek, and to take the necessary measures to have Zoe legitimated. The mother, who had never thought of herself, was thankful that her child would be spared from encountering the civilised proscription that attends such as herself.

The change of climate caused a rapid improvement in Captain

68

Cleveland's health, and he was soon able to introduce his wife to the society and amusements of Paris. He purposed, after a little time, to take her over to England, and introduce her to his relations there. They had only been a year in France, a short time in Paris, when, returning from the theatre one cold, foggy night, the fair Greek caught a violent cold, to which she paid no attention; inflammation came on, which resisted all remedies, and her life terminated in a few days.

The first agonies of Captain Cleveland were terrible to behold—the very servants hid themselves from his presence; his grief was a sort of fury, he raged like a whirlwind through the house. For some days he was quite insane, and they were obliged to remove the body of his wife secretly for interment.

When he became calmer, the thought of his child began to soothe him, but he was summoned almost immediately to resume the active duties of his profession; and then came the perplexing thought, what was to be done with little Zoe?

Captain Cleveland had a brother in England, a clergyman of the Established Church; a good, benevolent man, with more common sense than belonged to his gallant and reckless brother; they had not met for many years; but Captain Cleveland could think of no better plan than to intrust his child to the care of his brother Oliver, at least until he could give her a proper home with himself. He wrote to his brother, who made no sort of difficulty; and Captain Cleveland determined to go with her and place her in his brother's hands; but a peremptory summons to join his regiment frustrated his intentions, and he was obliged to trust her to the care of the French *bonne* who had lived in the family since the commencement of Captain Cleveland's connexion with Zoe's mother. A handsome annuity was settled on Nannette, upon condition of her remaining with Zoe. Mam'selle Nannette, as she was called, was a good-natured, simple soul, devoted to the child, willing to follow her to the world's end, and to England included, which was very heroic, as she had a great idea that the English were a species of ogres, who lived on raw beef-steak, and were constantly drunk, whilst the weather was one everlasting fog. Captain Cleveland could only accompany them to the vessel, where he left them, with innumerable blessings. The same day, after making his will, and leaving

Zoe all he possessed, he departed for Bombay, where his regiment was then stationed.

It was an evening in May, when the Rev. Oliver Cleveland, closing a volume of Bishop Hall's "Contemplations", said to his sister-in-law, who was knitting at a little spider-legged table by the fire, "that he thought their guests must soon arrive".

"Well, every thing is ready," replied the lady, who was a tall, thin personage, of very erect and stately carriage; her face had a sort of demure sedateness, a pair of round, hazel eyes that looked as if they never shut, thin, compressed lips, and when she spoke it was in a precise, even tone of voice; there was an air of stately affability about her, as if she was on her guard against being proud, though at the same time she thought it her duty to keep every one at their proper distance. Her lawn handkerchief and clear muslin apron trimmed with point lace, were of a whiteness seldom, alas! equalled by the washerwomen of our own day.

The tea equipage was arranged on a bright, walnut-wood table, and a prim, demure little girl, of ten or twelve, was presiding over it; that was her daughter, who, under her bringing up, was fast becoming a pattern of thrift, decorum, and domestic management. They were assembled in what was called the "Tea Room", the joy and pride of Mrs Martha's heart, whilst it was the admiration of all the parish. The walls were panelled and painted white, according to the fashion of that day, and around hung various family portraits, who, one and all, seemed to have been peaceable persons, of substance and respectability—altogether, ancestors who were a credit to their descendants. An air of comfort pervaded every thing—a point not always achieved by emphatically tidy people, and which proved Mrs Martha to be a genius in her own way.

The rector was a grave, important-looking man, rather handsome, and fully impressed with the idea of the dignity of his office. He was highly orthodox, always scrupulously dressed in clerical costume, rather addicted to making Latin puns, not insensible to the charms of good living, slightly pompous in his manner, but thoroughly kind-hearted, and looked up to by every man, woman, and child in his parish. Being possessed of a handsome private property, he had a good deal of weight among the county gentry.

The parsonage, which had been built at the time of the Reformation, was a long, white building, with a kind of farm-yard behind, containing barns and sheds; before it was a garden, laid out in long grass-plots, and straight, well rolled gravel walks. An avenue of tall trees led along one side of the garden, which had been tenanted by a colony of rooks from time immemorial. The church, which was divided by a meadow from the parsonage, was an ugly, whitewashed building, not unlike a large barn, with a little one joined to it at one end; it bore marks of having once been a Catholic place of worship, though the stone carved work was grievously defaced, and the stained glass remained in the windows only in fragments. Such was the family and home to which Zoe had been consigned.

"I hope", said Mrs Martha, breaking silence again, "that the mother of little miss died penitent, poor thing."

"For what?" said the rector absently, as he turned away from the window where he had been standing since he last spoke.

"Why, for her shocking way of life to be sure; dear, dear, only to think of any woman being so shameless as to follow an officer up and down without being his wife; do you think she was really made an honest woman before she died?"

"I really don't know," replied the rector, "my brother says that Zoe will have all the rights of a legitimate child, and he seems just heart-broken for the loss of the mother; she was a Greek Catholic, and could get absolution I suppose."

"Well, I hope the child will not take after her," said the lady, "we must train her carefully, she must learn her catechism, and become a Protestant the first thing. I wonder what that Ma'mselle Nannette will be like, those foreign women are never like other people. We must teach little missy to leave off her outlandish ways and to behave like an English young lady."

"We must be kind to her, Martha, the poor child has no one but us to look to; above all, never speak of her mother but as a child ought to hear her mentioned; I need not caution you not to let a word drop before your own daughter; let the mother's sins be buried with her; God knows we have all sinned one way or other."

At this moment Sarah Anne, Aunt Martha's daughter, ran into the room from the garden gate (at which she had been standing to solace her impatience), with the tidings that a chaise was in sight, and coming down the lane, and that she was quite sure it was the strangers.

"Very well, Sarah Anne," replied Mrs Martha, "but how often am I to tell you that young ladies ought not to rush into a room in that manner, nor speak when they are out of breath; now remain here quietly until we return, that you may recollect another time."

Poor Miss Sarah Anne looked very downcast at this reprimand, but there was no appeal.

The rector put on his shovel hat, and Mrs Martha drew her stiff silk gown through the pocket-hole, and taking her ebony crutch-headed walking-stick in her hand, she followed her brother into the porch to receive the new comers.

When Zoe was lifted out of the chaise, she looked at her uncle and aunt with her large wild eyes, half shy, half frightened. The rector took her in his arms and kissed her, whilst Mrs Martha explained to her that she was her aunt, and that gentleman her uncle, and that they were very glad to see her, and then Mrs Martha kissed her too. Zoe did not understand one word of all this, as she could only speak French and a few words of Greek; a natural thing enough, but one that had never occurred either to the rector or his sister until that moment.

Mam'selle Nannette now stepped forward, she piqued herself on speaking English, but to Mrs Martha it sounded very like a personal insult to mangle a Christian language, as if it were no better than foreign gibberish, so her reception of Nannette was very stately indeed.

Zoe was soon seated at the tea-table on her uncle's knee, and plentifully supplied with cake and sweetmeats of all sorts; but the poor child was sadly tired, she could hardly hold up her head, and fairly fell asleep before tea was over; so Nannette carried her off to the comfortable bed-room hung with white dimity that had been prepared for her.

The rector was full of inquiries about his brother, and Nannette delivered the letters and messages with which she was charged.

Mrs Martha would fain have asked some questions concerning Zoe's mother, but she refrained; partly because Sarah Anne was not gone to bed, and partly because she conscientiously thought such a person was not fit to be named, whilst Mam'selle Nannette both tantalised and scandalised her, by continually mentioning her late mistress as a "real angel", but without going into any particulars. At length she begged permission to retire, as she felt fatigued, and after sipping some of Mrs Martha's spiced elder wine, she followed her charge.

"Well, sister," said the rector, when they were alone, "what do you think of your new niece?"

"Why, brother, she seems a nice little thing enough, but not the least bit like other children, she has such a gipsy look about her eyes, and then she is dressed in such a strange fashion."

"All that, my dear, is left entirely to your own management."

"But", ejaculated Mrs Martha despairingly, "what *am* I to do with that Mam'selle Nannette? The people in the village will follow her for a show!"

"Well, well, my dear, I must see that they don't; I will preach them a sermon on Christian behaviour and charity."

Next morning after breakfast, Nannette was installed into a large rambling apartment over the brewhouse, which Aunt Martha's contrivance had fitted up to supply the place of a nursery for Zoe, and a comfortable sitting-room for Nannette, where she might reign undisturbed by any of the establishment. There was a corner cupboard with glass doors, full of radiant-coloured china, and old glass curiosities, which Mrs Martha had foraged up from the sanctuary of her store-room; there was a bureau of some kind of dark wood clamped with brass, to hold Nannette's personal property; a large looking-glass slanted from the wall over the chimney-piece, surmounted with peacocks' feathers; a table with many legs stood in the middle of the room; a few tall, straight-backed chairs, and a little table and chair for Zoe, completed the furniture. We must not forget to say that Mrs Martha had discovered, in some mysterious recess of her store-room, a collection of wonderfully preserved old toys, which were handed over to Zoe with a strict charge not to break them.

Mrs Martha, with true English instinct, did all in her power to make Nannette comfortable in her house, but she never took cordially to her, which was not much to be wondered at. Yet she never failed to send "the poor outlandish body" a bit of any thing nice that happened to be made in the Rectory kitchen. Nannette, in spite of Mrs Martha's forebodings, was neither hooted nor followed for a show by the village people, but, on the contrary, became a great favourite, and was delighted with her little "ménage à l'Anglaise"; she tried to show her gratitude for madame's goodness, by clear-starching her lawn and ruffles in a style which was the envy of all the washerwomen of the parish.

Zoe, like all children brought up alone, had the gift of amusing herself, and made herself very happy among her playthings in her new home. But she was soon told that her life was not to be all play, and as soon as she had picked up enough English to understand what was said to her, she was taught to sew, and learn her catechism, as Mrs Martha had promised, "without missing a word"; a weary task both to teacher and learner, and not achieved without many tears. She was also dressed in a fashion more according to Mrs Martha's ideas of what an English young lady ought to be; her long hair was cut short all round, "to keep it out of her eyes", and she was instructed in the inscrutable mystery of sitting still, and taking care of her clothes.

Although Zoe showed small affection for her catechism, yet she "minded her book", and learned to read with a facility that astounded her aunt; any time she would leave her doll, to read to herself in the little gilt books which were amongst the treasures Mrs Martha had brought to light for her; every penny and halfpenny she could procure went to buy books, which she read over and over, till she had them by heart. "Little Red Riding Hood", "Hop o' my Thumb and his brothers", were her great favourites; she did not take to "Goody Two Shoes"; she had no sympathy with her. On Sundays, if she had been good at church, she was allowed to sit on Uncle Oliver's knee, who would tell her stories about "Joseph and his Brethren", and "Daniel in the Lions' Den", and many others. In fact, Uncle Oliver was her favourite; when she grew older, he helped her to weed her garden, and made a sod terrace round a heap of stones which she had piled up for the "Tower of Babel"; above all, he stood between her and many scoldings for "romping like a ploughboy", and other enormities of a similar kind.

We are sorry to record that the older Zoe grew, the more her aunt was driven to despair; Zoe could neither be made to look or behave "like other people's children"; she was now eight years old, much taller, and more developed than English children of that age, and her aunt was obliged to declare that, with her best efforts, she could "teach her nothing that she would learn".

One day Zoe had been shut in a room with strict orders not to stir off her stool until she had darned a large rent in her best frock; instead of doing this, she had employed herself in building a palace with the chairs and tables which she had pulled from their appointed places; Mrs Martha entered. Zoe, caught in the act, did not dare to move. "You little idle thing," said her aunt, "do you think you were sent into the world for nothing else but to play and read story books? God won't love little girls who don't take care of their clothes, and do as they are bid. Don't stand there staring at me with those great impudent black eyes: of course you did not make them, but you must be very good, and then perhaps people will forget them. Now put all those chairs in their proper places, and bring the knitting you did before breakfast for me to see." Zoe, looking frightened and ashamed, went slowly to the bag where the knitting was kept, and presented it to her aunt.

"Why mercy on me, child, what have you been doing?" ejaculated Mrs Martha, "if you have not gone and knitted the stocking that I fixed so nicely for you, all upon one needle. Oh for shame! for shame! You shall have nothing but bread and water for dinner to-day, and shall be sent to bed at tea time; there, take it away, I am sure I don't know what is to become of you," continued she, administering a sound box on the ears as Zoe came near her. The remainder of the day was spent in tears and disgrace. Uncle Oliver, although rather scandalised at her untowardness in female pursuits, was grieved to see her merry heart and cheerful face clouded by these perpetual worries; he had, besides, discernment enough to see that Mrs Martha was not exactly a fit preceptress for a girl of Zoe's disposition, and he determined to take her in hand himself.

"She does not seem to be cut out for a housewife," said he to his sister that evening as they sat at tea, "I will see what I can make of her as a scholar; I am much mistaken if she does not turn out something wonderful in that way; I have a theory of my own about education, and I will try it upon her; she shall be taught just as if she were a boy, and I will not have her plagued with sewing and darning any more."

Mrs Martha knew there was no appeal from her brother; but from that day she looked on the perdition of Zoe as a thing finally determined upon by Providence (she was a little Calvinistic in her notions), and walked away ejaculating, "Well, to see how the sins of the fathers are visited upon the children, it is just wonderful! Though I had her so young, and have done my best to train her, I cannot make her like an honest woman's daughter. Ah, Sarah Anne!" said she, as her daughter entered the room, "you have a great deal to be thankful for in being born in England, but you must try not to despise your poor cousin, though she is so ignorant and outlandish."

CHAPTER VIII

— · —

From that day Zoe was emancipated from her aunt's tuition. Her uncle determined, as he said, to educate her like a boy, and this, as it happened, was just the wisest course that could be taken. Her tropical organisation, and the strong passions that were lying latent within her, made it very requisite that her mind should be strengthened, and her intellect receive a steady discipline. But the plan had its disadvantages. The grave disapprobation of her aunt was not expressed in words, but she contrived that Zoe should be made to feel that she considered her conduct as not at all right, and nothing has such a debasing influence, as living in an atmosphere of vague censure.

Sarah Anne, several years older than Zoe, a thoroughly commonplace girl, who, without being tangibly vulgar, was coarse and common in all her feelings, had a great idea of her own dignity as "almost grown up"; and kept her cousin Zoe at a distance, as a mere child; but she disliked her to a degree very disproportioned to the contempt she expressed, she was never weary of sneering at Zoe's "exceedingly peculiar manners", and constantly prophesied that with poring so much over books, she would become an idiot.

There were several young people in the neighbourhood who visited at the Rectory, they looked on Sarah Anne as a sort of leader, and poor Zoe was completely sent to Coventry by these miniature women.

Zoe was naturally a very warm-hearted, affectionate child, and she would have loved both her aunt and cousin if they would have let her; but meekness and gentleness were certainly not her distinguishing virtues, so she repaid their repulsion with scorn, and as she was very expert in the art of aggravation, the hostilities between them were sharp and bitter. She insulted Sarah Anne's friends, and prided herself upon being as different as possible to all whom her aunt declared were "models of what young ladies should be". An Ismaelitish feeling was thus acquired towards every body round her, except good Uncle Oliver, whom she dearly loved, and whose heart she won by the credit she did to his "theory of education".

Zoe had a passion for knowledge, and her own energy was better than any theory ever invented. She had a talent for music, and her uncle was coaxed into sending to London for a harpsichord, and he gave her what instructions were needed at first, the rest she found for herself. Most of her time was spent in Uncle Oliver's study, where she forgot all the heartburnings and contumelies she met with in the other parts of the house. Zoe had, however, one scene of triumph where she had no rivals, and that was at the dancing school; there her beauty and grace gave her indisputable pre-eminence; she was not popular there, but she despised every one too much to care for popularity. "Take the good the gods provide thee", is the motto we all instinctively adopt, and Zoe was not slow to take on herself all the airs of a sultana in disguise.

Things went on this style till Zoe was fifteen. Letters, at rare intervals, came from her father, which constantly assured her of his affection; but immersed in the active duties of his profession, he never succeeded in coming over to England to see her. She wrote to him at stated periods, but, unless there is a community of daily interests, even the intercourse between a parent and a child becomes an abstraction. Zoe however secretly expected he would raise her from her obscurity, and produce her to the world as a princess.

Things went on without any incident worthy of record until Zoe was fifteen, when the grand state secret, the secret of Zoe's birth was, in an ill-advised moment, allowed to escape from Mrs Martha to her daughter!

Zoe, we are sorry to say it, had one day been guilty of some choice piece of impertinence, which had provoked the good lady beyond all bounds; and, looking after Zoe, who was sailing majestically out of the room, she remarked to Sarah Anne, with a sort of agitated laugh, "That, after all, Miss Zoe need not give herself so many airs, the daughter of a Greek woman who followed her father up and down without being legally married to him; and it is all owing to my brother's goodness that she has a roof over her head at all; but, poor girl, she is very ignorant, and we ought to pity her."

The exclamations of wonder, the torrents of questions that broke from Sarah Anne, first recalled her mother to a sense of the indiscretion she had committed. She was not an ill-disposed or malicious woman, and she felt very sorry for what she had done. She strictly charged Sarah Anne not to breathe a syllable of the matter, telling her, by way of security, that a great part of the scandal would fall upon her, as belonging to the same family; and, moreover, that her uncle would be seriously displeased if he knew of it. Sarah Anne, proud of her secret, promised every thing. At first she treated Zoe with the most perplexing condescension. Zoe was surprised, but soon settled it, that cousin Sarah Anne was only a degree more disagreeable than usual.

A week after the above occurrence, the two girls were sitting in the tea-room making up some finery for the ball which was given annually at the dancing school. Zoe was sewing on her dress some beautiful lace, which had been her mother's, and they were talking, girl-like, of their partners, which was rather a sore subject with the sedate Sarah Anne, so she said spitefully,

"You are making yourself very fine. I suppose you intend to captivate the squire's son."

"To be sure," replied Zoe, "and why not? True, that squire's son is an awkward booby, and does nothing but blush, but he is the best partner, and so, *faute de mieux!*"—

Now this "squire's son" was the Apollo of the neighbourhood, and the grand *parti roulant*. Sarah Anne, in spite of her strict propriety, had long felt a secret *tendresse* for him, but she had sense to see that he had no eyes except for Zoe; that was enough to pique any woman; but to hear her rival turn him into ridicule at the very moment she declared her intention of engrossing his homage, was more than female philosophy could stand; she tossed her head, and said,

"Ah, it is well for people who don't know themselves, that other people know nothing about them either, or else"—and she looked maliciously mysterious.

"Or else what, good cousin? Your sayings are as dark as those of the sphinx."

Sarah Anne looked provokingly placid, and kept silence.

"Speak out, good oracle," cried Zoe, in a mock theatrical tone.

"It is better for you not to ask," said Sarah Anne, "because I must tell the truth, and I don't want to hurt your feelings, though you care so little for the feelings of others."

"Sarah Anne," said Zoe, "do tell me what you mean, and I won't plague you again, and I will tell you something the squire's son said of you."

"It is perfectly indifferent to me what he either says or thinks," rejoined Sarah Anne, virtuously; "it is not necessary for the daughter of a respectable woman to attend to what young men say."

"As far as family goes, we are pretty equal," said Zoe; "the only point of equality between us."

"Indeed!" cried Sarah Anne, tossing her head, "*my* mother was my father's wife, *your* mother was only some Greek slave or wandering gipsy, who followed the camp with your father; so it is very natural young men may think they can laugh and talk with you as much as they please; when it comes to choosing a wife, the case will be rather different I fancy, with all your learning and stage playing accomplishments."

Pride, which was the foundation stone of Zoe's character, kept her silent for a few moments on hearing this astounding disclosure. At length, speaking with a forced calmness, she said, "Why was I not told this before, if it be true?"

"Because", said Sarah Anne, "my uncle wished to keep it a secret for the credit of the family."

"Then," rejoined Zoe, as she rose to quit the room, "if my uncle forbade you to repeat it, how dare you disobey his orders?"

She gained her own room, the door was bolted and her face buried in the bed, at the foot of which she knelt, before she gave way to her choking feelings. "Why was I ever born? what have I done to endure such disgrace?" was all she could sob out. For two hours she gave way to her uncontrollable emotion—then she rose pale and exhausted; opening the casement, the summer breeze came into her room; she wondered whether it were all true that she had heard; all that Sarah Anne had said was like a strange dream; there stood her looking-glass, giving the same reflection as when last, in her girlish vanity, she had stood before it, speculating on all sorts of grandeur as the inheritance of so much beauty. Then came considerations as to her future conduct—she was the same—she at least remained to herself; and the proud thought flashed on her mind to make for herself, in spite of all obstacles, a destiny equal to all her vague dreams. The hope of being reclaimed by her father, and proudly introduced by him to a brilliant assembly in some family castle or palace, where she was to be received with acclamations, vanished away; Zoe had dreamed her last childish dream,— she felt henceforth that her fortune must depend upon herself— and she felt a consciousness of power that assured her of success. A smile of determination was on her lips as she unbolted the door, and descended to join the family at dinner.

Cousin Mary Anne never once spoke, Uncle Oliver was full of talk about the hayfield, and aunt was settling the haymakers' supper. Nobody noticed Zoe. As soon as dinner was over, she went straight to Nannette; she found the old woman making up a set of ruffles for her darling to wear at the ball.

After a few words had passed, Zoe said, "Nannette, tell me about my mother, how old was I when she died?"

"Ah, Mademoiselle Zoe, I came to your mother soon after your father had rescued her from the pirates; that exploit made a great noise at the time; she was a lovely creature, and nobody could help loving her, she was so good."

"Why have you so seldom talked to me about her, Nannette?"

"Your papa did not wish it till you were older, mademoiselle, but I have her picture here, though you were not to see it till you were seventeen."

"Oh, Nannette, give it me now."

Nannette went to an old-fashioned black trunk which Zoe from a child had longed to see opened, it had such an air of mystery, it contained all Nannette's love letters, old-fashioned trinkets, China boxes set in copper rims, her will, and all that she held most precious in the world. She turned all her treasures reverently over, and took from the bottom of the trunk a green shagreen case which she placed in Zoe's hands.

"This my mother!" exclaimed Zoe as she opened the case, almost startled by the beauty it disclosed. "This really was my mother?" A tumult of feelings almost choked her, she kissed the picture again and again, whilst tears streamed down her cheeks.

"Oh, if she had lived! how much better I should have been than I am now; and I never remember her," continued she after a pause, "and I never even thought about her until this morning, but I shall love her memory now, and all the sneers in the world shall not make me feel ashamed of her." And she hung the miniature, which was set as a locket, round her neck.

"Ah, she loved you very much Mam'selle Zoe," said Nannette, "and her great grief in dying was to leave you."

"Was she really a Greek slave?" asked Zoe.

"Oh no, mam'selle, not a slave, the pirates had taken her prisoner and murdered her father, who was a Greek merchant, and very rich in his own country I have heard."

"No matter," said Zoe, "I should love her whatever she had been." So saying, she took leave of Nannette and rejoined her aunt and cousin. She was happier than she had been for a long time, her feelings were awakened for an object apart from herself, a spring of love gushed up in her heart which took away all bitterness.

"What is that? where did you get that beautiful ornament?" exclaimed both ladies at once when she appeared.

"It is my mother's picture," said Zoe, proudly.

It was no sudden flash of energy that possessed Zoe; she now knew her actual position, and felt that she had only herself to depend upon; she had received her first lesson in the importance of the commonplace people and things that make up the staple of the world—the importance of weight and impracticable stupidity. She saw she had no natural standing or position to fall back upon, and that so soon as her secret should be known, if those she had so much despised were to lift up their voice against her, she could not make her struggle against them; she saw that her very beauty and talents would be against her obtaining a footing in the "respectable society" of the world; and that she must have a position before she could make her gifts effective. Pride was the leading feature in her character, and love of influence her besetting vanity. From that day forward, Zoe became very worldly-wise, and set herself to become in manner and appearance less offensively unlike other people. She succeeded very well, as she had now a motive, but she could not sometimes help wishing she had been born stupid in her own right. In a few months the general cry was: "What can have come to Miss Zoe, she is so much improved!" Her aunt too was lavish in her commendations, though all would have been puzzled to state in what the improvement exactly consisted. Half the impressions made on people are by things so impalpable, that they vanish when they are examined closely, and re-appear the instant they have been explained away.

Zoe retained no spiteful feeling against her cousin; she was on too large a scale both for good and evil to have room for spite.

CHAPTER IX

— · —

Two years after Zoe became possessed of the secret of her birth, Cicely Dawson, the buxom housekeeper of Birly Grange got married, and went to legislate for a farm-house of her own; this event had important consequences for our heroine, or we should not have taken the trouble to record it. We must explain that Birly Grange, a rambling country house of rough grey stone, was the residence of the "squire", as he was called, the respectable parent of the youth who has already been mentioned; the "young squire" had been in love with Zoe ever since she was twelve years old, though he had always wanted confidence to tell her so; but now that she was grown up to be the most beautiful girl in the country, he could hold his tongue no longer. He stood almost as much in awe of Parson Oliver as he did of Zoe, so that though he was six feet high, and stout in proportion, he trembled at the bare notion of pleading his own cause, and he had strong misgivings that his father would not consider Zoe exactly the person qualified to succeed Cicely Dawson: but three days after the departure of that exemplary female, the household of Birly Grange had fallen into a state of confusion and anarchy not to be described. The squire had been kept waiting three quarters of an hour for his dinner; the men servants were in the house when they ought to have been out of it; the maids were flirting and romping when they ought to have been minding the dairy; the old squire was at his wits' end, and as he emptied the bowl of his pipe on the table, with an energy that broke it, he told his son, that he wished he would make haste and begin courting, for Birly Grange was going to ruin for want of a mistress to keep the hussies in order. This was an opening not to be neglected, and Master Will made a very sensible speech about good wives, and domestic duties, what would be required from the wife who was to be mistress of Birly Grange in particular, winding up with a declaration of his passion for Zoe Cleveland, and an earnest entreaty that his father would speak for him to Parson Oliver to use his influence with Zoe. The old squire listened with a patience that surprised his son. "You seem to have very sensible notions about marriage, Will, I must say, but I am not quite sure that Miss Zoe is just the wife best qualified for you; you could not cast your eye upon her cousin, Miss Sarah Anne, instead, could you? She is not just so handsome, or so pleasant in her ways, but she seems more likely to make the sort of wife you want, and wives should be chosen with an eye to the future, my lad; you know she will last you your life, unless, indeed, she should be taken away like your poor mother, but that we don't calculate upon when we marry."

"Miss Zoe has been brought up by her aunt yonder all the same as her cousin, only she has made different out of it," replied the son.

"May be so, may be so," said the old squire, "and I like the girl well enough, especially of late, she is not so fantastic as she was, but I don't like foreigners, Will, you can never feel sure of them, and though she is the parson's niece, still she is only half an English woman, and not the least bit like your poor mother, Will, and she was the best wife in the country; you could not just ask her cousin instead, could you?"

Master Will was resolute in declaring that if he might not have Zoe, he would marry nobody, and that if his father would not go and speak for him to the parson, he would try his fortune himself. The squire, who was a good-natured man and hated worry, put on his best drab suit with silver buttons and large silver buckles to his shoes, and mounting his black horse, rode off to the Rectory that very afternoon to do his son's bidding. He was shown into the study on his arrival, and unfolded his errand as well as he could.

Uncle Oliver found himself in a perplexed and painful situation. The family secret about Zoe's birth, could not be honourably kept from him. There was no help for it, so after a pause he said, "There is one circumstance, sir, connected with my niece, of which you are unaware, but with which you ought to be made acquainted before your son makes his proposals. I don't know exactly whether,—in fact Zoe is,—in short, my brother was not married to Zoe's mother until long after her birth; but he has taken every needful step to give Zoe all the rights of a legitimate child;—as you know, her mother died when she was a mere infant, and she has been brought up here under her aunt's eye, along with her own daughter."

He might have gone on much longer, for the old squire was fairly struck dumb at the disclosure of such a shameful piece of profligacy occurring as it were under his own eyes, and if the truth must be told, he was not a little scandalised at Parson Oliver for countenancing his brother's conduct, by allowing Zoe to associate with an "honest woman's" child.

"A vile jade!" cried he, as soon as his wrath found words; "were there no justices in those parts to take the baggage up, and hinder such a scandal coming to a credible family? Those impudent minxes have no natural feelings or they would never bring poor children into the world to be looked down upon for what is no fault of theirs! A saucy slut! I warrant, when all the mischief was done, she trapped your brother into a marriage to patch up her character a bit, but I'd have tented her! Oh, the jade! the naughty hussy! but I must say, parson, I don't think you have altogether done your duty in harbouring the daughter of an outlandish foreign tramp in a decent English parish, to say nothing of the shame of such a companion for your own lawful niece. It is going clean against Providence too, for what does the Bible say? but that children are to suffer for the sins of their fathers, to make the fathers more careful of what they do. I declare, how we do get deceived with outside show; I was getting quite fond of the girl myself! Poor Will little knows what an escape he has had!"

In vain did Uncle Oliver try to moderate his vehemence, the old gentleman would not listen to a word he said. To Aunt Martha's great surprise, he did not stop to take a tankard of ale in the parlour with her, and she saw him making his way across the yard to the stable, with a face much redder than usual.

Uncle Oliver said nothing to Zoe about his conference with the squire, but she was conscious of an increased kindness in his voice and manner whenever he spoke to her.

To his sister he was more communicative; she was a worthy woman at the bottom, and felt sorry for poor Zoe in spite of the discomfiture of her worldly hopes for her own Sarah Anne, which is saying a great deal in her favour. As to Sarah Ann, when she heard that the old squire had been to make proposals on behalf of his son for Zoe, she could not conceal her mortification, and her only consolation was, that Zoe was not to be married to him, nor even informed of the honour that had been intended.

Two days afterwards, as the whole family were sitting at tea, a horse was heard at full gallop splashing up the gravel walk, and the next moment the squire's son Will himself, entered the room, his eyes sparkling, and his whole appearance much agitated. He walked, gasping for breath, up to Zoe, and seizing her hand in both his, looked round with an air of defiance and said, "Look ye, Parson Oliver, neither my father nor you shall hinder me from marrying Miss Zoe, if she will only have me, though she may be the daughter of a stage-player or a mountebank from foreign parts! Miss Zoe has been brought up in England, sir, and I say she will make a good wife, and I will make her an honest woman and a lady besides; I should like to see who will throw her mother in her teeth! Let him do that dare!" added he, emphatically clenching his hand. "Bless your beautiful face," said he, turning to Zoe, "it was no fault of yours; I'll teach people how you ought to be treated!" He stopped for breath, and looked at Zoe for a reply to his generosity.

Her eyes were turned away, but her compressed lips, and the full vein starting on her forehead, and the flush that covered her face, neck, and shoulders, showed the struggle that was going on within. She snatched her hand out of his grasp and ran out of the room. A moment after, a heavy fall was heard over head, every one rushed to see what was the matter; they found Zoe lying insensible on the floor, she had fallen with her head against the fender, and the blood was streaming from her mouth and nose. The young squire, without waiting to see further, mounted his horse and galloped for the village doctor. Uncle Oliver, who guessed what had happened, loosened her dress himself, laid her on the bed, and sent every body out of the room. The doctor was announced, who satisfied them that there was nothing serious to be apprehended. Zoe had only fainted, the hurt she had received in her face was very trifling, and there would be no bad results; but what was the dismay of all to discover that, in his agitation, the foolish young squire had told all the particulars of the previous scene, and that it was now a matter of village gossip! However, he administered a composing draught, of which Zoe now stood in additional need, and left the house.

"You stay with me, uncle," said Zoe, as he was preparing to quit her, "I must talk to you before I go to sleep."

"Well, my darling, but keep quiet, and don't hurry yourself just now."

"I shall be better for it afterwards," said she. "It is well that all has happened as it has done, I see now how, do what I will, I shall always be looked upon in England; dear uncle, I will stay no longer in this land of forms and respectabilities, to hear my mother made the subject of brutal remark, and myself the victim of condescending notice. I will go to my father, he loved my mother, he will love me, at least, he will not reproach me for not being respectable. I want you to write to him this very night, and tell him all that has happened, tell him to take me home to him, no matter where."

Uncle Oliver tried to remonstrate, but Zoe was wrought up to a pitch of desperation, and sitting up in bed she said coldly,

"Uncle, you will write to my father, and write to-night, and advise him from yourself, to leave me here no longer, for I will not stay; and if you refuse, I will set off to-morrow, if I have to sing in the streets to pay for my passage to France."

Uncle Oliver saw that in her present state it would be useless to argue with her, so he wisely abstained, kissed her, and promised to do all she wished, if she would only sleep just then, and desiring Nannette to remain with her, he departed.

Zoe awoke the next morning nearly well, and having now a plan which she expected would put an end to all her mortifications, she was quite calm and cheerful at breakfast; as soon as it was over, she followed her uncle to his study, and said, "Well, is the letter gone?"

"No, my darling, but you see I wrote it as you bade me, I waited to see what morning reflection would bring;—you will not mend yourself, Zoe, by going to France, you will not find among strangers a home like this, nor can your father love you better than I do; be not impatient and petulant, my child, you cannot alter your lot in its essential point, we are all of us tried where we feel the most sensibly, or else it would not be trial."

"Dear uncle," replied Zoe, "do not talk to me just now, I cannot bear it, indeed I cannot. I will add a postscript to your letter, and take it to the post myself."

When Captain Cleveland received the letter he was more affected than he had been by any thing since the death of his wife. "Poor child," said he, wiping his eyes, "I ought to have foreseen all this, I have been very cruel to you, but you shall come and live with me, and never leave me again."

He did not write to Zoe, but he did better, he made arrangements for absenting himself from his official duties for a few weeks, set off to England, and arrived one fine evening at his brother's Rectory, as the family were sitting down to supper, before they had begun to calculate when they should receive an answer to the letter.

Zoe knew him at once, and flinging herself in his arms, sobbed passionately for some moments, unable to utter a word.

"My darling child!" said the captain, soothing her, "you shall come back to France with me, and shall never leave me again; you are the very image of your mother, your beautiful, good mother."

"Tell me about my mother," said Zoe. "Was she your wife? Am I really your daughter?"

"Yes, yes, you are my child, my own darling child, and your mother was better than any other woman I ever saw, and I have known a good number. You need never blush for your mother, but feel proud of belonging to her; since she died I have never cared to look at a woman."

Zoe's heart was lightened, there was sympathy between her father and herself from that moment; old Nannette was delighted once more to see the captain, and half out of her wits with joy at the turn things had taken, she began with great zeal to prepare her dear young lady's clothes for departure.

The captain and Uncle Oliver had much to talk about; Captain Cleveland was never weary of expressing his gratitude and delight for all that had been done for Zoe; but Uncle Oliver was very sad at the thoughts of losing his foster-child, and made his brother repeatedly promise that she should come and pay a long visit every year. Even Aunt Martha, when it came to the point, found she

89

loved Zoe a great deal better than she had ever suspected, and was more put out of the way at parting with her, than she had been for years, except by the great household catastrophe of the kitchen chimney falling down in a high wind. The poor young squire was nearly mad with love and desperation. Zoe did her best to console him by her gratitude for his chivalrous spirit in daring to persist in his suit in spite of what had struck every one else dumb with horror, but as she would not consent to marry him, her gratitude was not much of a solace.

The sensation caused in the whole village by Captain Cleveland's visit, his imposing appearance, and the almost veneration with which he regarded his daughter, very much softened down the virtuous indignation of the neighbourhood; now that Zoe was going away, in all appearance to fill a much more brilliant sphere than she had hitherto occupied, a great reaction took place in her favour, and every body was anxious to show her some token of remembrance and attention. The fact is, nothing puts people in such a good humour as a little bustle, in which every one is at liberty to interfere. Half the ill nature in the world arises from people being dull, and having nothing to excite them, and then the temptation to become sententious about their neighbours is beyond the virtue of human nature to resist.

Zoe's departure with her father was an event for the whole country round, and the people shewed their gratitude for it by finding out all sorts of good qualities in her.

Zoe went away loaded with presents, for which we are sorry to say she did not feel above half grateful: she had yet to learn the value of kindly dispositions, even with all the alloy of gossiping vulgarity.

CHAPTER X

— . —

Zoe left the Rectory under the idea that she was going straight to a perfect paradise. There are many ideas of paradise entertained by mortal men and women, all differing essentially no doubt, from the orthodox original. With girls of Zoe's age, paradise is the type of ball-rooms filled with adoring partners, all handsome, and all besieging her with declarations of love and marriage. Coronets and carriages are seen vaguely in the background, grouping themselves into a brilliant destiny, to which she is gracefully to yield, the fair victim of honours thrust upon her. Zoe's paradisaical notions took a still higher flight, she dreamed of becoming celebrated as well as grand.

She arrived with her father and Nannette at Bordeaux, where he resided. The sight of his apartment, No. 55, Au troisième, Rue de St Pierre, gave the first shock to Zoe's expectations. The rooms had done well enough for a *vieux garçon*, or a widower, who would naturally take all his meals at the *table-d'hôte*, and spend his evenings at a club or the theatre, on the principle of the old French lady, who said, 'Je vais au théâtre par économie,' viz., to save her parlour fire and candles. Indeed what else could poor Captain Cleveland do? He had no companion at home, and did not care for reading—people who have seen a great deal of active life rarely do. Zoe's looks showed her dismay at the sight of the *ménage*. The bare parquet, the scanty and shabby furniture; the tawdry hangings, and tarnished mirrors, with the untidy livery of the foot-boy; were enough to give disgust to one who had always been accustomed to the bright comfort, good order, and more than Muhammadan cleanliness of Aunt Martha's rectory.

Her father was so kind, and seemed so delighted to have her with him, that she did her best to conceal her feelings. She saw, too, that he had exerted himself to fit up her room in the way he thought most likely to please her. He had purchased a beautiful new harpsichord, and a wholesale supply of music. He had also commissioned the principal bookseller in Bordeaux to select a library proper for a young lady who had just finished a first-rate education; and the books, all bound alike in scarlet leather, were standing neatly arranged on two shelves. They comprised an odd jumble. They had been left entirely to the judgment of the bookseller, who, having understood from some book of travels, that English young ladies were allowed all the freedom of married women, made this selection with the idea of showing his acquaintance with English customs, so side by side with books of delicate rose pink morality were seen 'Les Liaisons Dangereuses' and 'La Nouvelle Héloïse'. Zoe heartily thanked her father for these promising appearances, and trusted, with Nannette's assistance, to get things into better order.

Captain Cleveland thought he had done all that was necessary for the reception of his daughter; and the very next day, after kissing her and telling her to make herself very happy, he went out as usual to his café. He was very proud of Zoe, and would have done any thing to amuse her if he had only known how; but he had lived the life of a *garçon*, so long, that he could not now alter his habits; besides, he found it very difficult to keep up conversation with a young girl for long together.

Zoe was not dainty about her eating, but the ambitious ragouts and amphibious dishes sent in by the *traiteur*, were so different from the wholesome appetising viands she had been used to from 'the neat-handed Phillis' at Aunt Martha's, that she ran some risk of being absolutely starved.

Still she did her best to seem contented, but worse remained behind! She soon discovered that her father held very strict notions about the propriety of keeping unmarried young girls shut up from all observation, and allowing them no sort of liberty: he would not even permit her to go out of doors with Nannette, unless he were also of the party, and he hated walking. Sometimes he used to take her a drive into the country, but what was that to a girl who had been accustomed all her life to an unlimited allowance of fresh air and active exercise? She once proposed to dine with him at the *table-d'hôte*, but it was a proposition she never ventured to make a second time. To all her entreaties that he would take her to the theatre or the opera, he turned a deaf ear, he totally disapproved of the theatre for young ladies, who were not married, especially when they chanced to be as beautiful as he assured Zoe upon all occasions that she was, by way of excusing his unusual care and anxiety. "Why," said he, "if I once allowed you to be seen in public and in full dress, we should have no more peace; all the young rakes and *petits maîtres* in the place would be parading before the house, and insulting you with *billets doux*; ah, my child! if you only knew as much of the world as I do, you would never wish to leave your own home. No woman ought to go to the theatre until she is married, and even then the less the better."

"I am sure I wish I could find any body to marry me," said Zoe, pettishly.

"Time enough, time enough, my beauty; you don't want to leave your poor old father yet, do you? why I have had you no time at all, I have hardly seen you yet."

The total absence of all society, and the idea that her exquisite beauty, about which she was so constantly hearing, and her accomplishments, of which she was equally conscious, were even more buried in France than they had been at the Rectory, did not tend to raise her spirits.

Winter came on, and her walks were entirely stopped, for her father was confined to the house by a violent rheumatic attack, which made him very testy. The rooms too, had to be kept at a high temperature, and Zoe grew really ill; her spirits, which she had struggled to keep up, at last gave way; she sat all day, except the hour when she either played at chess with him or read to him after dinner, with her feet on the stove, either sighing for the green fields and fresh air she used to have at her uncle's, or else in building castles in the air for the future.

What she had heard Nannette and her father say about the freedom of married life was not lost upon her, "I wish I could get free," said she to herself one night as she sat at one end of the large ill-lighted room beside the stove, whilst her father and his visitors, the only ones who ever crossed the threshold, sat with the candles at a whist-table deeply absorbed in their game, laughing and joking amongst themselves between the deals, and giving no heed to poor Zoe, who sat moping in the dusk. "My father thinks", continued she to herself, "that because I am well dressed and well fed, I am as happy as a queen; he little knows," thought she as she brushed away the large tears that had gathered in her eyes. She fell into a reverie, looking on the three friends who were with her father. They were about his own age, and all of them old bachelors; one was a retired officer of high family, but reduced fortune; the other two were brothers, Englishmen; one of them was an invalid, who resided in France, because the cold foggy air of England did not suit him, and his brother lived with him because they could not bear to be separated. All ideas of love, marriage, and handsome men, had been completely kept out of Zoe's head by her education; for Aunt Martha always impressed it upon her, as the height of indecorum in a well brought up young woman, to allow the idea of a lover to enter her head, until a proposal had been formally made and accepted, and she had the sanction of the higher powers "to keep company together"; even then she always seemed to consider it a sort of necessary evil, which young people would commit, and the less said about it the better. Since Zoe left England, she had always heard her father and Nannette speak of marriage, as the only honourable emancipation for a girl, and the only means by which she could be made partaker of the rights and privileges of a woman. Zoe had thus grown to look forward to being married, much in the same way that a schoolgirl looks forward to the holidays, or to "leaving school for good". Any sort of a husband who would have presented himself to her just then, would have been gladly accepted, no matter how old or ill favoured, if by that means she might have gained her freedom and a position in society. So much for false maxims instilled betimes, which could mould the feelings of a hot-blooded, passionate young creature into the semblance of those of a cold, calculating merchant! Circumstances and habit had, in those days, given to Zoe an appearance of coldness which deceived even herself; she never for a moment contemplated the possibility of falling in love, or entertaining the feelings she had read about in Ovid's epistles; no dreams of that sort ever entered her head.

This very night, at the moment we are speaking of, when she fell into a reverie, she was speculating, in the extremity of her *ennui*, whether it would be possible to convert either of the two rich English brothers into her husband; but no, they were both past sixty, and confirmed old bachelors, even the invalid was quite content with the hired nurse who knew his ways, and had lived with him for some years; he could not live without his brother, so there was no hope in that quarter, and as to the French officer, it was clear he could hardly keep himself, much less a wife. Zoe's pride was so completely humbled by sickness, solitude, and absolute want of air, that her next thought was to write to Uncle Oliver (corresponding with whom had been her chief comfort), giving him a little delicate hint, that when he next saw the young squire, he might tell him that she did not like France, and that she often thought of England, and sometimes of him!

The very next morning she put her resolve in practice, she knew that Uncle Oliver would do any thing in the world to get her near him again, so she considered the matter as good as settled. "At least," said she to herself as she rang the bell to send her letter to the post-office, "I shall be able to breathe the fresh air, and walk in the fields again."

The dingy footboy who answered the bell, carried a small wooden box in his hand which had just arrived for her from England; it was directed in her uncle's hand-writing. Zoe broke it open and found a bride-cake, white favours, and a letter announcing the marriage of the young squire to her cousin, Sarah Anne! He had at last followed his father's advice, and cast his eyes on her cousin, to the great joy of Aunt Martha and the young lady herself: he had stipulated that Zoe should know nothing of the matter until they were fairly married, as "she would be so surprised".

Zoe's colour came and went, she tore up her letter, and throwing it into the fire, she exclaimed, "What mean plan must I think of next to obtain my freedom!"

Out of humour with herself, thoroughly mortified, and seeing no hope of any change, her health began rapidly to decline. Captain Cleveland all of a sudden grew terrified, and sent for two physicians, who told him that change of air and scene were absolutely necessary for his daughter. Poor Cleveland was ready to go to the world's end if he could only get Zoe strong again. He asked her if she would like to go back to England, but no, she much preferred a tour on the continent, and they began the tour accordingly upon May day.

They had not been a week *en route*, before Zoe's colour began to revisit her cheeks, and her spirits resumed their old buoyancy. They were sailing up the Rhine, and Zoe, who had never seen really fine scenery before, was in a state of enchantment. She had the soul of an artist, and every sight or sound of beauty "sent to her heart its choicest impulses". Her father, who had been in too many different countries to be very susceptible to the charms of scenery, thought her almost mad, and could not refrain from entreating her to be "more moderate", but with very little effect.

One morning Zoe had placed herself on deck in her usual place; her father finding it chilly, left her under the care of Nannette, whilst he made himself comfortable down below. Zoe on turning round to speak to Nannette saw a gentleman who had just come on board earnestly regarding her; he was a gentlemanly-looking Englishman, of about fifty, much marked with the small pox, but in spite of that his face had, on the whole, a pleasing and intelligent expression.

He seemed perplexed as he looked at Zoe, and at last, approaching her, said, "Pardonnez, Mademoiselle, but you are so strikingly like a lady whom I formerly knew, the wife of Captain Cleveland, and yet I heard she was dead; in fact your ages would not agree. I beg your pardon, but I was quite startled by the resemblance."

Zoe was equally surprised. "My name is Cleveland," said she, "and Captain Cleveland is below in the cabin." The unknown gentleman uttered an exclamation, and darted away. After a few moments he returned with her father, who introduced him as Mr Gifford, an old friend of his, whom he had not seen for the last seventeen years.

The rest of the day was spent by the gentlemen in talking over old times when they were in Malta and the Mediterranean together. Zoe remained at her old post on deck, quite satisfied with watching the beautiful changes of scenery.

It was not till next morning Zoe heard that Mr Gifford was a

Catholic gentleman who had a large estate in Devonshire, that he was a widower, and that he had strong thoughts of entering the priesthood now he was free from secular ties. Zoe did not pay so much attention to this as she would have done some weeks previously. She was now completely absorbed by the excitement of travelling, and the novel scenes presented to her; for the time being all her matrimonial visions were banished from her head. She only felt very glad when she heard he was to join their party, because papa would have some one who could talk to him in his own way, which would keep him from so constantly lamenting after Paris and his nightly whist party.

"Poor Gifford!" said Captain Cleveland, "he knew your mother, Zoe, and admired her so much, that if she had been any other woman I should have felt annoyed; he got married however, himself, soon after we parted; he married some English lady of rank, who died in her first confinement, he tells me, and left her infant daughter to the care of a bosom friend and confidante, Miss Rodney, a prime old maid, and a thorough *dévote* by Gifford's account."

Gifford, however much he might have admired Zoe's mother, seemed to have transferred all his admiration to the daughter, for he was constantly at her side; he was full of information, and could tell her every thing she wanted to know about the places they passed far better than any guide-book. The sight of Zoe reminded him of many happy days, and brought vividly back the image of the only woman he had ever loved, though both she and Cleveland had been far from suspecting it; for Gifford was an honourable man and a rigid Catholic, who had no notion of disguising illicit passion under false names, or of pleading temptation as an excuse for a breach of friendship. He abruptly quitted Captain Cleveland and his wife when he found that in flight lay his only safety. Zoe was her mother over again, and there was no reason why he should resist the charm of being near her, he fancied that he looked upon her as his own daughter, and one of whom he would have felt proud. Zoe's masculine education had given a tone to her mind which showed itself in her countenance, he was astonished at the power of mind she discovered in conversation, for though so young, and with a judgment unripe, and her intellect altogether unmature, there was still the stamp of genius on all she said.

Whenever they were stationary in a place for a few days, he escorted her to all that was worth seeing, and showed an untiring patience in walking and driving that utterly astonished Cleveland.

They at length took up their abode at Koblenz, intending to remain a few weeks, as Captain Cleveland was threatened with an attack of gout. The day of their arrival, as soon as dinner was despatched, Zoe left the room to prepare for a long exploring walk with Gifford and Nannette, who never quitted her young lady for a moment.

"You will make that girl quite wild," said Captain Cleveland, half in an ill-humour at the idea of being left by himself. "I shall never be able to keep her within bounds when we get home again; she will never settle at home as she used to do."

"Oh, dear papa!" said Zoe, who entered just then, "I had quite forgotten that we should ever have to return to that odious Rue de St Pierre! Thank Heaven, however, it is still so far in the future as to be almost out of sight, or it would spoil all my pleasure here!"

Captain Cleveland gave something between a sigh and a groan of dissatisfaction, and applied himself diligently to his Turkish pipe for consolation.

As Zoe and Gifford went along, Zoe began to tell him about all her miseries at home in the Rue de St Pierre, about the hot rooms, and her papa's oriental notions of the necessity of keeping young ladies closely shut up and never seen;—finding that Gifford listened, and seemed to sympathise with her, she chattered on, and told him about the three visitors who had the *entrée* to No. 55, to play at whist when her father could not go to his club; she described their portraits and peculiarities at full length, till Gifford was obliged to stand still to laugh. Then she went on to describe the evening when, seriously believing she should die by inches for the want of air and exercise, she speculated on the possibility of persuading one of these ugly old men to marry her, "For then", said she, "I thought that at least I might walk out and be independent like a rational being, which it seems no woman on the continent is considered till she gets married; as papa says, what I shall do when I have to go back, I don't know; and luckily, just now,

I need not consider. Look, we are on the top of this hill—what a beautiful view!"

Nothing more was said or done during the remainder of their walk worthy to be recorded. When they reached home they found Captain Cleveland sitting with the chess-table arranged before him, and looking at his watch which was lying upon it.

"Why, you have been gone nearly three hours!" he exclaimed, when they entered, "where can you have been? Zoe, child, you will kill yourself with all this fatigue and racket; here, Gifford, now for the chess; I have been studying all this time an infallible mode to check-mate you."

Gifford sat down rather abstractedly, and soon received the promised check-mate, but it was not attended with the *éclat* the captain had anticipated, the fact being that Gifford was speculating upon a mate of a different kind. Zoe's random speech about the two old brothers, and the very modest requirements she expected from a husband, had given him the resolution to propose for her himself! Had he met with Zoe when he was surrounded by the formal conventionalities of his ordinary life, it is probable he might never have thought of doing any thing so hazardous; but now, he was in the midst of the most romantic scenery, cut off from every thing that could remind him of the world he lived in, the extraordinary beauty of Zoe, her naïvely expressed desire to become an independent married woman, all conspired to make him forget that he was as old as Zoe's father, that he had a daughter of nearly her own age, that he had formally notified his intention to sell his estate and enter the English College at Rome to study for the priesthood; every thing in short that, at another time, would have weighed with him, was forgotten. Nature seems to have a malicious pleasure in overturning the reputation for wisdom and gravity which it has taken a lifetime to build up, by suddenly inspiring some signal piece of temerity, at which the boldest would have held his breath. So it was with Gifford. His hour of folly was come, when it was written that he was to make a fool of himself in the eyes of all his acquaintance!

He made the most unaccountable moves in the next game, till Captain Cleveland, out of all patience, swept the men off the board and rang for coffee. However, before it arrived, Gifford contrived to make Captain Cleveland understand the secret of his ill play, and had requested his influence with his daughter.

"Make yourself quite easy on that score, my good fellow," said Captain Cleveland, "there is not a man on earth I would sooner give her to than yourself; and depend upon it that Zoe is too good a girl to make any objection. I will speak to her this very night."

Captain Cleveland, like many men who have been very romantic in their youth, had settled down into a most prosaic elderly gentleman: with him "the wine of life was spent". The death of his wife caused a gulf in his career, and when he recovered from the shock, he was no more the same person; all his feelings of youth and passion had been left on the other side. He was too continental in his notions of matrimony to see any thing but what was highly advantageous in the proposed alliance; and it may be doubted whether, at the bottom of his heart, he did not feel better satisfied to commit his daughter to a staid, respectable man, able to take care of her, than he would have been to see her in the hands of one who should be as young and passionate as himself when he first met her mother.

As to Zoe, her courage for matrimony had rather ebbed since she had become more pleasantly circumstanced, and she was startled when her father announced Gifford's proposal, and told her that it had been accepted by him.

Her dread, however, of returning to No. 55, Rue de St Pierre was too great to permit her to make any strenuous objection to what seemed her only resource.

"After all, papa," said she, "Mr Gifford is very good-natured; and he is not so very ugly either, at least not half so bad as either of the two brothers who used to come to play whist with you; and then I shall really be one of the 'county ladies' of whom Aunt Martha used to speak with such reverence. But it will be droll, will it not, to hear myself called mamma by a girl nearly as old as myself?"

So the matter was settled, and in three weeks from the walk and the games of chess above recorded, Zoe became Mrs Gifford.

Gifford had next to write two letters, which taxed his powers of diction to the utmost; one was to Miss Rodney, begging her to inform his daughter of what had occurred, and also saying that the whole party, including Captain Cleveland and Nannette, were on their way to Gifford Castle, where he requested every thing might be put in order for their reception.

The other letter was to the Superior of the English College at Rome, informing him of the change that had taken place in his intentions of entering the priesthood; and this was the letter that caused such a commotion in the refectory as we have before narrated.

Everhard, who shared the curiosity of the rest, was very far from suspecting the influence this marriage was to have on his own destiny;—meanwhile, as he is safe in college, we must still leave him a little longer, whilst we pursue the fortunes of our heroine. He is in the safe keeping of Fate, who never forgets or makes mistakes, but lets every stroke of good or evil fall precisely on the head for which it was destined, when the due season for it arrives.

CHAPTER XI

— · —

Success is the true "Tree of Knowledge"; there is no wisdom equal to that which comes after the event. When a man has accomplished any scheme which he has moved heaven and earth to compass, there first follows a pause, a lull, in the storm and strife of the passions that have been aroused, during which, he begins to doubt whether he has not been spending his strength for naught:—then the perception dawns still more forcibly that the object was worth all the pains and labour bestowed upon it, and he wonders why he should ever have felt so anxious about the matter; and finally, he feels quite sure that if it had pleased Providence to thwart the scheme, it would not only have been much better for him in the end, but now that his eyes have been opened by success, he could have borne a disappointment with edifying resignation.

Zoe and Gifford were married. Captain Cleveland's wish to see his daughter honourably settled in life, was thereby fulfilled. Zoe's desire for the freedom and privileges of a married woman, was also satisfied. Gifford was in possession of the woman he desired to make his own. Surely we must express ourselves ill when we record our wishes, or our guardian angels must be very stupid, for they never seem able to understand what it is we want; when they do their best to fulfil our desires to the very letter, we always find some mistake which renders them any thing but what we expected. So it was in the case before us. Gifford had not been married a fortnight, before all the sensible speeches that would or could be made by Miss Rodney, began to ring in his ears with the most appalling distinctness:—then he had a vision of the English College at Rome, with all the scorn and indignation of the ecclesiastical world, the world for which he chiefly lived;—then, almost as disagreeable, were the bad biting jests with which his imagination liberally supplied him, as what would certainly be made at his expense by every body. Twenty times a day he caught himself whispering all the unanswerable reasons that might be urged in defence for what he had done,—but somehow he could never succeed in satisfying a little malicious demon within him. Though he did his best to disguise what was passing in his mind, he was so abrupt and *distrait*, that Captain Cleveland began to doubt whether, after all, he had done wisely in marrying his darling Zoe to a man not only treble her age, but one who, from his monkish way of life, had contracted many peculiarities in his habits and temper.

As to Zoe herself,—but it may be questioned whether all women, even those who have married for love, would not, in the early days of their matrimony, if the choice were offered to them, gladly return to their former condition, even if it were thenceforth to be irredeemable spinsterhood for life: so poor Zoe's misgivings are not so much to be wondered at. But certainly, never did three people look less like the ideal of mortals crowned with SUCCESS.

They proceeded to Paris immediately after the ceremony, where they remained a few weeks, and arrived in England at the end of August, 17—.

When they drew near to Gifford Castle, Zoe's future home, both she and Gifford looked out for its turrets with anxiety;—she, full of hopes and fears of she scarcely knew what;—he, with some dread of the reception which it might please Miss Rodney to give them. He had only told her in general terms that he had made the daughter of his old friend, Captain Cleveland, his wife,—but he knew that Miss Rodney disliked utterly both naval and military men, believing them to be all reprobates, in virtue of their commission.

Gifford's dread of Miss Rodney is not to be looked at with surprise, nor altogether with contempt—for every body knows how much more influence disagreeable people acquire over us, than pleasant ones; if they are of the silent species, they are like a perpetual nightmare, and if they are of the violent and objurgatory, we dread them like a storm; either way we put ourselves to more pains than we would own, to keep them in their most inoffensive humour.

Miss Rodney was of the silent, sententious genus. On the receipt of Gifford's letter, she had put herself to a little martyrdom of prayers, confessions, and penances, to bring herself to a proper frame of mind to receive the wife whom Gifford had taken, as she conscientiously believed, under a special temptation from the evil one.

Some natural feeling too, there might be, at seeing herself deposed, for she had been a faithful housekeeper to Gifford, and a kind of mother to Clotilde ever since the death of his first wife.

Miss Rodney had, in her youth, been a noted beauty, and a reputed heiress. All her knowledge of the world was derived from six months spent in Paris, just after she left the convent in which she had been educated;—she had been thrown into the gayest circles at the time of the regency, where she was honoured with the notice of that fascinating reprobate, the Duke de Richelieu himself;—no wonder she believed the world to be very wicked indeed. Before, however, she had time to fall into much mischief, she was attacked by the small pox, which destroyed her beauty, but, as she firmly believed, was the means of saving her soul alive.

Almost immediately after her recovery, her father was utterly ruined by the breaking up of Law's banking scheme, and he died of a broken heart in a very little while, leaving his daughter nearly destitute. It was just then that her intimate convent friend, who had married Gifford, hearing of her situation, entreated her to come and live with them, and Gifford Castle had been her home ever since. After the destruction of her beauty, and worldly consideration, Miss Rodney gave herself up to devotion, as the handsomest means *de se tirer d'affaires*. Her ruling idea became, by degrees, to be self-mortification. Her steady self-denial and innumerable good works, might have challenged respect, had they not arisen more from the desire to benefit her own soul than from any feeling of benevolence to those around her. She farmed out, as it were, the troubles of this life, and endured patiently the many annoyances of her lot, hoping thereby to cover, not only her own expenditure in the way of sins here below, but to lay up a handsome treasure in

Heaven, which would enable her to make a respectable figure in the company of the world to come.

To do her justice, she always did thoroughly any disagreeable duty she undertook to perform, and she had prepared her young charge, Clotilde, very judiciously for the step-mother she was to expect. Every thing about the castle was in the most exact order for the reception of the bridal party, and when the carriage stopped at the great entrance, all the servants were drawn up in the hall to receive them.

Gifford was agreeably disappointed. It was like throwing oneself forcibly against a door to break it open, and finding it yield to a touch.

Miss Rodney was in the drawing-room, sitting in an arm chair beside a small table, on which lay an ebony crucifix, a gold snuff-box, and a book of devotions. She was determined not to hide her religion before the heretic new comers. Her dress was more like that of a Benedictine nun than a civilised costume. It consisted of a black stuff gown with one or two shawls, of the same material, pinned over each other; a black silk hood, which nearly covered her tight cambric cap; her powdered hair was turned back over a roll, and exposed in its full, unshaded dimensions, her large flat face, which was so painfully disfigured, that it seemed as if a burn or scald had assisted the ravages of the small pox; her mouth was quite distorted. She rose from her chair as Gifford entered, and tried to utter some proper phrase of congratulation, but burst into tears instead. Gifford had not been prepared for the expression of so much feeling, and his heart smote him for his unkind thoughts of her. She soon recovered herself, however, and received Zoe and Captain Cleveland with a dignity which would have been very dismaying, had not the door at that moment opened, and a slight, fair child entered. She was in black (for since the death of her friend, the old lady could not bear to see colours), her flaxen hair was parted, and fell in natural ringlets over her shoulders, forming a beautiful relief to the deep black dress, and ebony rosary which hung by her side. Gifford flew to embrace her, and presented her to his wife as his only child, Clotilde. Zoe, who had a natural love for children, was delighted, and putting her arms round her, said, "You are to be my little girl, and you must let me love you as well as your papa." Clotilde, who was crimson with emotion, looked at Zoe with a sort of shy astonishment, but she was too gentle to repulse her caresses.

Luncheon was announced, and the whole party repaired to the dining-room, where Zoe gracefully insisted upon the old lady retaining her place at the head of the table, but Miss Rodney was too great a stickler for etiquette to hear of such a thing.

After the repast was over, Zoe retired to what were to be her own apartments, in order to lay aside her travelling-dress; she coaxed Clotilde to accompany her, for she felt anxious to make acquaintance with the timid little being beside her, and her cordial sunny looks were not without their effect. Clotilde looked with amazement on all the treasures of vanity, which the maid was transferring from the trunks and packing-cases to the ponderous chests of drawers, but evidently she was not in the least tempted to possess any thing like them herself; she was, however, highly delighted when Zoe gave her a little ivory figure of the Virgin and child, and some coloured prints of different female saints, with a short account of each, written at the bottom.

"Now, Clotilde," said Zoe, "is it possible you can really prefer that trumpery to the beautiful new hat I chose for you myself?"

"Oh, yes, very much!" replied Clotilde. "Aunt Rodney has taught me never to desire the vanities of this world;—it was very good of you to bring me the hat, but I shall ask Father Mulgrave to bless this figure and these prints, and then I can put them into my oratory."

"Will you show me your oratory?" said Zoe.

"Oh, yes, if you will like it,' replied Clotilde, hesitating and blushing. "And you have not seen the rest of the house yet," added she, "I shall like to show you that and the grounds too, if I may."

Zoe assured her that she would rather see them with her than any one else, so they began their progress with Clotilde's oratory. It was a little room in one of the round towers, which stood above a steep cliff covered with wood and all kinds of curious plants, which the regions of Devonshire produce in such abundance. A beautiful view of Porlock Bay and the Bristol Channel was to be seen from the window. The room had once been fitted up as a chapel, but most of the ornaments had been removed to the larger one which Gifford had built when he first came into the property.

"Do you always live here by yourself?" said Zoe, "do you never wish for companions of your own age?"

"Oh no," replied Clotilde, "I am very happy, I wish for nothing, I am very fortunate in being kept from the evil of the world; Aunt Rodney says it is a dreadful place, a dreary wilderness, with the devil, like a roaring lion, going up and down in it. I am so glad papa has brought you here, you will be so much safer."

Zoe smiled, and promised the young saint a beautiful new piece of brocade to make a covering for her altar.

After this Clotilde led Zoe through all the principal rooms of the castle, which was on a very magnificent, but somewhat inconvenient plan. The great drawing-room had a raised daïs at one end, and the ceiling was covered with armorial bearings emblazoned in their proper colours, which took Zoe's fancy much. The furniture was in a style long since obsolete; all the chairs and tables had very thin legs and a great many of them, the hangings were faded, and the carpets scanty, but Zoe did not know much about furniture, and Clotilde declared it to be too magnificent to live amongst every day, and that she much preferred Aunt Rodney's little sitting-room.

When they had gone through all the rooms, Zoe proposed to join the gentlemen out of doors, to look at the grounds.

Gifford Castle was situated about two miles from the village of Culbone, on the confines of Devonshire; the road up to the castle lay through steep cliffs covered with woods, the hills towered above the castle on all sides, except the one open to the sea, to the height of thirteen or fourteen hundred feet, fretted with jutting rocks, and covered with trees of all kinds, grown to an enormous size. The castle itself stood like an eagle's nest in the cleft of a rock, the road to it was barely wide enough for a carriage to pass along; the thick boughs of trees twisting together from each side, formed a canopy, through which the "golden and green light" glanced like waves.

The wall-like rocks were covered with ivy and creeping plants; about half way up, a succession of table lands or terraces had been formed with great labour and expense, and laid out as flower gardens: from the sides of these terraces rose the walls of the old castle, nearly concealed by venerable trees, except at the great east tower, which stood high and naked on the very edge of the precipice, looking down on the sea beneath. The castle had evidently once been a fortress of considerable importance. Zoe was enchanted with all she saw, Gifford thought he had never seen her so charming, and grew quite in a good humour with himself, for the first time since he had been married.

When they rejoined Miss Rodney in the drawing-room, Zoe exerted herself very amiably to conciliate her, for which Gifford felt sensibly obliged. Music was introduced, and Zoe sang a little German hymn so touchingly, that the tears streamed from Clotilde's eyes, and even Gifford and Captain Cleveland were affected; but Miss Rodney was a deaf adder, not to be charmed. She never for a single instant relaxed from the formal ceremonious politeness she had maintained from the first. It does not require a long acquaintance to take a dislike to people—we daguerreotype our characters when we least think of it; and though Zoe had neither said nor done the least thing with which the most fastidious person could find fault, yet Miss Rodney felt by instinct that Zoe neither thought, nor felt, nor believed in a way she approved, and she determined that Clotilde should have as little to do with her beautiful step-mother as possible; indeed, she felt disturbed to see the good understanding that had already commenced between them.

Whilst poor Gifford was pleasing himself with the idea of the advantage Zoe would be to Clotilde, Miss Rodney had come to a very different conclusion.

The next morning she sent to Gifford to request him to give her an audience upon a matter of great importance. Gifford's heart sunk within him; however, he replied that he would wait on Miss Rodney whenever it would best suit her to receive him. The old lady did not make him wait long.

When he was seated in her parlour, he tried to make the interview less formidable by a few cheerful remarks. Now Miss Rodney had carefully abstained from telling him, either by word or look, that she highly disapproved of the wife he had brought home, for that would have been an infringement of her "act of faith, hope, and charity"; but she was not going to indulge him in conversation, as if he had done nothing wrong. She drily cut short his attempts to be agreeable, by telling him that her reason for taking up his valuable time was to inquire whether it were his pleasure that the education of his daughter should remain with her, or pass into the hands of Mrs Gifford. She spoke in that low, even, suppressed tone of voice which, whilst it seems determined to afford no handle against itself, reveals so much inward dissatisfaction. She grew more natural, however, as she pleaded to have Clotilde continued under her own care. She requested it as a favour. "For", continued she, "as it was at my entreaty she was kept from a convent, I am bound to see that her precious soul does not suffer by my human weakness; and I am doubly anxious that she should be kept from all the evil that is in the world."

In vain Gifford tried to point out the advantages that Clotilde would enjoy in being with Zoe. The old lady declared it was a snare of the evil one to wean her heart from religion, and that unhallowed learning would ruin her soul.

There seems to be a sort of magic or free masonry in the name of the devil, by which all who believe in his power try to frighten each other. Gifford did not feel altogether pleased to hear his bride classed among the agents of Satan, still the contradiction to it stuck in his throat; and now that Miss Rodney had taken such high ground, he could not find in his conscience to be disobedient, so he acquiesced, and it was finally settled that Clotilde was to be Miss Rodney's charge as heretofore.

When this was signified to Zoe, she remonstrated warmly, and even penetrated into Miss Rodney's own sanctuary, in the wild hope of persuading an ill-tempered *dévote* out of a piece of spite, which she had the letter of her conscience for calling a matter of duty. Of course Zoe was obliged to give way, for neither reason nor flattery made any impression on Miss Rodney.

Zoe found her post as mistress of the establishment a complete sinecure, for the old servants were too much accustomed to one regular routine to take any orders from a new comer. She took long walks with Gifford, when he went to visit different parts of the estate. When he was alone it was all very pleasant, for he was fond of making her understand his various plans of improvement; but when the steward was with them, which often happened, they fell into statistical details of draining and manuring, and new modes of ploughing, till Zoe in despair sometimes left them, to go exploring by herself; a proceeding which invariably made Gifford very angry, at what he termed her giddiness and indifference to his interests.

Still he was very fond of her after his own fashion, and never liked to go any where without her, or to have her out of his sight, though it might be that he would not address a word to her for a whole morning together.

We should have told the reader that, soon after his arrival in England, Captain Cleveland had gone into Essex to visit his brother, and Zoe was in great hopes that Uncle Oliver might be induced to return with him.

All the resident country gentry, who lived within a visiting distance, had called on Zoe, as in duty bound, and their visits had been duly returned; advantage had been taken of the moonlight nights to give state dinner parties in her honour.

The people were all dull and stately, as people who live always in the country, and have it on their conscience to keep up their dignity, must needs be; but Zoe was young, and too new to her part of "county lady", not to feel an interest in all that went on; besides, there were races, and assize balls, and assemblies in vague perspective, at which she was to be "patroness". Added to all this, she had to give dinner parties in return, which, we may as well say here, thanks to Miss Rodney's management, went off with great credit, according to the most rigorous etiquette. Fortunately for Zoe's character as a housekeeper, Gifford had laid his commands upon her not to interfere in any thing; he was a thorough Englishman, and had a great dread of any innovation in the economy of his dinner-table.

In this manner the autumn passed away and Gifford's long expeditions with his steward came to an end, to Zoe's great joy. Gifford had formed a plan which completely engrossed him, and allowed Zoe time to follow her old pursuits.

Although Gifford had given up the idea of becoming a priest himself, he was as devoted as ever to the interests of the Church. His present plan was to build a college on his estate, for the education of Catholic youths, and he entered into a correspondence with Rome, to obtain the sanction of the higher powers.

Meanwhile, Captain Cleveland returned home, but unaccompanied by Uncle Oliver, who could not leave his parish. Zoe was terribly shocked at the alteration in her father's appearance. He had taken cold in Essex, which had been succeeded by an ague, from which he seemed to recover, but no sooner had he returned to the castle, than he had a relapse. His constitution seemed altogether breaking up. The medical man who had been summoned from Minehead, gave it as his opinion that he was rapidly breaking; indeed, he continued to grow weaker and weaker throughout the winter. Zoe attended on him indefatigably; one day, early in March, he had been removed to his arm-chair beside the window, and Zoe remarked that he seemed stronger than he had been for some weeks; he shook his head, and said, "I should like to live to see my grandchild, but the will of heaven be done! You must christen it after me, Zoe, if it be a boy; if not, after your mother; and now, my child, whilst I am able, let me say a few words to you. You are not like most other women, Zoe, you are stronger both for good and evil, and it may be that you will be tried. Women like you, seldom pass through life easily. But, my child, whatever temptations assail you, just keep the plain, straightforward, right course, and it will prove wiser in the end, than any scheme you can find out for yourself. And don't fancy that your circumstances are peculiar; people always make mistakes when they fancy themselves exceptions.—Don't juggle with plain right and wrong. Never bring disgrace on the memory of your mother; I leave it with you for a sacred pledge. And now, my darling, I will lie down; this talking tires me sadly. I will go to sleep."

Captain Cleveland never woke out of that sleep, and the next morning Zoe had no more a father.

Zoe's grief was, at first, overwhelming. She was near her confinement; and the only thought that gave her any comfort, was the idea that she should not long survive him.

Losing a parent is like no other grief; it seems to break up the foundation of our resting-place here; other friends and connexions we form for ourselves, but parents are given to us by Providence when we leave that unknown world from which we are called forth; and when they are taken away from us, there seems to remain nothing more to stand between us and death. We may be rich in friends, and their voluntary affection may be very precious to us; but there is a sense of insecurity in it all, when we have lost the only love that was ours of right, and we feel that nothing but natural ties can supply the craving for natural affection. We have no longer a birthright of love in any human heart; they to whom we belong, have been cut away; we have lost the love that came to us with our life, and nothing remaining on earth can replace it.

Zoe continued for many days plunged alternately in a stupor of misery, or else in a paroxysm of grief. She had a sullen pleasure in thinking that the time was drawing near when she should be sure to die; but she was to be undeceived.

However hard mental affliction may be to bear, an attack of fierce bodily pain throws it into the shade, as Zoe found when her day of trial came. There is in acute bodily pain, something that rouses all one's energies to grapple with it; there is no instance on record of a person committing suicide either in a paroxysm of bodily suffering, or to escape the most severe surgical operation.

Zoe was half bewildered at the fierce reality of pain. "What, is all this horror of horrors a law of Nature that cannot be altered!" she exclaimed, between gasps of prayers for mercy, which she felt was mockery. It was not till after her child was born, and she lay feeble and helpless, that she had leisure to meditate on the strange capability of enduring for hours, suffering which once she would have imagined must quickly end in death. Zoe wept in utter weakness, not for herself, but at the thought of all the suffering and agony so many millions of women had borne before her. Her eyes seemed suddenly opened to all the misery there was in the world; she realised with a terrible and morbid vividness the varied forms of human suffering; poor girl! the very hospitals and operation-rooms seemed to open before her eyes, and disclose their secrets. Hitherto she had never thought about evil,—she had not wondered at it;—now, it rose before her in all its awful mystery. She brought to her recollection all she had been taught, all she had read of the well compacted plausible theories by which men, living at ease, and in health, have complacently endeavoured to reconcile and account for every thing. She turned for comfort to the religion she had been taught, but it seemed cold and forced, and to have no tangible meaning. The prayers and praises that were prescribed by all forms of religion, seemed to her only the aspirations of crushed slaves under the hand that lay heavy upon them. Wherever she turned for refuge, she beheld only dimness of anguish; and driven into darkness, she exclaimed in the frenzy of her soul, "Where is the All-powerful, the All-merciful, in whom we are taught to believe?"

When she recollected that even according to the Christian faith, all the complicated miseries of this life, to the greater number, are but the "beginning of sorrows", to be carried to a horrible perfection through all eternity after death—the calm, apathetic belief of Miss Rodney, and the placid acquiescence in this tremendous doctrine by the gentle, unruffled Clotilde, roused her hatred and disbelief in all religion, almost to insanity. She wondered how the purblind old confessor, believing all this as he professed to do, could rest contented in the midst of a world devoted to such horrible torment, thinking he had done his part towards saving it, by his mumbled prayers, his days of abstinence, and his droning sermon once a week; she was astonished that all living creatures did not realise their condition as she did. But as her strength increased, this morbid exaltation passed away. Her attention was diverted to matters more immediately pressing upon herself. Her little boy had an attack of croup when he was three months old, which left him very delicate; he was subject also to violent convulsions, which kept her in constant anxiety, and scarcely allowed her to leave him day or night. Added to this, before twelve months were over, she was confined a second time, and was long reduced to a deplorable state of weakness. The constant watchfulness which both her children required, and the bad nights and broken rest, seriously undermined her health. Gifford feared she was going into a consumption, of which there seemed many symptoms; the medical men recommended change of air both for Zoe and the children. Gifford, anxious to have further advice, and also, if the truth must be told, rather weary of the monotony of his matrimonial life, determined to leave the castle, and reside for some time first at Bath, and afterwards in London. The arrangements were speedily made. Clotilde was to be left with Miss Rodney at the castle, and in due time Gifford, Zoe, and the children, set off on their journey.

CHAPTER XII

— · —

All this time Everhard had been at college, completely engrossed in his studies; the days passed over one so like another to the outward eye, that the very nature of time seemed altered, and to bring neither chance nor change; all its work was being done within.

Everhard had become remarkable for talent amongst the most able, and for unwearied perseverance, more than all. A few extracts from his private memorials, will save a great deal of description. The first extract is dated about a year after his entrance into college.

"There are times when the heart is opened in written confession as it never is, never could be, to the dearest or most sympathising friend. It is not sympathy that we require at such times, it is to learn that which is lying hid in our own heart. The thoughts that oppress us have not yet taken a shape, but they are come too near the surface to be longer suppressed. In such a condition is my own mind at this moment; a fire burns within me, and compels me to utterance—but there is no friend to whom I could speak.

"Of all the field of human attainment that lies open before me, that of metaphysical philosophy is the only one that has charms for me. It promises to open all the treasures of wisdom and knowledge. I revel in the exercise of the fine-spun questions of the schools, my very senses seem quickened by the subtle dexterity and minute investigation they require. It is a mental gymnasium in which the gloriously gifted of the gods of old rejoiced to try their strength.

"Vague, dreamy feelings after beauty! What are they but childish plays? Graceful in youth, and not without a certain weak and ineffective beautifulness, but can Truth in all her majesty be compelled to disclose herself thereby? For the mind of a man aspiring to attain to the full measure of its stature, what is there to be desired or strived after but strength? Formerly I lived in my feelings, and used to value sensation and emotion beyond all things; now, any appeal to my passions would disgust me; all that cannot be proved, or give a reason for itself, I despise utterly."

"How deeply do I regret that the order of Jesuits is abolished; it would have been the height of my ambition to be one of the body. They alone seem to have had the full comprehension of how to grapple with men; they had a knowledge of all the mysteries of the human heart, and learned how to turn it about whithersoever they listed. Look at their schools; they turned out men able to make use of what they knew, not pedantic schoolboys, crushed under the weight of useless knowledge. There was something almost oppressive to the imagination in their mode of using their power, working together as one man towards the same end. Their motto was obedience to their head—their secret was obedience, and their success was the result of it. What a precision and certainty was there in all they undertook! To this hour the idea of a Jesuit impresses me with the idea of a darker and stronger power than I can express!

"He that would learn, must be obedient in all things, must empty his mind of self; it is the pressure from within, that prevents our seeing that which really is. We contract ourselves together; if we would really lay ourselves open to the influences around us, knowledge would spring up within us, and we should be bathed in an atmosphere of truth. If we were not darkened by conceit and self-fancies, we should be transparent, and the light would shine into us : we should open our eyes and see the world of God lying everywhere around us."

"'Become as little children,'—what meaning is there in that phrase! We must give ourselves up with meekness, to receive the instruction of those who teach us, or the light of wisdom can in no wise arise in our hearts. It seems to me that there is a sort of dullness, a simple-hearted, unambitious, but genial slowness, which may at first sight look like stupidity, but which in reality is far more hopeful, more capable of being transmuted into wisdom, than that adroit, brilliant cleverness which plays dexterously with the points and superficies of difficulties, making them puzzles and cramboes, to catch, not wisdom, but praise and applause, like that bestowed on conjurors and rope-dancers.

"I would not be unjust;—it may be that I despise this quickness and dexterity because it is not mine,—but it baffles and distracts me. I get no good at all from such men,—they make a sparkling light on the surface of a question, to leave all beneath in blackness of darkness."

"I blame others for being full of themselves, but am not I full of self also? Do I not feel it as a mill-stone round my neck, impeding my progress, and making base all I strive to obtain? Self! self!—the eternal presence of myself! Seek what I will, go where I will—self creeps like a leprosy eating into my soul! I know that I am a worm—that I am less than nothing; and when I contemplate the greatness which the heaven of heavens cannot contain, I know that I am an atom in creation, of no use, of no consequence to any earthly being, and yet I am absorbed in myself. I feel this wretched, worthless self, is more to me than all the wonders of the universe beside. I have an anxiety for its welfare that I cannot feel for any other thing. Why can I not look upon myself as I really am? I read books of devotion—I read the expressions of self-abasement, uttered by the holiest of saints and martyrs, individuals by the side of whom I am utterly worthless,—but I cannot realise these expressions, though they befit me far more than they who first used them! Oh, if I might but attain the grace of humility! If I might be utterly emptied of my self-love,—so that I could think honestly and soberly of myself as a mere tool to do any work the Almighty may be pleased to appoint for me,—oh, for this I would willingly and joyfully sacrifice all hopes of fame, power, success of any kind, that it may be in me to obtain. Oh, to be clothed with humility!"

The next entry is a year and a half later.

"What is meant by the pleasures of sense? What are those gross desires we are enjoined to subdue? It is not these things that separate me from God. I cannot understand the sort of need the saints of old felt for their savage penances, for their seclusion in rocks and caves, where they let themselves be wet with the dew from heaven, and the hair of their bodies grow like the skins of beasts. A sneaking, grovelling sensuality will eat into the heart, taking all virtue and strength out of it; but there must be a secret clinging to the accursed thing, if such mechanical aids are needed to cleanse the soul. There must be something gross and grovelling ingrained, when sensation is required to stifle sensuality. Unless the heart is in earnest to know no pollution, unless the determination to be pure springs up from the very centre of our being, there is no hope for us.

"That morbid beauty, the half sensual half intellectual guise which emotion takes, filling the heart with a luxurious melancholy, is the beauty of the charnel-house—a beauty not purified with life, but tending to dissolution, its form speedily to be effaced, and its beauty to be trodden out into slime and miry clay."

"Life! What is life? for what end was it bestowed on man? This question has been haunting me of late. I cannot answer it myself. Was it given that the holder of it might be happy? This mysterious and magnificent endowment for such a poor and impotent conclusion? It cannot be, for even I myself can scorn the idea of happiness. 'Majestic pain', an earnest labour, is far rather to be desired; they are indeed blessed, beyond happiness, who have a task given them to do, and who can work, not having their ownselves as the end and centre of their task, but who are willing to spend and be spent for the accomplishment of their labour.

"Let all desire for my own ease, for my own consequence, perish! Let me only find a work worthy to be done, that I may be able to press onward to the mark of my high calling. Let there not be a single feeling of my heart kept back from the perfect surrender I desire to make of myself unto Thee, oh my God! I desire only to be obedient, to do the work thou mayest appoint for me, to be as one with Thee!"

"Pleasure! happiness! There is an austere and majestic beauty in the abnegation of passionate and sensual emotion, which no indulgence of them can bestow, a keenness of perception, a god-like power. Genius is in its nature ascetic, the master and not the slave of passion. That genius which takes its rise in passionate sensibility, and the strength of indulged passion, has a certain earthly beauty indeed; but it leads to sickness and satiety. The glorious colours left by the departing sun, fade away into dullness and darkness.

"There is, if people only knew it, a voluptuousness in the subjection of passion, in the being king over one's own heart, of which they who yield to temptation never dream. It is like the perfect health which follows the rough training of a prize-fighter."

"They who cling to worldly prosperity as if it were the one thing needful to be desired after, who consider 'what they shall eat, what they shall drink, and wherewithal they shall be clothed' as the great problem that life was given them to resolve,—who look on their powers of intellect as the tools which are to obtain for them a portion like Benjamin's, seven times greater than that of their brethren,—these, and such as these, are destined to be servants and slaves to those who can renounce and trample on things deemed so precious. They are the kings of the earth, and in their ranks are found all who stand eminent above their fellows; 'whatsoever things are true, whatsoever things are honest, whatsoever things are of good report, if there be any virtue, if there be any praise,' it is achieved by those alone who belong to this class.

"Strong passions to teach the secrets of the human heart, and a strong will to hold them in subjection, these are the keys of the kingdom of this world and the next."

The reader will be able to gather from the above disjointed extracts, the prevailing tone of Everhard's mind during the first period of his college life. Neither his moral nor intellectual powers had come to maturity; but men change less than is imagined; their after life is only a kaleidoscope combination of the elements of their character at the period of adolescence. No event worthy of record occurred till about a year after the period of our last extract. When Everhard had been five years an inmate of the college, a letter from his brother came, which we shall lay before the reader, as it contained news of some interest.

"My dear Everhard,

"I have not written to you of late so frequently as I ought to have done, but I hope you will not set it down to any want of affection, as that is by no means the case; but I have had my mind a good deal occupied for the last three months.

"I think (and have no doubt but what you will agree with me) that as the head of an old family, it becomes me to marry (not but what my mother has presided admirably over all that belongs to the female province). When I was in London lately I met with a young lady, who in every thing seemed adapted to make me an admirable wife. She is the niece to Mr Gifford, of Gifford Castle, in Devonshire, who married a very beautiful Greek lady some years ago. Every body says Mrs Gifford is very clever, but to my thinking, she is neither so handsome, nor so in every way what a woman should be as Marian is. She has large flashing black eyes, which have a kind of bold, saucy look, very different from Marian's, which are light blue, very modest, and downcast, with soft brown hair. She is so gentle and amiable, I am sure you will like her,—nobody can help it, she is so good. She is rather romantic, and very fond of me, which, strange to say, I rather wonder at sometimes. I have had to write her a great many letters, for she likes those sort of things, and that has taken up a great deal of my time, and prevented me writing to you; you know I am not a great scribe. However, I hope the time is near when my letters to her may cease, for seeing one another all day long is much more satisfactory than the best letters that ever were written (and hers are quite beautiful).

"We shall be married, I expect, in a very few weeks from this time. My mother, of course, will continue to live with us, for the house would not seem to be right without her. I shall go to London almost immediately, for Marian's friends all live there. She has no parents, but resides with her uncle, Mr Gifford. He talks of coming to pay us a visit in the autumn, and of bringing Mrs Gifford with him. I hope we shall be able to make all comfortable for them, but I wish you could be here then, for I never feel quite easy with Mrs Gifford, though she is very gracious to me, but somehow she never seems to care about any body, and perhaps you might be able to talk to her in her own way, for of course any body would be glad to listen to you;—but Marian is not at all a fashionable lady, so you need not be afraid of her. My mother, I should tell you, is quite agreeable to the marriage, she considers it a very good connexion, and in these days it is the duty of every good Catholic to consider that we ought never to forget the interests of our religion in any thing that we do.

"I have new furnished the drawing-room. The little room that used to be your study, is fitted up as a private sitting-room for Marian. My mother will have a set of rooms to herself in the gallery that leads to the chapel.

"It is quite time I should end this long letter. My mother sends you her love and her blessing, and

"Believe me, dear Everhard,
"Ever and always,
"Your affectionate brother,
"LOUIS BURROWS."

Everhard lost no time in sending a letter to his brother, full of affectionate congratulations; he also conveyed a mark of consideration to his fair sister elect, in the shape of a splendid cameo necklace, though Louis, with a lover's pre-occupation, had neglected to inform him of the family name of the fair Marian.

He was glad that in his home things were going on so happily, but it was a happiness he regarded in his own mind with something like contempt. We make some further extracts from his private memoranda, and the reader can judge for himself.

"What a poor thing all the happiness of this world is! We often feel disposed to envy a man for being happy, though at the same time we should for ourselves utterly despise the thing that renders him so.

"My brother is going to be married : he seems overflowing with gentle pleasure and egotism: ever good-natured, he shows his disposition to make every one else who comes across his path a sharer in his happiness, that he may see nothing out of keeping;— but he can enter into no feeling unconnected with himself,—he can see nothing but himself, and the fair creature he has chosen for his bride. Has Heaven bestowed everlasting souls on men, and sent them upon earth for no better purpose than to marry and be given in marriage? Is the circle of man's aims and duties comprised in living in a country mansion, and doing the duties of hospitality to neighbours as full of conventionalities as themselves? to hunt, to fish, to preserve game, to legislate on turnpike roads, to send poor vagabonds to the stocks,—and after a life of sensual trivialities, to die, and lie under a painted monument? Is it the highest duty of which a woman is capable, to see that her house is well swept, her dinners well ordered, her servants well trained, and her children kept beautifully dressed? and yet, is not this the sum of what the majority consider life was given them to accomplish?—do all accomplish even this? True, there is in the world much more wanting to be done—but is it the people leading a secular life who will do it? The cares of this life, and the deceitfulness of riches, choke the inner life out of them.

"What is there that really deserves to have a life spent in doing it? What is there that will not prove in the end, 'Spending money for that which is not bread, and labour for that which satisfieth not?'

"I can feel no interest in the things of this world. How daily does my thankfulness increase, that I and my labour will be absorbed into the Church. What is there on earth to be compared to her?

"Is the love men bear to their wives and children to be compared to that which I feel for the Church? Oh, I feel, I know that I have it in me to devote to her all the energies of my nature. I only know that I am a man of like passions with other men, by the intensity of my love for the Church. She is not an abstraction, as the profane deem, but a living and glorious creature. What object should I have in all my strivings after wisdom and knowledge, if all were not for her sake? it is she who gives a meaning and a value to all I attempt.

"Even infidels are struck with the fascination of the Church, which, terrible in her beauty, stretches her influence from age to age, 'from the rising of the sun to the going down of the same'. As vitality pervades, and takes the shape of the visible universe, so does the religion which came down from God take the form of the Catholic Church, to make itself visible to mortal eyes. She works on, like the operations of the natural world, moving all resources, no matter how distant or how complicated, making them all tend to the furtherance of the same object : all under one wise and perfect governance, working unseen, without noise or confusion, and only recognised in the clear and perfect result : never wearying, nor stopping to wonder or glory over what has already been achieved, but continuing age after age in the same strong, grave, silent course, going on from strength to strength, as unsusceptible of change as the perpetual hills, or the everlasting framework of the earth itself. It is no wonder that 'nations come to her, and kings bow down before her!'

"What then must be her influence over the hearts of those honoured to be her servants? destined to be absorbed as living stones into integral portions of her glory and might!"

Our next extract is dated a year after the preceding one, and will serve to mark the change which was gradually working in his mind.

"It is well for me that my love for the Church, as an institution, is so strong and engrossing : for the love of religion for its own sake, which I had as a child, has of late been greatly modified.

"Four years of theological study have changed its aspect. From being a sacred and mysterious object of belief, it has come to be a collection of doctrines to be disputed, to be stated and proved by premises, to be handled, in short, like any other subject. The foundations on which its external evidences rest, have been laid bare to my eyes; they are to be defended against attacks; there are doubtful points to be skilfully covered, there is defective evidence to be supplied by elaborate argument. A habit of metaphysical subtlety has for ever stripped off the bloom of reverence and awe with which I formerly regarded religion, and it can never come back to me.

"Religion has no evidences independent of the Church; therefore the Church, as an artistical working out, an embodiment of vague doctrines, a gigantic frame work, whereby religion is made available to the wants of men, is all in all. We cannot be left desolate, not entirely orphans, whilst the Church remains with us."

Some months later.

"A strange state is coming upon me more and more. Is it that they who serve at the altar, are to have less faith in the oracles than they who worship in the outer court? My religion seems slipping out of my grasp; the more dim and impalpable that becomes, the more do I cling to the most holy and visible Church, that if so be I may merge myself into her, and by passionate clinging to her, I may press out all disbelief.

"I lay hold upon her with the desperation of a man, who by that grasp alone is suspended over the abyss. If my belief and trust in the Church give way, then indeed I shall fall, and go, I know not whither. Tomorrow is my ordination—I have passed my final examination—I have received compliments on my theological knowledge! Oh mockery, to buy theology at the price of religion.

"I will think no more on these things—After to-morrow I am a vowed servant of the Church—I will do her work faithfully—I have no right to my own judgment—I will make an 'act of obedience', and submit that, along with all my other gifts to her will. I will stay myself upon her, and will she not as a tender mother save me from this horror of great darkness, that is coming upon me?"

We find by the record of the college books that, on the 17th of April, 17—, Everhard Burrows was ordained a priest. The same day he was offered a professorship in the college: it was a great honour for one so young, and he gladly accepted it, as his inclination led him to prefer a college life to any more active or public career. Eight years had passed over between his entrance into the college, and becoming a professor in it.

CHAPTER XIII

— • —

Gifford, Zoe, and the two children, with the train of misses, ladies' maids, and other servants, proceeded at once to Chelsea, where Gifford had hired a handsome and commodious house, ready furnished, in a stately row fronting the river, and dignified by the name of the "Manor House". There was an entrance by a glass door into a large hall, paved with black and white marble, which opened on the opposite side by another glass door into a garden of very spacious dimensions for the neighbourhood of London.

Zoe was delighted with the situation, and quite scandalised the sedate Gifford by the eagerness with which she searched out all the traditions connected with the neighbouring localities, and which he declared were not fit to come to the ears of a respectable woman. But the current of Zoe's taste having for the moment set in for secret memoirs and scandalous gossip, his remonstrances were of no avail. One day he solemnly committed to the flames a choice French copy of De Grammont's Memoirs, which Zoe had that morning discovered in an old book shop, and which unfortunately fell in his way as he was waiting for her to come down to dinner. The flames were curling round it when Zoe entered hastily, exclaiming, "Dear me, Mr Gifford, what a terrible smell of burning there is here! Has any thing caught fire?"

"Nothing, madam," replied Gifford severely, "but what ought to have been burned long since by the common hangman; how often am I to declare that I will not have such books in my house?" At the same time he thrust the unfortunate book still deeper into its flaming bed.

Zoe was terribly annoyed, but as she saw there was no possibility of rescuing her book, she did not go into a useless passion; after a minute's silence, she said, "Well, I see you are determined, I shall make what you Catholics call an 'act of obedience'—but you will set the chimney on fire—do let the butler carry it into the kitchen, and let it finish burning there; the lower regions are the fittest locality for such a sacrifice."

Gifford, who had hardened himself in the expectation of a torrent of reproaches, finding both his wrath and his wisdom turned aside, looked a little confused, and perceiving too, as she said, that he had well nigh set the chimney on fire, he told the butler, who just then entered, to see to it, and walked silently into the next room to dinner.

Zoe did not once allude to what had passed, nor showed any discomposure; and by her self-control prevented a quarrel, in which even a good woman might have thought herself justified. However, we are bound to confess that she bought another copy of the same work the very first opportunity, and of which she took better care.

Gifford had, in his own way, both ambition and vanity; as a Catholic he could not enter parliament, which he would dearly have liked, being strongly addicted to making long expositions of his own views and opinions; he was a sensible, sound judging man, only very ponderous, but that did not prevent his being regarded as the leader of the Catholic party in England. His great object in visiting London, was to bring about the means of introducing a Catholic mission into Devonshire, and to obtain the requisite sanction for erecting a college on his estate. His annual income was large, and the economy which had marked the administration of Miss Rodney, enabled him both to support a handsome establishment in London, and to contribute largely to his favourite project.

All the leading Catholic families called on Zoe as soon as she arrived at Chelsea, and the Duchess of N—— offered to present her at the next drawing-room. Gifford was much gratified, and to Zoe's great delight, so far from making any objection, had the family diamonds reset, and made her a very handsome present, in addition to the sum he usually allowed her, to meet all extra expenses; and, as he was in the way of being generous, he selected an elegant "esclavage"; an ornament in those days much coveted and fashionable, gallantly saying it was to make amends for his rudeness in burning her book.

Zoe was, as we have told the reader many times, eminently beautiful; but as the costume of that day is not in accordance with our present notions of the becoming, we shall not describe her court-dress, but only declare that it was in the most approved fashion, and of the most costly material, and that she looked lovely in spite of it. Her appearance at court caused more sensation than any thing that had occurred since the presentation of the two fair Gunnings. In the evening the French ambassador (a personal friend of Gifford's) gave a large assembly, at which Zoe reappeared more radiant than in the morning; all the most noted men of the day crowded to be presented to her, and her chaperone, the Duchess of N——, could hardly keep the peace among so many suitors for her hand during the dance. However, the Earl of March led her out for the first minuet,—and the company climbed upon chairs and tables to see how she would acquit herself. The old duchess, who since the time of Zoe's first coming up to town, had seemed to consider her as her peculiar *protégée*, had strongly impressed upon her the claims of courtesies and carriage; Zoe, feeling by no means clear of her proficiency, had taken a few lessons from a celebrated dancing-master of the day, and though her skill was not altogether transcendent, yet, thanks to her natural grace and beauty, her success was decisive; it would have warmed the heart of the master of her old dancing-school to see the honour she did to his instructions. When she was led back to her seat, the old duchess graciously commended her, for she felt Zoe's success partly her own property. The Earl of March kept his station beside her chair to prevent any other person making himself too agreeable. Zoe for the first time listened to the conversation of a well-bred man of the world, and was astonished to find, that without a single wise or even witty remark, it was so thoroughly agreeable; however, all the conversation she heard that night had a peculiar charm, for she had never in all her life before been among people who admired her. The sudden burst from freezing indifference to the tropical heat of insane adulation, was enough to have turned a stronger head. Possibly, had Zoe known how very thankful people in general, fine people especially, are for any thing new or piquant to flavour the monotony of their lives, she might have been less grateful for the interest she excited. After the cotillions were over, the earl bounded up to one of the card-tables, and addressing a heavy-looking individual who seemed half asleep over his cards, said, "Come with me, and I will introduce you to her;—get somebody to hold your cards, they cannot have worse luck than with yourself, so open your eyes, and come along to look at a miracle."

"Pooh," replied the other, rising lazily from the table; "she is like the rest of women, I suppose—they are all variations on the same air—who is this you are talking about?"

"Why, good heavens, where have you been not to have heard of the new Venus who has come to visit us, nor how we have been witching the room with our noble dancing? where have you put your senses?"

"Whilst you have been in the seventh heaven, I have been in inferno, losing my money,—so how should I know any thing about you. Is that her by that old dowager?"

By this time they had made their way through the crowd, and March presented his companion to Zoe, who recognised the name as belonging to one of the most noted men of the time. Though she said little, her eyes gave him a flattering welcome,—but the announcement of supper gave her no time for conversation; soon afterwards, Gifford, who had been prevented coming before, made his appearance to take her home. His relationship to the new beauty was quickly known, and caused many remarks on their incongruous assortment.

"The idea of that little ugly fellow, old enough for her father, being the husband of that lovely creature! *mais tant pis pour lui.*"

"My dear March, don't talk so loud, it is of no use to rebel against Providence. She is married any way, her husband holds her by divine right of legitimacy, which does not often sanction you; it is cheering to see virtue rewarded elsewhere than in copy-books."

"Is she not magnificent?" said the earl, paying no attention to his friend's discourse. "Since the Countess of Coventry, I never saw so lovely a woman; but she is a *coquette au naturel*, and Heaven help the man who falls in love with her! Ah, George," continued he, "if I had only your reputation now, I might present myself boldly before her to-morrow."

127

"Well," replied the other, "I can only say to you as somebody did to his son, who wished to be thought a great man, 'really be one'; so if you want a reputation, deserve it".

"*Merci, non!*" cried the other, laughing; "a reputation is a means, not an end, with a wise man; but see, my divinity is preparing to depart. I must not lose my privilege of attending her to the carriage." The graceful profligate moved off.

"Ay," cried a cynical-looking elderly man, who stood near, "you have met with your match. That woman is a thorough coquette, in spite of her engaging openness; she may have a heart, but it is out of one man's power to touch it. Heaven help any man, if she does chance to fall in love with him; he will have his hands full; we shall see the days of Dido and Cleopatra over again. But for beauty, she is nothing to the Countess of Coventry."

The current of Zoe's popularity had too strongly set in to be turned aside; and when she came down to breakfast the next morning, she was installed in the fashionable world as the recognised beauty of the season.

Henceforth, for some weeks, Zoe's life was one scene of brilliant success, amusement, admiration, and dissipation, which for a time dazzled her, and occupied every moment; but she was not among people likely to do her any good, or to obtain any permanent influence over her. Women gifted like Zoe often present instances of aberration from the standard of female rectitude. It is not that high talents are in their own nature inimical to the delicate and refined virtues, but they require, in proportion, a stronger and wiser guidance than they often get. The motives that influence the generality of women, do not touch women of high powers; they do not feel the obligations of those small moralities, the fear of "being singular", of rendering themselves the subject of "remark", which wholesomely qualify the love of admiration and display, in the generality of female breasts. They have more energy of character than is absorbed by the routine of duties women are generally called on to perform, and they have no channel in which their superfluous activity can be expended. Women seldom have their powers equalised and balanced by a thorough education, so it is not wonderful that one gifted with more strongly marked strength of character than the generality should have somewhat of the eccentric and irregular in her actions. Her strength resembles the undirected activity of a child, much promised, and nothing accomplished with it. Besides, women cannot, like men, correct their false and crude notions by intercourse with the actual world; from their natural position, they are prevented taking a broad view of things as they really exist. When a woman steps beyond her own domestic circle, into whatever scene she goes she is the subject of a social fiction: she is treated as a visitor, not as an inhabitant: therefore what a woman calls a "knowledge of the world" is only a fresh source of bewilderment, which, besides being in the highest degree undesirable, is confined to a coarse exaggeration of scenes, which undoubtedly do take place, but which lose their truth by being detached from the course of natural circumstances under which they occur. Women of the class we are describing have often a morbid curiosity for this kind of enlightenment; but it leads them no nearer to their object, viz., something to fill the void in their hearts and intellects. WHO are the only class of women who *know the world best*, who see it and mix with it in all its hard and appalling realities?

But this is a digression from the apology we were about to offer for the eccentricity which generally marks women of strong energetic character, who chafe against the harmless conventionalities which are a law to their weaker or better broken-in companions, whom they keep in a constant state of discomfort and fear, lest discredit should thereby be brought upon them. Such women are not wisely treated; if they were judged more kindly, and not looked upon with ill-natured criticism, ever on the watch to sneer and find fault, they would not only be saved from much heart-burning and bitterness of feeling (for no woman is insensible to blame whether deserved or not), but eccentricity would be kept from growing into faults of a graver kind, and they might mature into genial and valuable characters, who in times of trouble and distress would be able to support and guide those of a more fragile nature than themselves. Then would the strong sister amply repay to the weaker one the trusting forbearance she showed towards peculiarities she could neither understand nor sympathise with; at such seasons (and they are not of rare occurrence) would the weak ever find reason to rejoice that she had not fretted the strong-minded with petty unkindness; nor driven her out into the highways of the world, where she must have perished for "lack of knowledge". Zoe had no one to judge her kindly, not a single friend to deal honestly by her, and her eyes were not open to the real destitution as to every thing really to be desired in which she was living. Her life was divided between admiration and detraction; she was an object of curiosity and speculation to all, of friendly interest and regard to none. Her most extravagant admirers were those who said the bitterest things of her; no one understood her; her strong and undirected powers of mind had taken their bent at random, had struck root wherever they chanced to find soil. She had much crude information on many subjects about which women seldom trouble themselves, and was profoundly ignorant of the conventionalities of etiquette; yet it was a graceful ignorance redeemed from all appearance of *niaserie* by a coquetry which might have supplied a whole generation of the sex at once; with quick, artist-like perceptions of the beautiful, and strong passionate emotions gleaming up through all she said and did; but lying far down below the surface, so deep that they defied all the influences around her to rouse them up. For she was true to her own nature, and required something as strong, true, and integral as herself to move her, and she found no mate in the scenes around her; her innate strength kept her from contamination in spite of the handsome, well-bred libertines who surrounded her, and whose brilliancy was like the phosphorescent light streaming from corruption; yet she had an inordinate curiosity to see things and people as they really were, to know the world as women seldom have an opportunity of knowing it, and this kept her from being revolted at a tone of conversation, and a style of confidence, which men seldom feel inclined to address to a woman whose virtue keeps them in awe.

There was a constant speculation going on about her. She puzzled every one; those whom her peculiar style of beauty, and singularly tolerant manners, inspired with the most audacious hopes, were supremely astonished to find they made no way with her, though not a word of sentimental morality ever escaped her lips. She would talk brilliantly, and in a style which startled even the least severe women of society, and caused what they were pleased to call a blush, in the cheeks of women whose divorces and liaisons have become matters of history. Yet with all this, and married to a man whom she confessedly cared very little about, she was faithful in thought, word and deed—"the heart of her husband did safely trust in her"—and with reason. She was a devoted mother to her children, and never for an instant were either their comforts or their education neglected through her dissipation. Yet no one gave her credit for this, her correctness was never set down to her virtue, only to her being difficult to please.

Gifford was too full of his Catholic mission and his new college to pay her much attention. He was satisfied if she went into public, when he could not attend her, under the auspices of the old Catholic Duchess of N——, a worthy and thoroughly respectable old lady, who continued her countenance to Zoe, in spite of imprudences which would have consigned any one else to the extreme penalties of female reprobation, because she hoped to convert her.

The singular Lady Elizabeth Craven, better known afterwards as Margravine of Anspach, was her great ally. Topham Beauclerk, who had married the divorced Lady Bolingbroke, and of whom Dr Johnson said, "that his mind was all virtue, and his body all vice", was perhaps the only one of the brilliant circle that surrounded her, who really did her justice; at first, he made some pretension to being her lover, but he soon had sense to see that she was not the sort of woman he had imagined, and he had the magnanimity not to resent his want of success.

He stood up for her on all occasions, both among his own set at White's, and in private companies; he did his best to check all scandalous reports about her, and did her all the good in his power. An anomalous sort of friendship sprung up between them; he prided himself on making her his companion, and telling her all the scandalous news of the day; he gave her a great deal of good advice, and told her many truths that women seldom hear, and must have perilled the peculiar divinity which "doth hedge" a woman, before they can be in a position to find of use. He was at any rate a most fascinating companion, and introduced to Zoe all the people worth knowing of his acquaintance.

George Selwyn, as famous for his kindly disposition as for his wit, went a great deal to her house, and she had the honour of knowing Dr Johnson during the last year of his life. The following letter, written by Zoe to her Uncle Oliver, will give a better idea of her character and way of life than many pages of description. Our most indifferent actions have the impress of individuality; we may convey an impression not to be effaced for years, by an unconsidered word, a gesture, nay, by our very silence, and we, all the time, unconscious of having done or said any thing at all : it is never by our deliberate actions that we persuade others to estimate us.

"Chelsea, 17—

"Dear Uncle,

"Many thanks for your last letter, which ought to have been answered long since; but I have really not had time. I grant you that my time is filled up with trifles, but trifles are just as imperative for the moment as things of importance: on the same principle I suppose, that a fool is harder to deal with than a wise man. However, if you will scold me I shall be very glad, because the scolding must come in a letter, and I want to hear from you. You are very good in wishing me to come and see you—though you little know what you are asking for. I should certainly scandalise you, and drive poor Aunt Martha out of her senses; however, I will, if possible, come to you for a month in the autumn, and bring the children. I hope you will invite my cousin Sarah Anne and her husband and children: what a singular meeting it will be, and how the good man will bless his good angel that would not let him marry me! I give you notice, in order that you may not be startled, that I shall bring my finest finery, and my grandest manners to mystify them. Now, dear uncle, mind you arrange every thing well. I only hope poor little Sarah Anne will not have her head turned in good earnest.

"Like all other good people, you take great interest in the gossip about naughty ones. I shall of course tell you no tales about myself. I was at Newmarket last week; the Duke of Queensbury's horse won, and he was, besides, a winner to the amount of several thousand pounds, a matter of very little importance to him now, one way or the other; he would have been more thankful for his good luck if it had come some years ago. Topham Beauclerk says that there are a set of devils who preside over the dice, and who are named after the points, aces, sizes, deuces, and what not, and their duty is to come to every one who invokes them; but there are so many players calling out at once, that the poor devils, who cannot be everywhere at once, are obliged to go to people in their turn; consequently they often do not arrive till too late, and do as much mischief by their presence as they have caused by their absence; or come when the people don't care whether they come or stay away. As you have to deal with the devil and all his works, perhaps you can tell me whether this is really a fact.

"I had a grand party at my house the other evening, which, as the newspapers would tell you, is one of the most brilliant this season. The Countess of Cork was present, who is the most amusing oddity in the world. She never seems to mind any one but herself, and has very little patience, or ceremony either, with those whom she finds bores; but there is all the difference in the world between the piquant selfishness (for I suppose it must be called so) of a clever person, and that stupid indifference to every thing but yourself, which is the general aspect it assumes; one is willing to forgive a great deal to the person who has the grace to find us interesting, and one has hardly the philanthropy to wish that all the world should be equally well treated. Then there was the Countess of Coventry, a very good, respectable woman, but not specially handsome to my thinking, though she has the reputation of being a fine woman; but she is nothing to her predecessor, the beautiful Maria Gunning, who was her husband's first wife; those who knew her pay me the compliment of thinking me something like her. Then there was Lady Sarah Bunbury, who narrowly missed being married to the king; she is very clever, and certainly no one can deny her beauty; but I don't think she much likes me, she is always civil, but cold and stately. Lady E. Craven was here too, she is dreadfully picturesque, and has a mania for wandering about like Don Quixote's princesses. Selwyn, the wit, whose name you must know well, came also; he is a real good man, and he kept wide awake all the evening, which was a special miracle. By the way, Boswell will be in your neighbourhood shortly, and I shall give him a letter of introduction to you; he is worth your seeing for the sake of that great man. Tell Aunt Martha, who I know loves her novels, that I had Evelina, Cecilia, in one word, Miss Burney herself; she came with her father and one of her married sisters, and they brought the great singer, who is all the rage just now. I cannot say much that will satisfy my aunt's curiosity. Miss Burney is the most consequentially modest little damsel you can imagine; she seems to carry her fame about with her from a sense of duty, and to be almost sinking under the load; her bashful attempts to keep it out of sight, and to look unassumingly are truly comic. She receives all the ordinary compliments which people pay at first addressing her, *au pied de la lettre*; she is very little and young looking; not very pretty, but she has a pair of bright black eyes; and she dresses with exemplary neatness, and would not have a pin or a plait awry for the world. There were a crowd of other people besides, all of much value and importance, doubtless, in their own eyes; but you would not care to hear about them. The evening, altogether, went off brilliantly, and has raised the reputation of my parties even beyond what it was before.

"Mr Gifford is quite well, and in high good-humour, his college goes on prosperously; he made me a present of china on my birthday, which has made me the envy of all my friends, nobody, except Horace Walpole, has any thing to be compared to it.

"I must not forget to tell you that my portrait by Sir Joshua is finished, it is one of his best. Gifford finds fault with the dress, but what should he know about the matter?

"The children are quite well, the air of Chelsea agrees with them. Give my love to my aunt, and wishing you, dear uncle, all sorts of health and happiness, believe me.

"Your affectionate niece,
"ZOE GIFFORD."

One morning, not long after the date of the above letter, Gifford entered his wife's dressing-room. She was lounging upon a settee at the open window, sometimes looking at the boats which were passing gaily up and down, and occasionally on the pages of a book she held in her hand. A little table covered with a dainty breakfast stood beside her. The room was full of elegant trifles, and perfumed like the Temple of Spring itself, by a large vase of choice flowers that stood on a marble slab. The chintz curtains were blown to and fro by the breeze from the river, and the morning sun glanced merrily on the radiant colours of a paroquet which was screaming in its gilt cage for the allowance of muffin its mistress usually bestowed upon it at breakfast. All looked so fresh and pretty, that Gifford paused for a moment to admire it. At length he said, "I am come to beg some breakfast and a short *tête-à-tête* with you, for you are so *répandue* in society, there is no finding you alone any other part of the day." Zoe smiled graciously, and having quieted her paroquet, proceeded to do the honours of the breakfast-table.

Gifford had evidently something on his mind which he wished to say, but did not know how to introduce. Zoe did not assist him by expressing the smallest curiosity; at length, when he had finished his last cup of chocolate, and Zoe evidently had no intentions of remaining any longer over breakfast, he mustered courage and began, "You are now such a grand lady that I hardly dare ask your concurrence in a plan I have long entertained."

"Is it about that everlasting college?" said Zoe.

"No, madam, it is not. It is about a niece of mine, the daughter of my only sister, who has just finished her education, and is now of an age to be introduced into society. She is coming to London next Tuesday, and will come here for a short visit; if you do not find her very disagreeable, I should much like her to reside here permanently, and to find a home with us; but I am far from wishing to force her upon you if you feel any objection to receiving her."

"But", said Zoe, almost bewildered, "who is she? Where does she come from, and what does she come here for so suddenly?"

"There is nothing sudden in the matter," said Gifford. "When my sister died, I promised her that when Marian was of an age to leave her convent, she should find a home with me. She has been for the last few months with her father's relations, but they are not persons with whom she can advantageously remain. She is some years younger than yourself, but you need not fear a rival in point of beauty."

Zoe made a scornful mouth, and shrugging her shoulders, said, "Of course if you wish it, I can make no objection ; but girls of that age are a great annoyance. I dare say she will not be half so nice as dear little Clotilde, whom that old Miss Rodney keeps shut up in her stifling room. I wonder how you can leave the poor child by herself, without any companions. I think your niece would do her good if she went to keep her company; but we must make the best of her. I am sure I don't know where to put her, we have so little spare room, unless she takes Mrs Brown's room, and Mrs Brown must move up to the attics along with the rest of the servants. The Duchess of Devonshire's ball is next Thursday, so she had better come directly, that I may have time to get her a decent dress for the occasion."

"You are very kind, my dear," replied Gifford; "perhaps you will write to her yourself, and tell her she will be welcome; the poor girl is very timid."

"Ugly and awkward that means, I suppose," thought Zoe, but

she did not say so, she merely said, "Well, leave me her address." The hair-dresser was now announced as waiting—and the husband, quite satisfied with his success, retired like a wise man.

Zoe was as good as her word, she wrote a very kind letter, and on the day appointed, sent the carriage to meet her. When she arrived, Zoe ran down stairs with some anxiety to see what she was like. A fair, slight girl was standing in the drawing-room beside the window; she was not exactly pretty, but there was a pleasing expression in her blue eyes, and her soft auburn hair fell in large curls round her neck.

"Thank Heaven!" thought Zoe as she kissed her, "the girl is not vulgar at least. I can do with any thing but that. Now, my dear," said she aloud, "come with me and rest yourself whilst we get better acquainted. You will see your uncle at dinner-time. Is your luggage all gone up-stairs? We must lose no time in seeing after the ball dress, but we will talk whilst you take some refreshment."

CHAPTER XIV

— · —

Marian Gifford was in every respect the reverse of her brilliant aunt; she was a gentle and romantic girl, not more averse to the prospect of dissipation, than the generality of girls at sixteen. She made her *début* at the Duchess of Devonshire's much to her own satisfaction, in a robe of white paduasoy, brocaded with silver. Zoe's acquaintance, anxious to find favour in her sight, vied in paying atttention to her *protégée*, who, in consequence, had a great choice of partners.

Marian had a very tender heart, which was quite at her own disposal, and very much at the service of the first applicant—but unfortunately, she was not in the way of lawful lovers. Few, or none, among Zoe's set, were marrying men. The civilities that were shown to the niece, were for the sake of the aunt, who monopolised all the attention and admiration that any one had to bestow.

Poor Marian was not much to be envied; she went certainly into the best company, and had a sufficiently large allowance of balls, plays and masquerades, to have excited the envy of any Miss Larolles (vide 'Cecilia'); still Marian, after the first week or two, did not find much enjoyment; for though balls, and plays, and public breakfasts, may sound very gay and very dissipated, still there is nothing more flat and insipid when one has neither a special lover nor general admiration to give them a zest and significance. Marian found herself very dull, and not being a metaphysician, could not account for it.

She was thoroughly affectionate, and at first tried to be romantic about her beautiful aunt, but Zoe was too unimpressible ever to see it. She took great pains to make Marian understand that she must not make herself ridiculous by believing a man meant any thing by his civillest speeches, unless he made her an offer in plain words. She told her so many instances of men amusing themselves by flirting with young girls, without the remotest intention of marrying them, that poor Marian began to believe that a genuine lover was a blessing that only existed in novels.

Zoe, however, was very kind to her in her own way, took her everywhere, supplied her plentifully with dresses and trinkets, and never, by word or look, reminded her of her dependent position.

Zoe was too high-minded and generous to do any thing that showed a want of consideration;—but she was also too much occupied with her own affairs to take an interest in a girl of Marian's age; a real English girl as she called her; so poor Marian had no one to love her, and there was no one, except the children, to whom her love was of the slightest importance. The two children, indeed, were never easy when away from Cousin Marian, who would play with them for hours together, and would let them harness her to their carriage, and never weary of "being their horse"; still the heart of a girl of sixteen requires something more romantic to satisfy it.

At length, whatever Power it may be that has the office of rewarding the virtue there is going in the world, seemed disposed to acquit itself towards Marian.

She one night accompanied Zoe to a literary reunion at Mrs Montagu's. At first she had felt very much disposed to repine at the arrangement, because she wanted to go to the opera instead, as had first been arranged. We never know what is best for us.

She sat crushed into one corner of a sofa, listening with all her might to the speeches that were spoken by each one with laboured sprightliness, as a tribute to his own reputation for wit. She wondered in her ignorance why the same things could not have been said in a straightforward way, thinking, though she could not have put in words, that if insipid things must be said, they seem more respectable when they go a steady prose pace, than when they attempt the fantastic steps of a rope-dancer.

There were abundance of pictures and prints and curiosities laid about to be looked at, but they were on a table in the middle of the room, far distant from the corner where Marian was at anchor.

She had resigned herself to her lot, when her hostess approached from the other end of the room, followed by a good-humoured looking young man who seemed much afflicted with *mauvaise honte*. Addressing Marian in the most silken tones, she presented to her "Mr Burrows", spoke to her as "her most sweet, natural young friend", and assuring Mr Burrows that he would infinitely prefer her society to that of the more shining members of the gifted throng around, she glided off and left them together, with the comfortable persuasion on her mind that she had disposed of two of her dead weights for the evening.

Our old acquaintance, Louis, sat for a few moments silent before he could collect his senses to address his companion, but when he ventured to look at her, there was a sort of quiet, home-look about her, which infinitely relieved his embarrassment; and after another pause, he summoned resolution to tell her that the room was very full. The gentle assent that was given, emboldened him to say further, that he understood nobody came there but distinguished authors, or at least very clever people. This was said in a timid, half-rueful tone, which made Marian feel very much inclined to laugh, and she answered merrily, "Oh, no, they are not all authors, there must be some everyday people to look at them, and listen to the clever things that are said."

"Ah," said he, with a sort of little sigh, "I never read many books, and one feels the want of them when one comes to such places as these. Do you know the names of those who are here?"

"Yes," said Marian; "that is Miss Seward,—the thin lady who is speaking now; and that polite-looking gentleman is Mr Hayley; that lady in the red gown, is Miss Hannah More; and that elderly lady beside her is a very learned woman indeed, she is Mrs Elizabeth Carter, who translated Epictetus,—a Greek philosopher," added she, innocently, seeing that the face of Louis did not brighten as if she had conveyed any intelligence.

"Ah," said he again, "what a number of books there are one ought to read, and I never even heard of their names; have you written any thing?"

"No," replied Marian, half laughing; "I come here with my aunt, and for no merits of my own."

"Then we are equal," said Louis, greatly relieved. "I have a brother, though," continued he, "who has written a great many very learned books, and though you may not have heard of him, he is, I dare say, a great deal cleverer than any of the people here. I wish he were here, it would be in his way, and he could talk, and they would be glad to listen to him."

"I think," said Marian, colouring slightly, "that it must be your brother who wrote a book I like better than any I ever read; it is an abridgement from some large work of his, and my confessor gave it me when I left the country as the most valuable present he could make me. Is not your brother the Father Everhard of Rome?"

"Yes," said Louis, greatly pleased, "and it makes me feel quite friendly with you, to know you have read any of his books. I can hardly fancy we have only just met."

A very promising conversation ensued, in which he told her a great deal about Everhard, and the great person he was in the college at Rome, and the estimation in which he was held by the pope himself. As Marian seemed really interested in listening to him, he grew quite confidential, he told her about Sutton Manor House and the chapel, and that he hoped soon to have a resident priest; nay, he went so far as to tell her about the excellent coursing there was in the neighbourhood, and to give her a special account of his own favourite hunters. But suddenly he stopped in the full tide of his eloquence, and colouring like fire, said, "I quite forgot we are nearly strangers, and you must think me a fool for talking of my own things at this rate." He seemed half vexed at himself, till Marian thanked him for the forgetfulness which he was lamenting, and assured him it was very seldom any one talked to her about any thing in which she had felt so much interested; "The fact is", said she, "nobody here seems at all to care for what they are saying, they seem only to think how they may make fun of it themselves; and one gets so tired of people who only try to make one laugh." Then, in her turn, she told him about the relations she had left in the country, and found that he knew something about them; so by the end of the evening, when he handed her to the carriage, they both felt as if they had known each other all their lives.

"Why, Marian," said Zoe, as soon as they were seated, "you seem to have made a conquest; who is that you have been flirting with all night?"

"Oh, such a delightful young man, aunt, do you know he is brother to that Father Everhard of Rome, whose books you were reading the other day."

"Indeed!" replied Zoe, "I wish I had known, I should like to have spoken to him.—Is he clever?"

"Yes, I am sure he must be, he is so agreeable," said Marian. "I never had such a pleasant evening."

The consciousness of being admired always beautifies a woman, or at least, makes her look to the greatest advantage her case will allow. When Marian came down to breakfast the next morning, the glow of the evening before had not faded away. She was quite radiant as she gave her uncle an account of the party.

"Burrows," said her uncle, "Louis Burrows, why that is the name of the young man who brought me a letter of introduction yesterday, and I have invited him to dine here to-day."

"Marian, you are in luck," said Zoe, laughing, "you must mind and complete your conquest."

Marian was not a coquette, and yet it is an authenticated fact that she went up stairs a full hour before the dressing-bell rang, and came into her aunt's room when she was just descending, to beg that her maid might dress her hair, as she had pulled it down three times, and could not make it fit to be seen.

"Come, I will do it myself," said Zoe, good-naturedly, "you always look best when I dress you." Whether Zoe was successful in her undertaking is not recorded, probably she was, since Louis not only remained as late as he decently could, but contrived to find his way into their pew at chapel the next day, which was Sunday; and accepted with eagerness Gifford's only half expressed invitation to "walk in" when they came to the house door. In short, he contrived all sorts of excuses to be constantly in the way of Zoe and Marian wherever they went; lovers in those days were much more enterprising than they are now, or, as a good lady once said, "Love was the fashion then"; and matrimony too, it would seem, for Gifford very shortly received a formal request from Louis, to be allowed to pay his addresses to his niece. Neither Zoe nor Gifford raised any objections, in fact, the alliance was highly desirable in every point of view. So Louis came every day, and soon succeeded in making Marian in love with him to his heart's content. The children alone found fault with this happy state of things, for Cousin Marian had lost all inclination to sit up in the nursery, and had no more time to be their "horse". They both loudly expressed their joy when Louis had to leave town to make preparations for receiving his bride; but they soon found that matters grew worse; for the first few days after he went, Cousin Marian was very dull, and cried a great deal, which they did not at all like, and afterwards she was always writing letters, so, as Frederick, the eldest boy, said one day, they wished Burrows would come back, for he not only used to play with them sometimes, but cousin Marian always looked happy when he was there to talk to her, and keep her from being always writing. At length all was arranged, Louis came back to London, accompanied by his stately mother, who soon took Marian into high favour for her sweetness and docility. The house at Chelsea was in a bustle of preparation. In addition to her handsome outfit, Gifford had presented his niece with a thousand pounds as a marriage gift. Louis bought a handsome new family carriage, and the evening before the day appointed for the ceremony, a case of valuable jewels came directed to Marian. They were the family jewels, which the old lady had caused to be reset as her present to her daughter-in-law.

"Why, Marian, what is the matter with you?" said Zoe. "Louis will fancy that your heart fails, and that you are repenting, if he sees you with such a sorrowful face."

"I am so happy", replied Marian with a sigh, "that I feel quite afraid to think of it—it is almost like pain—what have I done to deserve so much? I have a sort of dread lest something should come between now and to-morrow. I never used to think much about death, and now it is the one thing in my thoughts."

Zoe looked at the young girl with surprise. She had always considered her as of a different nature to herself, and unable either to think or feel except in the most ordinary fashion: those few words seemed a claim to the sisterhood she had never acknowledged. There is the strong bond of humanity between both wise and simple, they are more alike than they fancy.

In a short time the lover appeared, and all misgivings fled before him.

The next morning rose bright and happy, a train of gay carriages full of wedding guests arrived: the important ceremony was performed, both according to the Romish form in Zoe's drawing-room, and afterwards, according to legal prescription, in the parish church of Chelsea. Then followed the wedding breakfast, after which the new married pair departed for their own home, leaving the ball which was to grace the day, to follow in its due season.

At length all was over, the guests departed, the lights in the dancing room extinguished. Zoe and Gifford were standing in the dressing-room we formerly mentioned; it was the only spot that had not been molested by the revels of the day.

"Poor Marian," said Gifford, "I hope she will not repent the step she has taken. She deserves to be happy."

"Poor Marian," said Zoe, "I think she is sure to be happy. I did not at all expect she would have made such a good match. How late it is. I am glad weddings don't come every day."

The day week after the event recorded above, Zoe found on her breakfast-table a letter sealed with black; it was from Clotilde, telling of the sudden death of Miss Rodney. It was very short, for the poor child was evidently in the deepest affliction; a few lines from the old priest gave a more particular account of the occurrence. The old lady had imprudently remained out of doors late in the evening, and caught a cold which had brought on a sort of croup, of which she died in a few hours. Gifford was much shocked, for he had a great respect for Miss Rodney, and knew how many worthy qualities she possessed; but he felt more than consoled in the idea that now they would all be obliged to return into Devonshire much sooner than he had dared to hope. The college was finished, and he was anxious to make the interior arrangements. He had grown woefully tired of the life of gaiety and dissipation he had been obliged to lead since their arrival in London, yet without this unforeseen event he would hardly have had courage to attempt to take his wife away from scenes in which she naturally found much more satisfaction than he did. It was with a slight trepidation, nevertheless, that he broke to her his wish to return at once to Gifford Castle; and he was both surprised and pleased when Zoe at once replied: "To be sure, we must leave London as soon as possible. Poor dear little Clotilde! how terribly lonely she must be in that old castle. I will write to her by this post to tell her she may expect us forthwith."

"I hardly expected to find you so willing to leave the scene of your triumphs," said Gifford; "but you are really very good whenever it comes to the point; what is the reason you take such pleasure in seeming worse than you are, as if you cared for nobody?"

"Because people are fools, and I feel a pride in imposing upon them," replied Zoe. "They are not worth wasting good feelings upon. I grudge even wearing real jewels for them. I rejoice when I can make them believe that my paste buckles are diamonds like my necklace."

"But that is a sort of insanity, madam; you injure no one but yourself, and you can have no satisfaction from it."

"You are mistaken," said Zoe; "there is great pleasure in feeling that I can see through all the people about me, whilst they know nothing at all about what I really am. What do I care whether they do me justice or not; so long as they can say nothing really bad of me, they may make as many observations as they choose; it is amusing to hear the nonsense they talk."

"Zoe, Zoe, you are like a child playing with fire, who declares that it does not care if it burn its fingers. You will be wiser some time, when you have ruined yourself in gaining experience; but *allons*—there is only an hour for writing our letters."

Zoe wrote an affectionate letter to Clotilde,—telling her that she should begin to make arrangements for leaving London that very day, and that she should quite rejoice to find herself in the old castle once more.

Zoe's preparations went on rapidly. She was too much of a woman not to have drawn some advantage from the alacrity with which she prepared to return into the country; accordingly Gifford had been made to reward it by purchasing a great quantity of handsome furniture to fit up her own apartments in the castle. This was all sent on before them. Zoe insisted, too, on taking back her French maid with her. She received an infinite number of perfumed notes containing odes, declarations, and desperations, in every approved fashion of elegance. She treated them all with great impartiality. She made them into a bundle, tied round with blue riband, and gave it to her husband, in order, as she told him, "That when she grew old and ugly, it might remain on record what a miracle of perfection she had once been!"

At length all was ready for their departure, and on a fine morning in August, the whole family started on their journey home.

It was a rich, mellow evening, the dark purple sky of night was blended with the golden and gorgeous light which the sunset had left behind, when the travelling-carriage entered the huge portal cut in the rock, which was the entrance to the castle grounds. The thick branches of the trees on each side kept out the little daylight that remained, except when here and there the rich gold light flashed from behind their dark boughs.

"How slow they go!" cried Zoe; "let me get out!—how delicious the air feels! It is like getting suddenly into one of Titian's pictures!" She was out in a moment, in spite of Gifford's remonstrances, and striking into a well-remembered by-path much nearer, but frightfully steep, she clambered up the flights of steps, and in about ten minutes she reached her garden terraces. The castle stood dark and shadowy in the deepening twilight, her pace gradually slackened, and she stood like one entranced. The glitter and noise of the scenes she had so recently left, contrasted strangely with the freshness and solitude of the place where she now was, and raised thoughts and emotions she had never known before. A feeling of reverence and worship arose in her heart, which made her feel as if all the latter part of her life had been one sacrilege; but she was aroused by the noise of the carriages entering the great court-yard, which reminded her that she had still a circuit to make before she could reach the gateway and join the rest.

They were not expected till the next day, and the old servants ran about in great dismay to light the lamps and set the things in order, whilst Zoe's French maid looked wildly about, thinking she had come to some bandit fastness.

Gifford, meanwhile, flew up the creaking oak staircase, and the flight of stone steps that led to Clotilde's oratory. There, unconscious of any arrival, or the bustle that had been going on, knelt his child before the crucifix, her fair hair falling over her throat and shoulders in full contrast to her deep mourning dress. She had been very lonely since Miss Rodney's death, and it was with a violent burst of tears that she flew to her father, and nestled in his arms.

Zoe and the two boys were not far behind,—they all joined in soothing her, and it was a happy group that sat down to supper in the old wainscotted dining-room that night.

CHAPTER XV

— · —

Mankind have ever fancied that they hold the reins of destiny; they have struggled, legislated, speculated, hoped, and feared, as if it had been laid upon each individually to keep the world from rolling to perdition.

Men are mostly divided into two classes, one who have their faces resolutely set towards the past, always prone to try the virtue of some "patent drag", and would keep peace by persecuting all expressions of diversity.

The other set incline to rush recklessly forward, always seeking some new thing, some special and compendious theory, for making men happy, and renewing the age of gold. Each set vigorously abuses the other, each accuses its neighbour of "being fatal to the interests of mankind". Meanwhile, the poor old world rolls on in her course, neither better nor worse for all this activity, which seems nothing more than the noise caused by the working of the machine.

In the early part of the 18th century these two parties were in collision. It had long been the fashion either to ask no questions, or to remain satisfied with the answers made and provided. There were then, as now, elaborate specimens of special pleading for the edification of such as inquired, all leading more or less ingeniously to the orthodox and authorised doctrines of the Catholic Church, for the Church legislated upon all points, whether of religion or philosophy; consequently, independent opinions and private judgment, when they happened to be at variance with the declared code, placed their possessor under a ban ; and the social brand that was placed on every one who dared to give ear to differences of interpretations, was enough to induce any but a saint or martyr to hold his tongue, or, at least, to veil his thoughts in discreet and doubtful words.

In this state of things, men were reduced to work off their superabundant activity by perfecting the mechanical detail of literature. Criticism was in repute and flourished; commentaries, notes, and quibbles, abounded on the glorious works of genius that had been written aforetime.

In matters of religion, men were obliged to find what nourishment they could for their souls in settling the Jansenists and the Bull "Unigenitus".

But a strong spirit of reaction was going on under all this.

The unbounded licence of manners at the time of the regency, prepared the way for a free utterance of opinion on all subjects. Voltaire arose, and the school of the philosophers and encyclopediasts. They attacked and turned into ridicule the outer works and external doctrines of Christianity;—they scoffed at scripture history, Church legends, and ecclesiastical authority, and destroying as they did with scathing wit, the *prestige* connected with those subjects, they imagined that they had entered a successful crusade against religion itself.

The genius and ability of the heads of the movement were unquestionable, but they gave in to a showy, uncandid, superficial way of treating their subjects, and it was no difficult task for the friends of Christianity to refute their cloudy declamations; still, they had struck a chord in the hearts of the people, and the belief in Christianity ceased to be what it had been of old.

Every candid mind felt that the theories set up by philosophers in lieu of Christianity, were false, wild, and impossible as a child's nursery-tale—yet every thinking mind felt also that there lay a deep truth amid all this error, though they might lack strength to distinguish it, and there was a feeling of sympathy with their speculations even in the hearts of those who might not agree to any one of their propositions.

Everhard lived when "infidelity", as the Christians phrased it, walked boldly abroad—when it was the fashion, the mark of a liberal education, to be sceptical.

The works of the encyclopediasts, of course, were read by him, for he was looked to by the Church party as one who promised to become their most powerful champion. He wrote a work, soon after he was elected professor, which had a prodigious success, and provoked a reply from Diderot himself; he had learning and eloquence, he could fight the encyclopediasts with their own weapons, and they felt that in him they had their most formidable controversial antagonist.

But whilst the orthodox party were loud in their praises, and the opposite party were forced into expressions of admiration at his skill, how did it fare with Everhard himself? He was heavy and dissatisfied, and disturbed at heart; he was conscious that those philosophers whom he had assailed with such energy, whose mistakes and false reasonings he had exposed with such pitiless sarcasm, had made at least one thing clear and palpable to him, had fixed in his heart a conviction from which he in vain endeavoured to avert his thoughts; he saw and felt that Christianity, and what we are pleased to call "revealed religion", as far as the external evidences go, rests on no better foundation than those of any other form of religious belief which ruled the world before it was promulgated, and has faded away from men's sympathies. He saw that, struggle to conceal the fact as priests and devotees might, the awe with which religious doctrines had hitherto been handled by the generality, was destroyed; the mystery in which they had been reverendly shrouded, was henceforth irretrievably rent away. He felt bitterly convinced that the Catholic Church—his idol the Church—was not a Truth, but only a form by which truth had once been made manifest, and finally almost obscured by ceremonies which had ceased to be transparent,—that it was ceasing to be the expression of men's adoration,—that it was no longer the form spontaneously assumed by their devotion. He felt wretched and confused; it seemed as if with the vanishing of the decaying temple, the God whose presence had once been felt therein, was passing away also.

When any thing strikes the mind as a truth, however distasteful it may be, or opposed to our former feelings, we have no option— the instant we see it as true, we are constrained to embrace it;—we cannot say we will or we will not—it is a necessity, and we must. The first distinctly recognised doubt is of the same kind; we may struggle against it as we will, but there it is, a wedge inserted into the very fabric of our faith, which splits to the foundation, and falls off from us, leaving us naked and trembling among its ruins. Everhard had loved his Church, had loved his religion as if it had been his life; it would have cost him less pain to have been a martyr than to doubt; he could have cried with Micah, "Ye have taken away the gods which I made, and what have I more?" But he was before all things a sincere man. That which had now come upon him, seemed to raise to distinctness a thousand voices which had for years been murmuring within him; that which was within was leagued to that which was without; all the misgivings of old against which he had struggled, now flashed clear into distinct disbelief. But who may paint the distracted, discordant thoughts that crowd into a heart which is beginning to be severed from its life-long worship and belief? The fear—the uncertainty—the tossing to and fro—the soul cast adrift from its anchorage—no God—no light— no hope—yearning after its old religion, yet having no faith to cling to it—and nothing to supply its place! All the dark questionings which hitherto had been kept like evil spirits bound in the depths by the power of the ineffable name, now that the spell which had held them was broken, rose up to have their time of torment—they came sweeping over his bewildered mind, till he trembled at the blasphemy which was in his heart, and loathed himself; but there was no escape. Who was there to deliver?—on whom now could he call? Oh, God!—hast Thou indeed made all men in vain! He flung himself on the ground in agony, and gave vent to his anguish in groanings which are not to be uttered.

Day after day passed on; but no light broke on his darkness; the very foundations of his being seemed broken up, and out of course; he was desolate, but the calm of desolation was not yet his. In this state of mind, the thought of John Paul Marston came across him, and completed the measure of his perplexity. "Is there no differ- ence", he exclaimed, passionately, "between right and wrong? Is every thing alike? Have I all my life been wrong, and he, the hypocrite, the sensualist, has he been right? Surely I have cleansed my heart in vain, and washed my hands in innocency?"

But his mental struggles at length affected his health; he was seized with a brain fever, and lay for many weeks between life and death.

When Everhard began to regain his consciousness, he had a confused idea of being in a state of "mortal sin"; he seemed to labour under a terrible nightmare of crime, of which he could give no account to himself.

> "Deeds to be hid, that were not hid,
> And all confused, he did not know
> Whether he suffer'd or he did,
> But all was sin, and fear, and woe."

His bodily weakness was, however, too great to allow him to think collectedly, and after many fruitless efforts to arrange his thoughts he gave up the attempt, and resigned himself to that dreamy, passionless state, which the entire prostration of bodily strength brings along with it. This again gave place to the irritable impatience of imperfect convalescence, that most weary condition in all this weary life.

When he at length left his bedroom for the first time, and descended to his little parlour, the sun was streaming through the open casement, but shaded by large vases full of flowers and green branches, which some of the students had arranged, in order that all might look cheerful to welcome him back amongst them again. A spring of joy gushed up in Everhard's heart as he looked out on the glorious prospect, a pleasurable sensation of existence poured in upon him, for the time bearing down all sense of sorrow.

The Prince de Ligne says, that one of the three happy days of his life, was the one on which he first went abroad after having the small pox. Everhard experienced the same kind of feeling, he wondered what it was that could have made him wretched; but in that self-same hour, it seemed as if that burst of joy had only raised him up, to cast him down still lower into the depths from which he had for a moment emerged: a sudden darkness fell upon the face of nature, he recollected that he had not now the God towards whom beforetimes in such scenes as the present, he lifted up his thoughts; he had no religion now to give significance to the appearance of nature: the prodigal wealth of life and sunshine, which pervaded all things, had become to him only a vast enigma;

and the broad surface of beauty spread over all, barely concealed the dark and inscrutable abyss over which it was flung. The thoughts of his past life, and all the labours in which he had delighted, rose up before him, striking his mind with a morbidly vivid conviction of their worthlessness. What was there now left for him to do in the world? He wished in his heart that he had died as he lay sick upon his bed.

The next day there was high mass in the chapel, at which he had to assist to return thanks for his recovery. He ascended the altar and heard the organ pealing "*Gloria in excelsis*", and he felt himself an apostate, having no part nor lot in the hopes and worship around him. All the reasons which had led him to this change had vanished for the moment; nothing remained but the sense of having by his own act cut himself off from the congregation.

To stand among the ruins of our home after it has fallen a prey to the spoiler, is a calamity so heavy that there are no words by which its bitterness can be expressed; but even that is a light thing compared to standing among the relics of a religion, under which we once dwelt in safety, none making us afraid, but whence we have been obliged to go forth, confused and trembling, to encounter the mysteries of life and death as best we may, alone, in utter ignorance, without either a hope or a belief to guide us, or any God to whom we may cry for help. This calamity was Everhard's.

The service proceeded until it came to the "*Agnus Dei qui tollis peccata mundi, miserere nobis*", the "*Dona nobis pacem*" came in notes which were the very embodiment of human misery and human appeal, in tones that gave utterance to all the inexpressible emotions of a soul prostrate before its God. Everhard's heart was cloven by that prayer; it was the voice of his own soul, crying in its agony; but WHERE could he go? To whom could he appeal? There was none that answered, neither any that regarded; "The God that heareth prayer" had for him departed thence. Then came the recollection of the blessedness he had formerly known at such seasons, when as a child, at the elevation of the Host, he believed that God had indeed descended to be bodily present with men; he felt that if this belief might but come again he could never know sorrow more.

Everhard's infidelity, apostasy as some might call it, was the strongest test of his sincerity that could be given—a test far beyond that of martyrdom. The whole economy of life was deprived of the clue by which he had hitherto guided himself, and his feet were left "to stumble amongst the dark mountains". Added to all this, there came doubts and misgivings whether, along with the support of his religion, he should not also be deprived of his moral integrity; whether, though at present his whole soul recoiled from the idea of sin, he might not eventually be "let alone" to plunge into all the unutterable pollutions that are rife among men. This fear haunted him like madness. Strange as it may seem, a sense of guiltiness for his unbelief pursued him; he had no religion, and yet his whole soul yearned after God.

To perfect his convalescence, which his mental uneasiness much retarded, he accepted an invitation from the Prince de B—— to spend a short time at his villa on the Tiber. A large party was assembled there, some distinguished foreigners, and several artists and poets, all were men of note. The princess, his wife, was there also, with a circle of ladies, rendering the whole place like an Armida palace. The gardens, which were laid out in the old Italian fashion, were filled with statues, fountains, and stately terraces; it was not in the heart of man to resist such enchantment, and yet to Everhard all seemed like the treasures that Solomon got together, to prove whether there were any thing good for the sons of men to do under heaven; and as the answer had once been obtained from Destiny, it seemed to him a strange infatuation to go on repeating it to all eternity. His invalid condition gave him the privilege of being much alone, and he availed himself of it to keep himself aloof from all the wit and merriment going on around him.

The window of his sitting-room opened on to a lawn of elastic moss, covered with wild aromatic plants; a little beyond was a grove of myrtle and orange trees. One evening he had been walking up and down the broad path beneath their branches, and when he emerged from the grove the moon had risen high in the heavens, surrounded by stars, and bathing all beneath in a flood of silver radiance. The glory of the scene struck upon Everhard, as if now, for the first time, his eyes were opened to behold it. His heart overflowed within him; by an uncontrollable impulse, he prostrated himself upon the ground in an agony of speechless devotion.

The absolute need of some Being to whom he might give

thanks—whom he might adore—pressed upon his soul, as upon a man who is suffocated for want of air to breathe. His passion found itself way in tears and inarticulate groans. The presence of the Invisible was upon him.

How long he had lain there he knew not, but he was roused by hearing the sound of voices and light laughter, mixed with the tones of a guitar, coming in that direction. He sprang up, and took quick refuge in his own apartment.

The spell was broken; but though he did not regain the rapture of devotion, the blessed influence remained behind, and for the present at any rate, the blackness of despair, "the darkness that could be felt", was lifted from his heart.

ZOE

VOLUME II

CHAPTER I

— . —

When Everhard returned to Rome, which was a few days after the occurrence related in the last chapter, the first thing he did was to send and request an audience with the superior. He determined to explain the change which had taken place in his views, and to submit to his decision the course he ought to pursue. A blind instinct of integrity alone remained to guide him: he saw his future course no further than this one step, this interview with the superior: as to how or where it would lead him, he was unable even to form a wish. The superior was in the apartment where Everhard had been received on his entrance in the college, and in which, with a beating heart, he had undergone his examination. The portraits of former pupils who had become distinguished men, still hung on the walls around, and Everhard's own portrait, in his professor's robes, had recently been added to their number, by the command of his Holiness himself.

The superior received Everhard with great courtesy, and expressed sincere pleasure at his restored health. Afterwards he began a light conversation on the topics of the day, made many inquiries after the Prince de B——, and showed much curiosity about the distinguished guests who had been of the party; but Everhard was constrained and absent, showing by his replies how little he had understood of the questions. He was thinking how he should introduce the object he came about, amidst the trivial discourse that jarred upon him like the sound of a revel on the ears of a sick man. At length, with a sort of half smile, he said, "You must think my illness has left me strangely imbecile; but the fact is,

I am come to speak to you on other matters than these. I came to speak to you about myself; to submit myself to your authority."

The bland, gossiping manner of the superior became instantly changed for a mechanical, business-like austerity, and, inclining his head slightly, he intimated that he was prepared to listen.

Everhard paused for one moment, and then, making an effort, he gave a distinct account of the change his opinions had undergone: not the process through which he had reached his present condition; for he instinctively felt that his auditor could comprehend nothing of it: but he spoke as to his superior in the Church, who had the power to decide on his future connexion with that body. "Now, Father," he concluded, "you will take what steps you see fit to dismiss me from among you. I submit myself unreservedly to you; for the solemn vow of obedience which I have taken, cannot be cancelled by any personal change of sentiment."

"My dear friend," replied the superior, in some dismay, "you must surely be labouring under the effects of your fever! What has come over you? You, our most able champion! you must not give way to these fancies. They are, no doubt, temptations from the Evil One, with whom you have so manfully fought, and he has prevailed to wound you. Do not give ear to them. We are all liable to such delusions; I myself, if I dared to give way, should soon be in your state; but I do not suffer my mind to dwell on those matters. Keep yourself quiet for a few days, and just make an 'Act of Faith', and you can pray to Our Blessed Lady to dissipate these shadows; but that, no doubt, you have done; and a—struggle against unbelieving thoughts, and—a—you will be restored to your right mind in a little while. We will not let you throw yourself out of the reach of succour. You must not depart out of the pale of the Holy Church for fancies like these. There is much work for you yet to do: the people must have a form of doctrines; a worship that will gather them together; and you can have no call to instruct them in subtle doubts, that lead to no result. Even if you did, you have nothing to give them instead of the religion they have been brought up in. Our Holy Church is a fold for the people, and they must be gathered together into it, or perish among the wolves in the wilderness. You are in an excited state of mind. Keep yourself quiet, and make an 'Act of Faith', as I said; you will find comfort from it no doubt. And now I have urgent business, and must pray you to excuse me." He accompanied Everhard a few steps towards the door. The interview was over, and in a few moments Everhard was in his room alone.

It is to be questioned, whether there is a matter of any real importance under the sun. We see what costs us days of anxiety and nights of sleeplessness, treated as a thing of no moment by people who are just as well able to judge of it as we ourselves. If one could only realise this, it would go far towards making us take every thing much more quietly than we do. Everhard felt that what had shook his inmost soul to the centre, was of no consequence to any one but himself. Two days afterwards he received a message requesting him again to go to the superior's apartments, who, after a few words of inquiry about his health and state of mind since their last interview, proceeded to inform him, that he had been appointed by his Holiness himself on a special and confidential mission to Paris, in which dexterity and despatch were both required: there were only a few hours to prepare for the journey. Everhard received his instructions, and in less than two hours he had quitted Rome, not sorry to have his thoughts diverted to other objects. During his absence a communication came from Gifford, stating that his college was now built, and entreating that some able and zealous man might be appointed head of it. Much was said of the opening afforded for a mission in that part of England.

"Everhard Burrows, the young professor in the English College, will be the very person to fill this position," said Cardinal Morosini, the friend and favourite of his Holiness, whom he had consulted on the subject of Gifford's request.

"I don't know," replied the Pope, doubtfully; "they tell me that all these controversies have shaken his faith. It is not wise to send uncertain men to fill places of trust, and if this Everhard takes it into his head to turn round upon us, we shall have our hands full, for no one could make head against him; and, besides, his defection would make less *éclat* where he is now, than if we elevated him to a conspicuous station; where it would not say much for our gift of discerning of spirits."

"There is a flaw in Everhard's faith, as regards religion, certainly," replied the cardinal, returning to the charge; "but not as regards the Church. He is not prepared to leave that; at least not at this present time, and it would be highly unwise to suffer him to depart from it; secure his allegiance by giving him a place of trust; his liberalism in matters of religion will recommend him to the people he is to go amongst; it would not do to send a bigot, as matters stand at present. This Everhard is an Englishman, to begin with; he will be able to conciliate and disarm suspicion and distrust, and establish the Catholic faith on a footing that can be made the most of hereafter. His works are in great repute in England, even amongst the most ultra Protestants; they look upon him less as a Catholic priest than as the champion of Christianity."

"Well," replied the Pope, "if we could but feel sure that he would keep his doubts to himself; but he has a strange mania for being sincere, which with him, as with every body else who takes it up, means saying the most inconvenient truths, at the most inconvenient times, to other people; and he has a disregard for consequences that is quite appalling. Truth is not a virtue intended to grow wild in the highways of the world; it ought not to be administered without due authority; otherwise it may act as a deadly poison; you know what Solomon said, 'I, Wisdom, dwell with Prudence.'"

"Everhard is an enthusiast in his own way, your Holiness," rejoined the cardinal, "and we want men of that stamp among us."

"There again," replied the Pope, "enthusiasm is too mighty a power to be trifled with, according to the caprice or judgment of one man; there is no directing it, or calculating on its effects. When great masses have to be moved, and the progress of events is on a large scale, enthusiasm is necessary. In early ages, when the machinery of society is coarse and simple, halting and hitching at every turn, it needs the outbreak of a wild enthusiasm to overcome the friction, and get the machine to move onwards at all. But, in the present day, where the affairs of the world are complicated by innumerable individual interests, where every thing is fine drawn and elaborated by a thousand different influences, where no single action is impelled by a simple motive, and the whole mechanism of life is so complicated, a burst of enthusiasm, no matter about what, would break up the existing order of things, and destroy in an instant the elaborate policy of years. In these days of ours enthusiasm is not safe. There is neither strength, nor knowledge, nor device left in the world to direct its course, to shape its ends; we are not strong enough to stand against its first outbreak; it would sweep every thing before it up from the foundations. Nevertheless," continued he, after a pause, "perhaps the best thing we can do with this Everhard will be to make him superior of this college."

So the appointment was made, and on Everhard's return to Rome he found all prepared for his departure, and his professorship filled up. After a most gracious audience of leave taking, he departed for England.

Everhard would have preferred paying a visit to his brother, before going to see his new college, but his orders were to proceed at once to Gifford Castle, as soon as he landed.

It was a bright autumnal evening when he drew to the last stage of his journey; he left his luggage to follow him, and getting out of the chaise, proceeded on foot towards the village of Culbone, in the neighbourhood of which Gifford Castle was situated.

The mountains were tinged with the hues of sunset, and the corn-fields were vying with each other in their golden beauty. The first thing that strikes an eye long accustomed to foreign scenery, on returning to England, is the peculiar freshness and richness of the green foliage; the green fields and trees of England are as peculiar to it, and as unapproached in beauty, as the sky of Italy.

It was a village holiday, nothing less than the Wakes; all the lower orders were abroad in their best and gayest dresses; the red cloaks of the elder women, and the many-coloured dresses of the young girls sitting in carts driven by their brothers and sweethearts, looking like gaudy beds of tulips, or walking along the road and seen glancing through the trees and tall hedgerows; the sounds of their laughing and talking resounded far and wide on the still air: now and then snatches of a song, shouted on the top of a rough, strong, but merry voice: the poetical-looking cottages with which that district of England abounds—all contributed to make Everhard feel, on returning to the land of his birth, that it indeed merited the epithet of "happy England". The sweet odours, that were borne to him on all sides by the breeze, intoxicated his senses. The face of nature again looked to him as he had seen it in his boyhood, she was again "a glory and a joy", and he felt that "light is indeed good, and a pleasant thing it is for a man to behold the sun."

It was not till night appeared in all her shades, turning to blackness what the sunset had left gold and purple, that Everhard fully awoke to the reality of his situation, and recollected that he must make the best of his way, or else his chaise and luggage would arrive without him at the castle. He quickened his steps and beckoned to a young man who was lounging near, to show him the nearest way.

In the castle, meanwhile, all had been hurry and business since the arrival of Zoe and the family. The great room, wainscotted with richly carved oak, was henceforth to be the drawing-room; an odd room for that purpose, certainly, with its four little corner rooms like cloisters peeping through fretted oak arches and balustrades; but still it was much more picturesque than the one that had hitherto figured as drawing-room, and which Zoe now took for the library. In a little time there was a most novel air of luxury and comfort which astonished the old domestics, and made them bode speedy ruin to their master from the extravagance of their mistress; though to do Zoe justice, the changed aspect of the whole place was much more owing to her own taste and personal exertions, than to any lavish expenditure. Sofas, couches, stands for flowers and shrubs, were all indebted to her hands for their graceful arrangements, which gave an air of *recherche* not always achieved by costly materials.

The children, assisted by Clotilde, planted flower-roots in the fancifully-shaped flowerbeds, and then they had their own little gardens where they might dig and plant to their hearts' content, undisturbed by any remonstrance from the gardener.

It was evening, and they were still working away at a fish-pond which was to match with a pyramid on the opposite side, when the elder boy, looking up, met the eyes of a tall, grave stranger fixed upon him with a mild yet somewhat absent look. He was leaning against a large tree, and had been silently watching them for some time with his thoughts far back in the past;—it was Everhard—and the present seemed like a revived scene of his own childhood.

The boy called the attention of the rest to the stranger, and Clotilde, who saw directly that he was a priest, invited him with great reverence to go with her to the castle. As they proceeded, Everhard tried to make friends with the children, but the boys looked shyly at him and lagged behind, peeping curiously at him when they were not seen, and looking in great confusion on the ground when he turned his head.

Clotilde regarded all priests with too much reverence to enter into any conversation with them, so they performed the short walk in silence. At the door they met Gifford, who, saluting Everhard with great courtesy, informed him that his chaise had just then arrived; he then conducted him into the house, where he proceeded to look for Zoe. They had to pass the chapel, the door was open, and they caught sight of a female form high up on the ladder, over which the light streamed in from a small painted window, making the figure look scarcely like an inhabitant of earth, for the mechanical contrivance of the ladder on which she stood, was almost concealed in the gloom; a silver lamp stood on a table near, which was covered with pictures and frames, and balls of crimson cord. Zoe was, indeed, standing as we have described, contemplating a picture of St Francis in the Wilderness, which had just been hung under her directions. On hearing the voice of Gifford, she quickly descended; her long hair, which was bound round her small Greek-shaped head, had half escaped from its confinement, and hung in heavy masses over her neck. The flowing Parisian *négligée* in which she was attired, the embroidered slippers, the bracelets on the round white arms beneath the hanging sleeves, marking the little hands which grasped a hammer, made a graceful and singular picture.

She received Everhard with a gracious cordiality, and apologised blushingly for having meddled with the chapel with what he might consider sacrilegious hands. Everhard told her that on the contrary, he was glad she took interest in such matters; and after viewing the new pictures, and also two splendid candelabras for the altar, the whole party proceeded to the drawing-room, where they had much conversation.

Everhard retired at night surprised at the interest he felt in Zoe; her very worldliness and coquetry seemed to sit upon her like graces. "Certainly", said he to himself, "she is far too good for the life she has hitherto led—full of passions and capabilities, which have as yet found no outlet." It is what may be said of many persons, for very few in the world have their passions adequately occupied; almost everybody has it in them to be better than they are, but it is only when we see beings so largely endowed as Zoe, wearing themselves out with the trifles of life, that the discrepancy strikes us forcibly enough to lament about. But Everhard was too weary with his day's journey to moralise that night, even upon Zoe,—still, it seemed as if a new element had mingled with his life.

CHAPTER II

— · —

The next day there were too many things to be done to allow
Everhard to bestow any thought upon Zoe, who would hardly have
believed her senses could she have known how completely the new
college and its arrangements occupied his mind. Zoe with all her
beauty, coquetry, and studiously arranged comings and goings, and
lookings and sayings, were quite lost upon him; but Zoe never
suspected the possibility of this, and accordingly, though she
desired beyond measure to take the third place in the carriage that
was to drive them over to look at the college, she would not propose
it herself, lest Everhard "should suspect something". She therefore
ordered her riding horse, and declared her intention of going in a
contrary direction to pay a morning call; Gifford only said, "Well,
my dear, if you prefer it, go there, and if you will order dinner half
an hour later, we need none of us be hurried."

Everhard looked perfectly indifferent, and was quite unconscious
that the arrangement was any thing but a matter of course.

The two gentlemen set off on their expedition, and Zoe annoyed,
she could hardly tell why, went to perform her visit in no very good
humour.

Gifford's intention in erecting a college, had been to supply a
place of education for the sons of the English Catholic gentry, so as
to obviate the necessity of sending them abroad; he hoped this
would prove a means of raising the Catholic body in England from
its depressed and broken condition. Trifling as the undertaking
may seem in these days, it was at that time a singularly bold step.
To keep silent evil tongues, and to avoid publicity as much as
possible, he allowed it to assume merely the appearance of a school

for Catholic boys, but it was regarded in head quarters (or they would hardly have sent over so distinguished a man as Everhard to be at its head) as the nucleus of a clerical seminary, where a class of priests could be trained and adapted to the genius and temper of an English mission.

Gifford had given the ground on which the building was erected, and had invested ten thousand pounds as a permanent endowment; he had also given the use of one of his valuable quarries for as much stone as was required. Contributions from other Catholic families completed all that remained to be done, and Everhard was agreeably surprised at the tasteful but unostentatious edifice which had been erected. There were accommodations for about thirty inmates, besides the president and four resident professors, who were to be appointed by Everhard. The grounds attached to the college were extensive and well laid out. Everhard warmly expressed his admiration, and congratulated Gifford on his success.

"It must", said Gifford, "seem strange in the eyes of the world, (if the world takes the trouble of thinking on the subject) to see one so distinguished as yourself, the master of a boys' school, but we do not judge things according to their outward appearance; if by your instrumentality this place is honoured to become a home where a race of priests may be trained in wisdom and prudence, to overcome the enmity with which Catholics in this country are regarded, it will be as noble a work as any that would sound your name from one end of the world to the other; and I feel convinced that our holy religion will yet raise her head even in this apostate land."

"I think so too," replied Everhard, "but it will be a work of time, the Catholics must live down the prejudices against them; modified views must be presented of their tenets, for Catholicism, as it exists in Italy, will never obtain a footing in England; it must adapt itself to the genius of the people.

"Protestantism in all its phases, is a system of negations; it has more affinity with scepticism than belief. No form of Protestantism can, for any length of time, satisfy the devotional feelings and aspirations of a nation. For the multitude, you must not refine doctrines too much, you must give them something tangible to believe, something that can take a quick and stringent hold upon their heart and conduct. The multitude, in all ages, require to have high truths dramatised in forms, creeds, and symbols, before they can be made to apprehend them.

"The Catholic Church alone, has taught the truths of Christianity, on a large scale, with any thing like success. As to the small number of men who strive to pierce into the heart of things, it is no matter what form of doctrine prevails, they must, and always will, believe in a different spirit to that of the mass. Their grand mistake has been in uttering their subtilised doctrines, to the gross, dull ears of the multitude, who can see, hear, and understand nothing, except through the medium of their coarse passions and sensual appetites; hence arises the herd of infidels, who make a mock at all religion; as if to disprove a tradition, or raise an objection to a creed, were an emancipation from the law of wisdom to which that creed or tradition endeavoured to give utterance. For myself, I consider that in coming here, I have undertaken the most awfully responsible office that can be laid upon a man, that of educating a body of youths, who may hereafter be called upon to instruct their fellow-men in religious matters."

Everhard ceased, and there was a pause for some moments; had the speaker been one with a less established reputation than Everhard, it is certain that Gifford would have found matter of scandal and cavil in what had just been said; but coming, as it did, from one who had so well fought the battles of the Church, he was fain to believe that it must be more orthodox than it sounded.

From the college Gifford took Everhard to see some improvements he had been making in that neighbourhood, particularly a hamlet of singularly neat and well-built cottages, inhabited altogether by Catholic peasants and their families.

"I have", said he, "drafted as many as possible of my poor Catholic tenants to my own immediate neighbourhood. I wish to have no party spirit, and the less intercourse there is between them and my Protestant tenants the more peace there will be. Neither side is as yet sufficiently well instructed to understand the beauty of mutual toleration. I expect much good from your labours amongst them."

As they rode home they passed a row of almshouses that Gifford had built and endowed for the widows of small Catholic tradesmen who had been left in destitute circumstances.

"You are in a fortunate position, Mr Gifford," said Everhard, with a smile, "and you are able to feel interest in all the objects that surround you, which is a blessing much more rare than actual prosperity. Many men have the materials of happiness placed within their reach; but not one in ten knows how to manufacture any thing out of them except *ennui*."

"Father Everhard," said Gifford after a pause, "I often think of the punishment of unthankful souls in Dante's 'Inferno', where they who perversely encouraged a gloomy disposition, are punished by being kept from the pleasant light of day, and condemned to plunge about in darkness and the bottomless Slough of Despond. When I first read that, I was much impressed by it, and I resolved in my heart never to give way to a spirit of repining or indifference to the blessings of my lot. I prayed earnestly that I might be kept from that sin, and I think it has, at least, been kept in subjection; otherwise—but listen: From my childhood I have loved every one more than any ever loved me in return. If one showed me but common kindness, I repaid it with affection. I could not exist without the sympathy of those around me; without loving them. For a long time I had a sort of faith that my love must of necessity cause me to be beloved again; the more insensibility I met with, the more I poured out my whole heart to melt and overcome it. There were some whom I called friends, and whom I loved too earnestly to be able to stop and examine what they gave me in return; but they had always a sort of half smile at my headlong devotion; and I overheard them laughingly boast of it to others, as a singularity, of which they hardly seemed to know whether to feel vain, or ashamed. I had a vague sense of outrage at this; but I could hardly make my feelings tangible even to myself. In a little while I grew older, and able better to understand the meaning of what passed around me, and I discovered that I was of no use, or value, or pleasure to those on whom I had bestowed affection that was without alloy. They did not know what to make of me; they considered me as eccentric, and their good will was dashed with contempt.

"When I first discovered this I was very miserable; more miserable than I have ever been, either before or since. It is such a sense

168

of helplessness that takes possession of us when we have loved with all our energy, and it has obtained no affection for us in return. After we have given our love to a friend, there remains nothing more that we can do for him: we have bestowed our most precious gift, and found it valueless. Do not mistake me; I did not indulge in any sentimental passion; the heart love I gave was to the companions of my own sex, to the members of my own family. I never fell in love, as it is called, but ONCE in all my life. At first, after my eyes had been opened as I have described, I am sure I must have become very disagreeable, for the worst feelings of my nature were roused; I became *exigeant* and distrustful. I tried to look upon myself as a kind of martyr; and yet, martyr is not the exact word; for I had a strange kind of admiration for the coldness and worldliness by which I was suffering. There seemed to be something clever about it; and I thought there was something very fine in being able to think one thing, and make people believe another. I was sincere and single-hearted literally because I could not help it, and not because I reverenced that 'beauty of holiness'. In this miserable plunging state I continued for some time, without enough sternness of nature to hate, and without sufficient faith in my natural impulses to live on in a spirit of love, when I met with such poor encouragement."

"Well," said Everhard, "and did you work your way out of this?"

"Yes," replied Gifford, "after a while I did; but from no thanks to myself. One day I was walking very disconsolately by myself, in a retired part of the park, when it suddenly flashed upon me, like lightning, that after all, there was really nothing in me to excite the love and admiration of men; that if I had been worth it, I should have had their love spontaneously, and without any striving on my part. You will think this sudden conviction an odd source of comfort; yet so it was. The instant I felt convinced that I was nothing, all the unreasonableness and anomaly of my situation ceased. I felt content to be as I was; all bitterness of spirit was effaced; I felt to lie still, if you can understand that. I now saw, for the first time, that to be beloved is not the highest motive from which a man can act. 'Do good, looking for nothing again,' rushed into my mind, and I saw how poorly and childishly I had felt. I had been tormented by a vague idea, that it was poor-spirited to do other than resent the slights which I had received, and that I ought not to do such a thing as love those who did not care about me; but now I seemed suddenly set at liberty from thraldom. I was relieved from all obligations to care about myself or my own dignity, and you cannot imagine the relief it was to me. I had no further concern with what people thought about me; I saw myself as I must appear to them, heavy in conversation, shy and awkward in manner, and wearisome to those I most wished to please. I perceived, in fact, that I was what people call a bore; and I felt that I was bound to have some consideration, and not inflict myself too much upon those who happened to be more amusing than myself. Since that time, it is wonderful how much better I have got on: there are some people who really care for me, and seem to set store by my friendship."

"Many more perhaps than you imagine," said Everhard, smiling. "Yes, Mr Gifford, the gift of humility is far more to be desired than either love or gold."

"Indeed you are right," said Gifford, with great *naïveté*; "but what I have been telling you is a mere matter of fact."

Everhard did not reply, for he had no wish to awaken the burden of consciousness in the worthy man. After another pause, during which they turned homewards, Gifford spoke again.

"Father Everhard," said he, "there is one thing that makes me very uneasy; it is about my wife. Mrs Gifford is a singular character, and I do not think that I have been quite wise in my conduct to her. I cannot understand her, and I fear I have not made her happy; she has many fine qualities, but she turns them to no good purpose; I have not the gift of drawing them out and directing them. I wish you would consent to spend as much of you time as you can with us; she worships intellect in all its shapes, and though she has very little sense of religion or belief of any sort, yet she has romantic notions about the Catholic religion, and would, I think, listen to a priest, when she would hear nobody else. She has, I know, long known and reverenced you, and is familiar with all your works; if any one can obtain a salutary influence over her it is yourself; you must be sensible that I cannot help being very anxious that she should not continue the infidel she is."

"Does she read much?" asked Everhard.

"A vast deal more than ever did a woman good yet," replied Gifford. "Women have no imperative and engrossing employments to work off what they read, or to correct their notions by practical experience; therefore they grow positive and extravagant, and their mind has no balance; it is a thousand pities she was not a man. It often frightens me to see a woman holding the views she does."

The conversation that followed was desultory; Gifford gave Everhard many particulars about Zoe, with which the reader is already acquainted, and this lasted till they reached home. Everhard knew nothing of women, and certainly he could not have commenced his acquaintance with a more puzzling specimen of the sex. On reaching the castle they found dinner waiting for them, and also two letters, one for Everhard from his brother, who was on a tour in Scotland with Marian, and the other from Marian herself to Zoe, full of wife-like admiration for the "angel of a husband" who had fallen to her lot, and expressive of her conviction that he must be quite as learned and clever as his celebrated brother, "though he was too modest to show it". Certainly there must be many virtues hidden under the matrimonial bushel, which the graceless and unbelieving world can neither see nor feel. The letter contained an earnest petition that Clotilde might be allowed to go and pay her a long visit as soon as she should be settled at home again; a postscript added by Louis himself seconded his wife's request; and poor little Clotilde, who had never been twenty miles from home in her life, did not know whether to hope or fear that the invitation would be accepted; all discussion was, however, by common consent postponed till after dinner.

Zoe had recovered from her temporary ill-humour, and was curious to know how Everhard and Gifford had spent the morning; she had a most amusing account to give of her own expedition; but the calm, grave manners of Everhard piqued her, for she felt that she made no impression upon him, or at least if she did, she could not discover what it was. She set herself to elicit some expression of admiration or surprise, some emotion, no matter what; she had not of late been accustomed to indifference, and she could not endure it. She uttered brilliant paradoxes, he listened with gentleness and did not contradict her; she talked sense, and he did not seem surprised; she had never before exerted herself so much to please, or produced so little apparent effect. This arose in part, undoubtedly, from the secluded manner in which Everhard had so long lived, and from his being so utterly unaccustomed to the society of women, which rendered his mode of addressing them both *gauche* and shy; he literally did not know how to keep up a conversation with them; Zoe, with all her beauty and brilliancy, positively bewildered him. It was not long before she perceived that this was the case, and it tended in some degree to pacify her; and it made her feel all the more interested, and all the more determined to conquer him.

As some time was still required to complete the arrangements for beginning the business of the college, Everhard remained an inmate of the castle for a fortnight longer, during which he made more progress with the nun-like Clotilde than with Zoe. Clotilde had still the appearance of being a child; her pale, sweet features and unconscious manner inspired Everhard with an interest he had never felt for any human being; her simple-hearted piety seemed to him like a reflection from the days of his own childhood, and to bring back the time when he wandered in the woods with Father Martin, listening to his legends. As to Clotilde, she soon invested Everhard with all the attributes of her most favourite saints; he went with her to visit her pensioners, and did not disdain to take an interest in the garden she had succeeded in coaxing at the top of a rock, and which she insisted was like the wilderness in which John the Baptist lived. Clotilde was the most complete contrast to her beautiful mother-in-law that can be conceived. She was more like a woman of the middle ages, than an educated young lady of the eighteenth century. She embroidered beautifully; was skilled in the mystery of compounding simples, cordials, and condiments of all sorts for the use of her poor sick people. She could certainly both read and write, but her acquaintance with books did not go beyond the "Garden of the Soul" and a few favourite books of devotion;— her ignorance, however, was graceful, and her sweet docile nature, made her heart far richer than her head. Full of all gentle and feminine instincts, she felt no desire for more extended knowledge, and Everhard could not help secretly hoping that Zoe would not spoil her by the endeavour to impart any of her fashionable accomplishments. Speaking of accomplishments, we forgot to state one that Clotilde really did possess; she danced beautifully; graceful she was by nature, and Miss Rodney, who retained enough of her aristocratic prejudices to think that an elegant carriage was the birthright and prerogative of a gentlewoman, had herself superintended the lessons of the master. Clotilde soon overcame her reserve, and trusted Everhard with all the little trials and scruples which could trouble so pure and gentle a heart.

One day as they were walking in the garden, she said to him, "I feel so glad that mamma is come back to live here, I like her so much better now than I did formerly; do you know, I fear it was very wicked, but she always frightened me, she seemed to be like one of those evil spirits who formerly used to assume the shape of beautiful women, and appear to the saints to tempt them; and yet she was always very kind to me; but now I love her very much, and don't feel afraid of her at all; perhaps I understand her better."

"Perhaps you do," replied Everhard, hardly able to repress a smile at Clotilde's simile, which had also occurred more than once to himself. During the whole time he remained at the castle, he kept aloof from Zoe with an instinct he could hardly account for; the consequence was that Zoe felt her pride engaged to subdue and punish such a defiance of her charms. She had no ill intentions; when she thus ventured on such slippery ground, it was in a spirit of mischief and curiosity, not of deliberate wickedness. Zoe was a proud, spoiled, petted beauty, and had led a prosperous life, which goes for a great deal in blunting the moral perceptions both of men and women. She had great talents and strong passions, and, alas! she had neither food for one nor employment for the other. A woman's wisdom always comes from love, and Zoe had never loved in the whole course of her life. Half the wickedness that gets committed in the world, arises more from the absence of some engrossing employment than from any special depravity.

In about a fortnight Everhard left the castle, and the business of the college began in earnest. Everhard was too much occupied in laying down rules for the management of the establishment, forming plans of study, and in giving to the whole undertaking a form and body, to be able to bestow a thought upon any thing else. Gifford often rode over to the college, but Everhard had no time to visit the castle. An accident occurred, however, that entirely changed the face of affairs.

One day, just before the commencement of the first vacation, Gifford was thrown from his horse at his own door, and his leg was severely fractured. On hearing of the accident, Everhard went over instantly. Gifford, who had a horror of the prospect of his long confinement, expressed such an earnest desire that he would spend the vacation at the castle, that Everhard could not find it in his heart to refuse; he had fixed to pay a visit to his mother and brother, and he felt great reluctance to give it up, but he consented at least to delay his visit to Sutton, and finally he came to the castle, from which, however, it would have been much better if he had stayed away.

CHAPTER III

— . —

There is a pleasure in being ill, or rather in the recovery from an illness, which none but the patient can tell. It is so soothing to one's self-importance to find our most unreasonable whims suddenly become laws to the whole household,—one's nightcap invested with all the virtues of a wishing-cap, as we listen to the reiterated entreaties from all around, to know "if there is any thing we could fancy". Then the pleasant little surprises of all kinds that we imagined; and the pleasant looks that greet us when we condescend to accept them; the patience that can translate our most unwarrantable "crossness", because there has been some trifling difficulty in obtaining the half of a star or the corner of a moon which it had pleased us to require, into "such a good sign of being really better"; and then our appetite (which the gods know is at that season singularly keen), how is it not tempted with unutterable dainties and *friande* morsels, all sorts of amateur cookery in our behalf, where Love himself has not disdained to turn the spit, and look into the stewpan! and all served up so gracefully on the small tray, covered with its delicate white damask cloth, arraying with more than mortal charms the moulds of crystal jelly and pure-looking blanc mange! Then there is the arrival of the doctor (the grand event in our day), who comes,—sits beside us—encourages us to complain, and listens. Oh, what can equal the blandness and sympathy of a listening doctor! We detail our minutest sensations with a modest pride at possessing so many indisputable claims on his attention; he is *our* doctor, we never realise the fact that he has other patients;—they only form the shadowy background of *our* doctor's reputation, skill, and immense practice; by a pleasant fiction we monopolise his sympathy, whole and undivided. Then there are the libraries ransacked for the new books to read to us, and the neighbourhood scoured for the newest of news! Ah, it *is* a reverse to come down from this to the ordinary accommodation of everyday mortals,—to hear the chilling words, "Oh, he is quite well now, and may do any thing"; which "any thing", by the way, is always bounded by an injunction to avoid evening parties, the night air, and to get up early in the morning. Till people have tried, they cannot know how affectionately one gets to feel towards the bed where we have lain so long!

This had been Gifford's experience of the last six weeks, and if the reader will look into Zoe's little library, which we have described as opening into the drawing-room, he will there see Gifford lying on a sofa, for he is well enough now to be removed there. Everhard sits on the other side of the sofa-table, arranging a chess-board— in the distance Zoe is extended on a couch, sometimes following the train of argument in a theological work of Everhard's, which she holds in her hand, and sometimes watching the calm Madonna-like figure of Clotilde, who sits in the window-seat under one of the tall Gothic windows, employed in embroidering a wreath of roses round the "sacred heart of Mary". Such a picture of purity and faith she looks, sitting there unconscious of any observation— now lifting her blue eyes from the golden sunset which seems to veil heaven and its hosts from her view, longing to pierce through them and mingle with those favourite saints and martyrs, with Christ and his mother, and all those wonderful and holy beings ever present to her imagination—Zoe longed to paint her. The book falling from her hands, startled Clotilde from her reverie. "What are you thinking about, Clotilde?" asked she. Clotilde blushed and hesitated, but on Zoe asking her with a smile, she answered, "I was wishing I had wings like the angels, to go and see them all, and poor Miss Rodney and mamma, who was so good, they say. I was thinking what a pity it is that we must die and be put in the dark earth, before we can have such great happiness; but so it always is, as our Church teaches—mortification first, and then——." What the "then" was, Zoe did not get to hear, for the door was flung open, and the servant announced "Mr Burrows!" Everhard started up, overturning the chess-board, and sprang to meet him. "Louis!" "Everhard!" was all they could either of them utter,—they had not seen each other since they parted in the inn yard at Coventry—how many years before? Then followed cordial greetings, exclamations of surprise, and inquiries from Gifford and Zoe after Marian.

"Oh", said Louis, "I was so disappointed when Everhard did not come (though I had hardly the heart to wish it when I knew the reason that kept him here), that I determined to come to him myself, for I could not bear to be any longer without seeing him. Marian did not much like parting with me, but she could not accompany me, because", said he, with a sort of half bashful importance, "the medical man thought it would not be prudent in her condition to undertake such a long journey. I have promised to bring back Miss Clotilde with me,—Marian has quite set her heart on having her, and she must stay until Everhard can come and fetch her back. Oh, Everhard!—my mother is so anxious to see you,—you cannot think how proud she feels of you,—she does nothing but talk about you, and the blessing you are to the Church, and the credit to us all."

It was long before there was space for any thing like continued conversation; but when they were seated round the tea-table there were many inquiries to be made, and remembrances of people as they were twenty years before, to be compared with the actual state of things, and much new matter to be communicated, that never had been dreamed of under the old *régime*. "Old Sarah Matchet, who used to keep the gingerbread shop, must be dead by this time," said Everhard.

"No; only bed-ridden. She lives with her grand-daughter, that pretty girl whose father got transported for sheep-stealing. Oh, I forgot; that is since your time. He was to have been hanged, but we contrived to get it commuted to transportation. You remember his wife; she used to be the prettiest woman in the parish; but soon fell off in her looks after she married that great good-for-nothing scamp, who broke her heart. She died of shame and grief soon after his trial."

"Do you remember Jack Bolt, who used to help us to get bird-nests, and make our fishing-tackle?"

"To be sure," said Everhard.

"Well, he has taken to poaching; he was brought up before me the other day for snaring hares: three pheasants were found in their feathers, lying behind his door. I was sorry to commit him, but there was no help. Poaching is no joke, and it is getting quite a common offence. Marian will take care of his family whilst he is in gaol."

"Let me intercede for him," said Everhard; "it seems to me such a hard thing to imprison a man for killing a wild animal belonging to nobody."

Louis looked up perfectly aghast at this heresy; but, recollecting that it was Everhard who spoke, he only said, "Ah, you are too tender-hearted, you don't understand these things. You remember old Stringer, the gardener," continued he; "well, he is dead— followed his own tree roses; but his son, to whom we have always been so kind, and considered him as belonging to the family; well, do you know, he has gone over to the other side!"

"What other side?" asked Everhard.

"Why the dirty dog has turned Protestant—no less! The new Irish rector, who came to the living on the death of the old man, is very zealous and evangelical as they call it now; he is very bitter against our religion, gives out tracts and Bibles; has a Sunday-school, and all that. He goes into all the houses to instruct the people, he says, and he got hold of Stringer, and, by some means, persuaded him to leave the religion of his forefathers, and to join their crew. I never was so mortified. Then the tea-drinkings at the Sunday-school, and the speechifyings there were about it, as if it at all signified what such curs as he believed! And because I turned him off, they made him think himself a martyr. He began to make speeches too, about the delusions of popery, and that O'Brian put it all into a tract, and got it printed, and distributed it about the parish, forgetting to say he was such a drunken dog nobody could depend upon him for a day's work, and that I had kept him on, out of respect to his father, till he disgraced himself by leaving his religion. So pitiful, too, when there are so few to stand by it in England!"

Zoe laughed outright at the indignant eloquence of Louis, and began to ask further particulars about the Reverend Horace

O'Brian, who had been the means of seducing such an ornament into the Protestant community.

"Oh," said Louis, "he is an Irishman, and full of blarney. He is a gentleman, however, as far as family goes; but his father was a renegade, and got a post under government for changing his religion; his son has got this fine fat living, and wants to make himself popular. People come from far and near to hear him preach: he is very bitter against us Catholics, declares we are dangerous to the country, and that to tolerate us is a sin against God. Considering that we are the only Catholic family in his parish, I must say it is very personal and ungentlemanly; but we must none of us complain of suffering for our religion."

"Is he handsome as well as eloquent?" asked Zoe.

"Yes, the women all say so; but for my part, I cannot endure those great, tall, black-whiskered fellows, with their white hands and drawling voices, as if it were a sin to speak bluffly and honestly. However, they say that Miss Smith, of the Hollows, admires him. It will be a fine thing for him if he can marry her; and then, I suppose, he will live at his ease, as his predecessor did before him. There is a cotton factory, too, established since you left, and print-works; besides, Sutton is as large again as when you knew it, Everhard. When you come you shall try to convert some of the people, for I cannot bear that fellow to have it all his own way. I tried to argue with him one day, but he could talk better than I could. I made nothing of him; but it will be different when he has to deal with you."

"Thank you," said Everhard; "but I do not want to get into controversy."

Louis remained a week at the castle, during which time, though the brothers walked, and talked, and rode, as in former days—a sense of mutual strangeness and restraint was between them. This was not to be attributed to any actual want of attachment, nor even to their long separation. On the side of Louis there was an instinct that he could not talk to one whose name ranked along with those of the fathers in the Church, as he would to a neighbouring squire, and the attempt to keep up to what he considered the mark, made him feel sadly *gêné*; then, too, he had interests and pursuits that had arisen since they parted; the chain of mutual association which holds members of the same family together, in spite of difference and tastes and habits, was broken between Louis and Everhard. Everhard, with every possible wish to be affectionate, felt that somehow his brother was a sad interruption to the pleasant mode in which the time had hitherto glided on. Zoe felt it too, and had naturally much less patience with the author of it; so she occupied herself in preparing Clotilde's simple wardrobe, in order that when Louis brought his visit to a conclusion, there might be no sort of delay. Gifford was the only one of the party who found any satisfaction in his presence; they were both amateur farmers, and they had a wide field of sympathy in the different modes of manuring and cultivating land, mangel-wurzel, and Swedish turnips, to say nothing of an improved plough that Gifford had invented, to which Louis became so great a convert that he promised to bring it into use on one of his farms. No wonder Gifford thought him "a very superior, sensible young man, with no nonsense about him". Zoe grew every day more impatient for the departure of this "superior young man", for he had quite lost all that awe of her presence, and the diffidence which had made him tolerable before. The dignity of marriage had given him confidence to speak his mind on all he saw.

The evening before the day fixed for their journey, Clotilde brought the embroidery of her "Sacred Heart" to a conclusion. She had worked it for Everhard, as a chalice cover for the college chapel.

"Really, Clotilde," said Zoe, "this is beautifully done. I wish you would work something for my library; all you do goes to the chapel. How many sets of vestments and ornaments have you worked in your time?"

"Oh," said Louis, "you should see Marian's work; this is nothing to what she can do; she too, has worked a set of vestments. You never do any thing, Mrs Gifford, you fashionable ladies are all for ornament, like the cups on the mantel-shelf."

"Mrs Gifford", replied Everhard, hastily, "is capable of doing much better things than sewing with coloured silks."

"No doubt," said Louis, "when she gives her mind to it; it may be all very well for people of fashion, but I confess I like to see English wives employ themselves in a rational manner. I think nothing marks a superior woman so much as being constantly occupied. There is Marian for instance: she is always up by seven o'clock in the morning; she spends all the morning regularly in the housekeeper's room, looking after every thing in the house, and making all the jellies, and preserves, and potted meats, with her own hands; and then, though she is so economical, and such a good manager, she finds time for work. Catch her when you will, she is always busy; she has begun a large carpet of a most beautiful pattern, as she says it will be something for her grandchildren to remember her by; and now she is making all her baby clothes with her own hands. I tell her sometimes, I feel quite jealous of her needle, and often beg her to give herself a holiday; but she says when a woman is married she ought to set an example of practical usefulness."

"But", said Zoe, gravely, "could not the housekeeper or the cook make the jellies? and it seems almost a pity to take the trouble of working a carpet, when there are such pretty ones to be bought."

"That may be," said Louis, "but if women did not occupy themselves in those matters, what better things would they do? I do not wish my wife to be a fashionable, fine lady; it is all very well for women to lose their time in reading books, and playing music, before they are married, but after that they have things of more importance to attend to, in looking after their house and family, and seeing that they are not imposed upon; but of course you will only laugh at such notions."

"Indeed," replied Zoe, gravely, "I am quite aware how liable we women are to be imposed on, and I quite agree with you, that if a woman is wise she cannot look too narrowly, or watch too strictly, in order to avoid it; and yet," said she, turning with a smile to Everhard, "it is not the delusion which gives us pain, but the discovery of it. I often think of the prayer of the poet, 'Long and deeply let me be beguiled.'"

"I think they must be very weak-minded, foolish people", said Louis, "who can prefer being deceived to finding it out, they then know what they have to guard against in future; now I will give you a case in point. Marian found that the butcher had made an over-charge of five pounds in his bill last Christmas. Now do you think it would have been better to go on being cheated, than to find it out?"

"We are imposed upon in many ways besides butchers' bills," said Zoe.

"Will you have a game of chess, Mr Gifford?" said Everhard, hastily.

"Why no, thank you, not to-night," said Gifford, "it is your brother's last night, and I want his opinion on this sample of wheat for seed, that I received this morning, when you have finished what you are talking about."

Ths broke up the conversation. Zoe went into the drawing-room, and began to practise some new music, which had arrived along with the "sample of wheat". Clotilde began to cut out some work for poor people, to take along with her; and Everhard seemed to fall into a reverie, as he stood leaning on the mantel-piece.

The next morning, at ten o'clock, the post-chaise came to the door, and Louis and Clotilde, having bade "good bye" for at least the twentieth time, got into it, and were driven off. Clotilde did not seem at all disturbed or agitated in going alone to visit one whom she had never seen. Ever since Louis came, she had seemed strangely anxious for the journey, and had shown an eagerness so different from her usual timidity, that Zoe was quite puzzled; but the child had formed a project, which had taken possession of her dear little heart; she had entrusted it in confidence to Everhard, and the reader shall know what it was all in good time.

After the departure of the travellers, things did not fall back into their old train; the spell was broken, Everhard was obliged to return to the college, and Gifford, who had grown very anxious to superintend some farming operations, got dreadfully impatient at being confined so long; interviews with his steward took the place of chess, he grew cross, and poor Zoe grew dreadfully dull, till she was almost tempted to emulate Marian, and work a carpet in sheer despair. There seemed nothing before her, but a long dreary six months of solitude; for she had grown too much accustomed to the society of one superior to herself, to be able to fall back into toleration for the second rate persons who formed the society of her neighbourhood. Complete solitude was far more endurable; so, shutting herself up in her boudoir, she began strenuously to rub up her knowledge of Greek, in order to read some of the Platonic philosophers, whose works Everhard had lent her at her own special request. She certainly found it rather dry work, but she persevered, and read as hard as if she were going to be examined for her degree.

One fine morning, however, about three weeks after his departure, the door of her library opened, and "Father Everhard" entered. The thrill of pleasure which Zoe felt, was quite worth all her previous *ennui*; till he came back, she did not know how very much she had missed him. There was nothing extraordinary in his visit; he had come to inquire after Gifford, and pay his respects to the family; but, somehow, Zoe had not expected him. She had feared it would be as it was before, when he got back to his business at college; so the sight of him was gratifying in more ways than one. Gifford, who was now able to ride about in a low carriage, was just setting off; he looked in however for a moment, was delighted to see Everhard, and begged him to come very often; but he had an appointment with his steward just then, and could not delay any longer. Zoe and Everhard went to the hall-door with him, to see him start, and then returned to the library together.

CHAPTER IV

— · —

Whether Everhard had less business than formerly to occupy his time, we do not know, but it is certain that his visits to the castle were much more frequent. Sometimes he came to examine into the progress the two boys were making under their tutor; but the tutor of Gifford's children was a dull plodding man, who disliked interference. Sometimes he came to see Gifford, but it soon grew to be a habit about which he ceased to give any reasons to himself.

When Gifford was at home and disengaged, they sat in the study, at other times they were in Zoe's little boudoir. Every day he felt himself more strongly attracted to the strange, beautiful being who had thus come across his path. He felt his mind grow, and his perceptions become clearer, under the quick and glancing impulses of her genius. She unveiled for him the resources of his own mind,—she gave a force, and meaning, and use to learning, which till now had lain crude and inert. He was startled by the intuitive perception she seemed to have of the state of his mind; her voice seemed the "voice of his own soul, heard in the calm of thought";— his intercourse with her calmed down into mature thought, much that, experienced in solitude, and seen only from the fitful light of his own feelings, had become fantastic and exaggerated. A man is in an unhealthy disposition when he fancies that he has a monopoly of any peculiar feeling or opinion; if it be true, other people have known it also. When Zoe spoke, he found she looked from the same point of view as himself, and this is the secret of all sympathy. The crust of reserve which his isolated and anomalous position had caused, was broken up; he began to speak and feel more truthfully and naturally than he had done for years; a strain seemed taken off his life, and his mind put forth fresh growth. He was like a fertile soil, teeming with the seeds of life and vegetation, basking for the first time in an atmosphere able to draw them forth, and bring them to perfection.

Zoe on her side, with all her undisciplined and undirected powers, was gaining strength and knowledge by working in the mine of Everhard's attainments. He was the first person she had ever met with in the least qualified to obtain an influence over her. Women like her are only to be influenced by those they can recognise as their masters. Still there were other elements at work; there was too much of the priest and Jesuit about Everhard to permit his making her in so many words his confidante; much of what Zoe knew about him was tacitly assumed. She always felt that there was a point beyond which she could not go, and this, to a woman of her disposition, was the charm of his influence, for it must be remembered that Zoe was a coquette in grain.

The first annual examination of the scholars was about to take place, and the castle was expected to be full of company, as Gifford had made open house to the friends of the youths who were in the college.

Zoe, with a brilliant party from the castle, went to grace the occasion.

In addition to the usual phenomena, the boys had got up a Latin play, for which Zoe had invented and furnished the dresses. Then there were English recitations, and several essays on various subjects; amongst others, there was a theological thesis read by one of the boys, which obtained great applause.

Gifford had marquees erected in the grounds, and entertained the whole college. In short, it was a very splendid affair, and found its way into the county newspapers; but as there were no "reformation societies" in that neighbourhood, it only passed for a liberal and friendly entertainment, and not for a "Catholic demonstration".

When the bustle had subsided, and the students were dismissed to their different residences, Everhard found time to visit the castle, to which he had been a stranger for the last few weeks, owing to the accumulation of college business.

Zoe was alone when he entered the boudoir. "You see," said he, with a smile, "I dedicate to you the first fruits of my leisure."

"And, according to your brother Louis, you get nothing but the fruits of my idleness in return," she said. "After all, I begin to think his way of employing women is the best, and I don't know but what Marian does more good than I do."

"Since when have you thought so?"

"Oh, I am only beginning to wonder whether it may not be. It is very little use that can be made of what we any of us do. I don't know what we come into the world for, I am sure. It is that fine exhibition at your college the other day, that has set me thinking about it. Cobwebs to catch flies, seemed about the pitch of its utility;—that thesis on theology, which was the best thing, only set me wondering whether that youth, as a *man*, would ever be able to find his way out of the labyrinth of absurdity in which he had been walled up."

"Would you not have young men instructed in their religion?" asked Everhard.

"Creed, you mean," said Zoe. "With all the fine things that are said and sung about religion, as it is called, there is a want of frankness that disgusts me. The priests of all creeds never tell their own experience, or their own belief; they fight for the side they have taken vows upon, they pretend to argue, but it is all make-believe,—they are pledged to a foregone conclusion, and nothing beyond that can be got out of them; they are especial pleaders, retained for a cause about which they feel no personal interest. I have seen first-rate preachers descend from the pulpit, where they have just spoken like angels, to whom all the mysteries of the invisible world are laid bare; and then, like actors, come off the scene, speak in the dialect and with the feelings of men of this world. Do you think, if they were interpenetrated with the truth of those tremendous mysteries about which they discourse, if they realised the fact that the eternal welfare of those who listened to them probably depended on the faithfulness with which they should instruct them, that heaven or hell were the stakes.—Oh! if they really believed all they preach, how would any priest or preacher be able to sleep in his bed under the tremendous responsibility, and with the declaration ringing in his ears of, 'Surely the souls of these men will I require at thy hand!' But they do not believe what they talk about; they grow sleek and rich, and live to an untroubled 'old age'!"

"You are warm, lady," replied Everhard, somewhat disconcerted.

"I know I am," said Zoe. "I am out of patience when I think how insincerity has grown into the heart of the most sacred things; if people would only speak simply their own belief, and tell the feelings and principles which influence their own life, they would not infect each other with practical atheism in the way they now do."

"But", replied Everhard, "the people, the majority of those who live in the world, must have a form of doctrine, something definite by which they may shape their belief. They cannot see the force of moral truths, until they are promulgated from authority; made dogmatic,—enforced under a penalty,—'thou shalt and thou shalt not.' 'Cursed shall he be who doeth this,' and 'blessed shall he be who doeth' so and so. If it were not for these stiff creeds and commandments, enforced by blessings and cursings, we should either get nothing done at all—the world would relapse into a state of anarchy—or else mere notions of expediency, of social convenience, would become the highest recognised motives of action. They who are enlightened, have in all ages seen more in those religious doctrines which so move your scorn, than the ignorant mass of people, those 'poor,' to whom the gospel was sent; they have always believed in the essence, and not in the form; but for the people we must beware of refining too much, lest they lose the active principle, along with the coarser elements.

"Those legends and miracles which form part of every religion that has ever been promulgated, are to the uninstructed, literal truths—mere matters of fact—whilst to the more intelligent, they are only types of truth. All religious forms are but the shell which covers the spiritual meaning, the body by which it is made manifest. Do not take away from the people that which they have, until you can give them power to discern something better. There are many who realise, as you call it, their belief, and who are far happier and safer under it than you in your scepticism."

"That may very possibly be, Father Everhard; but why are the people who do not believe, to go on pretending that they do? How can it be either wise or healthy to go on making believe, as St John

187

says, 'neither entering into the kingdom of heaven themselves, nor suffering men to enter it?' For we are told by the same authority, 'that nothing which maketh or loveth a lie', shall find a place therein; and surely to profess a form of belief for the sake of looking respectable in the eyes of that part of the world where we happen to be thrown, is the most pitiful of all false pretences. Then your argument does not always hold good, for we have lately seen in France how delighted people are when it becomes the fashion to throw off all religious belief, because the generality imagine that with a religious creed they may also throw off those moral requirements that press upon their vices. They can disprove a legend or tradition, and then they imagine that a moral law is thereby rescinded. How much better to teach people that whatever it is really right to do, would have been equally right and equally imperative upon them, even though Moses never had delivered the ten commandments."

"Your plan", replied Everhard, "might do for Utopia, but it would never work here. Who shall begin the crusade against the doctrines of religion? Where, in the present state of society, would you find people who have not taken up some set of opinions or another; and though there are men who would be willing to ruin their prospects in life for the sake of religion, you would hardly find one man who would do so for the sake of that which was none.

"In the working out of your plan, if it were attempted, sad scandal would arise; men are not refined enough in their consciences to do right for its own sake alone; they are too blind and gross to feel the influence of an abstract idea, unsupported by some extraneous notice; they cannot see beyond the present moment, and will not act against their apparent interest, unless there be a penalty attached, or a future reward annexed. Your doctrine would be a cloak for every kind of ill deed, under the plea (for they are a perverse generation) that each man thought it right. The greatest seasons of anarchy have been those emphatically described, as when 'the people did each man what was right in his own eyes.' In fact, mankind have deceitful hearts and corrupt consciences; it is useless to try to argue with them on abstract grounds; the actual working of their wickedness must be provided for in the best way it can be done; and if you take away men's belief in religion, such as it is, what can you propose as a practical restraint instead?

"You see there is much to be considered, and the peace of Christendom ought not to be rashly disturbed; begin your labours by bestowing a pure heart and understanding upon the world, and after that you may begin your crusade against the creeds, as soon as you please, without the risk of doing much mischief."

"Well," said Zoe, "I must have the last word in right of my sex; I don't see how people, if left to themselves, could contrive to be much worse than they are now, under the government of a religion that not one in ten bestows a serious thought upon, and that not a great proportion amongst those who do think on the subject, believe in at all. Don't you think it would be possible to teach people, and to make them feel that to do right is to act wisely, even in a mère worldly sense? We cannot see the event of any action we undertake; we do not know the consequences of our most trivial act,—we are so much mixed up with the detail of affairs, that we cannot see the end to which they tend; our reason is not strong enough to grasp the plan of our life, our instinct is not pure enough to be depended upon; we are like those unlucky animals which are placed as the connected link between two species, without the full capacities of either. Our conscience seems to have been bestowed as a balance. If we would but simply do what is right, and dispense with the cumbrous machinery of policy and second motives—if we would but eschew the false wisdom of expediency, there would not be so many elaborate blunders committed; we should be wiser, and bid fair to become greater that we have ever yet been.

"I never heard of a system either of philosophy or religion, that could solve all the difficulties and perplexities of our position in this world; they all fall to pieces, and get themselves disproved in the common wear and tear of life; we have to fight for the creed or system we adopt; we are obliged to make laws for its furtherance and preservation; instead of finding it what it professes to be, a teacher and guide for ourselves; it is a regular King Log, without King Log's inoffensiveness. Oh! if every one of us would only act by what we honestly believe to be true; do, in simple truth and singleness of purpose, that which in our own soul we feel to be right; instead of trying to impose on those around us, by making them think us a little more of this, or a little less of the other, than we really are; oh! what a strain would be taken off life! We should respect ourselves, and love our neighbours, instead of despising them for looking so much like our secret selves!

"If men honestly believe any sort of creed, let them believe it in all peace; what I am complaining of is, that those who do not believe in it, make a pretence of following their example. It was by having a firm belief in the doctrines they preached, a faith in their internal convictions of what ought to be done, that your saints of old achieved their wonders. They did not act with an eye to men's approval; they saw work lying to be done, and they did it.

"'We are not careful to justify ourselves,' was their motto, and must be the watchword of whoever seeks to act up to the gift that is in them, if in their turn they would fulfil the work they were sent into life to do; and no man *can* work who 'holds a lie in his right hand'."

Zoe had risen from her seat, as she uttered these last words, her face glowed, and tears of passionate earnestness flashed in her eyes. Everhard did not feel at all disposed to dispute her claim to its being the "last word"; her words burnt into his heart like lightning; he remained for a moment gazing at her, after she had ceased to speak, and then hastily averted his looks. At that moment, Gifford entered, "Ah!" he said, "I am so glad to find you here, I was afraid you would be gone; farmer Ball, down in the hamlet, is dying, the doctor does not think he will live out the day, he is quite sensible at present, and very anxious to receive the last sacraments. They were sending off to the college when I got there, but I promised to send you, as I could be quicker than their messenger."

"How very sudden," said Everhard, "I saw him only two days ago, and he seemed quite well then."

"It is inflammation of the bowels," replied Gifford, "and they fear that mortification has already begun. I ordered a horse to be prepared for you, as I came in, and here it is at the door."

"Is there nothing that we can send?" asked Zoe.

"Oh no, he is past all that now; but you can go over to-morrow to see the family."

Everhard had departed whilst Gifford spoke, without even saying good bye; and Zoe was left alone to meditate upon the efficacy of the "Last Sacraments".

CHAPTER V

— · —

When Everhard arrived at the college, after closing the eyes of poor farmer Ball, he found a packet that had come during his absence; it contained a most flattering letter of thanks from the pope himself, for all his exertions at the college, and expressive of the high sense entertained of the value of his services in England; concluding with a personal request that Everhard would find time to edit a translation of the principal works of the Fathers of the first four centuries.

It seemed, as if all his honours had conspired to come at the same time, for during the evening of the same day, another parcel came containing a gold chain, which had been sent by the University of Göttingen for his work on Philology, with a diploma conferring on him the degree of doctor in their university. A very short time previously, Everhard would have been gratified by all this, but now thoughts had been aroused by the conversation of the morning, that none of these things could still. He sat gazing at the chain and letters for some time, and then, impatiently sweeping them into a drawer, he exclaimed bitterly, "Would that I had never been born!"

That same evening, Zoe, according to her usual habit, was reclining on the little blue satin sofa, thinking over her morning's conversation with Everhard, and speculating upon the peculiar and hasty manner in which he had averted his head when she finished speaking; but she could not make any theory about it that satisfied her. "I wish", thought she, "Gifford had not come in just then; I wonder when Father Everhard will be coming again, I shall be able to make it better out then."

Tea was now brought in, and with it, the post-bag. Zoe opened it with all the eagerness that such an event always causes in a country house. To her great delight, she drew out a highly-scented, and elegant looking letter, that bore the Parisian post-mark. It was from a certain Lady Clara Mandeville, who, in London, had been Zoe's bosom friend and confidante: a clever, witty, unscrupulous, good-hearted woman. Zoe was precisely in the humour to enjoy any thing coming from her. She read the letter over twice, and when the tea-things were removed, and Gifford had departed to play chess with the tutor, she sat down to answer it. Her letter, thanks to the great carelessness and indiscretion of Lady Clara, we are enabled to lay before our readers, who, of course, share that usual infirmity in human nature of delighting to hear matters which were intended to be specially kept from them. If Lady Clara had done as she ought to have done, she would have put this letter into the fire the moment she had read it. But Lady Clara did not understand the responsibility of confidential letters; she always either left her friends' letters on the chimney-piece, for the benefit of the footman, or else she made them into very broad spills, and when she wished to be very careful indeed, she put them into a desk which would not lock!

There are wonderfully few secrets in this world; "*tôt ou tard, tout se sait,*" said Madame de Maintenon, whose prudence almost amounted to genius. At the same time, if people would only keep their own counsel, and not confess all their indiscretions on paper, their secrets would stand some chance of enduring till the day of judgment, when the lawful term of their existence expires. If Zoe had only abstained from letter-writing, she might have gone to her grave with the reputation of a second Egeria, and the respectability of Theresa Tidy and Mrs Chapone rolled into one! What our readers are going to think of her now, we dare not anticipate; we can only say, that our own sense of propriety received a severe shock when we read this letter; and let it be remembered that we are beforehand with them in the expression of our grave disapprobation. Zoe has been arraigned at the bar of our private judgment, and reprimanded accordingly. The letter which has caused us such a virtuous sensation, was as follows:

"Dearest Clara,
"Yes, here we are settled down into what you call our prison. I

assure you it is no prison to me, after so long a residence in London, where I had begun to forget the natural colour of daylight.

"The only London thing I miss, is yourself. What would I not give for one of our old *tête-à-têtes* just now! one cannot write down one's feelings, they look so absurd; at least mine would to-day. Poor dear Clara! you thought when I came down here that I should find nothing to do, but to take to moralising with Gifford (who really says some good things now and then), or to saying my rosary with Clotilde, or feeding poultry. When a woman can find no mischief to do, your doctrine is, that her vocation is over, and she had better go to heaven at once. I fear my time for going to heaven is as yet far distant, for I feel the greatest possible vocation for mischief at this moment. Good heaven how I write! I, talking of mischief, who have turned a deaf ear all my life to every thing in the shape of love and lovers, and with fifty admirers sighing after me, have lived as soberly as the ugliest German frau. To change the subject, let me tell you how I have furnished the wild old halls here. I have contrived to make them look as splendid as those of Madame de G. The couches, the fauteuils, and marble tables, and those splendid candelabras, and Dresden vases look brighter than ever, in contrast with the oak and ebony wainscotting. Now try to fancy that great, dim room, I have so often described to you, fitted up with every luxury of fashion and tasteful furniture; try to fancy you see me, dressed in my last pink cashmere *negligée à la sultane*, and *coiffée à l'abandon*, reclining on a velvet couch in a huge alcove, carved all over with Gothic grinning faces, furies, flowers, and griffins entwined; and sitting on another couch opposite to me (with a table of books between us), fancy a tall, large, earnest-looking man, of—(no matter what age, I don't know), in black from head to foot, oftenest in a cassock, in deep conversation with me. He is the head of Gifford's new college here, and was sent from Rome express, where he was held in wonderful estimation.

"I can't tell you how this man interests me; with all the learning of the Sorbonne, he is as ignorant of the world (at least of the world of women) as a young child. So much genuine feeling, not mere sentiment, such freshness and originality of thought! And he is as modest, nay, even blushes like a woman; he has got a habit of silence, yet at times he breaks out into the most touching eloquence. Above all, his passions have never been broken up, to this day he has never known the meaning of that most hackneyed word, '*amore*'. Shut up from boyhood in a cloister, he has been kept clear from all the fascinations of our sex, and never tampered with by any excitement whatever. If he could be made to love—how different from those *roués* of young men, *blasé* with pleasure, old in worldliness before they reach the term of middle life; oh! how I have always loathed them all. Courtly, graceful, despicable things, I hated them with a more genuine hatred than such fictions of men deserved. It was all very well to let them rave about me and my beauty; they were the fashion, and I chose to be in the fashion with my lovers as well as with my fans and jewels; but how tenfold more loathsome would they all seem now.

"I have already told you that Father Everhard is a priest, and consequently bound down by a creed, as far as words and outward expressions go: he seldom says in words that he thinks with me, but how I am learning to read his thoughts. Now, Clara, do not imagine that I for the first time in my life am going to fall in love, after keeping free from it all these years, and passing for a cold English woman,—love is a word quite out of my vocabulary; but I do confess that I would rather have the friendship of this man, than the love and rhapsody of the whole sex besides. It is a strange providence that has thrown him in my way, and I hope to put him in my power. What I wish is, to make him taste a happiness he has never yet known nor dreamed of. I shall be his keeper, and he shall never do any thing of which he can afterwards repent; meantime, he is too unsophisticated to dream of any danger in our long *tête-à-têtes*, he remembers that he never came here at all, during the first six months of his residence at the college, and now he comes once a week to visit me,—there's all the difference.

"Do get his celebrated work against Bayle, Diderot, d'Holbach, and the encyclopediasts: he handles them like a giant: and yet what creed does this man hold in his secret soul? not much more than they, if I read him aright; but I think he does not own his doubts even to himself. At all events the man puzzles me, and to study him is the only occupation I feel inclined to attend to.

"Write to me, dear Clara, and let it be one of your wittiest letters. Do you ask *pourquoi*? Why then, because I want to read it to Father Everhard. What a quaint name, is it not? and yet I am beginning to think it the most graceful combination of letters in any language.

"I have nothing to tell you that you would consider news, unless it be that Clotilde is gone on a visit to Gifford's niece, who was married whilst we were in London, to Everhard's only brother. We have had monsieur le mari for a whole week here, such a contrast, oh, ye gods! A regular English husband of the most insipid kind, and Marian, from what he says, must have settled down into a most intolerable specimen of female respectability; but they seem very happy together, and no doubt consider each other a great blessing.

"Once more write, write, write, and soon,

"Ever yours,

"ZOE GIFFORD.

"P.S. I forgot to tell you that poor Gifford met with a serious accident some time ago, which confined him to the house for nearly two months: he is quite recovered now. Really I made a capital nurse, and liked it moreover."

CHAPTER VI

— · —

What would become of the world without the Devil?

Under all the different systems of religion that have guided or misguided the world for the last six thousand years, the Devil has been the grand scapegoat. He has had to bear the blame of every thing that has gone wrong. All the evil that gets committed is laid to his door, and he has, besides, the credit of hindering all the good that has never got done at all.

If mankind were not thus one and all victims to the Devil, what an irredeemable set of scoundrels they would be obliged to confess themselves!

But men, not content with laying the blame of all their wickedness upon the Devil, likewise charge him with all their own folly and blundering stupidity.

When we consider, above all, the long sermons, all the ponderous books that have been levelled against him for so many ages, without, so far as we can perceive, making the smallest impression upon him, we are forced to conclude one of two things, either that he is utterly destitute of all gentlemanly susceptibilities, or else, "that the Devil is not so black as he is painted": for which latter opinion there is the authority of the old proverb.

For our own part, we are inclined to adopt the policy of the Spanish nobleman, who, when he made his last confession, removed his cap, and reverently styled him, "my good lord the Devil", every time he had occasion to name him. He was a prudent man as well as polite, for he considered that as there was some danger of eventually falling into his hands, civil words were best.

Our friend Everhard had however offered an insult to the said

Devil, far worse than the most bitter revilings;—he had actually brought himself to disbelieve in his existence altogether; and the Devil, though much enduring, was piqued into playing him a shrewd turn which seemed likely to set the question effectually at rest. We shall watch the progress of the struggle between them with great interest, for it involves a very important principle.

It is hard to say on which side victory will incline. Everhard has a strong desire to do right, and an upright heart, which is goodly armour for the soul. The match is not so unequal, if he will only rouse himself and put forth honestly the strength that lies in him. But will he? Can he? Is it strength at all that he has, or only a mist arising from the untried depths of self-confidence? Can a man who has no religious belief, have any moral strength? Is a sense of moral duty sufficient to keep him firm in the day of temptation? Can he pass through the fire and not be burned? Can a man in short, who has neither hope nor fear of any thing after this life, be a law to himself, and strive earnestly to do right, simply because it *is* right?

This is an important question, and can only be answered by the result. Everhard must fight it out. There is no one to whisper danger in his ear; fair-play even for the Devil!

Some time had now elapsed since the violent crisis in Everhard's religious opinions. He had become accustomed to the change; the strange fear and dread with which he had at first been haunted, subsided; he had ceased to perplex himself by obstinate questionings, and had sunk down half in patience and half in apathy, to await the result. The reaction was in proportion to the violent agitation he had undergone. We are tied to a centre, from which we advance in one direction to rebound as far in the opposite one, but we can only go the length of our tether any way. We should go mad, could we constantly see the things around us in their true bearing. Our perceptions cannot remain long on the stretch; our indolence blunts our feelings and blinds our eyes. A most merciful provision! So we continue to stumble amongst the mysteries that surround us, without being aware of them; or else we become accustomed to them, and they cease to surprise us.

Poor Everhard! he had, as the reader may have learned from Zoe's letter, got wonderfully into the habit of visiting at the castle; and yet he never went except when there appeared to be an imperative necessity for going. It had grown to be the most natural thing in the world to spend long mornings there; it seemed as if he could not do otherwise.

The acts that have in the end the most important influence over our life, do not appear at the time they take place, of a different texture to all the other acts that fill up the rest of our days and years. We understand the full meaning of nothing that we do, until it is over; and when the husk which shrouds the present moment from us, is burst by the event, then, and not till then, we become conscious of what it is we have really done.

Time glided on quietly; nothing occurred to open Everhard's eyes to the danger of such constant intercourse with a most fascinating and gifted woman. There was no one to dispute with him the smiles and conversation of Zoe, so there was no possibility of his being brought to consciousness by a flash of jealousy. A constant steady pressure, will throw down a stone wall in time; but it will take longer, and be more quietly done, than by a series of battering-ram assaults.

Everhard was so comfortable, and so well satisfied with the footing he was on with Zoe, that it never occurred to him to inquire into the nature of his sentiments for her.

It was a few days after the conversation recorded in a foregoing chapter, that Everhard, taking an evening walk, had wandered to some distance in the intricate mazes of a wood, that lay between the castle and the college. A sudden turning in the path, brought him unexpectedly upon Zoe and the two boys. They had their hats full of nuts, and had adorned Zoe's hat with a garland of cowslips and wild roses.

The children both bounded forwards at the sight of him, and began to talk, both together, about the delightful afternoon they had been spending in the wood, and all the wonderful things they had done. Zoe, who just then came up, seemed singularly disconcerted; she blushed, and tried to think of something natural to say.

Everhard remarked that it was "a very fine, cool evening", as he took out his handkerchief to wipe the perspiration from his forehead. Both of them were unaccountably embarrassed.

Luckily, Zoe had in her hand a new French work, which had just been sent down from London. She turned hastily over the leaves, wondering she could think of nothing to say. Somewhat ashamed of being silent, she began to read aloud a passage she had found at random. It was singularly *mal à propos*. The passage went to prove that people always take to religion when they have been unsuccessful in love, and that religion is the only thing that does not seem insipid after it.

"I wonder whether that is really the case," said Zoe.

"Yes," replied Everhard, smilingly, "there is one great point in which religion is far better than love (not that I profess, or, indeed, ought to know any thing of such matters). In religion we have no need to suppress or disguise our feelings; we may utter every thing without restraint."

"And why may we not do the same when we love?" asked Zoe.

"Because", said Everhard, "that would too often be followed by the loss of the beloved object. The Deity is the only being before whom we can be perfectly true; for He is the only being who can comprehend all our infirmities, and who will not misunderstand us."

"Should we not also", said Zoe, "love better those whom we love already, for knowing their weakness; knowing them as they really are; than when they keep themselves shrouded in motives of which we are ignorant. Should we not love them better for being quite sure that all we see and hear really is?"

"No," replied he, "we must be content to believe it so. Knowledge is not for this life, faith is our element here. There is no man living who is so far exalted above his fellows, as to make it safe to trust him with a human heart laid bare before him; even our own is hidden from us; the instinct of concealment lies at the very foundation of our nature, and we always suffer when we neglect its impulses. The moment we suspect the extent of our influence over another, a disposition to tyrannise and give pain is aroused; and that not so much from cruelty, as because none are strong enough to bear the burden of the entire and clinging love of a human heart, without staggering under it. God, who made us, is alone strong enough to bear with us. He alone can be loved with safety. He will not weary of us, nor throw us back upon ourselves when our affection is the most ardent."

"You are a true Jesuit," said Zoe, with a slight shrug of

dissatisfaction. "You, at least, never told your secret thoughts, and never will."

They walked towards the castle in silence. When they arrived, Gifford was in the library reading the "London Gazette". He was delighted to see Everhard, and would not hear of his leaving that night. All his objections were over-ruled, and a servant was despatched on horseback to the college with a message, to say that he would not return.

Gifford, as soon as they were settled, proceeded to inflict the whole of the ponderous leading article upon Everhard *aux petits coups d'épingles*, along with his own comments upon the same.

Zoe, when she found she could no longer have all the conversation to herself, stretched herself on the sofa, where she appeared to be busily employed in cutting the leaves of her new book, but from time to time, she contrived to throw such glances upon poor Everhard as perfectly bewildered him, and contributed not a little to reduce him to that state of passiveness which is the perfection of a good listener; Gifford thought he had never met with such a good one before!

Was the Devil in the wood that night or not?

CHAPTER VII

— · —

We must now for a short time follow the fortunes of Clotilde. A family visit to a dull country house seems, at first sight, a reasonably peaceable adventure, promising nothing beyond a great trial of patience, and threatening nothing worse than an attack of *ennui*; but in this world it is a rule absolute, that every thing must be judged comparatively; what are little matters to one, become things of importance to another, so that it is hard to say whether it is that every thing is trifling, or that nothing is trifling; people are apt to speak of things as they find them. Any way, this journey was a grand event to Clotilde, not only because it was the first she had ever made, but also because there was a design, that lay very near her dear little heart, and this journey was to be made the means of accomplishing it. What this design was she had imparted in solemn confidence to Father Everhard, and had begged his blessing upon it; and it was a delightful sensation to her, to know that every step taken by the four post-horses brought her nearer to the scene of her undertaking.

At length the carriage drove up to the entrance of the Manor House, about eight o'clock in the evening. Marian, who had been expecting them since noon, or rather looking out for them, as they could not in reason be expected before the time when they actually arrived, rushed into the courtyard to welcome them. Clotilde was half smothered with kisses, and dragged, without giving her time to get rid of any of her mufflings, into the parlour, where the fire was blazing brightly, and the table laid for supper. Dazzled by the sudden change from darkness, Clotilde did not at first perceive a stately old lady dressed in black silk, with a bonnet of the same upon her head, and a white shawl pinned over her shoulders, who occupied a large three-cornered arm-chair on one side of the fire-place. It was Madame Burrows, somewhat less active than when she was last presented to the reader, but still erect in her carriage, and her faculties as vigorous as ever. She rose from her chair to embrace her son, who presented Clotilde to her. The old lady looked at her with a keen, scrutinising glance, which might have been expected to disconcert her, but Clotilde had been used to Miss Rodney, so she only curtseyed very reverently, and cast her eyes to the ground.

"Ah! I like your manner," said Madame Burrows, abruptly; "you have been well brought up, and have none of the flippancy of the young girls now-a-days. How is your father and Mrs Gifford?" continued she. Questions and replies followed each other rapidly, Louis was the speaker by common consent, and he had much to tell. The old lady listened to his accounts of Everhard, with a dignified sort of satisfaction. He was also very warm in his praises of Gifford, declaring him to be far the most sensible fellow he had ever seen. Somehow, very little was said or asked about Zoe. Supper, however, now interrupted the torrent of conversation. Marian had herself superintended the cooking of the woodcocks, and the delicious spiced beef had been prepared with her own hands, expressly against her husband's return. Whatever people may say or write about the comforts of tea, on coming in from a journey, our own opinion is, that on such occasions a dainty, well-appointed supper-table is a far more satisfactory sight: and could our readers have looked in at the parlour where they were all assembled, it would have been a sure and certain mode of converting all who differ from us. Marian was a first-rate house-keeper, and had a thorough understanding of what is meant by comfort. One way in which she showed her love to her husband, was by studying his dinners and suppers;—a stronger hold upon men's tender sensibilities than they might be willing to acknowledge.

As soon as supper was over, Clotilde, being very tired with her day's journey, was conducted to a charming little bed-room, where a bright fire was burning in a grate surrounded by curious Dutch tiles. A large old-fashioned looking-glass stood opposite, on its embroidered white muslin toilet-cover. A crucifix with a cushion of Marian's own working before it, stood in a recess on one side of the fire-place, and a small carved ebony clothes-press occupied the other. There was a mixture of old-fashioned quaintness and homely comfort, that gave it an extremely attractive air. "Oh, how very comfortable it is!" cried Clotilde, as she looked around. "I never saw any thing so delightful!"

"I hope you will be comfortable, too," said Marian, kissing her, "and make yourself very happy with us. If you want any thing ring your bell—our room is close by, so do not be alarmed or feel lonely. I am so glad you are come, we shall be so happy together. I am sure we shall be great friends. If you should feel tired, do not get up in the morning, and I will bring you some breakfast." And with another kiss, Marian bade her "good night".

Clotilde first examined the room, and the old-fashioned portraits on the wall, representing Everhard and Louis at a very juvenile period of their career, and Madame Burrows as a little girl dressed in pink brocade and a lace cap, playing with a lamb in an elaborately curled white fleece. Having finished her examination, and satisfied her curiosity, she sat down for a long time in the large easy chair, gazing on the fire in a profound reverie; her musings were not unpleasant apparently, for her face brightened, her lips parted into a smile, and raising her eyes, which were full of soft tears, she prostrated herself before the crucifix, and remained long at her devotions, then, like the Lady Christabel,

> "Her gentle limbs she did undress,
> And lay down in her loveliness."

The next morning she did not require the promised breakfast, but was up and dressed when Marian entered the room. "Why, how early you are!" she exclaimed. "I hope you slept well; don't plague yourself about unpacking, which is a hateful job, only a degree better than packing. Faucit shall put all your things into the drawers—she is quite a treasure, she does every thing for me." Clotilde left her keys for the "treasure", and went down stairs with Marian.

After breakfast Louis went to see after his farm, promising to take the ladies a drive at noon; and Marian in the full pride of a married woman, took Clotilde to see her house, and all the wonders of her still-room and dairy. An air of the most shining cleanliness and comfort pervaded every thing. Louis was quite right when he boasted of Marian as an excellent wife. Then there was the garden to be explored, which Marian had brought into the most splendid order, for she delighted in gardening; but now, as she said it was a bad time to see it, there were so few flowers. Clotilde gave all the admiration that could possibly be claimed; but she was thinking how she should introduce her scheme to her cousin. "Your gardener turned Protestant and forsook his religion," said she, suddenly, in reply to a speech of Marian's, about a plantation of monthly roses.

"Yes," said Marian, "and he was quite the hero of the village for it; but I think he is a little bit repenting now; his wife, whom he married for her money, is a great deal older than himself, and a fierce evangelical; she leads him a terrible life, for a pious shrew is a formidable person to deal with."

"Where does he live? Do you ever see him?" asked Clotilde.

"No," replied Marian, "Mr O'Brian takes charge of him, and would be very sorry to see the face of either you or me in the house of any of his flock. The man has turned shoemaker since he left us, and as long as Mr O'Brian and his congregation are his customers, it is not likely he will ever come near us."

Poor Clotilde felt terribly disappointed, but she did not despair. "Do you know," said she, "I am sure we ought to try to reclaim him; it is terrible to allow a soul to fall away from the true faith without an effort to save him. I have thought of this poor man, and prayed for him night and day ever since I heard of his terrible falling away, and I feel convinced that if I could see him and speak to him he would hear me. I have had an assurance given me that it will be so; only last night," said she, in a solemn tone, and crossing herself as she spoke, "only last night after I went to bed I lay awake meditating on this affair, and I suppose I must have fallen asleep, for the blessed Virgin appeared to me in a dream, with stars under her feet and a crown of stars upon her head, and she looked sweetly, though with great majesty upon me. I did not hear the sound of her voice, but I felt it in my heart. 'My child,' she said, 'be constant and fear not, there is a crown laid up in heaven for you,' and then her garment seemed to touch my cheek as she rose up in the air, and vanished out of my sight; now you see, I must go to see this poor man, and try to convince him."

"But", said Marian, almost bewildered by Clotilde's earnestness, "what will you say to him? What excuse will you make for calling at his house?"

"Our Blessed Lady will put it into my heart what to say," replied Clotilde; "only tell me my way to the village, and where he lives."

Marian saw how fully impressed she was with the idea that had taken possession of her, and besides, she was too good a Catholic to throw obstacles in the way, even if it would have been of any use: so she contented herself with saying, "Well then, remember, if Mr O'Brian complains, and Louis scolds, you must look to it, and get me out of the scrape: so, that understood, you must go across the fields there, and over the bridge by the row of oak trees, which will bring you to the village, and the first house you come to is Andrew Stringer's; it is a little red cottage in a garden with palings before it, and he is a shoemaker, remember. You will have a better chance by yourself, than if I went with you, and besides, mamma will be dressed by this time, and want me to help her down stairs to the parlour, she does not like to have any one but me." As they had now reached the end of the park, they separated, Marian returning home, and Clotilde pursuing her way across the very field, where, in days long ago, Everhard had met with his memorable adventure in search of the mushrooms.

In spite of the assurance with which she had spoken, poor Clotilde felt sadly perplexed how she was to introduce herself and her errand, "Surely", cried she, "Our Blessed Lady, who inspired the idea, will not abandon me in my need!" Scarcely had she uttered this exclamation, than it seemed as if Our Lady really intended to vindicate the faith of her votary, for Clotilde heard sounds of sorrow, and on looking round, perceived a girl who might be about twelve years old, sitting upon the grass, apparently in great pain, and sobbing bitterly, whilst a baby that lay in her lap, was screaming an accompaniment.

"What is the matter, my good girl?" asked Clotilde, going up to her. The child wiped her eyes with her blue pinafore, and only sobbed the more, without speaking.

"If you will only tell me what is the matter, I will try to help you," said Clotilde again, at the same time taking up the baby, and trying to pacify it.

"What is your name, and where do you live?"

"Susan Brown," said the child, still crying, "and I live with the shoemaker's wife, to take care of the baby, and I was getting over that stile, and my foot slipped, and I can't walk on it at all, and missis will beat me when I get home—Oh!" here a fresh burst of tears drowned her voice.

"Let me look at your foot," said Clotilde, stooping down; it was terribly sprained and swollen, "My poor little girl," said she, "you must not try to walk, sit still here, and I will take the baby home, and send some one to carry you. Where does your mistress live?"

"At the red cottage, the first you come to in the village; but tell her I could not help it, and don't let her beat me." Clotilde did her best to comfort the poor girl, and then, scarcely able to contain her joy, she set off with the baby in her arms. Here was an introduction not only to the renegade shoemaker, but to the heart of his redoubtable wife also. Clotilde felt as if her way were indeed being made plain before her. On coming near the "red cottage", Clotilde saw Mrs Andrew Stringer standing at the garden-gate, looking up and down the road, with a look of mingled crossness and anxiety; "Only to think of the idle hussy," she muttered, "that poor baby will be famished to death, it has never tasted since morning, poor lamb! Ah! but I will give it her well!" On perceiving a strange lady carrying her baby, she looked very much surprised.

"Your little servant has met with an accident," said Clotilde, "she is not able to walk home. I have brought the baby, and promised to send some one to help her."

"I am sure your ladyship is main good," replied the woman, taking the child from her. "You must be tired to death, carrying such a load—will you condescend to come in and rest awhile?"

It is needless to say that Clotilde gladly consented. The neat little kitchen with its white floor sprinkled with red sand; the eight-day clock; the curiously carved oak settle with its pink gingham cushion; all bore witness that the owners of the house were well to do in the world. A row of thriving plants in bright red pots, stood in the well-cleaned window; and in the black-leaded recess of the chimney, were a dazzling array of shining pots and pans. A "no Popery" tract lay upon the dresser, and a broadside was fastened against the wall, having a flaming many-coloured print of a beast at the top, which would have defied Cuvier himself to classify: it seemed a complication of scales and claws; a serpent's tail; and more heads than could conveniently be counted, each furnished with an unlimited supply of horns. It appeared in a very lively condition, as it was represented in the act of executing a *pas de bête* peculiar to itself.

"Ah!" said the woman, complacently, when she perceived that Clotilde's attention was drawn to this wonderful production. "That is a representation of Popery; what a blessing it is, as dear Mr O'Brian says, that we live in a Protestant country, and are saved from its ravages!"

"I wish, wife, you would not talk such nonsense; that beast is no more like Popery than you are, and I ought to know something of it," cried a husky voice from within, and a man in a leathern apron and a red shiny face came into the kitchen.

"Aren't you ashamed to expose yourself before quality in that way?" said his wife, in an angry tone. "But you will bring us all to shame before we die."

The man seemed somewhat abashed, and was slinking off, when Clotilde hastily called him back, by inquiring whether he could make ladies' walking-shoes.

"Indeed can I," said the man, "since I left off being a gardener, I have had nothing better to do."

"Do you make for many families about here?" asked Clotilde, by way of beginning a conversation, as he knelt down to measure her.

"Yes, pretty well—but all the family at the Manor House go to Coventry for what they want, and it is a good twenty pound a year out of my way; but it's no use hoping," added he, with a sort of sigh.

"Why not?" asked Clotilde.

"Because, d'ye see, I used to be gardener there, but I turned Protestant, and ever since, none of them will speak to me. Mr O'Brian says it is because it is in the nature of Popery to be persecuting; God knows! It was a good berth whilst I had it, and this I will say, that a more liberal, open-handed gentleman never stept than the squire."

"Do you regret turning Protestant, then?" asked Clotilde.

"Why as to that d'ye see," replied he, looking round with rather a perplexed air, "there are many things beside religion that go to make one glad or sorry. I don't know—but, you see Mr O'Brian has such a power of strong words, one cannot think one is wrong when one listens to him—but I often think of the old place, too."

"You remember Father Everhard when he was a boy, do you not?"

"Ay, for sure do I; they say he is grown a grand man now, and much made of by the Pope himself; many is the bird's nest I've got for him and his brother, Mr Louis, and many is the fishing-rod I have made and mended for them;—but, may I be so bold as to ask if you know him?"

Before Clotilde could reply, they were interrupted by the entrance of his wife, who had been herself to see after her "little hussy of a servant", and who now returned, followed by a labourer who carried the poor child in his arms. Clotilde's experience amongst her pensioners at home, made her quite *au fait* at all required to be done. She made a fomentation, applied it with her own hands, and promised to come again in the afternoon with a proper lotion.

"It is some lady who is come to visit at the Manor House," said the wife, as soon as she was gone, "it is little they will let her bring from there."

"Well, what success?" cried Marian, as Clotilde, radiant with smiles and flushed with exertion, entered the breakfast-room.

"Oh, there seems quite a way opened for me," said Clotilde, and she began a detailed account of all that had happened.

"I fear it will only prove a way to my store-room," said Marian, laughingly; "however, you shall have the benefit of all I can do for you."

"I fear the promise of our custom for boots and shoes would do more to turn the heart both of Andrew and his wife, than all your missionary efforts; for his wife is a thrifty body, and has a dangerous taste for getting rich," said old Madame Burrows, from the corner where she was knitting a lamb's wool stocking: the ball of worsted rolled on the floor, and Clotilde hastened to pick it up. "You are a good child," said Madame Burrows, complacently; "but take care

208

how you meddle with these people, it may have more consequences for you than you think."

Clotilde was too full of her schemes, to pay any attention to the good lady; indeed if warnings of any sort were ever heeded till too late, it would be contrary to the order of nature; wisdom has grown so used to calling aloud without attracting attention, that the good lady would be actually embarrassed if any mortal chanced to turn his head at her first summons.

Clotilde went in the afternoon, followed by a footman carrying a covered basket, such as the shoemaker well remembered in the days when he lived at the Manor.

Clotilde dismissed her attendant at the entrance of the village, and went alone to the cottage. Andrew and his wife were both very civil, the little girl was lying on the settle, in great pain, but her face brightened up when Clotilde entered. She charged the woman on no account to allow her to walk, and that she herself would pay some one to hold her baby for her. The woman curtseyed down to the ground, but seemed rather surprised at so much generosity, and, like all vulgar people, began to think there must be some motive at the bottom of it. When Clotilde turned to Andrew and gave him a beautiful clasp knife that Father Everhard had sent him as a remembrance, she pursed her lips, tossed her head, gave an uneasy cough, and finally said, "That certainly it was very good of the gentleman to recollect her husband so long, but that she must say"—what, has never transpired, for Andrew himself stopped her by fairly drowning her voice in the expression of his own satisfaction.

Clotilde soon after took her leave, promising to return again. As she went out at the gate she heard Andrew saying, in an angry voice, "I tell thee what, I never did beat thee, but if thou dost not hush directly I will."

The next morning it rained, and as it was impossible to go out of doors, Marian and Clotilde sat at their work in the breakfast-room. Marian was employed in making some marvellously small and dainty lace caps, whilst Clotilde was getting on with the carpet, which Marian had begun to have some fears of never being able to finish, so she hailed with rapture Clotilde's offer to undertake the remaining portion of it.

They had been industriously employed for some time, when Marian, looking out on the weather, said, "It has set in for the day, we shall have no visitors to interrupt us."

At this moment a ring came to the hall door, and the old butler putting his head into the room, said, with a look of great astonishment, "It is Mr O'Brian, ma'am, the rector himself, I saw him come along, and I just made bold to see you, if you would please to be at home to him."

"Mr O'Brian!" screamed Marian. "Surely, Maurice, you must be mistaken, what *can* he want here? Clotilde, this comes of your going after these people yesterday, what must we do?"

"Oh, let him come in!" said Clotilde. "It is not for us to shrink from seeing him; let us at least hear what he comes for."

"Ah! you are not a married woman," said Marian, "what will Louis say? Still, I can't help feeling rather curious to know what he comes for, and, as you say, one ought not to be rude; so, Maurice, we are at home; and pray make haste, for there is his second ring."

Marian and Clotilde sat looking towrds the door in silent expectation.

"I hope Louis will not come in till he is gone," said Marian; "perhaps I have done wrong, but it can't be helped now."

The door opened, and Maurice ushered in the "Reverend Horace O'Brian!" He placed a chair for him, looking on him all the while as if he had been some highly curious beast, for Maurice had never come so close to a Protestant clergyman in his life before; and could hardly persuade himself to leave the room; indeed, the footman declared that he saw Maurice with his ear to the key-hole a full quarter of an hour after he had shown the Reverend Horace O'Brian into the room. At this accusation, Maurice only "phawed", and, with all the dignity of a butler, ordered the footman to mind his own affairs.

The Reverend Horace O'Brian was left face to face before two ladies whom he had never spoken to, and between whom and himself there existed a sort of theoretical hatred. But the Reverend Horace O'Brian was a tall, graceful, singularly handsome man, with a magnificent pair of large black eyes, one glance of which, as he bowed with a deprecating air to the two ladies, considerably modified the stately reserve with which they had prepared to receive him.

"You, doubtless, are surprised at my intrusion," said he, in a bland, silvery tone of voice; "but the kindness of Mrs Burrows towards one of my parishioners yesterday, has given me confidence to request her assistance again. A family, consisting of the father and mother and two children, came into Sutton by the coach last night; the poor man is this morning too ill to proceed on his journey; I was sent for and saw them, their case is really most distressing. The man belongs to a respectable family in the west of England; but disobliged all his friends by marrying a young woman who was a Catholic. He was then in a good way of business, but losses and casualties which he could not foresee, reduced him to difficulties, and finally to bankruptcy. His friends would do nothing for him, and they were on their way to Preston, where she has friends who promised to assist them if they came there; it seems really as if every thing were against them, for first the children fell ill, then the wife, and now at last the husband, who has been ailing for some weeks, but who would not own it, has been taken so much worse that I fear he will not be able to continue his journey for some time, if, indeed, he ever recovers, for he seems quite broken down with sorrow and anxiety: he is a superior man, and has evidently been used to good society. I shall try to raise a little money for them, but I thought that if you or Mr Burrows would call to see them, a little comfort would cheer them even more than money, and besides," concluded he, with a slight emotion perceptible in his finely modulated voice, "you have most nobly stepped forward the first, to give the hand of fellowship to necessity without consideration of sect, and I am proud to follow such an example in well-doing."

Long before he came to this point, all prejudice against him had faded away from the minds of his hearers. Clotilde eagerly declared her intention of going down that very afternoon, whilst Marian, with more matronly prudence, assured him, "that she would speak to Mr Burrows, who, she had no doubt, would be most happy to do any thing that lay in his power."

The conversation then took a general turn; having learned from Andrew that the young lady came from Devonshire, he began adroitly to speak of the country about there: he had an intimate friend in the neighbourhood of Gifford Castle; on mentioning his name, it proved to be an acquaintance of Gifford's who had often dined there. Behold then, an acquaintance already struck up, and the blushing Clotilde talking at her ease, to one who was not only a perfect stranger, but a Protestant clergyman.

To Marian he spoke of his children, and the melancholy lonely life he led at the great Rectory; he asked her advice most deferentially about the management of his children, whether it were better to send them to a school, or to have a competent person to attend on them at home. He stated his perplexities about them; lamented in the most feeling terms, that there was no superior woman living near, amongst his congregation, to whom he might apply in the many emergencies where a man could not advise. He spoke of his sisters, and said how much disappointed he had been, that they both refused to be buried alive, as they called it, in Sutton; and, finally, remarking that he had trespassed terribly on their time, the Reverend Horace O'Brian rose, and, with a graceful bow, glided out of the room, having fascinated his auditors as completely as heart could wish.

"What a very superior man!" exclaimed Marian, the instant the door had closed upon him.

"Yes," said Clotilde; "and how uncharitably I have judged him," continued she, in a reproachful tone. "Dear Marian! let us go and see these poor people this very afternoon."

"With all my heart; and I will try and persuade Louis to return his call; it quite does one good to see such an intelligent person."

"And oh!" cried Clotilde, "if we could but convert him too! Who knows for what purpose he has been brought here?"

The Reverend Horace O'Brian went home, which he reached pretty nearly wet through. "Humph," said he to himself, as, enveloped in his dressing-gown, he threw himself in a luxurious *fauteuil* by his study fire; "I think I have made an impression in that quarter, and it shall not be my fault if I do not get a footing in their house. Clotilde is a nice little thing, and will be as well endowed as a queen dowager, Montague says—"

Here his musings were interrupted by Alice, his housekeeper, who bore in, with her own hands, a tray of dinner on which she had exhausted all her skill in cookery; for she had a sort of *prescience*, that on such a miserably wet day, a good dinner would be more than usually welcome.

"Thank you, Alice, this is delicious; and how are the children?"

"Oh, sir, they are well enough;—but are you sure you have changed every thing that was wet, and don't you think you have taken cold? You ought to consider what will become of the parish if any thing should happen to you; but you are just so venturesome."

Whilst the handsome rector eats his dinner, and pacifies the anxiety of his housekeeper, we will tell the reader a little of his history.

The Reverend Horace O'Brian was the nephew of an Irish earl, and the eldest son of a man who had changed his religion for a clerkship in the Treasury. He had been educated for the Church, because the reversion of the rectory of Sutton had been promised to his father for him;—he himself would much have preferred pushing his fortune in the army, but as it was the Church who opened her arms for him, he was obliged to take the good the gods provided, and be content. He had been very extravagant at college, and contracted many debts; his only hope of liquidating them was from the economies of his living, and this tended in some degree to reconcile him to his lot.

Till he was fairly installed in his new career, the idea of self-control or self-denial, had never occurred to him, not even in the lowest form, that of refusing a present gratification to obtain a greater after a while. He was rich in that species of genius, which is the result of a strong passionate temperament; he had a vivid susceptibility to external influences; a love of luxury, that seemed rather an innate and artist-like perception of the beautiful, than a vulgar love of gratification; he was rich in poetical and general impulses; his whole being was saturated with a sense of pleasure; and he shrunk from pain, either endured or inflicted, as an anomaly in nature. But there was no sternness of principle to keep all these gifts from running to waste.

There is a period in the life of such beings as these, when all the possible perfections of humanity seem invested in them; they have a richness and ripeness peculiar to themselves; but they "hold in perfection but a little moment", they have no principle of endurance within them, and they shrink from pain, which is the secret source of all the excellence that is manifested in the world. They are cowards at heart, and cowardice is the root from which all base and craven deeds spring.

To this class belonged Horace O'Brian. Forced into the Church from motives of expediency—examples of time-serving, and subserviency to the powers that be, constantly presented to him, disguised in the epithets of prudence and wisdom—no one lesson of honesty or honourableness ever taught him from his cradle upwards—nothing like conscience or duty ever recognised in his hearing;—but carefully taught that to "rise in life", was the first and last duty of every man who was not a fool—placed in an uncongenial profession with the injunction to become a bishop— buried in an obscure provincial town, in order that the income of the living might pay his debts, and the practice form his style for a higher sphere—the great wonder is, that the Reverend Horace O'Brian was not an irredeemable scoundrel. Hypocrisy seemed forced upon him by circumstances. We are bound to say that he was kind and attentive to his parishioners, who all idolised him.

His sermons were eloquent; he had a perfect voice, a graceful delivery, and a very flowing and flowery style, so of course he could not well help becoming a popular preacher. He was a zealous no popery man; not because he had any antipathy to Catholics or their doctrines, but "no popery", happened to be the government watchword just then: to say all in one word, the Reverend Horace O'Brian did not think the Church the profession for a high-spirited gentleman; he hated it from the bottom of his soul, and nothing but the hope of rising to distinction, kept him patient in the ranks.

It was the weariness of *ennui*, and the wish for something to break this monotony, that inspired the sudden whim of calling at the Manor House. He had a curiosity to see Clotilde, whom his friend Montague had mentioned as a little saint, who was to be the largest heiress in the county.

We had almost forgotten to say, that when a mere boy he had made a run-away match with a beautiful girl of low family, with whom he had fallen madly in love, and whom he could not obtain on other terms. His father was highly incensed, and only forgave him when she died (quite providentially, as he thought), the year after their marriage, in her first confinement, leaving him the young father of twin girls: the children of whom he spoke to Marian.

CHAPTER VIII

_ . _

"Who do you think has been here?" exclaimed Marian, the instant Louis entered the room.

"Pshaw! how should I know?" replied he, pettishly (for he had just come in, hungry, and wet through besides); "I wish you would tell them to be quick with dinner, instead of chattering about your visitors; I suppose, as usual, it will be half an hour before we get it."

Whenever we are peculiarly exalted in our imaginations, we are sure to be within a moment of running our heads against some prosaical post that stands ready to mar our swimming progress; so it was with Marian and Clotilde, who were both thrown from their complacent frame of mind by the casualty of a husband coming home out of sorts, and wanting his dinner before it fell due. In an instant Mr O'Brian, his grace and his gentleness, were swept away like the properties of a wrong scene on the stage. Marian left the room to persuade the cook to do the impossible about dinner, and Clotilde shrank into a corner, feeling that her dreams for the comfort and conversion of various individuals were not _couleur de rose_, as they had been a few moments ago, but had decidedly assumed a very leaden-coloured hue. However, by the time Louis had divested himself of his comfortless attire, dinner was announced, and, still more luckily, he found the soup and game unusually excellent; so that when dessert was on the table, he had relapsed into his normal state of good humour.

"Well! who was it you were beginning to talk about just now? you women have no discretion, but begin to talk of just what runs in your head, when a man is tired to death, and thinking of his dinner; now I can listen, who was it?"

"You will never guess," said Marian; "and I am not sure when it comes to the point, that you will be very much pleased either; we have had Mr O'Brian, of all people!"

"A very great piece of impudence in him; and how came you to receive him?"

"Oh," replied Marian, "he made many apologies for intruding, but he wanted your advice and assistance in a very distressing case that has just occurred. A man, who has been quite a gentleman, and is of a good family, is lying ill at a little ale-house in the town, his wife and two children are with him, they are in the greatest distress; his friends have thrown him off, because he married a Catholic; he has met with the cruellest misfortunes, which have reduced him to absolute beggary, and they were on their way to some of her relations when he was taken ill. Mr O'Brian called first to thank us for our, or rather Clotilde's, kindness, yesterday; and, also to ask if you would do something for this poor man."

"Ay, ay, I suppose this poor man might starve, before he or any of his set would help him."

"Oh, no!" cried Clotilde, "on the contrary, he said he had already called on him, and intends to make his congregation help him."

"And," continued Marian, "he spoke very prettily about not wishing there to be such a line of demarcation between Catholics and Protestants; but both to unite in doing good; he spoke so respectfully about you, and was so gentlemanly and intelligent, that, though I was as stiff as possible at first, I could not help quite liking him before he went away."

"Well, and what did you say to him?"

"Oh, of course I said I could do nothing till I had asked you, but that I was sure you would do all that was right."

"Ah, Miss Clotilde," said Louis, half smiling, as he turned towards her, "this comes through you. You have quite a vocation to be a sister of charity, you bring work of that sort wherever you go. What is your opinion of this, madam?" said he, addressing his mother, who had not spoken.

"I did not see the gentleman," replied the old lady; "but though you have no right to turn aside from a work of charity, the less dealing you have with Mr O'Brian, the better. I think he wants to get a footing here; but go by all means, and see the poor man."

When they rose from the table, Clotilde was in great haste to get ready, and hurried Marian unmercifully, who, content with having obtained the requisite permission, would have delayed till the next morning, in the hope of a finer day; but Clotilde, like all quiet people, when they are set upon a plan, was very obstinate, so accordingly they set off.

They found the sick man and his family exactly as Mr O'Brian had represented; but they did not find Mr O'Brian himself; and Clotilde had a vague sort of feeling that she did not find so much interest as she expected. It is a bad thing to be impatient; she should have waited till the next morning, as Marian proposed.

The next day, Louis came home in high good-humour, saying, "Well, I have seen your Mr O'Brian, and I must say he is a very gentlemanly fellow; how one does get prejudices into one's head! I have asked him to dinner to-morrow, and then we can settle the best means of setting this poor man up again in the world; it is a hard case, and O'Brian spoke very sensibly and liberally about the matter."

The next day, the Reverend Horace O'Brian duly arrived to dinner. With his graceful and adaptive manners, he soon won the heart of his entertainers; even Madame Burrows, who had been inclined to distrust his advances, was charmed by his deference towards her, and pronounced him, in Marian's words, to be "a very superior young man, indeed", and was as cordial as the others in hoping to see him whenever he could find time.

During the whole visit, he scarcely spoke to Clotilde;—there was no need of it, for the looks he bestowed upon her from eyes that actually seemed to give light, took the full effect he intended they should upon the unsuspecting child. When he took his departure, she felt as if all his conversation had been directed to her alone, and expected that Marian would rally her upon the circumstance; she, therefore, made her escape as soon as she could; but Marian, to whom most of his words had been addressed, only remarked to her husband, when they were alone, "Is it not strange that Clotilde should attract so little notice? How different she is from Mrs Gifford, who attracts every body towards her."

"No, my dear," replied Louis, "not every body; but no doubt Clotilde and she agree all the better for not clashing. Clotilde is a sweet little creature, and to my mind, worth a hundred of her step-mother any day."

The O'Brian acquaintance thus auspiciously begun, went on prosperously, and a decided intimacy soon sprung up. The great interest felt both by Marian and Clotilde for the children cemented it.

At first, Mr O'Brian felt some scruples as to what his congregation might say, if he allowed his children to go to a Catholic house; but Marian met them one day, near the park gates, and beguiled them in, along with their nurse, to see a beautiful peacock she had recently added to her poultry yard. They were delighted, and gave their papa no peace till he promised to take them again to see the peacock and the pretty ladies.

Marian offered the park and gardens for their walks, and O'Brian, who was devotedly fond of his children, could not bear to disappoint or thwart them; so it soon grew to be a matter of course that they should go down every day to the Manor House.

They were lovely children, and it did not need their father's influence to make them darlings wherever they came; Clotilde was passionately fond of them, and could not rest with them out of her sight. Fortunately, Marian was propitiated by the respect Mr O'Brian showed for her judgment, and the half-confidential manner in which he talked to her about his affairs; nay, more, asking her advice on one or two occasions, and following it! Otherwise, it is possible she might have felt annoyed by her young companion being so completely engrossed by her convert's *protégés* and children, as to have very little time left for working at the carpet, or talking to her.

It was one morning, about six weeks after the eventful dinner, that Mr O'Brian walked into the oak-room, where the ladies usually sat. Marian was at work, and Clotilde, with the two children before her, was teaching them to dance; her back was to the door, so she did not perceive his entrance, but went on with her lesson; she stood with her dress raised above her instep, and her little flexible foot pointed before her; she was laughing with gentle merriment at some blunders of the children's, and was bidding them "try again", when the little ones bounding away, calling "papa! papa!" caused her to turn round in too much confusion to hear his well-turned compliment on the graceful sight he had so unexpectedly witnessed.

He did not distress her long by his observation, for he at once turned to Marian, saying, "I should hardly have ventured to intrude thus early, but I want Mrs Burrows to do a good action, and I know that can never come unseasonably to her. In my Sunday-school there is a young girl, very superior to the general run of Sunday scholars, whom I am anxious to train for a higher service than that of the farmers' families about, or the tradesmen in town; in short, my dear madam, if I could place her with you, my most sanguine wishes would be met; she would be thoroughly trained, and to have been under your care, would be of itself a recommendation; a servant of your training would be indeed a treasure."

Marian smiled, and asked what sort of situation he wished her to become qualified for.

"I am desirous she should obtain a reasonable proficiency in every household department; I must say my request sounds audacious, but in time she would become useful to you."

"Oh!" said Marian, "let her come by all means, I am quite glad to be made useful. Of course I need not say she shall attend both church and school regularly: I am sure Mr Burrows will feel gratified by the confidence you have in us."

The business was graciously concluded, and they proceeded to talk of other things, and finally adjourned to the garden; for the children had all along kept pulling at Clotilde's gown, to tell her that she had promised to show them where they might dig a garden, and build a castle for their great doll; so, to keep the peace they all went together to lay the foundation. Clotilde, who was very expert at this sort of architecture, was obliged to remain with the children, whilst Marian and O'Brian walked on, for standing spectator is cold work in a March wind. Marian was just as well pleased to have all the talk to herself. There was a comfortable complacency in the idea of having influence over Mr O'Brian, and to have him talking to her, as if she were his greatest friend; and as she did not much care to hear what all the world beside might listen to, she naturally preferred a *tête-à-tête*;—all women do. All this was without the smallest infringement on her sense of married woman propriety;

she was too thoroughly ENGLISH in all her notions, to have an idea of the possibility of caring for any one except her own husband; hers was nothing more than the truly feminine love of being made much of. She often thought, if he were a Catholic gentleman instead of a Protestant clergyman, that Mr O'Brian would just suit Clotilde; but, as there seemed no prospect of this, she was content to enjoy the present good without entering into the metaphysics of it. And Clotilde? Clotilde was happier than she had ever been in her life before; she asked no questions, and we can give the reader no information beyond; it had never been put into her head to analyse her emotions; and her nature was too single to feel any interest in that sort of occupation. "Nothing but Frenchwomen", as a friend of ours once said, "can analyse their feelings at the time they are passing."

In the afternoon of the day when the visit above related took place, Clotilde said she would take the children home herself, and afterwards go and see Andrew the shoemaker, and call on the Catholic wife of Mr O'Brian's *protégé*. Marian was too much fatigued to accompany her, so she and the children set off together.

Her scheme of conversion seemed to be going on prosperously, though the method she pursued has not reached us; she had completely tamed the ultra Protestant wife; who always, when speaking of her, remarked that "She was a very gracious young lady, and 'had the root of the matter in her', though she was a Papist."

Possibly the patience with which Clotilde listened to her ardent accounts of Mr O'Brian's goodness and greatness, and learning, might have had their effect; indeed, Clotilde never seemed so well pleased as when he was the theme of her discourse; besides, Clotilde had plagued Marian into giving Andrew an order for sundry pairs of boots and shoes, so perhaps the favour she found was not quite miraculous.

From Andrew's cottage she went to call on Mr Woolgar, as the sick gentleman, Mr O'Brian's *protégé*, was named; he was much better, though still very weak; his mental anxiety had caused a relapse more than once, but to-day he was in good spirits; Mr O'Brian's representations had stimulated either the pride or the compassion of some of his rich relations, and they had contrived to procure him a situation in the excise, and had sent him money to prosecute his journey; so that now all he wanted was bodily strength, which he seemed in a fair way for gaining. There again Clotilde had to listen to all that could be uttered in the praise of mortal man, and that man, Mr O'Brian; she said very little herself, but she was a wonderfully patient auditor; every body knows how insipid it generally is to listen to the praises of other people.

During her stay with Marian, she had discovered many poor people standing in peculiar need of assistance, and it was to the cottage of one of these, that she bent her way on leaving the Woolgars. Her timidity with Mr O'Brian was so great, that she could never address him without blushing and stammering to a most painful degree; and yet he always contrived to discover her wishes with regard to her *protégés*, and all that it would please her to have done for them, in a way quite wonderful; and then the poor people had often to tell her, in the most artless way, all the beautiful things Mr O'Brian said of her.

This afternoon, as she left the last cottage, and turned her face homewards, she was met by Mr O'Brian himself; it was beginning to get dusk, so without making any question about the matter, he turned back to accompany her. He had never on any occasion been struck dumb in his intercourse with her; on the contrary, he had always, when he had an opportunity, poured forth his most eloquent and graceful conversation for her benefit: he had never paid her a single compliment, but every look, tone, and word that he addressed to her, was flattery itself.

On this occasion, however, his genius had deserted him; he walked by her side, slowly and in silence; at length he ventured a sigh, and exclaimed, "How happy you are in your religious feelings! What would I not give to be like you!" Then, in a confidential tone, which he had never assumed before, he began to tell her that he had gone through many struggles in his mind, and had felt great difficulties before he could bring himself to embrace his present profession. After a pause, he added, with hesitation and apparent difficulty, "Miss Gifford, how shall I tell you that every year of my life, I feel myself more and more drawn towards the religion of my fathers. I preach against Catholicity; I have spoken bitterly of its professors; but it has been in the hope to drown the secret voice of my own heart. I have never thoroughly examined the doctrines of the Church, because I fear to be convinced. My call at the Manor House, was from an impulse I could neither resist nor explain; I was restless and unhappy at heart. I did not foresee what the consequences would be to myself," added he, in a lower tone, and with a passionate glance at Clotilde.

Clotilde was, on many accounts, too troubled to speak; Mr O'Brian himself seemed agitated, and they walked on in silence; at length, with a sort of forced calmness he spoke: "Will you keep my strange confession a secret? You are the only being to whom I ever opened my heart; you are like one of the saints in heaven, you can pity and pardon my inconsistency!"

"I will pray for you," said Clotilde, in a broken voice; "God knows we all need His help."

They had by this time reached the inner park gates that led to the garden; they both stood for a moment, he took hold of her hand and pressed it gently, very gently;—she looked up for a second, and saw his burning eyes fixed upon her face with a look of passionate tenderness, enough to change a saint of snow or marble into a most yielding woman. "You have been sent for my guardian angel," said he, in a tone so low, that it might have escaped her ears, but it did not. "I cannot go in with you," added he, in an abrupt hurried tone; "I am too stunned to see any one." Then, once more pressing the hand he still retained, he struck into a bye path amongst the trees, which immediately concealed him from view.

Clotilde walked as in a dream to the house, and went straight up stairs to her own room; she did not take off her walking things, but sat down on a large chair.

When the tea bell had rung twice for her, she was found by Marian in a deep reverie. Marian succeeded in rousing her by numberless exclamations of extreme astonishment as to "Where she had been, and what she had been doing so long in the dark?"— Clotilde returned very *distrait* answers. When they emerged into the full lighted dining-room, Marian was quite startled to see the soft troubled dreaming look, which had taken the place of her usual sweet and composed expression of countenance. She scarcely spoke the whole evening, but remained plunged in a happy abstraction. Marian did not say to her husband, when Clotilde had retired, "I wonder whether Mr O'Brian has said any thing to her?" but she thought, "I will soon find it out if he has."

CHAPTER IX

_ . _

When the Rev. Horace O'Brian reached home, he saw a post-chaise driving away from the gate.

"Mr Montague, sir, is come whilst you have been away," said old Alice, as she opened the door; "he is in your study. I asked him to have some dinner, but he said——"

Her master did not stay to hear the end of what she was saying, but strode on,—"Why, Montague, my dear fellow! where do you come from? Who ever expected to see you here?"

"Oh, I have a few days' holiday, and a little business in this neighbourhood, and I wanted to see you; so _me voici_; is it a supernatural appearance? I made love to Mrs Alice in your absence to find me a bed, which she has done; but she is so used to her master's sweet speeches, that mine sounded very tame, I fear, after them——"

"Has she given you any thing to eat?" interrupted Horace.

"She offered it, but I prefer waiting for one of her delicate _petit soupers_, to efface the memory of a villainous dinner and British brandy;—so now sit down in peace, I have a thousand things to say. Here, I have taken your own peculiar chair, and it is too comfortable to resign, so you must find yourself another."

The new comer was a tall dashing-looking man, with large red whiskers and a shrewd, good-humoured expression of face; he was a London barrister in good practice, and Horace O'Brian's most intimate friend.—They had not met for a long time;—consequently, for the next two hours they chattered like a couple of women. At length, after the supper which Mrs Alice served up punctually at nine o'clock, had been duly honoured, there was a pause, during which both gentlemen lighted a cigar; and Montague, setting his feet on each side the grate, said abruptly, "All this time you have not told me one word about Miss Gifford; what are you going to do with her?"

"Faith, I hardly know," replied O'Brian; "it is lucky you are come, or in another week I should have been in love with her beyond redemption. I am in love with her as it is, whilst I am with her."

"Oh!—have you said any thing to give her an idea how matters stand with you?"

"N—o, I don't think I have at all committed myself."

"I suppose you mean you have kept clear of an action for breach of promise; but I know it's not in your nature to see a girl day after day with impunity, for you never can resist an opportunity for love making. How far have you gone? She is a good little soul as ever lived."

"So she is," said Horace; "I don't know when I have been so much occupied as I have been the last six weeks; I think I fired the train this afternoon, and her sweet little innocent heart is ready to surrender at discretion."

"Have you summoned it?"

"No, I tell you; I have not committed myself at all."

"Then you still have an idea of Miss Smith, of the Hollows?"

"Yes, I suppose so,—as soon as I can get my courage up. I have had great difficulty to keep her pacified, for she did not like my getting intimate at the Manor, only I told her I thought they would, some of them, turn Protestant. I don't know how I shall keep up with them if I propose to Miss Smith; I should be very sorry to lose them, for they are the nicest people in the parish—Clotilde out of the question. I don't see, after all, why I should not marry Clotilde; I like her better than Miss Smith, and I am sure she is very fond of me. What is your idea?—why should I not?"

"Miss Gifford's fortune is as large as Miss Smith's," replied Montague, deliberately, "but Miss Gifford is a rigid Catholic, and Miss Smith is the favourite niece of the Bishop of L——; both ladies are willing to accept you, by your own account, but you like Miss Gifford rather the best; I dare say she is the nicest, for you have good taste; but so far, it has only been a love and idleness sort of affair, because you were *ennuyé* to death, and the girl was in your way; if you marry her, you will remain rector of Sutton all your days, with a faded popularity, and no possibility of regaining it; if you marry Miss Smith, you will have all her uncle's influence to push you on; and the Church must be a bore of a profession if you have not the hope of rising in it. I think I have stated the case pretty fairly; you must decide for yourself."

At this instant, so critical for the prospect of both ladies, old Alice came into the room with a note that a groom had brought on horseback from the Hollows, with orders to wait for an answer.

"At this time of the night! what can it be?" said Montague, whilst Horace broke the seal. The note was as follows:

"Dear Sir,
"Will you favour me with a copy of your sermon on the 'Two Witnesses', and if you have your book on the 'Mystery of Iniquity', please send it also. I am writing to my uncle, the bishop, by the early mail, and wish to enclose them. Excuse my troubling you at this late hour, and believe me in Christian regard,
"Truly yours,
"MARGARET SMITH

"P.S. The Dean of——died last night."

"That's what I call having a friend!" said Montague, after he had read it, "that clinches the matter; send the man off, and go and see her to-morrow."

"But after all," said Horace, "it is only a chance whether she succeeds; I don't want to marry her for nothing; and then she is so horribly evangelical and dogmatic."

"Well, man, you cannot have every thing; in matters of such importance, you must not stand upon trifles, but strike the balance with regard to the whole. What are faults in Miss Smith will be virtues, or at least conveniences, in the wife of a dean. And now let us go to bed, for I am tired, and Mrs Alice will not thank us for keeping her up any longer. To-morrow, remember, we are to commence the campaign in due form."

The friends separated. "At any rate," said the Reverend Horace O'Brian to himself, "I may go to sleep now, and need not think of any thing till morning."

The next morning when he descended, he found Montague playing with the children, and they were telling him about Miss Gifford, and the beautiful house she was building for their doll; they sprang to their father as he entered, crying, "Papa, you must be very quick with breakfast, for Miss Gifford told us to come very early, and bring the great doll, to see how high the house must be made. Oh Alice! Alice! bring breakfast quick."

"But, my queens," said Horace, taking both on his knee, "don't you see it is raining?"

"Then we will be carried," said they both together, "and you will come and fetch us. Miss Gifford is always pleased when you come, her eyes get quite bright, and she always kisses us, though she won't come into the room till you have been there a long time!"

"Don't you wish, Susan," said the other little one, "that Miss Gifford lived here, and then we could have her all the day without going out in the rain?"

"So much for disinterested affection!" said Montague, laughing. "No, your papa and I are going to see Miss Smith to-day, and we will go and see Miss Gifford to-morrow; which do you like the best?"

"I don't like Miss Smith," said the little one, with a petted toss of the head; "she is so cross, and tells us not to make a noise. We won't go to see her, will we, Susan?"

"No, we will go to Miss Gifford, now directly; ring the bell, papa, and tell John to carry us."

"Poor things!" said Horace, "I know who they would like for a mamma!"

After the noisy little ones had been despatched, the horses were brought round, and despite the rain, the gentlemen set off to pay their *devoirs* to the niece of the bishop.—"Turning out such a morning as this, ought to mollify the heart of any woman," said Horace.

"No doubt it will take due effect on Miss Smith," said Montague; "it will not do to wait till the vacancy is filled up to pay your homage,—you must go, for once, in faith: to-morrow, no doubt, we shall hear something definite about the deanery."

"Well," said Horace, shrugging his shoulders, "what must be

must; but what a farce to talk of men having a free choice in matters of matrimony!"

After a ride of about six miles, they arrived at the Hollows, a large old-fashioned English country house. An air of prim decorum reigned around: one felt the atmosphere of propriety before the green gate that led to the carriage sweep had closed. Their ring at the hall-door was answered by a demure-looking servant man, out of livery. They were shown across a hall paved with black and white marble, and with family portraits let into the walls; from this, they were ushered into a drawing-room, handsomely and heavily furnished. No expense had been spared, every article was the largest and handsomest that could be got for money; but not a particle of taste or fancy was to be discerned. A few religious books, expensively bound, lay on the table, mingled with Missionary Registers and Tracts; a large work-basket, filled with Dorcas clothing, stood beside the black horse-hair covered sofa; and in a corner of the said sofa, sat Miss Smith, herself—a tall, severe-looking woman of thirty, in a brown stuff gown, made high in the neck, a precisely plaited ruff round her throat, and a pair of black kid gloves, with the fingers cut half off completed her costume. She put down her work as the gentlemen entered, and received them with a formal curtsey, to which, as regarded Horace, she added a stiff shake of the hand.

"I don't wonder that Horace felt frightened," thought Montague to himself whilst he felt that his own dashing air was terribly out of keeping with all around him; indeed, the chaste eyes of Miss Smith did not seem to know where to turn for refuge, and she showed her embarrassment by becoming more cold and stiff than ever. But if the dashing Montague were struck dumb, the graceful Horace showed himself more than equal to the emergency; he addressed Miss Smith in a tone of confidential and almost brotherly esteem, nicely pitched between gallantry and respect; mentioned the audacious-looking Montague as "his oldest friend, who had unexpectedly arrived the evening before, and who was anxious to be presented to one who had so often been mentioned between them, as a lady to whom he was under great obligations, for her wise and Christian counsels".

Montague felt himself blush, but Horace did nothing of the kind.

The conversation then turned upon parish business, religious intelligence, and clerical matters of all kinds; the lady showed a great deal more shrewdness and good sense than Montague expected, but he was wonder-struck at the information and interest his friend Horace contrived to display; the fact was, that Horace O'Brian never could help trying to please the company he was in, after their own tastes. The lady then inquired with marked curiosity about his Catholic friends at the Manor, and especially whether the young lady from the south were still there. To all this Horace gave the most unembarrassed replies.

"I have my doubts", said Miss Smith, "whether a Christian be justified in holding social intercourse with any who are partakers in the soul destroying doctrines of the Church of Rome. You know St Paul is very strong upon the duty of keeping ourselves separate from all who do not hold fast 'sound doctrine'; and are you not afraid, too, that some of our weaker brethren may be offended and stumble, by reason of your intimacy in that quarter? The only fault your friend has, Mr Montague, is that he is too zealous; where there is good to be done he throws himself headlong, without considering the consequences."

Horace tried to say something in favour of the excellence of the family at the Manor House, but Miss Smith listened with impatience, saying, when he had concluded, "Well, my conscience will not permit me to have any intercourse with idolaters; we are distinctly warned against it in Scripture, so my duty at least is plain; I will pray for them, and if they require any sort of assistance, I hope, as a Christian, I should give it; but we shall never prosper as a nation till Catholics and Catholicism are rooted out of it. Our rulers have much to answer for, in treating them with so much indulgence as they do; when the fires of Smithfield are again kindled, and judgment falls on this lukewarm nation, they will learn wisdom, but too late. If we examine the history of our country, we shall find that in exact proportion as Catholicism has been put down, the nation has prospered, and every concession on grounds of expediency—"

Here the door opened, and the demure servant-man announced luncheon.

In the hospitable cares of the table, Miss Smith's anti-Catholic enthusiasm calmed itself down. On rising from the table the gentlemen prepared to take their leave. Leading Horace O'Brian a few steps towards the window recess, the lady, premising that he must consider what she was about to say as perfectly confidential, told him that the very last letter she had received from her uncle, made mention of him, saying that he might confidentially look for preferment the very first opening that occurred; and that Mr O'Brian might depend on having his influence, as the Church required more servants of zeal and ability like his. "I do not wish to rouse false hopes in you, Mr O'Brian, but I know you are not influenced by worldly motives in desiring a more extended sphere of usefulness, so that whether preferment came or not you would be contented; but I think I may speak confidently, when I say, that the vacant deanery will be yours, and I wish to be the first to offer you my congratulations. It cannot fall to one more worthy of it in every way!"

Horace O'Brian looked as if he were dreaming, and did not speak.

"You will not mention this till the appointment is officially announced; but I could not resist being the first to tell you good news."

The Reverend Horace O'Brian did not say much, but the looks that came from his magnificent eyes were unutterable, and Miss Smith was as well satisfied as if he had replied in the most orthodox fashion.

"What was the old girl saying in that cold window-place so long?" asked Montague, when they had cleared the green gates, and were safe from the possibility of a listener.

"An official secret," said Horace, smiling with a radiant complacency he could not suppress.

"That you are to be the new dean?" said Montague. "Well, I thought as much."

"So, she said," replied Horace, "but God knows whether it is not all woman's talk."

"Oh! no fear of that—there was a sort of bridling satisfaction, a mysterious importance peeping out at every pore, all through our visit. I set it down at first, to your fascinations, but the riddle is read now,—it was this secret, and indeed it was one worth telling. Aren't you glad now that we went this morning?"

"Yes," said Horace; "but I am thinking how I am to let poor Clotilde down gently, and get out of the Manor House connexion; it is clear the fair lady will not brook it."

"'Sufficient to the day is the evil thereof', as she would tell you. Let us now think only of getting out of this cursed rain."

When they reached home they found a letter written by the bishop himself confirming all that Miss Smith had said, and concluding with many compliments on his zeal, talent, and disinterestedness in never putting forward any claims to preferment.

"Well," said Horace, "this time yesterday I never expected this! Believe it or not as you will, for the last month I have actually forgotten there was ever such things as bishops and Church patronage: I did not even know, or had forgotten that the old dean was ill."

"Well, my dear Horace, I heartily congratulate you, but don't let Miss Smith get scandalised at me when she is Mrs Horace O'Brian, or I shall wish that your predecessor had lived to the age of Methuselah; now let us have a bottle of your prime claret, and we will make an unclerical night of it."

"Well, my darlings, and how did you enjoy yourselves yesterday?" asked Horace the next morning, at breakfast.

"Oh poor Miss Gifford," said Susan, shaking her head, "she was so sorry about your not coming to fetch us."

"Why, what did she say?"

"Oh, she said nothing, but she went quite pale and grave, and did not laugh again the whole day; and once she looked as if she were crying, and she told us the story of the 'Babes in the Wood'. Will you come and see her to-day, papa, and make her laugh and dance with us as she used to do?"

"Yes, my darlings, we will go, and you shall go with us."

"Oh! that's right," said both little ones together, clapping their hands, "and now, Susan, let us show papa the last step Miss Gifford taught us."

"Upon my honour," said Horace, "I don't half like facing her."

"Nonsense, my dear fellow, these sort of things happen to all of us; put the little creature out of her misery at once; there can be no difficulty now you have made up your mind."

Clotilde was sitting alone, working, when they entered. She did not dare to look at Horace; but she could neither control nor conceal the deep joy that the sight of him caused her.

Marian was called, Montague was introduced, and the conversation turned on general matters. Contrary to his custom, Horace spoke a good deal to Clotilde, but in a cheerful, indifferent tone; the unexpressed tenderness of a lover, had given place to the polite, kindly good will of a mere acquaintance. Kindness pains more than cruelty when it is given us instead of love.

The heart of Clotilde seemed turned to stone, but she could not have explained the cause of her pain. She raised her eyes with a grieved questioning look to his; he quailed under her glance, and abruptly proposed a walk to show his friend the grounds. He went first with Marian, and Montague tried to engage Clotilde in conversation; his family lived near Gifford Castle, and Clotilde had often seen his father; at another time she would have been delighted to hear of home; now, she could neither speak nor listen, and to prevent her trouble becoming too apparent, she feigned to busy herself with the children. Montague, who suspected the reason, left her in peace, and joined Marian and Horace, who was more confidential than ever, and fuller of his expressions of regard; he was detailing the stroke of good fortune he had met with. "Though", said he, with his sweetest smile, "I feel almost tempted to regret it, as it will, of necessity, remove me from my latest found, but most dearly valued, friends. I shall not continue to reside in Sutton. I must look out for a curate to take my duty here; and, perhaps, you will show him a little attention for my sake, that I may not seem to be altogether separated from you. Montague, my dear fellow," said he, turning abruptly to him, "ask Miss Gifford to show you the cedar walk, it is worth seeing."

After Montague, in obedience to a sign from his friend, had withdrawn, Horace began (with a little real embarrassment, it is true, but still that looked all the more natural) to hint to Marian that his preferment, which had so unexpectedly fallen to him, would enable him to realise a secret desire he had entertained for years. "You," continued he, "with your fine sensibilities, will enter into my feelings; so long as there was a possibility of being suspected of a worldly motive, I did not breathe a word of my attachment to the lady, for she was rich, and her connexions gave her great influence, whilst I had only the income of my rectory. You are the first of whom I have made a confidante. I determined not to speak until I had obtained so much that I could not be suspected of wanting more; now all difficulties are removed, and will not *you* wish me success?" he added, in a gentle tone. But Marian was in no humour to do any such thing; she was disappointed and annoyed. Though she had never allowed to herself that she expected Mr O'Brian to propose for Clotilde, the idea of his thinking of any one else offended her extremely, and none the less because it was unreasonably. So she answered in a constrained tone, that Mr O'Brian was not one likely to meet with a refusal. Horace went on, "I am obliged to leave here to-morrow to wait upon the bishop. After that I shall have to go to London for a few days on business, so that this is the last walk we can have in this happy garden for some time," and the Reverend Horace O'Brian sighed.

He could never bear to see people suffer pain, and he was really uncomfortable lest Clotilde should take matters seriously. The visit to London, and the business with the bishop, were just improvised on the spur of the moment to get out of the way of being obliged to witness—his own work.

The remainder of the visit passed without any thing occurring worthy of note, except that as they were all standing in the dining-room, where Horace had risen to take leave, Marian alluded to his approaching absence, and Clotilde's lips turned pale with the agony she endured;—he hastily shook hands with her, and looked another way. Proper messages were left for Louis and Madame Burrows; the children were to remain till after lunch, and at last Horace and his friend were fairly gone.

He drew a deep breath as if he were relieved from a painful burden, but did not speak until they reached the spot where he had parted with Clotilde two days before, and then he exclaimed, "Would to God, Montague, all this had come a week ago;—it would have saved me from feeling like a great scoundrel!"

It is curious to see the practical value that is put upon love in this world; it may be a very precious thing; but it is no matter what wealth of love is lavished on a man—unless it can do somewhat towards realising whatever object it may be that he desires in life, it is worthless and importunate in his eyes. If he desires money—love is good for nothing to him. If he be ambitious—the most devoted love seems insipid folly. No—if a woman wants the love of any man, let her bribe him; if she cannot give him that which his soul desires, her love will be very ineffectual.

CHAPTER X

— · —

"I cannot believe that Mr O'Brian really cares for the lady he is going to marry," said Marian, that same evening as she sat at work. "From his manner ever since we knew him, I should never have suspected him to be an engaged man, should you, Clotilde?"

Clotilde was standing before the fire; she felt herself go dreadfully faint at Marian's speech, and raised her eyes instinctively to the mirror above the chimney-piece, to see if her countenance betrayed the shock she had just received; but it bore no trace of the suffering within. She gained the sofa as soon as possible, and sat down, but she had no power to reply to Marian's question, who, however, went on without waiting for an answer.

"I am quite put out of the way about the matter. I know it must be that Miss Smith of the Hollows,—people talked about her for him a long time ago, but I thought it had all gone off: our acquaintance, which has been so pleasant, will just die away, for I know Miss Smith would as soon go to the stake as set foot in a Catholic house, or allow any belonging to her to enter one either. Oh, Louis!" exclaimed she, as her husband entered the room, "Where have you been all day? There is such news for you! Mr O'Brian is made a dean, and is going to be married! He came here this morning to tell me all about it; he is going away to-morrow to see the bishop, so it will be ever so long before we see him again."

"Indeed!" said Louis, "you *do* surprise me! I am sure I congratulate him very heartily; but are you quite sure he is going to be married—who is it to?"

"Oh, I am sure I don't know," said Marian pettishly; "he did not mention her name, but I fancy it must be to that Miss Smith; he told me it was to a lady to whom he had long been attached, and who had great Church influence. To my mind, there is something quite shocking in the idea of a clergyman marrying, even though he be only a Protestant. Mr O'Brian has had one wife already—I have no patience with him, I declare. His manner is quite changed already—he is not half so interesting as he used to be; and to think of those poor little darlings having such a step-mother set over them—an evangelical old maid, like Miss Smith!"

"But, my dear," said Louis, gently, when she had run herself out of breath, "how do you know it is Miss Smith? I heard that she admired him, but I never knew that he admired her."

"Oh, I am quite sure of it," said Marian, "by the way of speaking; he preached all those no Popery sermons to get favour with her and her uncle the bishop; besides, the dear children said that their papa and his friend went all in the rain to see her yesterday—it is of no use to persuade me out of my senses."

Here her eloquence was cut short by the entrance of tea, and Clotilde, terrified lest Marian should suspect what was passing in her heart, exerted herself to talk with an energy that quite surprised her hearers. After tea she offered to read aloud; but the efforts she made were too great to allow of their continuance, and she seized the first moment in which she might retire to her own room. But even when alone, she did not dare to relieve her dismayed heart by tears; she felt that if she once gave way, she must break down altogether, and the idea of allowing any one to suspect her feelings seemed shameful to her dear little innocent soul. She was bowed down with a strange weight of humiliation and disgrace, but it was all crushed down into a hard, confused sense of wretchedness; she did not dare to look into her own heart, for it required all her strength to keep every thing below the surface.

It was no self-love, or wounded pride that made her fancy she could never look any one in the face again, but a true womanly instinct of delicacy and shame. With all this there was not a particle of bitterness against the man who had deceived her with a vain show of gallantry and sentiment; no, she laid the blame in perfect good faith upon her own ignorance of the world, and her own presumption in having thought it possible that such a man as Mr O'Brian could care about her. It is always much easier to think ourselves wrong than one we love. It would have been no comfort to Clotilde could she have known that Mr O'Brian was a graceful good-for-nothing, who did not deserve one thought from her pure and loving soul. She knelt down before the crucifix, but could not utter a single prayer: she knelt, mute and motionless—feeling as if she were turned to stone. When she lay down in bed, she fell into a stupor that continued until daylight; she was roused to consciousness by a paroxysm of dry hysterical gaspings, which were succeeded by a violent shivering which lasted for some minutes, and left a sense of tightness across the throat which almost prevented her breathing; but no tears followed.

She appeared at breakfast, looking much as she always did, except that her eyes seemed larger and more opened than usual. She was surprised to find how easily she mingled in conversation. Her usual timidity had quite abandoned her. The fact was, she was hardly conscious of any thing that was passing around her, and once or twice she wondered how it was she could laugh so much more than she used to do.

During the day a message came from the Rectory, to say that the children had gone with their papa, and none of them would return for some weeks at least.

"Well," said Marian, in a vexed tone, "our intimacy with Mr O'Brian grew up like the 'Bean-stalk' in the child's tale, and it seems it will die away as rapidly—all gone off in this way at a minute's notice! One would think a dean never died in the Church before! You seem to take it all very quietly, Clotilde; but I am not such a saint, or perhaps I am too sensitive; but I own I feel hurt—I wonder whether preferment always turns things topsy-turvy in this manner? but it is all to curry favour with Miss Smith. Now that he has hopes of rising in the world, he is afraid of hurting his chance by allowiing the poor children to come here. I have no patience with double dealing and time-serving."

Marian's indignant conclusions were not exactly logical, and had Mr O'Brian overheard her, he might have proved beyond controversy, that she had no grounds for what she said, and that he was an exceedingly ill-used man; still there is an instinct in the heart of sincere people which seldom leads them wrong, and Marian had blundered on the truth, though she could not have explained how;

but Mr O'Brian's own conscience would have borne her out could she have obtained speech with it.

Near three weeks passed over, and then Marian's attention was roused to another subject.

"I am sure there is something wrong with Clotilde," said Madame Burrows one day when she and Marian were alone, "I have been watching her, she eats nothing, and I don't like her liveliness, it is not natural, and I can't understand her going so often into her own room. You should pay a little attention to her, my dear."

"I think, ma'am, you are mistaken," replied Marian, "she seems to have a little cold, but she does not complain; she feels lost without the children, I dare say."

"Without the children's papa, I am afraid," said Madame Burrows. "I wish he had never come into this house."

No more was said just then; but the change in Clotilde was too marked to be much longer overlooked. Her hysterical attacks had become more frequent—she always went to her own room when she felt them coming on, and the very day after Madame Burrows had spoken, Marian, passing along the passage, heard a singular noise in the room: she hastily entered, and saw Clotilde kneeling at the foot of her bed, her head buried in the clothes and convulsed with a nervous spasm that seemed to tear her delicate frame to pieces. Terribly alarmed, she was on the point of speaking, when Clotilde's head fell back, and the blood streamed from her ears and mouth. Marian had just time to catch her in her arms before she fell upon the floor. Assistance was speedily summoned,—a medical man was almost immediately on the spot, who pronounced that Clotilde had burst a blood-vessel, and that her only chance of life was in being kept perfectly still. It is possible that the poor child owed the continuance of her reason to this sudden prostration of bodily energy. A letter was immediately despatched to Gifford Castle, with information of what had occurred, and entreating both Zoe and Gifford to come with all speed.

CHAPTER XI

— · —

At Gifford Castle, meanwhile, things had been going on in the usual course; Gifford improved his estate, and the college prospered under Everhard, who continued to come to the castle to profit by Zoe's conversation; and Zoe? she had begun more and more every day to feel, that for a woman there exists that which is far more precious than the admiration of the world. Her proud coquettish heart was touched at last, and she felt abashed before the pure womanly instincts that now, for the first time, gushed up in her heart. Nothing teaches humility like love. The more conscious she became of her influence over Everhard, the more earnest was the desire she felt to make herself worthy of him; her manners became soft and timid; an indescribable air of womanliness tinged every action, and made her attractions more irresistibly subduing than ever. Gifford could not account for the change, but he thought it very delightful; a true love for one, makes the person who feels it, loving towards all the world, and Gifford came in for his share.

"Ah!" exclaimed Zoe, one night when the post-bag was opened, "a letter from my uncle! I hope all is well. Has had a bad winter," said she, reading aloud—"wishes to see me and the children once more before he dies—hopes I will not delay long—in short, has set his heart on seeing us at Whitsuntide; that is a grand time at the Rectory, I know; Aunt Martha used to be in her glory then. Well, Mr Gifford, have you any objection? Poor old gentleman, I feel as if I had neglected him sadly."

"My dear Zoe, how can you say so; you write to him at least once a fortnight, and it is not a month since you sent your Aunt Martha that splendid shawl; you are always in extremes."

Zoe was only conscious that her thoughts had been occupied by neither her uncle's health nor Aunt Martha's shawl; and that, in fact, she had almost forgotten their existence; so her self-reproach was not so wonderful as Gifford seemed to think.

"Well," said Gifford again, after a pause, "Whitsuntide falls early this year, it will be the week after next; suppose we go next week, and stay a week there, Father Everhard will join us, and we will all go to Sutton, and bring back Clotilde; I am getting anxious about the child; she seldom writes, and never expresses the least wish to come home again, and for her that is not natural; I should like to know what she has been doing."

"Oh," said Zoe, "Marian is more of her own age than I am, it is no wonder she finds her a nice companion. I wonder how she is going on with her converts, she has not mentioned them lately."

"Well, I have felt strangely anxious about her lately," said Gifford.

Everhard had been long under a promise to go out to the castle and stay a few days; his arrival now put a stop to the conversation; Zoe forgot every thing else, and even Gifford's anxiety was suspended for a while.

"Why, Father Everhard, we expected you to dinner," cried Gifford, as Everhard entered the room. "How comes it that you are so late?"

Zoe said nothing, but looked exceedingly well content to see him at all. She knew very well that his college arrangements would not let him get off before: he had not told her so—but she had found it out by some means or another.

The scheme of their journey was talked over, and Everhard promised to join them.

As they were sitting at tea the next evening, Gifford received a letter that made him very silent for awhile.

"Any bad news?" asked Zoe.

"Exceedingly annoying," returned he; "I am summoned on a special jury case, and I fear I cannot get off; it will detain me a couple of days."

"What is it about?" asked Zoe.

"Oh, you won't understand it—it is a trial about some patent for a new plough, and I suppose they fancy I must know something of the subject because I once made an improvement. I little thought it would bring this plague on me. I am very sorry I have to leave you," he said, turning to Everhard, "I had quite looked forward to this visit; however, I will be back as soon as possible; you must promise to stay, and you must make up for what I lose of your company now, by giving us a few days more."

There was nothing for it but to submit; indeed, Everhard had no desire to refuse.

The next morning Gifford departed in great hopes that he would be able to return the day following.

Everhard and Zoe were left alone.

It was a mild, beautiful day in early spring; they were out the whole day rambling about the grounds, enjoying that delicious sense of strength and pleasure that the first days of spring bring back to every body, though they may have fancied themselves as dead to pleasurable emotions as the trees and fields in winter seem beyond the hope of fruit and blossoming. We once heard a lady say, "that in spring she always felt as if it were a sin to be without a lover!" which, however shocking to one's sense of decorum, was only a compendious way of expressing what every body has felt: the uselessness and waste there seems in that overflowing sense of animal life and happiness, when we have no object to whom to dedicate it.

Everhard and Zoe were excessively happy all that day; the boys had a whole holiday; even the tutor forgot his pedantry and dignity, and condescended to enjoy the sunshine with an awkward, grotesque sort of satisfaction.

After dinner they all rambled together in the woods till evening set in, and then, to crown the delights of the day, the boys remained up to have supper with their mamma and Father Everhard.

When the tutor and the children had retired, Everhard and Zoe left the somewhat chilly dining-room for her warm boudoir. There was no light except what came from the fire, and an antique bronze lamp at the far end of the room.

A sense of sadness fell upon Everhard, as if it were the rebound of all the delight he had known that day.

Zoe was in high spirits, talking even more brilliantly than usual, and this jarred upon his present mood; he sat with his elbows on a table at a little distance, watching her earnestly. It was very far from being the first time he had been alone with Zoe, and in that room too; but now he was conscious of a feeling he had never known in her presence before—strange fancies of what his life might have been had he never been a priest. The happiness of the day had left bitterness behind. He felt that he had been mocked with the appearance of intimacy, and of belonging to the being before him, whilst it was nothing more than an accident which must cease almost directly: he felt bitterly, that whilst to him she made up the sum of all worth calling *life*, he had no hold upon her; if he were to be separated from her on the morrow, she would not have a single day overclouded by his absence; he desired passionately to become something to her—to make a bond between them, that she could not deny,—which might endure for life; what was to be its nature, he did not contemplate. These, and a thousand other vague thoughts, made his answers to Zoe absent and abrupt; his evident preoccupation at last seemed to infect her, and her lively gaiety gave place to a conscious silence, during which, for want of something better to do, she moved from the sofa to a fauteuil, and placed her feet on a white footstool. The light from the lamp now fell exactly upon her face, and like all persons who do any thing in embarrassment, she felt directly how much better it would have been to sit still in her old place; but that passed away.

She sat with her eyes fixed on the fire, in a reverie; she was dreaming too; all her coquetry was subdued; the feeling and impulses which all her life had either been crushed down or unheeded, now made themselves intelligible. The memory of all her schemes for getting Everhard into her power, now seemed like sacrilege, and she despised herself; she fancied that he must see to the bottom of her vain, frivolous soul, and despise her too; she looked up for an instant as if to ask pardon. Their eyes met—and he saw those glorious eyes upon him, soft with tears, and the whole countenance full of timid love and gentleness. Joy, almost like fright, flashed across Everhard; he could not turn away, but remained gazing upon her; words were needless, and prudence was vain; the secret of their souls had transpired in that one look.

At this critical moment, both were startled back to reality by the clang of the castle clock.

"Dear, how late," stammered Zoe, hardly conscious of what she said. Everhard did not speak a word, but staggered to a side-table where the night-lamps were standing, took one, and with a husky "good night", left the room.

Zoe remained standing where she was, altogether stunned and bewildered;—she, too, had seen Everhard's look; but she was afraid to believe in its meaning; on the contrary, the abruptness with which he had quitted her made her fear she had displeased him. A sentiment of modesty, unknown till now, made her cheek burn with shame, at the consciousness that she must have betrayed herself to him. After a while she took her lamp and went to her own room where her maid was sitting half asleep over a novel, waiting to undress her. Zoe could not bear to see any one, so she pettishly told her to go to bed, since she could not keep her eyes open.

She did not expect to sleep, but emotion is of all things the most exhausting, and she had scarcely laid her head on the pillow before she fell into a deep heavy sleep.

Everhard, all this time, was sitting in his own room, bewildered, stupefied—suffocated by emotions which had broken their bounds in his soul for the first time.

That look, and the expression of Zoe's countenance, had torn the veil which had so long concealed from him the danger of his position. He could now deceive himself no longer,—he felt that she had penetrated his secret,—that they understood each other— and what was to be the end of it? There was but one course left for him to pursue, and no consideration was needed to discover it;— he must leave the castle,—leave the neighbourhood. He must see Zoe no more.

Many men in Everhard's position might have come to the conclusion of the necessity of this step, but there was this peculiarity in Everhard's case, that he was perfectly sincere in his determination to carry it out; for he was not one who ever trifled either with himself or others. But with all his determination to do right, he could not resist yielding himself for a while to the delicious consciousness that he loved and was beloved again; it was a feeling he could not just then even try to conquer.

It was two o'clock, and Everhard still sat in his arm-chair, looking into the dying embers of the fire, when he was startled from his meditation by cries of "Fire": the great bell of the castle was rung to summon the out-servants, and the noise and confusion reached even that distant part of the building.

Everhard started up: his first thought was of Zoe, but he recollected that the apartments of the boys and their tutor were above his room, and the whole was separated from the rest of the house by a long gallery, the door of which was locked. Zoe's apartments were on the other side of the castle; he knew she would not escape till the children were safe,—that her first thought would be for them. He rushed up-stairs, and found the boys, who had been awakened with the noise, crying bitterly. The tutor, who had lost with fright the little bit of sense he ever had, was helplessly trying to dress himself, without being able to put on a single article the right way.

Everhard dressed the children with his own hands, hurried them down the staircase, which was happily of stone, saw them out of the castle by a side door (which had been made for their convenience), and telling them to make the best of their way to the gardener's cottage, he returned to rescue Zoe. He went with all speed along the gallery, which was beginning to fill with smoke. A bright, flickering light, was visible under the door; he struggled for a few minutes without being able to open it; but the sound of a woman's voice screaming wildly for help, gave him renewed strength, and, throwing his whole weight against the door, it gave way, and Zoe, just woke out of her sleep, rushed into the gallery, and ran to where he stood. It was too dark for her to distinguish him, but she knew him by instinct.

"Oh, Everhard, the children?"

"They are safe—safe in the gardener's cottage."

"Thank God!" she gasped, and fell an insensible weight in his arms.

The surprise, the alarm, the possible danger, were forgotten, he only felt the warm, palpitating burden which lay upon his bosom; he was too much overpowered by his sensations to move—they stupefied him—the intense enjoyment amounted to pain. He, who in his whole life had never touched a woman, now had a whole life of passion melted into that moment.

He crushed her into his arms with ferocious love. He pressed burning kisses upon her face, her lips, and her bosom; but kisses were too weak to express the passion that was within him. It was madness like hatred,—beads of sweat stood thick on his forehead, and his breath came in gasps.

How long a time passed he knew not; but a thick volume of smoke, and the heat, which was becoming almost intolerable, recalled him to the danger that surrounded her. He hurried down the stone staircase, intending to get out by the same door through which the children had passed; but in the darkness he missed the turning, and went up and down different passages, not knowing whither he went. At length he reached a part of the building to which neither the smoke nor the alarm had spread: it was the chapel. A light burned before the altar,—he bore her to the steps, and sprinkled her face and hands with water from a vessel that stood near. Zoe opened her eyes, and saw Everhard bending over her. The colour rushed over her face and neck. Everhard made an effort to turn away, but, almost unconsciously, he fell on his knees beside her; and the next moment Zoe's burning arms were round his neck, and her long hair fell like a veil over him. Everhard's brain was in a whirl, and his veins ran fire, as he felt her warm breath upon him.

Zoe was the first to recover from the delirium of the moment;— she struggled to disengage herself from his arms, and seizing a large shawl which had fallen on the ground, attempted to cover herself with it, exclaiming,

"Oh, Everhard, what will you think of me? I have made you hate me—despise me. Forgive me for letting you betray yourself, it was the last thing you desired to do."

The sound of her voice in broken tones, recalled Everhard to his senses; the force of long years of the habit of self-control was not lost in this trying moment; with an effort almost superhuman he suffered Zoe to disengage herself, and retreated against a pillar at a little distance; he twisted his hands in each other, and stood crushing himself against the stone, whilst a spasm of sharp pain attested the energy of his efforts to master himself.

Zoe, meantime, lay crouched on the steps of the altar, she did not dare to raise her eyes towards Everhard. There was a long silence. At length Everhard said, in a hoarse, broken voice,

"Zoe, you know now the power you have over me. I love you as man never loved woman yet. It is you who have saved both of us this night; I must remain here no longer. God bless you."

"Oh, Everhard, before you go, tell me that you have not lost the esteem you had for me."

"Oh no, no," cried he, passionately, "you are more than mortal!"

The sound of voices and the trampling of feet was now heard, and, for the first time since they entered the chapel, Zoe and Everhard recollected the danger from which they had fled.

A crowd of frightened maid-servants rushed into the chapel, and, with loud cries and great confusion precipitated themselves towards the altar to beseech all the saints in heaven to assist them. Everhard exerted himself to calm them, and committing Zoe to the charge of one who seemed the least distracted, he left the place to render assistance where it might be needed.

The fire had broken out in the room of Zoe's maid, who, as the reader will remember, had been dismissed to bed because she could not keep her eyes open; her candle had not been properly extinguished, and the bed-clothes had been set on fire in the course of an hour or two. She awoke frantic with terror, and rushed to her mistress's room, filling the place with her shrieks. Her room was opposite to the gallery door, and it was thence the flames and smoke were issuing that met Everhard when he burst upon the landing-place. Zoe, suddenly awakened out of her sleep, had only one idea—to save the children. She ran headlong through the thickest of the smoke to reach them by the nearest way, but must have been suffocated in a few moments had not Everhard so opportunely come to her aid.

When Everhard reached the scene of the conflagration, he found that the butler had taken the management of every thing, and shown great promptness and presence of mind. The fire-buckets belonging to the castle, and the stable buckets, had been obtained; the great cistern was luckily nearly full of water, and by passing supplies of water from hand to hand, the fire had at least been kept from spreading. Two rooms were completely destroyed; but, owing to the great thickness of the castle floors, the flames gradually died away, when there was nothing more in the rooms to feed them.

Everhard was very active in rendering assistance; the exertion required, and the danger, were at that moment congenial to his feelings. Soon after he arrived at the scene of action there was a cry that the flames from the window of one of the burning rooms had caught the window-frame of Zoe's dressing-room, which was on the opposite side of the court-yard.

"If that room catches, the missis's jewels and clothes and nick-nacks must go, and what will she do then?" said the butler, in great dismay.

"And, if it once gets there, it will spread to the library and all the oak work, and then nothing can save the place, it will burn like a chip," cried another voice; "our buckets will be no better than thimbles."

On hearing this, hardly waiting to ascertain the nearest way to the dressing-room, Everhard rushed forwards; leaving the servants to their exclamations, he sprang on the burning window-frames, tore down the hangings, and prevented the flames spreading in the room.

Zoe's jewel-box lay on the toilet-table, and the ornaments she had worn that day were scattered about. Everhard collected them all together, and carried them to the boudoir, locked the door, and took away the key with him.

It may be noted here, that when Zoe had leisure and composure to look over her jewels, the only articles missing were a miniature of herself, set as a bracelet-clasp, and part of a small gold chain which she well remembered to have had round her neck on the evening she and Everhard were together. She recollected, too, that in her embarrassment she had snapped it in two. It was supposed that these articles had been lost in the confusion; but Zoe's heart told her where they were religiously treasured, and she placed the broken links that remained of her chain, in the most secret drawer of her cabinet; she prized them far beyond all her other possessions put together.

In due time some degree of order was restored. The maid-servants left the chapel, and hastened to see whether their "boxes" were safe, and whether they had lost any thing.

Zoe went straight to her bedroom, having been first assured by the gardener that the children and their tutor were safe in bed at his cottage, and that his dame had given the poor things something warm to drink, to keep them from taking cold. Set at ease on this point, she locked her door, and left all things in the castle to arrange themselves as they best could.

Everhard had burned himself seriously in his efforts to extinguish the flames in Zoe's dressing-room; but, regardless of every thing, he was indefatigable in endeavouring to restore some sort of order. He despatched a special message to Gifford with tidings of what had occurred, and made every possible arrangement for the comfort of Zoe and the household, in case Gifford should not be able to leave his special jury. At six o'clock in the morning he went to Zoe's maid (the girl whose carelessness had caused all the confusion) and gave her a sealed packet for her mistress, with strict injunctions to deliver it into her own hand.

It was late before Zoe's bell rang. She looked wildly round as she took the packet from the maid.

"Where is Father Everhard?" she asked, hastily.

"He left the castle, ma'am, hours ago. I saw him go down the way towards the wood directly after he had given me that parcel; he looked very pale and strange: no wonder, poor gentleman, after all he has gone through this blessed night."

"What did he say?" asked Zoe.

"Nothing at all, ma'am; only to be very particular you got the parcel as soon as you awoke."

"Very well; you may go. I shall not get up yet; I am tired." And Zoe locked her door against every one.

CHAPTER XII

— · —

When Everhard had done all that was possible towards restoring order in the castle, he found his way back to the silence of his own room; he sunk into the chair he had left, stunned and stupefied. He was in the state of one who has taken opium, not altogether unconscious, but with senses too dull to be impressed by what passes either within or without.

If for a moment a flash of recollection aroused him, it died away into a crowd of voluptuous sensations, that held him like a sleeper on enchanted ground.

The cold light of morning at length broke the spell—he started up in search of writing materials, and wrote a few lines to Zoe, but without feeling fully alive to what he was doing.

He made up the note, and the key he had taken from the door of her boudoir, into a packet, and gave it to Zoe's maid, with strict orders to put it into her mistress's own hands, when she rang her bell. This done, he left the castle.

The deed, which it had cost him a few hours before so much emotion to contemplate, was now accomplished. He had left Zoe, and he had no idea of ever beholding her again. Now that it had come to the act, he felt *nothing*—he could not realise that it was done.

Every thing within him was confused in passion. Thought, feeling, emotion, all molten together, were glowing and heaving heavily below the surface.

The sun had risen when he left the castle, the morning air struck refreshingly upon him; he walked on at a rapid pace, without well knowing whither he went; he was only sensible of the relief afforded by quick motion, to the hot unrest within. Rain in a little while began to descend, and he was soon wet to the skin; still he went on; the need of violent exertion seemed to increase upon him. He had wandered from the direct road, and got among the mountains, he did not know when or how; but walked at random for many miles, insensible of hunger or fatigue.

At length, when it grew dark, he found himself in a wood he knew, about four miles from the college. Wearied out in body and mind, his clothes soiled and torn, he reached the gate. He went straight to his own apartment. The inmates of the college were at supper, so he escaped without seeing any one.

It seemed as if a whole lifetime had passed since he left, instead of three days.

If it were not that night, with its quiet shadow into which sorrow and joy are equally absorbed, stood between men and the need of any long continued thought—they must go mad—but there it is, an unfailing refuge, marking the end of every day, however long or weary.

Everhard flung himself on his bed with an intense feeling of thankfulness, that some hours of oblivion would blot out the consciousness of life.

But the hour of awakening cannot be escaped, and Everhard opened his eyes to feel that life and its requirements pressed heavily upon him.

A quantity of business had accumulated, even during the short time of his absence, and which, for a while, was something to shield him from himself.

But that also came to an end, and he was alone to meditate on what it behoved him to do. He was alone with Conscience, which, dull in its perceptions, and uncertain in its counsels, whilst the act is still to be done, is bitter, wise, and distinct, when all is finished.

Everhard's passion for Zoe, that for so long had blinded his eyes, and blunted every other sentiment, was for the moment suspended, or rather for the moment it was satisfied; and, in that lull of passion, the last three years of his life rose clear and undistorted before him. In a few moments his conscience had scanned the work of years— it had gone back through the whole period of his life—and what was its record?—What did all the costly array of genius, learning, labour, and patience, which had been at work for seven and thirty years, bring forth?

He had learned his religion—to find that he could not believe its creed; he had acquired honours and dignity in the eyes of the world—by a profession he had ceased to esteem; he had cared so much for ease and indolence—that he had allowed himself to be prevailed on, by second motives, to continue in a post where he was obliged to shut his eyes on his own consciousness. At that very moment he was in the act of supporting his life, by teaching what he believed to be false; he had taken charge of young minds, depending entirely upon him, for their direction, and he had neither been honest in teaching them to believe, nor sincere in telling them to doubt: and all this for what? Because, in the first instance, he had shrunk from encountering some vague inconvenience,— because, not seeing clearly what good he would do elsewhere, he had listened willingly to the smooth temporising of those who had never, like himself, had the responsibility of sincere and upright instincts laid upon them; he had wilfully shut his eyes, and been guided by sophistry, which, at the very time, he knew to be sophistry; and now the plating and varnish of expediency had melted off, and the mocking, miserable, worthlessness of that which he had permitted to beguile him of his integrity, lay exposed. There he stood, in the prime and vigour of his life, having acquired, and done nothing with his acquirements—having obtained a clear insight, and applied it to no purpose—having trifled with himself till he had frittered away his integrity—having tampered with his sense of right and wrong, until now, when he was tossed with passion, and needed all his energies to bear him through a temptation that few have escaped unscathed—he found himself left alone, with an enervated will, and bitter self-contempt in his heart.

Even the thought of John Paul Gregory brought shame to him: for he, at least, had used his abilities to the purpose he conceived best, and he was a strong, unscrupulous, worldly man—something at least; whilst Everhard felt bitterly conscious that he was nothing.

The cloud which had shrouded him so long from himself, cleared away, and the meaning of the last few years revealed itself to him.

The days, which as they passed along, had seemed merely vehicles to contain the routine of things which are essential to work the machinery of the world—the common employments which life was given men to transact—days which, as they passed along, seemed so quiet and dreary, now assumed to his eyes the look of reproving angels, whom he had allowed to escape, without constraining a blessing from them. The little motives which had governed him—the little difficulties which had clogged and impeded him, inducing rather than compelling him to go on up to the present day—all stood in array before him. He was like one who, from an eminence, overlooking a tangled and intricate path through which he has been travelling, sees at once all he has done, and all he might have done. He felt as if he were deteriorated to his very core.

The strength and reality of his love for Zoe, made him thus acutely sensible of the falseness and worthlessness of all that had so long influenced him.

One thing, after a while, evolved itself from this chaos, and became clear and plain to him; and that was the necessity of having done with his present mode of life; with as little delay as possible, to emancipate himself at once and for ever from the thraldom in which he was dwelling.

At this juncture a person came to see him on some business relative to the college, and he was called back to the actual working of the things around him. He felt puzzled to know how to begin to disentangle himself; so altogether unconscious that it was any other than what it ought to be; the machinery all worked on without hitch or flaw; all was gentle and well-ordered, offering a practical epigram on the tumult, and uncertainty of his own mind. All things in daily life work thus to a smooth surface. Even the most calamitous and startling events do not fall on us and crush us suddenly, but drop by moment's fall; and each moment has a natural connexion with the one that went before; and each as it comes finds its place beside us and around us, taking its shape gradually; it is not till all is over that we see the event moulded to its full proportion, standing out from the web of the day or year, though at first it looked no different from the common stuff of time. And *this* is the grand difficulty of life; we know not what we do, whilst it is being done, and therefore it behoves us in this dimness of uncertainty, to be sure of ourselves at least: to live each moment sincerely—so that, whatever the result may be, we at least can be at one with ourselves.

Everhard was again roused from his meditations by the physician of the college, who came to tell him that a sudden and alarming change had shown itself in one of the students, who had been unwell for a few days, with what at first seemed nothing more than a slight cold; he had expressed an earnest wish to see Everhard; and the physician added his own opinion that the symptoms had become so severe, that he feared the poor youth could not last many days.

Everhard was dreadfully shocked, and lost not a moment in repairing to the bedside of the sufferer, who was the most promising youth in the college: full of talent, of a singularly amiable disposition, and remarkable for his scrupulous attention to his religious duties. Everhard had, however, remarked an eager unrest about him, as if he earnestly sought, rather than found comfort in them; he had seen that the youth was not at ease in his mind, but he had shrunk from any attempt to dispel his reserve, from the consciousness that he should not well know how to counsel him.

When Everhard entered the room of the patient, he saw him half raised in bed, with a look of intense anxiety and fear upon his features; the mouth was open, and the lips swollen and discoloured. As Everhard approached, a gleam of joy shone from his troubled eyes, but it faded almost instantly. Everhard spoke a few kind words, but the youth did not appear to listen to him, but seizing Everhard's hand, said in a sharp, fierce whisper,

"I sent for you, to tell me how I must die," and he fixed his eyes on Everhard with a look of despairing earnestness, beneath which he quailed. "How", continued the sufferer, "is a living man to face death? Give me some belief, some word of strength, where my soul may take refuge in this extremity. I heard the doctor say, though he was a great way off, *but I saw his lips move*, that I could not live many hours, I *feel* I cannot."

And the poor wretch absolutely swelled with terror at the thought, and shuddered till the bed trembled beneath him.

"Oh, Father Everhard," he continued, "I have dreaded death ever since I can remember. I was a very little child when I was first told what death meant; I did not think much about it at the moment, but the next day when at play, I suddenly recollected what I had been told—that I must die—that it might happen to-day! I threw down my toys, screaming with terror—I did not tell any one what was the matter, for they could not help me, and I did not like to speak of it.

"I grew very anxious to hear about God and religion, but somehow it never went to my heart, I never felt comfort in it, as I heard other people talk of having, and the thought of death was never out of my mind; often have I awoke in the middle of the night, with the horror of death upon me, and have leaped out of bed in a frenzy. All my life long I have lived in the shadow of death; I never was gay or happy for an hour, but the thought of death, at whose mercy I was darkly lying, has sprung up in my heart to torture me. I wonder that every one who knows he is to die, does not go mad."

"But", said Everhard, trying to soothe him, "did you find no comfort in your religion?"

The sufferer cast on him a look of impatience and despair, then, as if the words rent his heart, said in a hard, dry voice,

"No. I have tried to believe it, I suppose I do believe it; but death is a greater reality than religion, and swallows it up. I have prayed, I have tried to live up to its minutest requirements, but it has done me no good—tell me," he exclaimed, with convulsive energy, "*what comes after death?* and then, perhaps, I shall not fear it so much!"

A spasm in the throat came on that almost choked him; it was terrible to see him struggling and wrestling for breath; when it passed, he lay panting and exhausted, the sweat standing in beads on his forehead. Everhard wiped it away, and held a cordial to his lips. The dying youth went on:

"Father Everhard, is there no deliverance? why do all the doctrines I have been taught seem to have no meaning? say something that I can feel. Those words are ringing in my ears all day—'After death, the judgment'—say something to drown their sound. Oh! you know not what it is to be writhing and struggling for every breath you draw, though you know your life is wasting away with each one. You once said a word in one of your sermons that has clung to me like pitch; you said, 'We know not where we shall be, nor what we shall be: Death is the last fact of which we

254

can be certain.' Oh, father! you cannot realise what it is to be swept out of life, to be 'driven into darkness', to be *alone* there, for none may enter into the kingdom of death with us—oh—." And he groaned with anguish and horror.

Everhard had not spoken whilst all this was being uttered, for he felt what a miserable comforter he must be; at length, he gently said,

"The dead who have gone the way before you far outnumber the living; is there no thought to which you can cling? The Church never abandons her children—she does not cease to gaze after you even when you can be no more seen; every week, in the place where you have worshipped, will your name be borne in prayer before that Being in whose hands are the souls of men. You will be in your Maker's hands then, as now. Can you not trust Him?"

"I tell you," said the dying youth, impatiently, "the promises of the Church do not touch my heart, but I fear the threatenings; for I believe those, and they deal with the world after this, a 'land of darkness where no man dwelleth'! But it seems that neither can *you* do any thing for me to help me; I must bear my burden alone."

He turned impatiently and contemptuously away; a spasm came on more violent than the last, there was a fierceness of terror in his aspect, that made him look like a dying beast in agony; gradually the face assumed a fixed and stupid expression, the eyes grew set and heavy; he appeared to sleep.

The doctor and nurse had come up, the former shook his head, and said, "Poor fellow! he will not be conscious again, even if he should awake."

It proved to be so. Everhard remained by his bedside several hours; the youth never stirred. At last he opened his eyes wildly, and called, "Mother, mother!" in a hurried voice; there was a gurgling in his throat—and he was dead. What he had so much feared, had come upon him in very deed.

"Is it with such mysteries as these that I have paltered?" said Everhard to himself, as he gazed upon the body. "I am here, pretending to give these youths the strength to meet an hour like this!"

He felt like a sleep-walker suddenly awakened, wondering and trembling at the position in which he found himself.

That very evening Everhard sent off to Rome his resignation of the presidency of the college, resigning at the same time his priesthood, and connexion of every sort with the Church.

Everhard had no fixed plan of life marked out; now that he was uprooted from the spot where he had been placed by destiny, he lay like a loose weed on the surface of the world. Two ideas only were distinct through all the chaos of thoughts and feelings within him; one was, to put an end at once to his present mode of life, the practical lie he was enacting every day; and the other was, that he would go away, where there would be no possibility of meeting Zoe again.

Early the morning after, Gifford rode up on horseback to the college; he entered Everhard's apartment in great agitation.

"I could not go away, Father Everhard, without thanking you for all your exertions the night of the fire; it has come at an awkward time, but that has happened which puts every thing else out of my head. I am come to tell you myself, because I could not rest in the house whilst they got the things ready. Read that letter; it came last night from your brother. My poor child! my poor Clotilde! she is dying! I cannot make it out—there is more in it than any one suspects—I ought never to have let her leave me—I shall be off in an hour—Zoe goes with me. Till we get to Sutton and see her, we cannot know what had best be done. I see you feel for me, but you don't know what it is to have a child dying—you don't know all that Clotilde has been to me—how my life is bound up in hers."

Tears choked Gifford's utterance; Everhard just glanced over the letter, which conveyed the information already known to the reader of Clotilde's illness, and entreated that Gifford would come over directly, if he wished to see her alive.

Everhard was inexpressibly shocked, now that it seemed likely Clotilde was about to be removed for ever; not the "for ever" of a mortal arrangement, but by the irrevocable separation of death; he felt as if he had never known or valued the gentle child before; he could only press Gifford's hand in silence, there was no comfort to be spoken; he tried to speak of hope, but the words choked him.

"I must go now," said Gifford, controlling himself; "the carriage will be ready to start by the time I reach home. Now, good bye; you are a friend I may cling to a little while longer—you will not be taken from me yet. I shall find you again."

Everhard could not tell him that there was almost as little probability of his seeing him again as that he would find Clotilde. Once more pressing Gifford's hand, he only said, "Now and always, you are sure of my regard, as long as I continue in this world."

Gifford was mounting his horse, and seemed absent and unconscious: he turned, however, before he galloped off, to say, "I will write to you before I sleep to-night, to tell you how I find her."

CHAPTER XIII

— . —

It was late in the day before Zoe left her apartment; when she descended to the drawing-room, the children were there, and in meeting them every thing else was for the moment forgotten. They were enjoying, childlike, the excitement of the confusion that had been produced, and the holiday which was consequent upon it:— every one in the house had something to tell about Everhard's courage and activity. At first it was soothing to hear his name, but it soon became intolerably oppressive, and she once more retired to the solitude of her own apartment.

Early next morning Gifford returned. It was fortunate there were so many persons anxious to talk at once, and to give their own history of all that had happened, or Zoe's abstraction and silence might have called forth some question.

What had passed within the last few days, had removed her beyond the sphere of any thing that surrounded her; she hardly knew whether she was in the body, or out of the body, but remained plunged in a sort of stunned amaze. There was no desire to see Everhard again—that time had not come yet; for, after the first gush of mutual acknowledgment, there is a fullness of satisfaction which desires nothing—it is a lull before the storm of passion rises to toss the soul—a calm, that love never knows after.—At night, however, she was effectually roused from herself by the arrival of Marian's letter, giving an account of Clotilde's illness. When we love one person intensely and happily it warms our heart towards every body who crosses our path, we bestow on them a portion of the tenderness that overflows our heart. Never had Zoe felt such affection for Clotilde as possessed her at this moment; never had she appeared so gentle and lovely, as in her attempts to calm the grief of Gifford, and to suggest hope and comfort. She was as anxious to start for Sutton as he was; and it was quite as much with a view to save him from the torment of waiting inactively till the preparations for their journey could be completed, as with a desire to convey information of their movements to Everhard, that she prevailed on him to ride over to the college, promising to be ready to set off by the time he got back. She was as good as her word, and when Gifford, who had ridden full speed, returned from seeing Everhard, Zoe was standing on the hall steps, waiting for him to hand her into the carriage.

During the whole of the long journey she exerted herself to soothe Gifford, and to prevent his mind dwelling on the painful cause of their journey: perfect success was not to be expected, but she made a day pass over, which would otherwise have been utterly unsupportable.

It was evening when they arrived at the Manor House: Louis and Marian met them at the carriage door.

"Clotilde is better—out of danger," said they both at once, in reply to Gifford's look of speechless interrogation; "but she is settled for the night, and it will be better for her not to know of your arrival till the morning; we are obliged to guard against every thing like sudden motion."

Gifford, with Zoe, followed them to the dining-room, relieved from some portion of the anxiety that devoured him.

When Zoe retired, Marian followed her to her room, and evidently seemed to have something she wished to say. Zoe led the way by asking whether there was any secret cause for Clotilde's illness.

"These mysterious seizures are altogether so different from what I should expect from her, and she used to be so calm and composed that breaking a blood-vessel was the last accident to be apprehended for her."

Marian agreed that it was so, and then proceeded to give the history of the O'Brian acquaintance, and the change that had been visible in Clotilde ever since the last day he came to wish them good bye.

"What sort of a man was this Mr O'Brian?" asked Zoe.

"Why, we all of us were much deceived in him. At first, we were inclined to believe him rather a superior sort of person to what you might expect in a Protestant clergyman. I own I never felt so sure about him as Louis and Mrs Burrows seemed to be; but you know I have almost too much penetration, so in Christian charity, I am obliged sometimes to shut my eyes on my own suspicions; in this case, I regret very much that I did not trust my own judgment, for he has proved to be, as I always thought him, a very shallow man."

"Did he seem to pay much attention to Clotilde?" asked Zoe.

"No," said Marian, "I must say he always seemed to prefer a little intellectual conversation with me; he was not at all given to flirting with young girls, to do him justice; and I cannot help being surprised that Clotilde, with all her propriety of sentiment, should fall ill on account of a man who never professed to care any thing about her; and he a Protestant clergyman besides. I think the natural shame she must feel, disturbs her more than any thing else; but of course I have felt too much delicacy to let her see that I have any idea what is on her mind, for she is not yet in a state to be reasoned with, on the want of modesty of which she has been guilty."

Marian cordially detested Zoe, whom she had been taught by her husband to consider as a highly reprehensible female; so this rabid decorum is to be attributed rather to a desire to let Zoe feel that she had only herself to blame for the breach of feminine etiquette into which poor Clotilde had fallen, and also to prove the vast superiority of a respectable English wife over a flashy foreigner, as she had learned to think Zoe. She did herself great injustice—for, in spite of the disapprobation she now indulged herself in expressing, nothing could exceed the affectionate and gentle kindness she had lavished on Clotilde ever since her illness; but as she told Louis afterwards, she could not resist "speaking her mind rather severely to Mrs Gifford".

When Gifford came to his dressing-room, Zoe lost no time in telling him all she had heard from Marian. They talked it over together, and agreed that total change of scene was the only thing from which any benefit was to be hoped; and Gifford declared that as soon as Clotilde could bear the journey, they would all go on to the continent, and travel about for some months. "Do you, my dear," continued he, "try to comfort the poor child under any morbid notions of propriety Marian may have tormented her with; a pure and loving heart like hers is not to be judged by conventional notions."

"Conventional go-carts are only good for people who cannot walk alone," said Zoe.

"That is not precisely an aphorism I would give by itself to young women," replied Gifford; "there is a value, and a beauty too, in a graceful allegiance to conventionalities that you never perceived; and I am far from wishing Clotilde to be as indifferent to them as you are yourself. Still the strictest conventionality is only the tithe of mint, anise, and cumin—there are many weightier matters of the law: but self-control, however shown, is advantageous to all—to women especially."

"But I am sure I love Clotilde all the better," cried Zoe, "now I know she has so much real feeling. I was afraid it had all hardened down into goodness, that was too transcendental to be used on any body. I quite respect the dear little thing for her struggles to keep every thing to herself; and that odious Marian had best not try to preach any of her maxims in my hearing. Clotilde shall be well and happy again under my auspices."

"God grant it!" said Gifford, sighing.

The meeting next morning with Clotilde was very affecting. She was more composed than could have been expected. She was much altered, and seemed shrunk to the size of a child of twelve years old; her face was as transparent as alabaster, but her eyes and whole countenance wore an expression of womanliness and sensibility they had never worn before.

She was not allowed to speak many words at a time; but she appeared happy that they were come. Home love is never so precious as to those who are bowed down under the burning load of ill-requited love; though there is a remorseful feeling for having preferred the selfish caprice of a stranger to the steady affection which has endured from childhood, which has been as natural and never failing as day and night, and depended on no gratification of vanity or self-indulgence to call it forth.

Zoe was a capital comforter; she understood, or rather practised (for she had no theory) the difficult act of making people really feel better for the hopeful, comforting things she found to say to them:

261

her words did not fall on the ears as words without meaning; people in the most obstinate grief had found themselves believing what she told them. She gave Clotilde the benefit of all her genius that way; and Clotilde, who had nourished her hidden love, and let it consume her heart, found herself making a *confidante* of Zoe the first time they were alone, and pouring out all her trouble, and shame, and devoted affection.

It was as Marian had said, the idea that there was something undefinably shameful in bestowing an unsought love, together with the utter impossibility the poor little thing found in helping herself, which had been by far the most painful part of her sufferings; for she was too unfeignedly humble ever to have expected that such an incarnation of all that was grand and beautiful as Mr O'Brian, should ever have loved her as she worshipped him; but she feared that in their last interview, when he left her at the park gate, he had seen how very much she cared for him; and she had a morbid fancy, that disgust at her want of feminine modesty was the cause of this changed manner the next time they met. She told Zoe all this, though she had fancied it was a thing she could never mention, except in Confession; and she was much relieved and surprised to hear herself praised for the strict propriety and dignity with which she had behaved all through the affair.

It is said that people can always teach others what they thoroughly know themselves—but Zoe could not teach Clotilde her own ideas about the Rev. Horace O'Brian; and she was fain to leave it to time to bring her a right understanding on that point.

Clotilde got well enough to leave the room, and was allowed to walk about the garden; but as the expectoration of blood had not altogether ceased, the physicians would not consent to her being removed.

One morning, about a month after Zoe had been at the Manor, Marian knocked at her door before she was quite dressed, and having been called with the "come in", which is *de rigueur* before either polite people or evil spirits can enter through a closed door, Marian came in with a face of most perplexed importance.

"What is the matter?" asked Zoe.

"Oh, Mrs Gifford! the butcher is just come up from the village, and has brought the news that Mr O'Brian was married this morning to Miss Smith! I could not think what the bells were all ringing for. How shall we break it to poor Clotilde? She must know it some time, and I thought I would just come to ask you what we had best do."

"Thank Heaven! the fellow is fairly married out of hand!" cried Zoe. "I was afraid he would go dangling on and keep us all in suspense; I know Clotilde better than you do; she will perhaps feel a little nervous at first, but she will soon get over it—it is the very thing I would have prayed for."

"Then you will tell Clotilde, for I really don't like to face her, poor thing. I wonder whether Mr O'Brian will send us cake and gloves. I am sure I won't eat a morsel of it if he does. So he must have been at the Rectory: but he has never been near us—a sign of what he thinks of himself in his own conscience. I suppose we shall never see the children again, and I was very fond of them. The stepmother they have got will soon break their spirits, poor things."

Whilst Marian ran on in this way, Zoe made haste to finish dressing, and telling Marian not to wait breakfast for her, she went into Clotilde's room.

The first object that met Marian's eyes when she descended into the breakfast-room was a triangular parcel, done up in writing-paper, and tied with white satin ribbon. Upon the parcel lay a note, directed to her, in the hand-writing of the Rev. Horace O'Brian. She opened it with the intention of being more aggravated against him than ever; but she read it through every word, and at the end said, with something like complacency, "Well, I always maintained that Mr O'Brian was quite a gentleman, at any rate; really it is very polite of him, I must own. Here, my dear, read this—of course you have heard the news." Louis took the note and read as follows:

"Dear Mr and Mrs Burrows,

"I am sure I have your congratulations on attaining the object of my dearest hopes. You, better than most others, know the value of domestic happiness—indeed, 'the fire-side enjoyments' I have shared under your hospitable and truly English roof, will never be effaced from my memory. I am not without hopes, too, that my present blessings may be the means of enabling me to labour in a more extended sphere of usefulness for the good of that Church of whom I am an unworthy member. I have been so overwhelmed with business, that, though I have made many efforts, I have not been able to get to see you, and I am at last obliged to say farewell on paper. Farewell I fear it is likely to be for some time, as I must reside at my deanery, in ——shire. May I venture to hope some day to see you there? My curate will reside at the rectory, and perhaps you will extend to him a portion of the same indulgent hospitality that you have shown me. The children often speak of you and the amiable Miss Gifford. If she be still with you, pray convey to her my kindest regards, and wishing you both every thing that is to be desired, either in this world or the next, believe me, my dear friends,

"Yours most sincerely,

"HORACE O'BRIAN."

"A letter of straw!" said the straightforward Louis, throwing the perfumed note down with a grunt of dissatisfaction. "He has a palavering tongue, and will get on in the world; he may get to be a bishop, but he will never succeed in making himself an honest man, according to my notions of honesty. As to what he says about the Church, it is all fudge. I know what he has said to me about Catholicism times without number, but there's no knowing what such fellows mean by what they say. Put that cake out of sight, and don't let Clotilde see it, and let us have some breakfast."

Zoe was hardly prepared for the emotion Clotilde showed when she was informed that the marriage had actually taken place.

"I am very weak," cried she; "but you will see I shall be better soon. You are very good to have so much patience with me; now go down to breakfast, I had rather be alone for a little while."

This was quite natural, and Zoe indulged her; but she went up again after breakfast. She insisted on taking the note with her to show Clotilde, who read it quite through, and then gravely said, "I think, mamma, you are quite right after all in your opinion of Mr O'Brian—he is very specious, but he is false without telling lies. I am glad he is married, it sets every thing at rest."

"You are a good child," said Zoe, kissing her, "and now come and take a little turn in the garden, the fresh air will do you good."

After this day Clotilde scarcely ever mentioned Mr O'Brian to Zoe; she seemed to have determined on a resolute effort to efface him from her heart; and she succeeded quite as well as could reasonably be expected. They began to talk of their intended journey, and Clotilde began to take an interest in it.

At length the time for their return to Devonshire was fixed for the week following; they were only returning to make the needful preparations for their tour.

Zoe's heart beat with perplexed joy; she had not received a syllable of intelligence respecting Everhard. At the bottom of her heart she was convinced he would endeavour to avoid her—but would he keep his resolution? Should she not at least see him once more before they left England? These questionings were put an end to in a way she had not calculated upon.

Gifford received a letter in Everhard's hand-writing; he read it half through, and then retired in manifest perturbation. Zoe knew not what to think: at length he put his head into the breakfast-room where all were sitting, and requested Zoe to come to him.

Zoe, without being actually sensible either of fear or guilt, was troubled at the seriousness of her husband's demeanour.

"What is the matter?" she asked anxiously, when they reached his dressing-room.

"Read that letter, Zoe. I fear you have been in some degree the cause of his determination."

Zoe trembled violently in spite of herself, and she gazed on the writing for some moments, utterly unable to distinguish a single word.

"Let me take it to my own room," said she, "I cannot make out his hand well."

"No, no, there is no need, I will read it for you."

The letter contained only a statement of Everhard's determination to give up the control of the college, with a frank statement of the private opinions which made it impossible for him longer to remain a member of the Church of Rome, or of any church. It was written in a dry, suppressed tone of detail, as if he had feared to colour the actual facts by the smallest expression of emotion; but at the conclusion all his feelings broke forth.

"And now, my dear, kind friend, adieu. Judge me kindly, for, God knows, the fear of being misunderstood and condemned by you, is the most painful feeling that oppresses me. I cannot live without your esteem—I know your value. Your opinions and belief differ from mine; but, thinking as I do, can I take any other step than the one I am taking? Ought I not rather to fear your contempt for not taking it long since? But though late, I am now under the control of a stronger power than the desire or fear of any mortal thing. A hand is upon me; I must do that which my own soul tells me is right, otherwise my heart would break at this moment;— continue your friendship to me, if you can; I never have been, and never will be, unworthy of it, so help me God!"

There was no mention of Zoe in the whole letter, till within three lines of the end.

"Tell your noble wife that I shall venerate her memory to the last hour of my life. Two such women as she were never created in the world. Tell her to act up always to the mark of what she was intended to be. And now, farewell. Write to me, even if it be in anger—let me hear from you once more. If you can remain my friend after all I have told you, I shall feel that I have been called upon to sacrifice very little.

"Do not mention the contents of this letter to my mother or my brother; I cannot expect them to understand me, and I would rather they heard all from myself."

Zoe had sunk on a chair, her head buried in her hands, and was almost convulsed with the violence of her emotion.

"I fear, Zoe," said Gifford, gravely, "it is you who have encouraged him in this perilous course; you are a free thinker yourself, and you have undermined him."

"He is good and noble," sobbed Zoe, almost choked with emotion, "I am weak and erring; it is he who has strengthened me. What was I before I knew him? He has made me all that is worth any thing. No, no, I have not perverted him, he cannot be perverted."

Gifford had never seen Zoe so moved before, and he hardly knew what to make of it; but he was pleased to see any thing like a display of natural feeling in her. The secret meaning of her last words did not strike him. The idea of being jealous of either Zoe or Everhard never occurred to him; and, indeed, could he have known all that was in Everhard's heart, it would have increased rather than shaken the esteem in which he held him. A man who can stand firm in the moment of unsought and almost overpowering temptation, is not a man to be visited with the conventionalities of distrust and jealousy.

Gifford had once been tempted, like Everhard, and he had met the temptation as Everhard did; had it been necessary for Gifford to know all that had passed in the chapel, he would still have felt as sure of Everhard's loyalty as he did at this moment.

"Well, well, Zoe," said he, "do not distress yourself in this way. I did not mean to blame you, as you seem to imagine; and though I think Everhard misled in this matter, what am I that I should presume to judge another? He is not a man who will act from unworthy motives; thinking as he does, he cannot act otherwise than he is doing. I would not be the one to stay his hand. I shall write to him by this post."

"God bless you for that, Gifford," said Zoe, in a broken voice.

She went to her own room, and no one saw her again for the rmainder of the day. Gifford brought the letter when he had written it to ask her opinion, and also to know if she would add a line.

"No," said she, "only say from me, 'that he knows all that is in my heart.'"

At the time appointed, the Giffords, with Clotilde, left Sutton Manor, but when they arrived at Gifford Castle, Everhard had left the college some days previously.

CHAPTER XIV

— . —

Everhard's preparations for leaving the college were soon completed.

The last day came of his communion with that Church, which, from boyhood, had been the one object round which his hopes grew, and which alone gave a meaning and value to his life; but the things that at a little distance look overpowering, and utterly beyond human strength to endure, come to us broken up into moments and seconds, and those not full fraught with consciousness of suffering, but divided by little details of indifferent occupation, accompanied by intervals of comparative freedom and forgetfulness. Sorrow is not continuous—it comes in bursts and paroxysms of passionate grief, but between whiles there is a lull of the pain, when we are much more comfortable than we would own, even to ourselves; indeed, it is to be questioned whether any ever had a season of affliction without at times accusing themselves of insensibility and want of feeling. Nature is a tender mother to us, and bestows a breathing space of ease in the midst of the sharpest pains.

Everhard was surprised to find that all things connected with his departure went on with business-like precision and quietness; and that the reality was much more tolerable than that vague dread of reproach and querulous remonstrance, which had haunted his imagination like a nightmare. But when all was ready, and nothing remained for him to do but to bid farewell to his pupils and the inmates of the college, he felt that as much suffering was laid upon him as he could bear.

On the evening fixed for his departure, he entered the chapel where all the inmates of the college were assembled for vespers, just as the benediction had been pronounced. In a few words—for he was almost suffocated with emotion—he announced that he was about to leave them. At first they were stunned with surprise, for no whisper of the approaching change had reached them; then an irrepressible sound of lamentation arose from all parts of the chapel; many of the neighbouring peasants were present, who had reason to remember his labours of love amongst them.

Everhard could not go on with his address; he concluded abruptly, and almost rushed from the chapel. The carriage in which he was to travel was at the private entrance gate; he entered it without venturing to look round him; as it rolled away, he buried his face in his hands, and did not again raise his head till he was many miles on his way.

He was then adrift in life, and alone.

He proceeded at once to London, and from there he sent his mother and brother the first intimation they had received of the step he had just taken.

By return of post, he received from Louis exactly the sort of letter likely to be written by a slow, commonplace, conscientious man, suddenly called upon to pass his judgment on a line of conduct amenable to none of his received notions of right and wrong. Louis had never had a doubt in the whole course of his life; his opinions were all packed and portable; to doubt, in matters of faith, he considered a mortal sin, the magnitude of which prevented him from clearly seeing any facts or modifications; he was too much horrified and terrified to use his judgment. Everhard was, in his eyes, transformed into a monster of blasphemy, with whom he could not soon enough disown all ties of brotherhood.

Marian, of course, held an exaggerated version of her husband's opinion—nay, she went so far as to indite a letter, entreating Everhard to return to the bosom of the Church he had quitted, and requesting a statement of his reasons for what he had done; the whole concluded with a luminous exposition of how very easily every body might believe if they only would—consequently, how exceedingly wicked it was to indulge any sort of doubt. "Infidel! being only another name for Satan!"

Everhard found sympathy where he had least expected it. His high-spirited mother, in spite of her strong Catholic feelings, was touched with the sincerity and boldness of her son; indeed, it may be questioned whether she did not love him more now in the day of his shame, than ever she had done in the season of his distinction. Her natural affection for him seemed suddenly aroused. She wrote to him for the first time in her life—not, indeed, approving of what he had done, but exhorting him not to mind what people said, and to be governed by his own conscience. In order, too, that he might not be absolutely starved into any sort of unworthy compliance, she settled an annuity of fifty pounds a year upon him, securing the continuance of it after her death, for she had not forgotten all her habits of business. She enjoyed this act of free will so much, that we fear it quite swallowed up all her orthodox horror at his heresy.

It would be very possible to fill a volume, were we so inclined, with a delineation of Everhard's feelings at this crisis—of his sentiments for Zoe—but those we are not anxious to dwell upon.

There is in all strong affection, a purity, an intense reality, that exalts the individual in whom it burns, to a point of excellence he could never have attained by any other path. Love, rightly conceived in its highest manifestations, ceases to be a mere passion; it becomes a worship, a religion; it regenerates the whole soul; till a man has found an object to love, his faculties are not developed; they lie curled round himself, crude and dwarfed; he may have the capability of becoming great and noble, but he *is* neither, until the divine fire is kindled within, burning up all worldliness, selfishness, and the dross of sensuality, that eat like cankerworms into the beauty of man. Kindling into newness of life all that lies dormant of good and beautiful—melting down all incongruities and littleness—destroying all unworthy aspirations—giving energy to walk through life with unwearied and unfaltering steps—"it makes the reptile equal to the God". The laws of mere conventional morality cannot be applied to a manifestation of the passion like that of which we speak. To love rightly, is the highest morality of which mankind is capable; no man can make an approach to true greatness till he can love—till he has loved.

True love and high morality are the same.

Everhard had lived near eight-and-thirty years; but now he was admitted into an inner world, and he found that all the doubts and struggles and spectres of despair amongst which he had so long buffeted, were only so many phantasms guarding the portals of this true world, wherein springs this fountain of new life. He did not give himself up to a crowd of intoxicating sensation:—it was too firm a reality for childish dreams. Strong passion has strength and sternness in it.

Everhard had not exercised the mastery over his passions all his life to let them at last degenerate into mere sensations and reveries. He had controlled himself in the hour of peril, and God knows that the victory he then carried over himself, had torn him as with wild horses. Rest was impossible for him; he was possessed by an energy like a devouring fire,—he panted for some obstacle against which to contend, to wrestle, to break himself;—he was transformed into another being. His former passive, contemplative habits were now incomprehensible: he felt a burning desire to be engaged in labour which had others, not himself, as the end. He looked round earnestly to find some actual thing to do—an occupation in which he might spend his life. He was full of the energy of self-sacrifice; but how was he to make it available?

Everhard had not been so many years a member of the Catholic Church without becoming imbued with a profound veneration for the practical;—he had pacified his conscience to remaining in communion with her so long after he had ceased to be a believer, because he did not see how he could reduce to practice his newly awakened thoughts and views. And now that he was at last set free—that the world was all before him, wherein to work out and realise the still somewhat vague principles for which he had forsaken a well beaten path—when, after removing the old landmarks, it was necessary that he should be able to "show a more excellent way", and feeling as he did the responsibility involved in setting up as a guide—standing face to face with the great Want; with the consciousness of his own weakness, his own shortsightedness, or rather utter blindness; and feeling that his own earnest desire to do right, his willingness to use up all his gifts of intellect, to spend and to be spent in the service of his fellow-men, was all he had to set against the almost illimitable task—no wonder he was ready to exclaim with him of old, "What am I, that thou shouldst send me!" He had no enthusiasm to hurry him along without feeling the ground under him—no specific panacea for the regeneration of mankind, which he might administer right and left, with full confidence in its infallible virtue. He had only a firm conviction that men might be made better than they are: that each one, even the wickedest and foolishest, has capabilities lying dormant which need only to be spoken to, to be roused: the persuasion that if they could be made to feel that there is the bond of brotherhood between each and all, and that they are not a mere assembly of individuals each set up on his own separate interest—that it is the birthright of each man to have his powers of mind and body developed, and to have the means given to him of becoming all that he has the capacity in him to become. This may seem a very trite conclusion to be dignified with the name of conviction—the only peculiarity was, that to him these things were not a formula, they were in his heart, and had force and energy to influence his life. No new doctrines are ever promulgated to the world. It is only that the world becoming accustomed to the droning of wise sentences, gets not to listen to them, but goes on its own way, not disbelieving—not contradicting—but never minding; till suddenly it strikes on the heart of some that these words have a meaning, and that it behoves to reform life by them; and this conviction sinking into their hearts, they strive to arouse the rest of the world; and these old truths come pouring forth in fiery words till the hearts of those who listen burn within them, and their minds and consciences become enlightened;—these old truths new cut and sharpened, take hold "like goads driven into the wall", and the world goes on with new vigour for a while.

All that Everhard felt had been said over and over again, in better or worse grammar, and in tongues not a few; but he felt the weight of their truth, and set himself thereby to work it out into practice, and to make others feel it as a moving principle. He was too old to have ardent visions of universal happiness, when the world should go on like well-oiled machinery; he did not draw pictures of the millennium he wished to bring about; he had no bright hopes, but rather a stern despair—a resolute knitting together of all his powers and energies—determined they should crack and break before he would desist from his labour, whether it were little or much that he was fated to accomplish.

Everhard was decidedly before his age, and the first step was to try to speak out loud and clear till

> "The word be wrought
> To sympathy with hopes and fears it heeded not."

But in the beginning of every great mortal and practical movement the originators of it have to put their hands to the mechanical drudgery and detail, till more labourers come to the harvest. Everhard, therefore, did not busy himself in literary labours alone for the improvement of mankind.

In a tour he had once made through the mining districts of Wales he had been struck with the horribly ignorant and degraded state of the inhabitants; a set of white heathens, with more than heathen grossness and brutality.

He determined to fix himself at T———, one of the wildest iron districts in South Wales, entirely inhabited by a working population. He chose that wild place because "no man cared for them": there was no place of worship, and if the people were nominally under the care of a clergyman he was many miles distant, and ignorant even of their language. The people knew nothing of religion, nor had any idea of a God except to swear by.

He went down there accordingly, and at first took up his abode at a little ale-house, the master of which spoke a few words of wretched English; he made him understand that he was come to live in the neighbourhood, and, with infinite difficulty, that he wanted to lodge in some cottage where he might have one room to himself. This at last he found in the house of a woman whose husband had been killed by an accident the week previously; she had only two children, who both worked in the coal mines. It was a miserable hovel, built of rough grey stone; the room allotted to Everhard had a sloping roof, the bare rafters were black with smoke; the roof in many places let in the rain; the walls were covered with rough plaster, which had fallen off in many places; there was, however, a tolerable fire-place, for all the work people were allowed what coals they pleased; and, by dint of patience and contrivance, the room was made habitable. The walls were white-washed, the roof was mended, and so were the windows; the floor was cleaned, which was by far the most difficult matter to get achieved, for the woman could not be made to understand the need of it; and, finally, Everhard's modest luggage was transported from the ale-house. The furniture he had brought with him consisted merely of a bed, a table, and a few chairs; but notwithstanding, when they were arranged in the room, and a view of Gifford Castle (which Zoe had drawn for him soon after he came to the neighbourhood) hung against the wall, along with a few other pictures and prints—a bright fire in the grate—there was a look of home and comfort which spoke very highly for Everhard's powers of practical genius. He felt that he had achieved at least the first step of his journey forward. He drank his coffee that evening with peculiar zest, and something almost approaching to buoyancy of spirit.

It would doubtless have been much more agreeable for Everhard if he had settled in a cottage all to himself, but he felt that all attempts to labour amongst the people till he could address them in their own language would be in vain; and, besides, living with a family gave him a sort of influence; over few certainly, but still these few were constantly at hand, and he was brought at once into contact with the people he came to serve, and was one amongst them. It was not long before he could make himself understood in what at first sounded their horrible jargon, and in a little while longer he actually discovered beauties in it. He took his meals with the family, and endeavoured to catch the leading features and habits of the people—He kept no correspondence with the world he had quitted, but gave himself up wholly to the work he had undertaken;—very little he found to attract, and very much to repel. In attempting to ameliorate either the temporal or moral condition of those who cannot help themselves, and who, from the long continued and heavy pressure of their condition, are grown almost insensible to their misery—to endeavour to impart knowledge to those who are so imbruted by ignorance that the human features are almost obliterated by "the mark of the beast"—has in itself nothing attractive; nothing to realise the rose-coloured visions of dilettante benevolence, which must be seduced into deeds of charity by the cant of the "delights of an approving conscience", and the "glow of virtuous benevolence".

True "workers in well-doing" require to be made of sterner

stuff. They who seek to raise men from the degradation we have described, must expect to feel as if they themselves were becoming polluted by the task; they must be prepared to dwell in an atmosphere of thickness and grossness—to be in contact with every thing that is "common and unclean"; they will have to create human sentiments and human feelings before they can appeal to them; they must look for no gratitude or appreciation of their labours to cheer them on, but instead, stupid indifference, or malignant misconceptions;—no "approving conscience", will carry a man through such things as these. Even the hope of thereby working out his own salvation, would hardly be sufficient; nothing but an overpowering sense of the ties of brotherhood with this debased manifestation of humanity—and even then, with the eye fixed on Heaven, and the hands and feet toiling on the earth amidst the loathsome details, nothing could keep a man on day after day, labouring at the practical minutiæ of a grand scheme, amidst all that is uncongenial, distasteful, and unutterably wearisome, with the sense of becoming as it were tainted with the surrounding environment; nothing, we say, could enable a man to go on, but the overpowering conviction of the necessity and urgency of the case, visible in its very loathsomeness. No afflatus of self-complacency can afford support to a man in a course like this.

We once remember to have seen in a gallery of pictures, a colossal head of Christ, by one of the Carracci, the embodiment of all that could be conceived of divine made manifest in man, with enough of mortal suffering and deep human feeling to make it visible and comprehensible to our sympathies. Close beside this there hung a gem of the Dutch schools—a painting of "Boors Carousing"—a scene of unutterable beastliness, minutely detailed. "And was it for the sake of such as these", we exclaimed, "that Glorious One lived and died!" We felt to realise, as if for the first time, the task that was laid upon Him. He could discern the cry of the outcasts "lying in wickedness", though audible only in their wretchedness, rising up to the great God of all, passionately appealing, "Doubtless thou art our Father, though Abraham be ignorant of us, and Israel acknowledge us not; thou art our father. Thy name is from everlasting." He heard that cry, so "He was their Saviour."

That cry is still rising from the earth, and woe to all who close their ears against it.

Everhard dwelt more than a year in that wild place; he soon found that all his hope must lie with the children; it was vain to try to move the parents, so he founded schools where both boys and girls might get humanised; he tried to infuse a spirit of love and fellow-feeling among that wild, selfish, and deceitful race; he went from house to house ministering to the wants of those who were sick, or who had met with any accident. He had to travel considerable distances on foot, for the surrounding district was thinly peopled, and the cottages lay apart from each other, or else in small and distant hamlets; but wherever he heard of want or sickness, there he went.

Gradually something like order and human feeling began to appear in this rude district; his labours among the children told on the parents; who, in their turn, touched by the unwearied kindness he had shown, became more accessible to his efforts to produce more civilised habits amongst them. But this progress was so slow and the improvement so gradual, that nothing but an eye constantly watching could have discerned it at all.

In the evenings Everhard was occupied with writing a work, by means of which he hoped to touch some answering chord, and call out from the midst of the world other workers holding their views.

A mighty engine was, however, even there at work, though he knew it not. The followers of Whitefield and Wesley had long been going about over all parts of England, causing a sensation that has not been known since the days of the first preaching of Christianity, and by far the greatest movement that ever originated in the bosom of Protestantism.

One Sunday morning a coarse, hard-featured collier appeared in the village where Everhard had taken up his abode, and in the open air he began with a loud voice to preach against the wickedness of men. Men, women, and children soon gathered round him. He showed in words of coarse, homely energy, the awful nature of their sins, and the terrible doom of the ungodly and the sinner.

It was a beautiful calm summer morning, yet there were no bright flowers, nor trees, nor any of the sights and sounds that make the glory of summer. But instead, the smoke and flame of the furnaces, the black, sooty atmosphere, the bare hills, and heaps of scoria and shale piled up around, till they nearly hid them in the distance. The wretched hovels of the village, the wild brutish looks of the people, the women with fierce shrill voices, their hair streaming over their shoulders, the men unwashed from their week's labour, enveloped in the smoke of their pipes, sturdy, brawny, and impassable.

The preacher went on, pouring forth his terrible denunciations, with all the minuteness and energy of intense conviction; a fear fell on the whole assembly, dogged men sobbed like beaten children, women screamed and fainted; the preacher still went on, taking no notice of the impression he produced, except to heighten the terrors of his discourse, by declaring that, if the mere tidings he brought were so terrible, the reality would be infinitely worse.

"Who", shrieked he, throwing his arms above his head, "who among you can meet the devouring fire, who can dwell in the everlasting burnings?"—he abruptly concluded his discourse, saying, "if any among you wish to escape this doom, let him come and hear me to-night, when I will point out the way 'to flee from the wrath to come'."

During this morning, Everhard had been absent in a distant district, visiting a man who had been seriously injured by a bucket full of melted ore falling over his legs; he had a great reputation as a doctor amongst the people, it was the only one of his qualities they at all appreciated.

When he returned home in the evening he found a crowd, still greater than that of the morning, gathered round the preacher. Curious to know what could have thus moved his usually stupid flock, Everhard joined the throng.

Though the "way of escape" was the theme, still the punishment of the wicked formed the chief staple of the discourse:—the shrieks of the women, and the groans of the men were redoubled. Everhard was both startled and shocked, he came forward and tried to restore them to composure; he might as well have spoken to the roaring of the sea. He had never witnessed popular emotion—the spectacle of a large assembly of people, moved by a common feeling, violently aroused—and there was something great and fearful in it.

Those men who have dwelled in well digested theories, and well balanced speculations logically arranged, cannot recognise their own principles, when translated out of their trim grammatical sentences, into the fierce energy and jar of action. They are astounded that what worked so cleanly in the theory, should make such tumult and confusion when it begins to take effect.

Everhard had, ever since his arrival amongst this people, been striving to implant some principle of action higher than their brutal passions, and to wean them from their degrading vices. He had made scarcely any impression; here was his wish in the process of being realised before his eyes, and he saw in it nothing but confusion, and a horrible distraction, that he desired at all costs to put an end to: as if such rugged natures could be touched without a convulsion of nature, such as "when the melting fire burneth, and the mountains flow down, at its presence".

It was no passing excitement. The next day there was to be seen the spectacle of shaggy men, writhing under the fury of an awakened conscience; women, sitting in the houses, wringing their hands and weeping bitterly under a sense of wickedness they could not have explained. The eyes of all seemed suddenly opened to a consciousness of the unutterable loathsomeness of themselves and their ways. Many rushed frantically to Everhard for instruction and consolation; but he could do nothing for them:—his calm words seemed mockery to their excited feelings. Everhard could have spoken wisely and well to philosophers, but he did not know how to deal with these rugged ones, under the first tumultuous heavings of the imprisoned life within; he was terribly perplexed, and not a little relieved when towards afternoon, they one and all set off in a body to be present at a field preaching which was to be held at a village about five miles off.

The next Sunday another preacher came to T——. He followed in the track of his predecessor, but he was a man of more refinement and education; he was a pale, placid, grey-haired man, with a peculiar collectedness and solemnity of bearing, as if he were ever pondering on the depths of an inscrutable and awful mystery;— earnestly, as from the depths of his own heart, he told them of his own experience from the days when he was a drunkard, an adulterer, and given over to sin. He spoke like one to whom all the secrets of the human soul were laid bare, and each of his hearers felt as if he were the individual addressed. The whole of the assembly flung themselves upon their knees, demanding with loud cries "what they must do".

The hitherto calm figure of the preacher was swayed to and fro as by the spirit within, the wind lifted up and blew about his grey locks, and his eyes burned like lamps: hitherto he had been almost overwhelmed with the sense of the importance of his mission, now he seemed to rise superior to the crushing responsibility, and not a word that he uttered was lost upon the multitude.

"Such", exclaimed Everhard, as he turned away, "ought the first teachers of rude men to be! It needs words of fire and thunder to rouse them, before they can become conscious of the 'still small voice'."

He did not attempt to meddle with the tide that had now set in. He felt that for the present, the work he had set himself to do, had been taken out of his hand. He therefore contented himself with remaining quietly, in readiness to step in when the discouragement of reaction and fatigue should come on. But he was not at all aware of the trial that was in store for him.

Preachings and prayer-meetings had become matters of regular course. Everhard and his schools and quiet instruction soon became objects of distrust to these fiery-hearted enthusiasts. First, the number of his scholars dropped off; then, the attendance ceased altogether. People under high excitement resent calmness in another, as an insult; and Everhard's conduct during the recent "Revival", as it was called, more than obliterated the memory of his goodness and labours. All the people in the village of T——lent a willing ear to the counsel of the preachers that Everhard should be requested to depart from amongst them.

Accordingly, one night, after a prayer-meeting, which had been held in the house of the widow where Everhard lodged, the two preachers who had first come amongst them, proceeded upstairs to Everhard's room. At first, they looked a little embarrassed, as if they hardly knew how to speak their errand, when it came to the point. At length, as Everhard began to lead the conversation to indifferent subjects, the one who had preached the first Sunday, said resolutely to his companion, "Brother, we did not come here to hold vain conversation, we came to declare our message—to say to this man, that he is endangering the souls of this people, teaching them that they can do good works of themselves, and that they can cleanse their own souls from sin;—a device of Satan's to keep them in his chains! Therefore, we are come", said he, abruptly addressing Everhard, "to bid you depart from amongst us."

"Really," said Everhard, with some haughtiness, "I must be allowed to manage my own affairs, and I shall neither go, nor stay, at the bidding of any man. I have resided here many months, endeavouring to instruct these wretched people; you, apparently, are come with the same intention, and if we can co-operate in our plans, it will be better than opposing each other. Their welfare lies very near my heart."

"We dare not, we may not," exclaimed the other, vehemently, "we may not be unequally yoked with unbelievers; rather do you depart from amongst us, and trouble us no further."

"By what authority", said Everhard, indignantly, "do you interfere with me?"

"By the authority of our Master, who commands us to make our faces as flints, against the snares of the evil one. You are under the curse of Elymas the Sorcerer, when he withstood the preaching of Paul. You are blind to the truth, and wise in man's wisdom. Under the guise of helping their poor perishing bodies, you have sought to slay the souls and pervert the hearts of these sheep, who have been without a shepherd; but their eyes are now opened, and they are enabled to cast your gifts from them, and to bid you depart."

"Yes," cried his companion, taking up the word, "Satan will not willingly give up his prey, and he has placed you here as a hindrance to the great work that has begun; but the prey shall be taken from the mighty, and the lawful captive delivered. Wherefore I order you, in the name of our Master, to depart, and trouble us not."

"I certainly shall not depart at your bidding," said Everhard, calmly; "and as for troubling you, what have I done? and of what do you complain? You, who have drawn upon yourself the odium and ill-usage of the world, shall not follow the example of that world, and persecute others, the instant you obtain the power. And what is it but persecution, to denounce me in your sermons, and to attempt to drive me from my roof?"

"You judge with man's judgment, and we are not careful to justify ourselves. Depart, I say, at once, lest evil befall you!"

They both turned and left the room.

The next morning, when Everhard walked out, there were stern fanatic faces scowling at him round the door; but he passed on without staying to note them. He went to visit the man who had met with the accident; he was now nearly well. He was sitting beside the fire-place when Everhard entered, with his legs raised on a sort of wooden rest, that Everhard had contrived with his own hands. One of the visitors of the evening before was sitting with him; he had a small patch of dust on each of his knees, and he evidently had been working up the invalid to take some desperate resolution; for he scarcely returned Everhard's salutation, but sat like a man waiting the moment to fire a train, and disguised his embarrassment under a more surly manner than usual. Everhard took no notice of the preacher, nor did he show any surprise at the peculiar demeanour of the sick man. He only said cheerfully, "Well, Williams, you seem quite better; a few weeks and you will be able to walk about as well as ever, and go back to your work. I have brought a fine strengthening drink, that will make quite another man of you."

"I trust I am another man, Mr Everhard, and that I have been renewed in heart since you were here; this good gentleman has been telling me grand news—oh, but we are poor perishing sinners!"

"Yes," said Everhard, gently, "and I hope when you get about again, that you will refrain from drunkenness and debauchery, and not ill use your wife."

"There is something more important than all that required," ejaculated the preacher.

"Undoubtedly," replied Everhard; "but that, at least, will be a beginning."

"Well, sir," interrupted the man, glancing, however, to the preacher for support; "I have to thank you for all you have done for me. I can't say but what I should have been badly off without you. I might have died; but the soul must come before the body, and you can do no good to that, for you are yourself an unbeliever, and an enemy to salvation; and I beg you will never come here again. I dare not have aught to do with you, nor your gifts either: so, good day to you—here, wife, help me to the next room."

Everhard was positively confounded; he was a stranger to personal insult, and the language and insolent tone of the man brought the blood tingling to his cheeks; and then the feeling that the heart of the people, amongst whom he had laboured, was turned against him, till they looked upon him as an enemy, was more bitter than any thing he had ever experienced; the tears stood in his eyes, as he said—

"Why, Williams, what possesses you?—When have I ever tried to do you any thing but good?"

"Ah!" said the man, gruffly, "Mr Simpson here can tell you, that Satan knows how to bait his hook, with fair pretences—no, no, don't come here again, or ye may be apt to rue it."

Everhard attempted no further parley, but, first depositing on the dresser the basket he had brought with him, and which contained various things for the use of the invalid, he took up his hat and left the house. As he turned away, he caught a glimpse of the preacher, with his eyes and hands elevated, as if giving thanks for the discomfiture of the emissary of the Evil one.

Everhard walked rapidly away; but at a turning of the road, he was stopped by the wife of the man he had just quitted. She was a coarse, hard-featured woman, and one who had always seemed the most rough and abrupt of all his people. Now, she was evidently under strong emotion. She made a humble apology, though in homely words, for the insult he had received in their house. Everhard assured her of his hearty forgiveness; still she stopped, and hesitated, as if there were something more to be said. At length, twisting her apron, she began:

"If I might make so bold, I would say to you, sir; though it is a sin and a shame for our lips to speak the word, when ye have been more like an angel than a man amongst us; but something has come over the people, and they are not themselves, and I think ye had better just take them at their word, and go: for there is mischief intended against you, if you stay any longer. They talk of pulling down the place ye lodge in, which would be a sore loss to the widow, and a great shame for our people; so ye had better just go, and don't bear ill will to the poor ignorant creatures; we shall not all forget your goodness, and God will bless you for it, some time."

She spoke with great rapidity, looking round every moment, to see if she were observed, then dropped a curtsey, and disappeared round the hill.

Everhard pursued his way quite bewildered with the events of the morning.

When he reached his own dwelling, a group of men and women were standing at a little distance, talking loud and eagerly; they stopped when he came near, and looked at him malignantly. The instant he set his foot within the threshold, the widow, who had evidently been waiting for him, began in a shrill, whining tone to say, that he must go away directly, for that the preachers said he must not stay any longer, and that the people threatened to pull her house down, if she harboured him: and then she complained bitterly of the ill-will she had already got from her neighbours on his account, and that she hoped he would consider it, and pay her accordingly.

"Peace, woman," said Everhard, with dignity, "I will not stay to trouble you any longer. Is there any one who will carry my luggage to the nearest town?"

"Oh ay, there's Griffiths Williams has a horse and cart, if ye would make it worth his while: but the people will be none so fain to let ye have any thing of theirs; however, I'll go see." Everhard went up-stairs to the room he had so long occupied, and began to pack up the few articles he intended to carry away with him: the furniture he left for his landlady, "for, poor woman, how should she be wiser than the rest," thought he:—at this moment the old woman entered, with the news, "that neither man nor boy would touch or carry aught belonging to him, that as he came without their asking, he might go away without their help." There was a malicious grin on her face as she said this, for now she felt sure of falling heir to the table, and chairs, and bedstead.

"Be it so then," said Everhard, "I will carry what I want myself. This furniture I always intended to leave you at my departure, keep it now; there is the money I owe you, and now God bless you, and good bye." He took up the bundle of his things, and lifting it to his shoulder on a large stick, turned to go away.

"You are not going in anger I hope, sir," stammered the woman. "I hope you bear me no ill-will—I am sure—"

"No, no," interrupted Everhard, gently, "you know no better, why should I be angry?" He had to pass through the group of people who were waiting to see him depart. There was not one amongst them who had not cause of gratitude to him; a simultaneous shout of derision greeted him as he appeared, which was followed by a storm of hisses and groans; one bolder than the rest sent a handful of mud after him, and there is no saying how far matters might have proceeded, had not the shrill voice of a woman interfered, crying that they had turned him out, and that now it was a shame, not to let him depart peaceably. It came from the widow, whose heart had been softened by the gift of the furniture, and perhaps also a little, by Everhard's mildness. Her appearance turned the current, for every one was curious to hear all he had said and done, and they prepared for a gossip; but they were disappointed, for the widow went back to her house, and standing with the door in her hand, looked at the people and said, "Well, so you have driven him away, and now ye'll be satisfied, and we shall see if them as comes in his place will be better"; with that, she went in, and shut the door upon them.

Meanwhile, Everhard pursued his journey, in a state of mortification and bitterness of soul, not to be described; towards eight o'clock in the evening, he arrived foot-sore, and utterly exhausted both in body and mind, at an inn in the town of Cardigan.

CHAPTER XV

— · —

When Everhard entered the inn yard he sat down on a little stone bench beside the wall, feeling more utterly miserable than he had ever been in his life before; he had eaten nothing since early in the morning, and the harassing scenes of that day, combined with the immense bodily fatigue he had undergone, were too much even for his athletic frame. He felt desire neither for food nor rest, and wished for nothing except to be left in peace; this, he was not destined to be, for the landlord was too true to his vocation; approaching the place where Everhard had been sitting for some time almost insensible to every thing that passed, he twisted his white apron round his waist, and putting his hands into their respective pockets, he stood for a minute considering how he should address him; then, without asking what he would have or whether he would come into the house, he only said, "You've just come in time for supper, and we can give you a good bed; you'll have come a good step seemingly."

As Everhard did not notice him, he took up the bundle which had fallen off the seat, shook him by the shoulder to rouse him, and told him to come into the house.

Everhard reluctantly obeyed, and the landlord seeing that every thing was left to his discretion, felt that it would be against his conscience if he were not to give his almost insensible guest, the supper that would figure the handsomest in the next morning's bill: which after all was the best thing that could possibly be done, and Everhard revived enough after it to ask for a bed, where he forgot every thing in deep sleep, which held him fast bound till it was too late on the following day to continue his journey.

Nature is very good to those who are dutiful children, and live according to her precepts; she can minister to a mind diseased and "erase a written trouble from the brain", or at least, do a great deal towards it. Everhard only awoke to a state of semi-consciousness, in which he ate and drank whatever his host put before him with a dreamy sense of satisfaction: he seemed wrapped round with poppy and mandragora, for no recollection of his recent annoyances crossed his mind till he arose the next morning, feeling strength and energy enough to encounter any thing and every thing.

Our philanthropy blushes whilst we write it; but the predominant feeling in his heart was gladness to be relieved from the need to live amongst barbarians, trying to love and civilise them. We fear the zealously self-denying reader will be shocked at this; the only plea in mitigation which can be urged, is, that the last crowning grace in doing good, is to allow the persons concerned to profit by it their own way; and if it really be their welfare that we are labouring at, we can bear to see it accomplished, even if our efforts are set on one side; a tolerably delicate test this, of our motives for activity. Everhard felt that the wild people he had laboured amongst were likely to get much more good from the ministrations of the field preachers, than from his, and he felt no sort of wounded vanity in seeing the labours of others more successful than his own: he only looked round to discern in what other sphere his services might be available. Nevertheless, there is no denying that he was very glad his duty seemed likely to lie amongst educated beings, with whom he might hope to feel some companionship.

He paid his bill and mounted on the top of the stage-coach that passed through the town to London.

Arrived there, his first care was to write to Gifford, giving an account of all that had befallen him; he knew that Zoe would see his letter, and that it would say to her all that was needed.

His next business was to find a publisher to give to the world the book he had written during his sojourn in the wilderness. This was no difficult matter, thanks to his widely extended reputation, and the report that had gone abroad that for secret reasons he had left the communion of the Church of Rome. Curiosity was on the *qui vive* to see the work that was now announced, the public making sure that it would thereby be enabled "to pluck out the heart of his mystery".

It was published at last, and with wonderfully few delays and vexations.

If Everhard had once longed to get among educated beings, he was now tempted to wish himself back amongst his "barbarous people". Words can hardly express the storm that burst upon his head.

The book was in the hands of every reading person almost as soon as it was published; and one simultaneous yell of horror and execration followed!

The periodical press was let loose against him; preachers of all denominations warned their hearers against his pestilential doctrines; he was indicted for blasphemy by the Society for the Suppression of Vice; he was threatened with a prosecution for treasonable and seditious tendencies; every lie that hate, rage, and calumny could invent was propagated in every direction. His name became on a sudden a byword and term for opprobrium. It was first insinuated, and then asserted, that he had been expelled from the Church of Rome, stripped of his gown, and degraded from his priestly office, for foul and monstrous crimes. The Romish clergy, indignant at his desertion, raised their voices to swell the outcry against him. Not in England only was the tumult raised. The name of Everhard had been known and reverenced all over the continent; and as wide as had been his reputation, so wide now spread the hatred and abuse that was lavished upon him.

In the heart of every man whether savage or civilised, there is a chained devil; but when any thing occurs to rouse its malice and fury, the civilised devil is the most terrible to deal with.

Everhard's bold heart almost quailed under the storm he had conjured. He was not prepared for it, he had not the least idea that he was uttering aught but the most natural truth. And he imagined that the words he spoke were so self-evident that they needed only to be said, for all men to give ear to them! The *naïve* and unconscious simplicity with which he delivered doctrines that made the hair of all who heard them stand on end, would have seemed comic to any one who had been cool enough to observe it. Poor Everhard had never once considered whether he were shocking prejudice or not. It had more than once struck him that he was uttering common-place truisms, and he had accordingly thought it right to make a grave apology for his want of originality. He was perfectly thunderstruck at the commotion he had raised, and was inclined to think all the world had suddenly gone mad.

It may seem incredible in these days that one book should ever have excited so much attention, but it must be remembered those were the palmy days of "Legitimacy" and "Divine Right"; consequently, when it was a point of religion to believe that whatever was, was right. Any one who then dared to lift up his voice against the existing order of things, became a marked man. There had been as yet no sympathy called forth for such daring; the people joined in the outcry, "deriding the tears of their prophets".

The first preachers of any great truth, they who first attempt to make it articulate and intelligible to the world, must expect to be martyrs for their pains. They who lead a "forlorn hope" must be prepared to fall in the breach, and with their bodies prepare a way for those who follow to pass over in safety. They who are amongst the first who listen to the preaching of a newly detached truth, are hated and persecuted as enemies to the human race. When that truth has made itself a place in the consciences of men, then, they who do not embrace it, are persecuted in their turn. The duty of mutual toleration is almost the only truth all parties are unanimous in refusing to recognise.

It cannot be denied that very good advice had been given by Everhard in his book, and that the public had much better have followed it, than employed themselves in abusing him for telling them what he intended for their good. However, it was a fine opportunity to try his own prescription upon himself, and he did not find that his philosophy at all hindered him from feeling very miserable under the ban of social reprobation to which he was consigned. None of us can live without the sympathy of our fellows.

CHAPTER XVI

— · —

The Giffords were all ready to leave England in a few weeks. Zoe hastened the preparations, for now that Everhard was really gone, all her energy of self-control seemed prostrate. The light that had brightened her life was taken away—and all was chill and desolate. It was well for her that the active exertions required to get all arrangements made for a prolonged absence from England, left her not a moment for musing. She went about with a weight indeed at her heart, but she could not stop to cherish or brood over it.

Their plan was to travel up the Rhine, through Switzerland, the Tyrol, and some parts of Austria, then to pass over into Italy. They were to take up their abode at any place that struck their fancy, and remain for weeks or months, as the case might be; in short, as Gifford said, for once they were to have no control except their own inclinations. The boys were to travel with them; but there was a scheme for placing them at some of the German schools, and coming back for them before they went into Italy.

Gifford furnished himself with excellent letters of introduction, in case they should feel disposed to enter into society; but at first, change of scene was all they wished for.

To those going abroad for the first time, the people who live in foreign countries are much less objects of interest, than the countries themselves. Nothing could be more delightful than the programme of the whole affair; but two hearts among the party were heavy with sorrow, and that was more than enough alloy to prove that schemes of enjoyment oftenest take their rise in suffering, and are intended for distraction rather than pleasure.

The party crossed to Ostend, and for several days travelled

without remaining more than a night in one place; but the weather was lovely, and the scenery most beautiful. It is not in the heart of man to resist the healing witchery of nature. The sight of a beautiful country—the fresh pure air—can efface nearly all the ordinary sorrows to which mortality is liable, and even those that nature cannot banish, she makes fainter. There are times, certainly, when the brightness of all around seems a mockery, but that passes away; and even in the heaviest afflictions, there are moments when we are fain to confess, "that light is sweet, and a pleasant thing it is for man to behold the sun".

Zoe's heart turned again and again to the memory of Everhard. In the midst of the prodigal display of loveliness that surrounded her on every side, a sense of intolerable loneliness fell on her, and "she turned from all it brought to all it could not bring". Still, as she lived more and more with scenes of grandeur and beauty, with no object to come between herself and nature, strength and health arose within her. Her own egoism, her own sensations, were swallowed up: she stood before the unveiled face of nature, and the "awful loveliness" overshadowed her whole being. A humility born from the constant presence of greatness, sprung up, she no longer murmured at "wandering companionless" through life, she forgot herself; it was not in expressions of humility, lip-deep, for she was not conscious that she had become humble; but she ceased to think of what she was, or what she was not.

After this, came the time when the recollection of Everhard, of the noble love of which she was the object, became the life-spring of her soul; she did not wish her lot differently cast, she could rejoice in his love, without repining; it was her most precious heritage; she loved him nobly and greatly, and to make herself worthy of him, was the aim she placed before her. The more a love is purified from mere emotion, and does not depend on the intoxicating sensations of presence or absence, it becomes dignified into a religion; nothing poor or trivial can live along with it. All coquetry, vanity, desire of admiration, were burnt up out of Zoe's heart. Her beauty was more dazzling than ever; and it seemed as if her powers of mind had been increased a hundredfold. A massive simplicity, took the place of her former meretricious display;—a

magnanimous transparency of character, made her appear surrounded as with a halo of moral beauty.

She was like one of Plutarch's women;—for she had much more
of high pagan virtue about her, than any thing approaching to
modern Unitarian morality.

She found companionship where she least looked for it. Gifford,
with his honest and gentle affection, had a sympathy with her
higher intellect, that she was far from expecting; but there is an
elective affinity in all truths, they make the weakest akin to the
strong.

Zoe did not *love* Gifford, but she lived more happily with him,
than she had done since their marriage, and felt a real regard and
respect for him. As to Clotilde, she took refuge in her religion; the
same process which made her mother-in-law a contented strong-
minded woman, only increased Clotilde's desire to leave the world,
and enter on a religious life, in which she might be absorbed into
her religious duties. Her gentle heart had received a wound, from
which it would never recover to become strong and happy. Her
only source of pleasure during the tour, was in going into all the
churches and small way-side chapels they passed. The splendid
music of the cathedrals, raised her soul to heaven; and the wild
scenery in which chapels are often placed exalted her imagination,
till her devotion seemed scarcely that of a being belonging to this
world.

They remained for some weeks at Como; and Clotilde wandered
about all day on the borders of the lake. A chapel was near the
house they occupied; at night she would go and kneel before the
altar, often remaining there till day broke.

There is a comfort in the Catholic religion, that soothes a
wounded heart, as the unhappy themselves only know. All modes
of human affection transfer themselves without difficulty to religion:
they three find a haven and refuge for the frail beating heart that
contains them. There is so much of human feeling in the Catholic
religion, so much that makes itself tangible to human sympathy,
that the mourners seem to be restored to the very objects of which
they have been bereft.

The Giffords travelled through Italy, and reached Rome to be in
time for the Services of the "Holy Week". All Clotilde saw during

this solemn festival, the splendour, the music, wrought up her feelings to the highest pitch; every thing that was in the world seemed coarse and drossy. She looked back with something like remorse to her brief dream of passion;—nothing but the pure ecstasies of adoration and self-dedication seemed worthy of her aspiration. Even her tenderness for her father seemed deadened. She was weaned from all that was earthly; but such a sweet, unselfish deadness to all the world, was surely never seen: it was the indifference of an angel, or a seraph.

When she broke her purpose to her father he was in a sad strait, unwilling to oppose the decided vocation of his daughter for a religious life, and yet very grieved to resign her to what, so far as he was concerned, would be a living death. With infinite sweetness and patience she laboured to overcome his objections, she prevailed on Zoe to use her influence. Her confessor (a man who had also the spiritual direction of a convent) used all his eloquence, and at length a tearful consent was obtained from Gifford.

Clotilde entered the Convent of Santa ——, on her noviciate, and the family remained at Rome during the whole period.

At length the day of her Profession came. Gifford had clasped her in his arms for the last time, had felt her his child for the last time. His spirits had sunk dreadfully, even since she first entered the convent, and he had suffered the more, as he fancied it was sinful to resist such a distinct call from Heaven. His health had given way in the struggle, though no one suspected how deeply it was affected.

On the day of her Profession, he had scarce strength to support himself to the church where the ceremony was to take place.

To indifferent spectators, the ceremony is almost overpowering, and to a tender father, struggling between a desire to retain his child, and a sense of the holiness of the vocation she is obeying, the suffering can only be conceived by parents in a like position. But when she lay on the ground covered with the black veil, and the chorus of the nuns rose in thrilling melody, realising dreams of the songs of Heaven, Gifford's fortitude was overpowered, and he was carried from the church in a deep swoon.

The ceremony ended, and the long procession of sisters passed into their convent;—the gate was closed, and the gentle, tender-hearted Clotilde, knew not that her father was even then dying.

When Zoe could leave the church, she hastened to the place where Gifford had been removed. She was shocked at the alteration apparent in his countenance. "It is all over, is it not?" said he, as she approached him.

"Yes," replied Zoe, sadly; "but she knows not of your illness; dear child, it will be a sad trial not to be able to come to you."

"No, no, Zoe;—it is all arranged by infinite goodness. I was unwilling to resign my child to the service of God, and now he is taking me away from her. I have not even had the merit of the sacrifice;—may he pardon the unbelief and the slow-heartedness of his servant, and accept me in my last hour, amen!"

The physician here appeared, and declared that there must be no speaking; taking Zoe aside, he informed her that the patient was reduced to such a deplorable state of weakness, that he feared he could not rally. Zoe could not account for this sudden manifestation of debility, but the physician told her that it was not uncommon in old people, and even in those of middle life, mental uneasiness, combined with health that was not strong, sometimes prostrated suddenly, where no definite disease existed.

Zoe, who had hitherto been incredulous of danger, was seized with horror; she reproached herself bitterly for her blindness, during so many months. Now that she seemed on the point of losing him, she found that Gifford was much dearer to her than she had ever imagined. Gifford was much affected by her tenderness and grief, but he had for some time felt a presentiment that he should not live much longer, and had silently arranged all his worldly affairs. He called Zoe to him the morning after Clotilde's Profession, and put a sealed parcel into her hands. "This is my will," said he; "I know that all I have requested will be complied with, and you will find I have not been insensible of your worth. Oh, Zoe! I have but one wish for you, which is that you would think of religion as you ought—you will need it in your last hour. Whilst you live a very little religion seems enough; but believe me, it requires a great deal when you come to die."

He was too weak to speak more, and soon after he fell into a sleep, with Zoe's hand in his. In the afternoon the priest came and he took the last sacraments; he lay afterwards for a long time apparently insensible to all that passed; at length opening his eyes, he fixed them on Zoe, and articulated with difficulty, "Tell Clotilde I desire her prayers, tell her that I send my blessing, and that I die happy." He seemed for a few moments in prayer, and then his lips ceased to move, and half-an-hour afterwards he departed without a struggle. He died so peacefully that those around him could not tell the exact moment when he ceased to breathe.

After the funeral, Zoe opened the paper he had given her. It was a condensed abstract of his will, made before he left England, and simply worded, in order that Zoe might have no difficulty in comprehending it.

The children were left with many testimonies of esteem to Zoe's sole management, executors and trustees were named for the property which was charged with an ample jointure for her, together with as much of the furniture of Gifford Castle as she chose to take, along with certain articles of valuable plate, which were specified. A certain sum was to be allowed to her out of the estate for the board and education of the children, and a singular request was introduced, carefully guarded from being in any way a command: it was, that if it could be arranged, his great desire was that his sons should reside under the same roof with their mother until they were married. Several touching marks of affection were scattered through the will, which affected Zoe deeply, and she bitterly reproached herself for having been so insensible to his value. She resolved, however, her future conduct should show her worthy of the trust he had reposed in her.

Affairs required her speedy presence in England. She took an affectionate farewell of Clotilde in the convent parlour, after which she and the boys left Rome, and proceeded on to England.

ZOE

VOLUME III

CHAPTER I

— · —

John Paul Gregory Marston had prospered in the world since last
we met with him. He had become rich by the death of various
relatives, he had risen in the Church, and contrived to make himself
much more comfortable in it than ever he had expected. His talents
for business, his love of bustle and excitement, his genius for
managing his own intrigues and those of other people, had recommended him to the attention of the higher powers. Though English,
he liked neither the country nor the customs; Italy was his delight.
He had sufficient credit to get himself appointed one of the resident
bishops in Rome; and he was often employed on secret missions
and in various confidential affairs.

He was as great an *athée* as ever; but instead of ridiculing the
Church and her doctrines as formerly, he now spoke of sacred
matters with the most scrupulous and decorous consideration: in
fact, he felt it incumbent upon him to treat with respect a Church
which had behaved so exceedingly well towards him. He contrived
to enjoy almost unrestrained licence of conduct, so that the fierce
and terribly sincere invectives which formerly used to break from
him, were not now needed as a relief to the unbearable constraint
of his profession. He never disguised from himself that he was a
hypocrite and a profligate, but he did not consider it necessary to
take the whole world into his confidence. His self-complacency was
not in the least ruffled by the consciousness that he was a hireling,
body and soul; on the contrary, he felt a real satisfaction in forcing
those who he knew saw into his real character, to treat with him as
an honest man. He never attempted to put a varnish of integrity on
his own conscience, for a villainous sort of sincerity lurked there in

spite of all his sins; but he would tolerate nothing short of the most immaculate reputation from the world. There was a tacit conviction on the mind of every body who knew him, and nobody could say they were exactly imposed upon, yet no one spoke ill of him; his great ability was a safe common ground on which all his debatable qualities were merged. After all, when a man is endowed with real strength of character, when he is able and decided in all he undertakes, has an object and pursues it (no matter whether the object be good or bad), he is to be recognised as a man of character, and he is one who has the stuff of virtue in him though it may be shown in a perverse sort of fashion. Strength is the main element of virtue. The very wickedness of a steady purposed, strong minded man, is worth more than the virtuous tendencies of a weak one, that never grow to be actions, but are mere feeble indications; they have no principle within them, and the merest accident may convert them into active vices. Weakness is the only state for which there is no hope, either for this world or the world to come.

John Paul Gregory was certainly not to be called a good man, but he had the seeds of redemption within him.

He was in London at the time Everhard's book made its appearance; he had come over on a private mission, which at that time seemed of great importance, but which has long since been consigned to the impenetrable secrecy of oblivion. Attracted by the name, he made enquiries after the author, and found that it was indeed the very Everhard who had been his school-mate and fellow-student at college. They had long ago lost sight of each other, but John Paul Gregory still entertained a latent regard for the man so utterly unlike himself, and whom he considered as an amiable visionary who would never do any good with his talents. There was a boldness, a magnanimous temerity, in Everhard's book, which excited his sympathy, and he resolved to pay his old comrade a visit in the very teeth of episcopal decorum.

He accordingly drove in state to the obscure street where Everhard lodged—for he gloried in never seeming ashamed of any thing he did.

He was shown into a little dark parlour on the ground floor; the house was on the shady side of the street, and though it was a reasonably sunny day elsewhere, not a glance of the sunlight visited any thing except the chimney-tops on the opposite side.

Everhard was sitting over the small fire, ill in body and depressed in mind. He had not heard the bustle in the street, nor had he paid any attention to the bustle in the house, until the door was thrown open, and the handsome, portly, and somewhat blustering, form of John Paul Gregory entered, seeming to fill the little space between the four walls, full and overflowing.

Everhard actually shaded his eyes with his hand, to see if it were really a vision of this world that stood before him. John Paul Gregory enjoyed his perplexed look of astonishment, and, grasping his hand, cried, "You see it really is I myself. I only heard you were in London this morning, or I should have found you out before."

"How you found me out now", said Everhard, "is a marvel; you really are the kindest-hearted fellow that ever lived. I can't tell you the good it does me to see you;—how did you get to know where I was?"

"I inquired, to be sure," replied John Paul; "when people really want a thing, they can always get it; and the instant I knew that you were to be seen, I wanted to see you, and here I am in consequence."

The beginning of conversation between two people who have not seen each other for a length of time, is always tumultuous; and, for the first half hour, many things were asked and told, and nothing was finished. John Paul Gregory told Everhard that he was a bishop and a sort of ambassador; but both parties were too impatient to go into details.

At length, when the first ferment had a little subsided, John Paul said; "Well, but Everhard, you have not explained how it has come to pass, that such a sober person as yourself has set up a character that is frightening the whole world from its propriety."

"Yes," said Everhard, "I almost wonder at your daring to come near me."

"Why, faith, perhaps the daring gave a relish to my desire to see you. The folks at home may just say what they like; if they make a grievance, I shall tell them I came to bring you back to the right way. But seriously, what have you been doing? I heard that you had left the Church, but nothing further. Do you remember the talk we had the first night you came to the college? Well, I have grown wiser since then, but you—you have progressed into one of those wise fools, whom the world always takes great credit to herself for having produced, after she has starved them to death, or worried them to death, with hard words;—broken their hearts in short, which is the only style of persecution tolerated in these days. Tell me all about yourself, and as we shall get on all the better for having some thing to do, give me a cup of the coffee you used to be so famous for making long ago. It is the only thing I drink.—But what a confounded noise! I should have expected that such a place as this would have the virtue of being quiet at all events!"

The fact was, that the sight of a carriage had warmly excited the curiosity of all the inhabitants of that street: and the rumour that it was "the Pope's own carriage", had stimulated their Protestant sensibilities to the highest pitch; by this time, mud and stones began to be thrown, and their orthodoxy would have proceeded to very inconvenient lengths, had not John Paul made his appearance amongst them; his good-humoured English look made a favourable impression upon the mob—the offending vehicle was allowed to drive off, a few dextrously interposed good words and jokes from John turned the current in his favour, the people began to cheer, and wisely retreating at the climax of his popularity, he retired into the house, and rejoined Everhard.

The coffee was ready. "Well now, Everhard, your history!" said John Paul, as he sat down. "Don't be diplomatic about it, tell me all the secret passages."

"You will hardly understand me, John Paul," said Everhard, smiling.

"A great compliment to my discernment, certainly, but pray let me try."

Everhard proceeded to tell him all that could be told; but, of course, the most important part remained of necessity unsaid—a proof that the truth is never to be extracted in words; the most sincere and truth-telling men can only speak a part of it—indeed, to tell all things exactly as they are, would often require more imprudence than sincerity:—a want of reticence is not truth.

When Everhard came to a conclusion, John Paul said, "Well, you must be left to fate, for clearly there is no use in Providence concerning itself any more about you. You have thrown away advantages which might have raised you to the highest dignities, and surely, even your appetite for doing good might have been satisfied by the legitimate opportunities which would have fallen to your share; why can you not apply your talents to ends that are already shaped out, instead of working in the dark, wasting both your time and talents upon Utopian experiments and schemes for regenerating the world, that would be scouted as fantastic even in Utopia itself, believe me; and instead of spending your strength in the endeavour to make men better, just employ one half the trouble in trying to make the best of them as they are; you would not only get more credit for your labours, but the rogues themselves would feel infinitely more grateful to you.

"There is such a press of business in the world, motion is generated till the whirl is enough to set the world in flames; and any one who is mad enough to want to stop the whole machine, in order to try some new patent wheel, to make it roll more smoothly, will only be thrown down and trampled to death for his pains; and the machine will go on in its old way all the same.

"Do you think that theories logically shaped beforehand, will ever shape the facts that come after? In short, my dear fellow, I cannot bear the idea of your wearing your life out for nothing in this way. Just leave this 'friend-of-man' nonsense, and consent to do some practical good in your generation; cast in your lot with mine, and trust me, you shall find plenty of employment for your talents after your own heart. You shall command all my credit to reconcile you to the heads of the Church, we will make easy terms with your conscience; leave this horrible hole, and come home with me.

"I am making no vague promises, I am assured that I can do all, and more than all I say. The Church would rejoice to get you back again, and your reconversion would be even a greater credit than if you had continued an unaltered allegiance; there would be more orthodox joy over the repenting sinner, than over ninety and nine dutiful sons like myself. I will not let you go back to the ranks I promise you, before I have secured your own terms; so you see you will risk nothing. Your consistency shall not be endangered till it is made clearly worth your while to abandon this *canaille*, whom you have so unaccountably taken it into your head to endeavour to raise to the rank of Men in the scale of creation. Believe me, who have to work with mankind, that no infusion of noble sentiments, will take effect on those in whom they do not rise spontaneously. That which is vice will remain vice still, when you have done everything; and as to calling such pitiful wretches brothers, where is the family likeness? I could say to you, as the slave-owner said to some mad methodist who asserted that negroes were human beings like him, 'Do you mean to tell me these niggers are men!—Only look at their *calves?*' It is of no use getting up a sympathy for people who cannot help themselves. Those who have any good in them, will raise themselves, without any need for you to sacrifice yourself to preach the gospel of love and fellow-feeling; those who make themselves of use, always get consideration in the world, quite as much as they have any right to expect."

"I have no patent scheme for regenerating the world as you seem to fancy," replied Everhard. "But I would have each man recognise the necessity of being true in whatever he does, if he would obtain any enduring good. I have no creed to preach; but I would have each man honestly profess that which he really does believe, and not lay out his whole soul to obtain a 'piece of silver and a morsel of bread', by pretending to be what he is not.

"You say if I will go along with you, I may gain opportunities of usefulness which are sealed to me in the position I now occupy. Too long I allowed myself to be blinded by maxims of expediency, too long I listened to second motives, and remained year after year in a position where I was obliged to act that which to me was a daily lie—because I persuaded myself there was this or that little bit of visible good I had it thereby in my power to transact. Believe me, John Paul, much that is not palpable to the senses of men, has a deep and permanent influence upon their souls, both for good and bad.

"It is not the obvious and tangible which is the all-important;— that which informs the spirit of man, is more to be accounted of than that which acts upon him bodily. Any way, we are not made responsible for the result of our actions, but we *are* responsible for bringing a pure mind and an earnest sincerity to every work we undertake, whether it be great or small;—it is only in proportion to our individual truthfulness, that the evil resulting from our blindness and incapacity, is not accumulated to our condemnation.

"I may seem to you to be wasting my energy in baseless schemes—to be doing nothing, in short. Certainly I have no result to show you for my labours—but I have at least made myself a true man. I have emancipated myself from that so far I have reason to consider false;—I am able to have faith in singleness of motive, and to tread under foot all temptations to expediency. I am thankful to have been enabled to make that which is within me, light, and to walk in some degree according to it; and I can truly say, that the price I have to pay in worldly comfort and reputation, to attain this, is not worthy to be named, though, till I go down to the grave, I must feel humbled at the recollection of the years during which I walked in the paths of expediency.

"What the work will be that I may be called upon to perform, I know not. It is possible that I may have no visible success in my teaching—still I must go on;—a way will be opened for me; and even if it is appointed to me to sit apparently idle, I am willing to do so. I can submit to think that my labour is not indispensable. He who is the ruler of all things, has all means in his hand. If work be given to me, I am willing to spend and be spent for it;—if nothing appointed for me, it is well also. 'They also serve who only stand and wait.'"

"Everhard," said John Paul, as he rose to depart. "You are only an elaborate fool, with all your wisdom. You talk like a rational lunatic; the world would just stand stock still, if you and such as you, had the management of it. Believe me too, it is only when things come to a stand still, that danger is to be apprehended; so long as they go on, no matter how—things will not fall to dissolution as you call it; but come, I have been talking in the vague quite as much as I have reproached you for doing. I cannot expect you should give up your *beaux principes* for general propositions; and whilst you have been talking, I have been thinking what actual and specific thing I can offer you.

"Come along with me, leave your goods and chattels a legacy to your landlady. There are certain private negotiations on foot with Spain, a special envoy is to be dispatched in a very short time, and you shall accompany the concern as secretary. In spite of all the

303

foolish clamour that has been raised, you are known to be a man of talent and practical ability. I know I can obtain the appointment for you, because I happen to be able to give value received. Once set going, you must infallibly rise; and as you are no longer a Catholic, there will be no obstacle about religion; all the compromise that will be required of you is, '*tais toi, Jean Jacques, on ne te comprend pas*'; and you know Solomon himself, your great oracle, says, 'there is a time for keeping silence'. Will you say 'yes' at once and come along with me to dinner?"

"John Paul," said Everhard, "you are a staunch friend, but you cannot help me, you must leave me to my own ways. The frank kind-heartedness you have shown this day has cheered my heart, and you must be content with having done that. Independently of everything else, the post you offer would not suit me, nor should I suit it; and besides," continued he, smiling, "you have overlooked the terrible impeachment it would be on your sagacity, to put an unbroken reformer into government harness! You must leave me as you found me, and yet not altogether so, for the sight of your friendly pleasant face has cheered me more than you can tell."

"Pshaw!" interrupted John Paul, impatiently, "then the devil may take you for an obstinate—but no," added he, softening, "you're a deal too good for the devil or any of his servants, for I think nearly all the people I have to deal with belong to him—myself amongst the number. But I can stay here no longer talking sincerity, I must be off to play Punch and Judy at a grand diplomatic dinner. I leave London in a fortnight, and I shall not be able to see you again, I know, so it is of no use making promises. God bless you, and if ever you should grow wise enough to do good to yourself, let me know, and it shall go hard but I will serve you."

He grasped Everhard's hand once more, and wrapping his cloak round him, he strode off in the gathering dusk.

"What a fine fellow he is, in spite of every thing!" said Everhard to himself as he gazed after him.

That night's post brought Everhard a letter from the Giffords, giving an account of their travels:—they had landed the day before at Leghorn—Clotilde was much better, the change of scene having had a most beneficial effect upon her spirits, and she was now in all respects like herself; "except", said the letter in conclusion, "that her affections now seem entirely weaned from every thing on earth;—she could hardly feel less interest in worldly matters if she were a disembodied spirit."

There was a postscript from Zoe, only a few words; it said—

"Everhard, if your book has only strengthened the heart of one individual, as it has strengthened mine, you will not have written it in vain. If ever I grow to be worth any thing, I owe it to you:—do not let yourself be discouraged, for it shall surely be well with you."

CHAPTER II

— . —

The obloquy to which Everhard was exposed did not prevent his acquaintance being sought by many men of consideration and talent. They were most of them men who, like himself, were under a sort of social ban, for entertaining more liberal opinions than beseemed the then fashion; for that was a time when any tinge of liberality, either in politics or opinions, was accounted synonymous with a breach of morality. None of his new associates were possessed of the calm good sense, or the entire purity of motive that distinguished Everhard. There was a touch of idiosyncrasy in their lucubrations and best digested schemes for ameliorating the world. Still they were seekers after good, and mutually tolerated each other. Everhard believed that he beheld in them a type of better things, for the whole world.

That which is religion amongst the people, has, in the first instance, been entertained as philosophy in the schools. When philosophical truths spread amongst the mass of the people, they always take the guise of religious doctrines, and at length grow to be received like the common light of day; but the first teachers are always persecuted for atheists, or at best are looked on as setters forth of strange gods.

Everhard saw many of his liberally-minded friends fall away, and join the ranks of the divine right of the legitimacy in possession, rather than endure tangible inconvenience for the sake of what they had too little faith to consider as any thing better than abstract theories.

Everhard was surprised and grieved, but he was willing to bide his time.

One of his new friends, a gifted and fiery-hearted man, was on the point of undertaking a tour through Germany, not then recognised for the store-house of wisdom it has since been found. He was very anxious that Everhard should accompany him, who gladly acceded to the proposal, and they started accordingly. They travelled mostly on foot, and stopped whenever they found matter worthy of attention. They were furnished with letters to many men of note, but their own names were in themselves a passport.

Everhard was surprised to find that much which he had believed peculiar to himself, many views which he believed he had been the first to set forth, were, in different terms perhaps, but in substance held and taught there, as matters of course. Everhard found himself now for the first time for many years entirely emancipated from the strain of a false position:—he had neither to endure clamorous abuse nor the heated atmosphere of his own reputation; he was there amongst his brethren, dwelling as kings amongst each other, in a majestic simplicity of thought and speech. Everhard had never before been thrown amongst minds of a calibre equal to his own; now he lived in daily intercourse with men greater than himself, and in his own line. He felt his powers mature every day; and in the exercise of them he found rest and peace.

When his friend was on the point of returning to England, Everhard decided to remain behind. "I have no ties of any kind in England," said he, "and I can truly say with the disciples, 'it is good to be here'."

"What are your plans?" asked his friend. "Do you intend to do nothing to distinguish yourself? Whilst one lives, one must strive for something; what you write here will never be known in England unless you have singular luck; here you can make no impression, you are overshadowed by mighty men of renown; what is there in this world worth obtaining but fame? What could lead a man of noble mind through the drudgery of life but the hope that his name will live after him? and if you remain here, what will become of your hopes of teaching the world, and showing it is a more excellent way?"

"But", said Everhard, "I shall learn myself; and that is certainly better than beginning to teach. It is because I am here amongst greater minds than my own, that I desire to remain, and finally, as to fame, perhaps it may be the fault of my indolence, but strife and turmoil are my aversion. I have no taste for struggling, I would earnestly desire to obtain excellence, but whether I am recognised as the possessor of it, I do not and cannot care a straw; and then, my dear friend, it has been my lot to get not fame exactly but applause certainly, and all for things of which I have now grace enough to be utterly ashamed; besides, one cannot feel very anxious about what is such a mere accident. It would make no difference in my feelings for you, if the whole world were to begin and clap hands, nor would it make me think less of you, if it were to begin to hiss like an army of geese; believe me, my friend, your desire for fame is an alloy to your genius—is a drawback on your greatness; be, do—achieve, to any excess of which you are capable, but let the fame take care of itself; if you really *are* great, what does it signify whether you are called so or not?"

"My dear Everhard, begging your pardon, you talk like a fool; how can one work, strive, attain, as you call it without a motive? Reverence from one's fellows, honour and worship after one has passed away from this world, are the rewards assigned to him who labours to excel his fellows, and why, if I am willing to go through the labour, should I not enjoy the reward of my labour? You talk like a child; you say you are not ambitious and you say the truth, therefore you cannot understand what you are talking about; one throb of generous ambition, one kindling feeling of the god-like frenzy, and you would throw your wisdom to the winds for ever; once braced and nerved for the struggle—gods! the thought is worth a life. Heroes are not made of such stuff as you are. I shall go back to England, and girding on my armour, I will overpass and trample down all competitors; there is no room for soft and amiable feelings, you must tread upon your rivals if you would attain the pre-eminence." His eyes gleamed fire, his teeth were set, his hands were clenched and stretched forth, he looked like one who would neither take nor show quarter, but who would rather attain his aim and die.

"You look like an impersonation of Energy," said Everhard, as he gazed upon him.

"Ay," said the other, his muscles relaxing as he spoke in his ordinary manner, "Energy is the only deity a man ought to worship.

But don't let us argue the last night we are together; we shall not agree, and it vexes me that you won't enter into my feelings: unless I struggle, I stagnate, and than that rather a thousand times death!"

"Well," said Everhard, smiling, "we must each work in our own way, and we each supply that which the other wants;—your fine, bold, positive actions will make more sensible impression on the world, than any thing I can expect to achieve; the positive always tells more visibly than the negative; still, both are needed, and I must be content to be that which I am; you cannot put your spirit into me, so we must each find work fitted for us."

Everhard's friend gave a half contemptuous shrug, and the conversation was changed. In a few days he departed for England, and Everhard remained behind.

The small annuity on which he had contrived to live in England, was, in the part of Germany where he took up his abode, more than ample. He was by no means condemned to inactivity, for where the disposition to do good exists, opportunities abound everywhere. He certainly was more occupied in learning than teaching; still he could not but be sensible, that he contrived to be of more actual use in the world, than he could flatter himself with having achieved during any other period of his life. His powers of mind expanded to their natural growth, and in the adequate employment of them he found rest and peace;—for it is the sense of inneffectual effort, the striving to reconcile ourselves with an ill-understood task stretching before us day after day, that wears out the heart-life of man. If we once could discern what was required of us exactly to do, it is not the greatness of the task that would frighten us (for we are capable of immense drudgery of labour); but it is left to us to discover our own work, and set our hands to it as best we can, and this makes the weariness of life. We spend half our strength in beating the air, and we seldom have the satisfaction of feeling that we have wisely and adequately bestowed our labour; that which we ought to have done still remains undone, and we are devoured by unrest and vague remorse. The only happiness worthy to be aspired after by men, is to see clearly what lies before them to do, with the disposition to set themselves diligently about it.

But without impugning Everhard's zeal in well doing, it must be confessed that it was his passion for Zoe which tinged his life with gladness:—it wrapped him round as with a bright cloud, through which none of the sordid evils of life could pierce. No communication ever passed between them; but he had no sense of being distant from her, her image coloured and vivified his whole destiny. The possibility of distrusting her, or of fancying that her regard could change, never occurred to him: he was too much engrossed in passionate love for her, to have any time to think whether her regard for him was of the same fervour. To be permitted to love her, to be able to dedicate himself to her, was all he required. The miniature which he had carried off on the night of the fire, was to him like that Talisman of old, which enabled all who held it, to throw themselves from precipices and to pass on unhurt:—it did far more, it kept him from all the evil that infects life—from that despondency and sense of disappointment which eats even the strongest hearts—and from all vain desires, for to him who has the gift to love intensely, what has the world either to give or withhold?

Everhard went on his way, clothed in the panoply of perfect love; and the tumult of this weary world, did not come nigh him. Singular as it may seem, he was not tormented with any desire to see Zoe, or to be near her. The relationship in which they stood to each other, was perfect and unbroken, and he did not wish for it to change.

Strong passion can create for itself a world amid perfect silence, and be satisfied to dwell therein:—but it must either be perfect possession or total separation. To have had occasional interviews with Zoe, could not have slaked the thirst of passion, and would only have served to make more visible the impassable gulf that lay between them:—they would have gained nothing but baffled hopes, aching desires, and all the tortures of unsatisfied passion.

He had lived calmly for several years—when he was threatened with an evil hitherto entirely unknown to him. His annuity, which was remitted from England, through a German bank, began to be exceedingly irregular, and at length ceased altogether; for the disturbed state of the continent rendered the communication between the two countries very difficult. His habits had always been of the simplest kind—still he had never known what it was to be in want of money;—it was a sort of thing he had never contemplated, for his money always coming in regular sums at stated times, he had grown to consider it a sort of natural production, as little likely to fail him as the air he breathed: and now that he found himself in a foreign country, entirely without resource, surprise and incredulity for a short time prevented him from actually looking his prospects in the face.

However, he did not allow it much to disturb him, thinking that he could easily find means to earn a living; but, as all who have tried can testify, that is no such easy task, when it is a hand-to-hand fight against starvation; and Everhard was reduced to terrible straits.

His friends were all poor; and besides, to live is a task that has to be renewed every day—so that even if he could have brought himself to accept assistance, casual help could only stave off the evil for a little while. He was fortunate enough to get work from booksellers: translations, school-books, copying of manuscripts, and all sorts of wearisome drudgery. He had written one or two works during his residence in Germany, which were much esteemed, and had been highly spoken of; but there was little money to be obtained by them; he struggled bravely on, however, working thankfully for daily bread when he could obtain work, fasting cheerfully, and enduring manfully every species of privation, with a sort of composed and unconscious stoicism; working in his intervals from drudgery, with undiminished ardour, at a philosophical history he had long had in hand, and which he hoped to make a work of solid and enduring worth.

He dwelt for months in a miserable garret, to which his room in the widow's cottage in Wales, was a palace. None of his friends in B——knew of his necessities: not that he would have been too proud to be assisted, but he never dreamed of talking of his own matters, or wishing for sympathy; and besides, as we said before, all his friends were themselves very far from rich.

At last, one day when matters were at the worst with him, for it was mid-winter and he could obtain no sort of employment from the bookseller, he had no valuables that could be sold and he had begun to think of the possibility of getting work as a day labourer in the fields, when he received a letter, informing him that he was appointed librarian to the College of G——. The handwriting was totally unknown to him, and he would have almost considered the whole as a mistake, had not there been enclosed an order on a banker in the town where he resided, for a sum of money more than sufficient to discharge all his debts, and to furnish him with means to appear with decency at the college. People must have been in want before they can understand the delight of being relieved from it. Everhard was entirely at a loss to know to whom he was indebted for his good fortune; he at last discovered that the bookseller for whom he worked, had accidentally mentioned him to one of the college authorities who happened to come to his shop;— it was one of those small things which have greater results than many actions done with solemn design.

Everhard joyfully repaired to G——, and found his new situation every way suitable to him. His book, which had been written under all kinds of hardship and privation, got itself perfected and brought to light, under auspices much more fortunate than he ever dreamed of.

Everhard had nothing left to wish for in the way of worldly comfort. Honour, consideration, friends amongst all the earth possessed of worthiest, these were now his; and he had the heart to enjoy all the blessings that were around him, which King Solomon adds as the crowning blessedness that can be bestowed on man.— Here we must leave him to return to Zoe.

CHAPTER III

— · —

Human beings cannot remain stationary; a constant expenditure of strength and effort is required even to retain their position; if once they fall into a state of negation, they recede, and lose the point they have gained. Life is a constant effort, a struggle against dissolution, and it is no wonder that every one, at times, feels "wearied with the greatness of the way", ready to sink down and die, if it so be that rest is not otherwise to be obtained.

Zoe, during the two years that had elapsed since she last saw Everhard, had experienced a peace and tranquillity far beyond positive happiness; she seemed to have obtained some high table-land in a serene atmosphere, and, in it she had hoped to dwell secure and peaceable for evermore; but these breathing spaces which we conquer for ourselves out of the struggle and conflict of our passions, are not intended as "secure habitations and quiet resting-places" for us to dwell in, but only as way-side tents, where we may recover strength, and from which we must ever hold ourselves in readiness to depart, and walk on in our life's journey.

Zoe's own thoughts and sensations had hitherto been the most important objects of her life; now, she had other occupation. Lawyers, executors, and matters of business, connected with the settlement of Gifford's affairs, threw her forcibly into a new channel, and by their tangible importance and peremptory claims on her attention, made every thing like sentiment and emotion seem very dreamy and unreal. It is quite impossible to entertain more than one current of feeling at a time.

She did not interfere much with the actual legislation of affairs, but it was necessary for her to be present, to understand, and to sanction, the different steps that were decided on for the advantageous arrangement of the property till her eldest son should be of age.

It was late on in the winter, before every thing was settled. As Zoe wished to remain near London, there was some talk of letting Gifford Castle, but to this she strenuously objected, and, accordingly, a couple of old servants were placed in it to keep the place in what order they best could.

Zoe could not conquer her reluctance to see the place again, but she sent down for all the furniture that was connected with old associations, and took a handsome house at Richmond, in order that the children might have the benefit of pure air, for she determined not to send them to school, but to superintend their education herself with the assistance of masters.

Her first step was to get rid of the tutor, and she contrived to procure him the situation of librarian to an old Catholic gentleman, for which he was much better calculated than to instruct children. Her establishment was handsome and substantial, but by no means conspicuous; her love of stylish display had long since been worn out.

Many of the people she had formerly known, were either dead or dispersed, and there were not many with whom she felt anxious to renew her old intercourse. She now felt ashamed of the things in which she used to delight: her staunch old friend the Duchess of N——, still lived, however, and had a house not far from Richmond. She no sooner heard that Zoe was settled in her new abode, than she paid her a visit. Much delighted the good old lady was, to find her *protégée* so much improved, and she failed not to attribute it to her own sententious lectures on the feminine proprieties, which had borne fruit in the seclusion of her residence at Gifford Castle; and as every body feels an affection for those who conform to their model, there was nothing too grand or too good for the old lady to do, to render Zoe's residence at Richmond agreeable. Her son was on a visit to her, and had brought a party of friends with him, the *élite* of these were drafted off, and carried to be introduced to Zoe by the complacent old lady, so that though she did not mix in general society, she saw pretty nearly all who were best worth seeing and knowing.

From Clotilde, she heard frequently, as she went on in her mild, placid, and most heavenly-minded course, unruffled by the smallest tinge of earthly alloy; her brief dream of passion seemed to have broken up all her deeper affections only to make her cling more intensely to the spiritual manifestation of hope in religion; her letters were worthy of St Theresa, or any of the virgin martyrs of old.

All this time, Zoe heard nothing of Everhard, except that he had gone over to Germany before her return to England. All trace of him seemed to have vanished; his brother Louis, and Marian, never mentioned his name, as they considered it a most painful and humbling dispensation of Providence to be connected with him at all.

Zoe endeavoured to persuade herself that all Everhard did must be right; she knew she could trust him implicitly, and she felt confident that nothing could ever supersede her in his regard. She had loved him, knowing they could never be more to each other than they were, for even though her ties might be broken, his must remain in force for life. He had broken his connexion with the Church of Rome, but his vows of celibacy had been vowed to God, and nothing could loose him from them, therefore there was no vague unsatisifed yearning in Zoe's bosom to become more to him than she already was; but she did feel oppressed and disappointed at the total silence he maintained; it was as if the grave had closed over him;—she felt that he might write—that he might counsel— that he might be her supporter through life;—he had touched all her womanly feelings, and it is in the nature of a woman to lean on him she loves. So long as Gifford lived, Everhard's silence had a majestic self-control and meaning, which now that she was free, it no longer retained. The past remained enshrined in her soul as a sacred mystery of which she might not speak without desecration— it was the secret source of her serenity and strength, but it was a thing apart from her actual life—it was confined to the "transparent prison of the past", and touched the present at no one point.

Everhard, poor fellow, supporting as we have seen his own struggling existence in Germany, could not communicate with her, and, besides, he found the thought of her a sufficient stay for his own soul, and he did not dream it could be different with her. He did not know women; he did not know that without any strong tie to the world except through their affections, the most exalted female nature requires some visible manifestation to cling to;— they are by the very constitution of their being, passive, receptive; in proportion as a true feminine disposition is developed, the positive, the active, becomes uncongenial to their nature; and in exact proportion as a woman becomes active, self-sufficing, subjective instead of objective, she is a grander character, of a stronger and more heroic mould, but she approaches the nature of a man, and loses her feminine empire over the hearts of men. With all her elevation of nature, Zoe was a thorough woman, and as the period from which she had last seen Everhard lengthened, the warmth and passionate energy of her sentiment for him, calmed down. At first it had surrounded every object with a halo of glorious beauty, but gradually that had subsided "into the light of common day". Her love for Everhard was as much a part of herself as her own soul, nothing could undermine it; but it had become a calm, grave reality, and no longer a passionate emotion;—her strong passions were slumbering and smouldering beneath a calm and serene exterior, and she felt as if nothing could ever rouse them more. A cold, majestic composure reigned within and without.

Her two children were all she could desire, and went on as well as human children could, both in body and mind; but the maternal instinct is only one passion amongst the many with which a woman is endowed.

Zoe might have had a great deal of society, but no one came across her path who interested her; when women have once known what it is to love, society for mere social purposes is very insipid except when there is *the one* to give a zest and signficance to its *fêtes* and *réunions.*

Well, and what of all this? As yet, candid reader, there is no predicating any thing, with any degree of certainty;—we have only wished by this unvarnished statement, to enable you to judge with fairness of events as they occur. Constancy, persistence of every kind, is the crowning virtue of man; but we suspect the physiology of constancy would present many curious anomalies, if sincerely recorded. Every thing in books is so varnished over with phrases, and cut out according to square compact maxims, that the human nature in books is as much like the human nature out of doors, as the yew-trees which ancient gardeners used to clip out in the shape of wigs and peacocks, resemble the trees in the woods and forests; or, as the dried and classified plants in a *hortus siccus*, look like those in a state of nature. Both cases may be improvements in the eyes of some people, but we are only speaking of the resemblance, and the amount of botany required to recognise them. Above all, we entreat the reader not to get out of patience, and abuse Zoe, till he knows what she is going to do: she may prove a miracle of constancy, for any thing he yet knows to the contrary. We would only suggest, in all humility, that more things go to make constancy that any one is aware of—till they try. A strong, vivid sensation, a vehement temptation, has, when it comes, a vitality and reality that make the most firmly believed and most emphatic maxims, seem very vague and ineffectual. Every body has an involuntary respect for whatever causes him to feel strongly, whether it be right or wrong (more's the pity). Whatever dignity the past may have, the present always overbears it in matters of feeling.

> "The present new and near,
> Are fetters to our soul, and must be here."

All this is a terrible digression, enough to weary the forbearance of the most gentle reader; but one comfort in writing a book, to be set against its many pains, is the privilege the author has, of saying his say without interruption;—the reader having also his remedy, of reading or not as it pleases him.

To get on, however, to what we began this chapter with the intention of telling the reader.

When Zoe had been a widow somewhere about eighteen months, she one morning received a letter from her old friend, Lady Clara Mandeville, saying that she had come back to England, and would be very happy to pay her a visit, if she would have her. Zoe and Lady Clara had not met for several years, their correspondence had died away, and their friendship had fallen into a sort of abeyance, but there had been neither breach nor coldness. People lose sight of each other, and renew their acquaintance in the merest accident. Friendships revive like torpid flies in the sunshine: it is hard to know when they are really dead. Persons whom we have once known with any sort of intimacy, are sure to reappear at intervals all through life.

Zoe was excessively pleased at the prospect of seeing her old friend again; independent of the cordial regard she entertained for her, Lady Clara was exactly the sort of person she wanted just then. A quick and cordial answer to her letter was immediately dispatched, begging her to hasten her visit as much as possible, and assuring her of the continued interest and affection felt for her by Zoe. While Lady Clara is making her journey, and Zoe is preparing to receive her, we will tell the reader something about her, for, as well as we recollect, he has not yet enjoyed the advantage of a personal introduction.

Lady Clara Augusta Mandeville, then, was a widow of some three or four-and-thirty, an age fatal to all mere prettiness, but an age at which all women of sterling beauty are in the full-blown radiance of their charms; their mind, too, if it possess any solidity, is then in full maturity; there is a glow of summer richness, which yet does not touch on autumn.

Lady Clara was the daughter of the Earl of Cheshunt, who had greatly embarrassed his affairs with gambling. Luckily there were no younger sons, or what must have become of them, with all the heavy luggage of family pride and family dignity they would have had to carry through the world with them! There was, however, only one son to inherit all that was left, by horses, cocks, dogs, cards, and two contested elections, in which the family candidate had been unseated on petition. The son having seen the evils of wanting money, and felt the annoyance of it, determined to be economical, and accordingly declined to increase the fortune of his only sister, beyond the three thousand pounds that came to her by his mother's marriage settlement. He also made other spasmodic attempts to overcome the spendthrift tendencies he had inherited from his father; but we believe there is no recorded instance of his having succeeded in economising at his own expense. Lady Clara resided with him for a short time after her father's death; but, not finding it a very comfortable home, she married, at the age of nineteen, Sir John Mandeville, Bart, a very rich and very infirm old man, who had married once before for love, and now wanted a wife to nurse him. Many respectable middle-aged females, who fancied their peculiar vocation lay in being "sisters of charity", were rather jealous at finding themselves superseded, and eased their feelings by declaring, "it went against their consciences, to see a young creature, like Lady Clara, sacrifice herself for money".

Of course it was a great consolation to their charitable bosoms, to find that Lady Clara contrived to make herself apparently very comfortable under her "sacrifice"; she had been accustomed to all sorts of disagreeables at home, and did not find her new situation by any means intolerable. She was endowed with the art of making every thing appear to the best advantage. Whatever befell her, good or bad, was sure to be placed in the most picturesque and imposing aspect; indeed, listening to her conversation was like reading a well-written novel; she was for the rest, thoroughly good-natured, very witty, and her manners were captivating to a degree that nothing human could resist their seduction; the only fault that balanced so many fascinations, was that she was not very placable when once offended. She had a great objection to having it thought she married for money, and always spoke of her husband as "her dear, darling Sir John". At eight-and-twenty, she was left a widow with an ample jointure. Adorers came upon her in regiments; but Lady Clara had no vocation for a second edition of matrimonial life; she determined to enjoy herself. Accordingly she took a large house in London, was presented at court "on her widowhood", as somebody maliciously said; gave splendid entertainments, assembled the best company, and was at the head of every thing that was brilliant and dashing. Her conduct during her husband's lifetime had been so unassailably correct, that no one now dared to gainsay any thing she chose to do; her reputation defied the most ingenious malice. Zoe and she had been very intimate, but Lady Clara went on the continent, just before Zoe returned to Devonshire, and so it had come to pass they gradually lost sight of each other.

"I wonder whether I shall like her as well as I used to do," thought Zoe, as on the morning appointed for Lady Clara's arrival she was arranging the flowers in her dressing-room. "One grows out of one's friends so sadly."

At this moment the sound of wheels was heard, and Zoe ran down to receive her friend, with some curiosity to see how the first glance would strike her.

A gay-looking carriage stopped at the door as she reached it, and a lovely creature, radiant with smiles and bird of paradise plumes, sprang out, before the two solemn footmen could let down the steps for descent.

"Oh, my dear Zoe! how glad I am to see you once more, and I hope you are glad to see me; how well you are looking! I was afraid I should find you in those odious weeds. It is so insincere to wear them, for no woman would make herself look unbecoming if she could help it. And what a beautiful place you have got! I am so glad to find myself here, that I shall commit all sorts of extravagances."

Zoe was almost overpowered with the torrent of words that poured forth without intermission; but, as soon as an opportunity was afforded, she assured Lady Clara of her own share in the gladness.

"How sedate you are grown!" exclaimed the lively lady.

Zoe laughed outright. "Every thing goes by comparison," said she; "but now let me take you to your room, perhaps you will like to rest a little before dinner."

"Oh, no, my dear lady, I hate the very word rest; poor dear Sir John was always talking about rest when he had his bilious fits, and most uneasy seasons those were to every body. But is this to be my room? What a pleasant one, and what a charming view from the window! Now sit down and let me look at you again;—well, I think I shall love you quite as much as I used to do, and, when the novelty of being together again is a little gone off, I shall be able to tell you all my secrets, and I have some very choice perplexities on hand, I can assure you, and I want to hear a great deal about you, too."

The two ladies had so many general matters to impart to each other, that they were kept well employed the rest of the day, without touching on any of the "choice perplexities" at which Lady Clara had hinted; and when they separated for the night they felt mutually pleased with each other.

CHAPTER IV

— · —

"Well now, Clara," said Zoe, the next morning, as they were sitting together after breakfast, "you have given me a great deal of general history about yourself; but my taste is for private memoirs; I would not give a straw to hear all that the rest of the world may know; do tell me what it is you really have been doing to amuse yourself since we parted?"

"My dear lady," replied Clara, "your complaint about my telling you nothing, is very consistent; pray, what have you told me? Or am I to believe that you have done nothing more *piquante* than teaching your children their lessons?"

Zoe blushed and felt annoyed; she had never yet breathed a word of the subject that lay nearest her heart to a creature, and the light jesting tone in which Lady Clara spoke, jarred on her feelings: she did not immediately reply.

"How pretty and demure we both look," cried Lady Clara again. "If I did not know how innocent I am, I should say that some devilry was coming. Come, my dear, there is nobody to edify by that proper-behaved look, and the only chance of two women not quarrelling when they are shut up together, is the excitement of their mutual confidences; without these, even if they did not quarrel, they would find each other very insipid."

"Well then," said Zoe, "insipid I fear I must be, for at this moment I am very badly off indeed; there is not a soul who comes in my way that I care a single straw about, and I really begin to find such calm work very stupid."

"I shall soon find out how far that is the case," said Lady Clara; "however, I am not sorry you have nothing on hand of your own, for now you will have patience to help me: there really is something I want to ask your opinion about."

"Well, what is it? You know you may depend on every thing I can say or do for you, so now begin."

"Why, after all, I have very little to tell you, and I am not sure you will feel any interest in the matter," said Lady Clara, playing with her snuff-box; "it really is nothing when you come to hear it."

"Well, but what is it?" said Zoe. "Do get on; you surely need not mind telling me any thing; it can go no further, for there is nobody to whom I can mention it, even if I felt disposed."

"Well then, I have fallen in love," said Lady Clara, "that is the summary of what I have to tell you."

"And am I to believe it is the first time you ever did such a thing? Who is it with, and what sort of a man is he? And what are the choice perplexities which surround the case? You said yesterday you would tell me; do go on without needing to have so many questions asked."

"Well then," said Clara, "you promise me it shall go no further?"

"To be sure," said Zoe, "now begin, begin."

"I am not at all clear that the man cares for me," said Clara, "and that is what provokes me. I don't even know where he is at this moment; I fancy he is in England, but I am not sure.

"Last May, I was at Spa; there were not many English families in the place, but after I had been there with my party about a week, an English clergyman arrived with his sick wife, and two of the loveliest children you ever saw—they were twins, and might be about eight years old. The father was not more than thirty, the most graceful and interesting creature you can conceive, but he looked constrained and *ennuyé* to death; at first, I thought he was in low spirits on account of his wife, but I soon found that his wife was a dreadful *gêne* to him; she was a cross, fretful, rigid woman, a great deal older than himself. How such a man could ever marry her, is a mystery to me; ill-humour is the only sin those evangelicals can commit with a safe conscience; they have always 'a sense of duty' to support them when they are inclined to be disagreeable, and this woman had the impertinence to treat her husband with the most solemn disapprobation, mixed up with the most provoking appearance of conjugal obedience and submission; she received all his

322

little amiable and gallant attentions with a sort of suppressed contempt, and really he was kind and attentive to her beyond expression; nothing could provoke him out of his good temper—it was quite beautiful to see him. As to the children, they were by a former marriage, and the present wife tormented them with collects and catechisms, and lectures on 'original sin'; she was constantly telling them about their sinfulness, and the natural evil of their hearts, till the poor things made a crime of every thing. Only fancy, one Sunday, as they were going from their mother's room, where they had been reading and saying their catechism all day, I met them on the stairs and persuaded them to come into the balcony of my room, where they might hear the band play, and see the people walking about. I showed them some pictures, and tried to amuse the poor things; at first they seemed in great glee, but suddenly one of them, who had been engaged with a book of plates, exclaimed, 'Oh, Susan, what will mamma say to us, these are not Sunday-books, and that is not Sunday music the people are playing.' The other little one looked frightened, but the nurse at the moment came to fetch them, so I was spared all further danger of getting the poor things into trouble. This, however, proved the means of my becoming acquainted with their too charming papa; he called the next morning to explain in the most gentle terms, his lady's peculiarly strict views about Sunday amusements, and to beg that I would not feel annoyed at the request he brought, that I would not invite them again on that day. I cannot help thinking that this was a pretext to make acquaintance with me on his own account, for I had caught him looking at me in a very earnest way several times. I can give you no idea how charming he made himself, nor of his graceful conversation; he certainly is, without exception, the clever-est man I ever met. He spoke very highly of his wife, and told me a great many of the good qualities she possessed, for his amiability and goodness of heart are beyond all praise; in short, Zoe, you may fancy I am partial, but I do believe he is perfect! The very tone of his voice is fascinating, and his eyes positively give light when they look at you. Somehow, we saw a great deal of each other. I don't know how it happened, there was no plan in it; every thing fell out as naturally as possible: he soon grew to consider me as a sister, and he often declared that if he might only have ten minutes' conversation with me during a day, it made him a different man. We used to talk about every thing: he told me all his concerns, and all his prospects in the Church (he will be a bishop some day I have no doubt), and I used to give him all sorts of good advice. All this time he never spoke a word that the whole world might not have heard, except of course, he would not have liked all his private concerns known, but I mean for any wrong there was; his wife might have listened and she could not have found fault. We were, I may say, the most sincere friends; and his friendship was far better worth having than any other men's love. Now, my dear, don't think I fell in love with him whilst he was a married man, because I am sure I did not think of such a thing, and I would have done all in my power to make him happy with his horrid wife. He always spoke very highly of her good sense and all that; he had married her entirely for her good qualities, and because he thought she would bring up his children wisely; but he was not prepared, as he said, for the unbending rigour of her manners. I can give you no idea what a stiff, tiresome person she was; she was always 'under arms', and never 'stood at ease'; what between her prudery and her religion, her thoughts seemed frightened out of their senses, and did not know how to find words proper enough to express themselves. She could never endure me, nor be decently civil to me. All this time I thought there was nothing the matter with her but disagreeableness; yet it seems she was worse than I gave her credit for being, and one day she caught cold or something, inflammation came on, and she died, after a two days' illness. Well, would you believe it, when she was dead, her husband (who I told you was full of feeling) seemed to have his conscience hurt, because he had not loved her enough; he was much affected by her death, and took her body to England to bury. I had been obliged to go away for a week on the day she died; when I returned he was gone, and nothing left for me, but a short and hasty note of adieu. I don't think up to this time I was in love with him, but now that his wife was dead there was no obstacle, and when he was gone I felt very lost, and I found I really cared about him more than I ever thought I should care for any one: when these things begin, they always go on *crescendo*. I had nothing to do but to think of him, and now that he was gone, the place seemed quite different. I might have written him a letter of condolence but I wanted confidence, and I did not like to come to England for fear he should think I was following him. I went travelling about and heard nothing of him; and now I am come to England and I am none the nearer to him. What am I to do? I never thought I should be such a fool as to be caught by a man who never committed himself. Do you think from what I have told you he cares any thing about me? What is your opinion?"

"Why, my dear," said Zoe, "you see a married man and a clergyman, was not likely to go and make an *éclat*; he might not love his wife, and she might be a disagreeable woman as you say; but a man's wife is his wife, and when there are children, men do not feel inclined to throw themselves out of the current for a mere sentimental fancy; and however much men may abuse their wives, they find a great deal of solid comfort beside them in general, and their situation is not so intolerable as to induce them to throw up their prospects in life on a sudden impulse. People are less led away by impulse than is usually supposed, and however men may profess to be victims of uncontrollable impulse, for the sake of producing effect, they are quite able to stop themselves during the whole progress of a love affair, if they feel so disposed; and in general they are very wary to keep clear of any circumstances that may entangle them. None but a fool as unstable as the sand will break up his entrenchments in life on an impulse. Your friend seems to have been very much on his guard all along. That he enjoyed your society, and found you very charming, there can be no doubt; but the very fact of his talking so much about his wife, and being so devoted to his children, proves that he had no notion of being foolish, or of allowing himself to be made uneasy by getting to care for you too much.

"Now that he is free, if he has any desire to renew his acquaintance with you, he can easily do it: you are not an obscure Mrs Smith or Mrs Brown, and the newspapers will tell him that you have returned from the continent. There is nothing to hold him back now, and if when you see him again you do not captivate him, and make him your slave for life—should you continue to wish it—why then, my dear, you will deserve to sigh in vain! No man ever escaped yet whom you wished to bring to your feet. I think your proposals are as good as you can possibly desire. Let us see, his wife died last May, this is August, so he may with decency pay you as much attention as he likes: you managed very well not to come to England till now."

"Ah, my dear Zoe!" said Lady Clara, sighing, "it is easy for you to talk so coolly, but I am very anxious; the mere fact that I have hitherto succeeded so well with men, is against me now; there is always compensation in these things, and just because I have flirted so much, and made men in love with me when I did not care for them, I shall fail now that I am in earnest."

"Nonsense, Clara, you only want me to contradict you. What is his name? I wish he were not a clergyman. I don't like the profession."

"He is a dean," replied Clara; "I am sure I don't see any thing objectionable in the Church, it is far before any other profession: besides he *is* a clergyman, and I cannot fancy him any thing else: one loves people, because they are themselves."

"Very true," said Zoe: "now what is his name, for the third time of asking. I am very curious to know what your future name is to be."

"Horace O'Brian," replied Lady Clara, "he is nephew to the Earl of Tyrone."

"Horace O'Brian!" screamed Zoe. "Oh, Clara, you must have nothing to do with him. He is as contemptible a rascal as a man in a civilised community can become, with a due fear of justice before his eyes; of course, understand me, he has done nothing *éclatant*, all his villainy has been *selon les règles*, and very gracefully transacted indeed; but when I think of his heartless conduct to poor dear little Clotilde, I cannot speak of him with any patience. It is his fault she is now in a convent, and it is no thanks to him she is not now in her grave. He wrecked all her worldly happiness, in order that he might have pastime for his *ennui*; I tell you what, Clara, more sins and cruelty are committed for the sake of beguiling *ennui*, to fill up that weary slough of despond with amusement, than from all the strong passions and vehement temptations put together. I have some charity for a man who sins heartily, and because the temptation is too strong for him, no matter what he does; but I have no words to speak my contempt for a man who is ready to do any thing for the sake of the excitement: and that is the way both men and women

326

sin the present day, they lay themselves out for sensations and have no idea of any thing beyond. It would be quite a relief to meet with a man who could commit good hearty crimes from the very strength of his organisation; but let them be the impetuous overflowing of undisciplined strength, instead of the morbid production of egoism and idleness."

"When you have quite finished your dissertation on grand wickedness, perhaps you will tell me in what way the Reverend Horace O'Brian has incurred your disapprobation?" said Lady Clara, haughtily.

"Perhaps you will think I speak more severely than he deserves," replied Zoe, "but I saw the misery he inflicted with my own eyes, and that makes me warm. He made love to poor little Clotilde, when she was staying with Marian, at the Manor House; and never rested till he had completely won her little innocent heart, all the while carefully keeping within the bounds, and never committing himself in words, and then, because circumstances occurred to make it suit his purpose, he went straight and married an evangelical old maid, who had powerful connexions in the Church; that was the lady you knew as his wife. I have heard she possessed many sterling qualities, and was a deal too good for him; no doubt she soon learned to rate her graceful good-for-nothing husband at his true value, for she was no fool. Clotilde's dangerous illness, and subsequent retirement to a convent, to say nothing of the severe mental suffering she endured, were the price of the Reverend Horace O'Brian's three months' amusement."

"So," said Lady Clara, with a heightened colour, "all this virtuous indignation resolves itself into a handsome young man's flirting with an inexperienced girl, who did not know the serious meaning to be attached to sweet speeches; and because he did not choose to sacrifice his prospects for life, he is to be abused in this manner! Really, Zoe, you, of all people have no right to talk; if flirtation were a capital crime, you would have been hanged long since. What possesses you to talk with such a rabid severity? If I recollect right, the very last letter I ever received from you, was full of projects for beguiling some unsuspecting Catholic priest into your snares, and you were a married woman at that time too! and here you give your tongue free licence to abuse poor O'Brian, though by your own account he never made any proposal to Clotilde. Girls ought to be taught, that whatever fine things men may say, they mean nothing till they actually make an offer, and then there would be many broken hearts kept whole. For my part, I think Miss Clotilde did quite the best thing, when she entered the convent; she was not at all fitted for such a man as O'Brian, she never could have understood his character, nor all that he required in a woman to make him happy. He is a very peculiar character, and has been misunderstood by almost every body; his wife was an odious woman, and he behaved beautifully to her—you don't know O'Brian as I do, and you cannot do justice to the noble and poetical temperament of his mind. You cruelly misjudge him; he is utterly incapable of any thing selfish or dishonourable!"

"My dear Clara," said Zoe gently; "I am very sorry to have annoyed you; I spoke warmly because I felt warmly. The affair with Clotilde is passed and gone; she is well and happy in her convent, so, if he behaves well to you, and makes you happy, I can afford to forgive him; but he is a slippery character, so take care of yourself, and consider your own feelings more than his, don't look at him in a grand heroic light, but treat him like a man whom you want to subdue into a submissive lover and a rational husband, treat him like a man, and don't bring any romantic generosity into play, and then you may do very well; but he is not the sort of character to stand too good treatment, it will all recoil on yourself, and you will repent of it if you get to care for him too much. I need not say that any thing I can do to serve you, may be depended upon; if we can but get hold of him, I have no fear but we shall make him do every thing we want. I will invite him here, and there are some splendid walks in the garden, and delightful shady seats and grottoes, where a man could not help making love if he were to try; for men don't like to lose good opportunities for making declarations, and they trust to fortune to get out of them afterwards, if they should happen to change their minds; besides, you never failed with a man yet, and you are not going to begin the first time you set your heart on success. Come, forgive my warmth of speech, and if he does not behave ill to you, I will not only forgive him, but take him into especial favour."

"Well," said Lady Clara, smiling, "I suppose I must forgive you, for the sake of your many virtues; but talk no more treason against him, if you wish to live in peace with me; it makes me feel as if I were doing wrong to listen to you. Is not Horace a very pretty name? There is something so graceful and high bred about it."

"Yes; but 'O'Brian' is not half so pretty as 'Mandeville'," said Zoe, maliciously. "But come, the children will have finished their lessons by this time; what do you say to a walk in the garden? I want to show you my shady bowers. I have taken to gardening lately by way of *'un plaisir innocent'*; but I cannot say it is much to my taste. I don't like the stooping down."

CHAPTER V

_ . _

"It is a charming place you have here," said Lady Clara, when they reached the garden. "It is a real shame such beautiful walks should be wasted on yourself alone, and no lover to have the benefit of them! What is the reason that people one does not care for abound, whilst those one can love are so scarce? Why should there be such a preponderance of stupid people in the world?"

"And yet," said Zoe, laughing; "every one of those stupid men is a Horace O'Brian to some equally stupid woman. One of my little boys was looking out of the window the other day, and suddenly exclaimed, 'Somebody loved that pig! come and see, mamma!' I looked, and saw a great, fat, dirty, white pig with a pink ribbon tied round its neck, driven along by a butcher's boy; as Frederick said, somebody had loved it."

"Ay," said Clara, "but the vexation is, that it is not always the right person."

"Well," replied Zoe, "love is never thrown away. 'The right person' is always very well pleased to see that we are _recherché_, and that a small discerning public is alive to the merits and charms which he is so fortunate in being about to invest in himself. Horace O'Brian will not set less store by you because you have already been sighed for in vain by so many other men. It gives a pleasant and complacent sense of difficulties overcome;—besides, it is always well to let them see you have a _corps de reserve_ of lovers."

They were passing through the lodge gate, as Frederick, the eldest of the boys, ran past with a printed paper, which his brother tried to get from him, "to cut the letters out to print a book with", as he said. The dispute was getting high, when they both appealed

330

to their mamma. "Let me see what it is you are quarrelling about," said she, taking the paper from them. "There, go away and play," said she, hastily, after looking at it; "and I will give you both a newspaper apiece, to cut up when we go in. I must keep this." Then quickening her pace to overtake Lady Clara, who had walked on, "You are a lucky person!" she exclaimed, joyfully; "read that— 'August, 3rd—Sermons will be preached—Richmond, by the Very Reverend the Dean of St——, on behalf', and so forth! What do you say to that? You see the right people do come sometimes. Perhaps he may know you are here, and have schemed this; and yet that is hardly likely. You only came here yesterday, and these things are always arranged long beforehand. To-morrow will be the 3rd, so of course he must arrive in Richmond to-night, as it would not be orthodox to travel on Sunday. I wish we knew where he would put up; however, there is nothing to hinder us taking a drive to-night to *reconnoitre.*

"Do any of your servants know him?"

"Oh, yes," replied Clara, "Vaughan, my maid, was a great admirer of him, so no doubt I shall hear through her if any thing is to be heard."

"Well, then," said Zoe, "my Abigail is going out this afternoon to visit some friend of hers, and your Vaughan shall go with her. If we can once contrive to let him know that you are here, it will be for him to act afterwards."

"But", remonstrated Lady Clara, "I feel to want confidence; suppose he should get to know that I am scheming to see him?"

"'Thus conscience doth make cowards of us all'," laughed Zoe, "it is very natural you should want confidence for yourself, but it is also natural that I should not want confidence for you, or else where is the use of having friends?"

"You are really good," said Lady Clara. "I only wish I could find somebody for you to take an interest in, and then you could keep me in countenance, and I should not seem so abominably engrossed with my own affairs."

"That you need not hope to do," replied Zoe, with a half sigh, "I am very well as I am; but now we had better go in; it will never do for you to fatigue yourself, you must be in brilliant looks this evening, and you had better begin to dress before dinner, as

331

recollect, Vaughan is to go out, and your dress is a matter of importance just now. What do you intend to wear?"

"I am sure I wish you would come with me and decide on a *robe de triomphe*; I have more faith in your taste than my own," said Clara.

The two friends were deep in discussion on the relative merits of a maize-coloured satin, and a delicate peach pink brocaded silk, when the hall door-bell rang sonorously, causing Lady Clara to start. "What is the matter?" asked Zoe.

"I don't know," stammered Clara, looking at the door, which opened, and a servant came in with a card which he handed to Lady Clara.

"'The Very Reverend Horace O'Brian!' Your heart was prophetic, my dear Clara, but don't tremble so violently, sit down a moment and drink this sal volatile;—do not keep the poor man in suspense any longer—if you would like me to see him, send me a message, and I will come."

"But don't I look very ugly in this gown?" said Lady Clara, going up to the mirror, "I don't like myself at all."

"Oh, no, you cannot possibly be better," said Zoe, "your heightened colour becomes you, and if you had dressed on purpose, you could have worn nothing prettier for a morning; but now go down or he will be getting vexed."

"What am I to do with the Very Reverend Horace O'Brian?" soliloquised Zoe, after Clara had left the room, "the man, with all his composed impudence, will feel awkward at coming into my presence, knowing all that he knows; and yet I want to make acquaintance with him for Clara's sake; I only hope he will behave better to her than he did to poor Clotilde; but things must just take their own course, she is a clever woman, and will be his match."

"Do come down," said Lady Clara, returning into the room, and looking rather agitated, "he has expressed a wish to be presented to you, and I thought I would fetch you myself."

"Well, and how have you gone on?" asked Zoe.

"I hardly know," said Clara, "I suppose as well as I could reasonably expect, but people never meet again on the same terms they parted. I have got on further in my sentiment for him, whilst he has been busy with other matters; but come down, and you will be able to judge for yourself."

The Very Reverend Horace O'Brian had grown handsomer than ever, since he last appeared before the reader; he had grown not portly but august looking, and a shade of dignity had been added to his still bland and insinuating manner. "I do not wonder at Clotilde nor at Clara either," thought Zoe, as she seated herself where she could view him at her ease, whilst she was herself shadowed by a curtain.

He entered into a light conversation on the beauty of the place; said that he had come to look for a furnished house, as he wished his children to have the benefit of good air, whilst he was obliged to remain in London. He asked Zoe about her family, and hearing she was educating them herself, entered on a graceful eulogy on home education. He spoke so nicely, and said such really good things, that Zoe got interested in spite of herself, and not only cordially offered her services to look out for an eligible place for the children, but volunteered to visit them, and see that they were well attended to in his absence; any thing connected with children found its way directly to Zoe's heart.

"I am very much indebted to those dear children," said Horace, with a smile, "they have made a way for me to the hearts of many valued friends, poor darlings, it is a blessing I hope they will retain, for they are getting of an age when the loss of a mother is a heavy disadvantage to girls; your boys are more fortunate, if one parent must be taken away, the father can be spared far better than the mother; girls require an understanding watchfulness, which a father, however he may desire it, cannot give; my children are my great worldly anxiety," added he, looking at Lady Clara.

The conversation then changed to London news, and he supplied the ladies with abundance of gossip—offered them tickets for a grand musical festival, that was to be held the ensuing week in Westminster Abbey, and promised to escort them himself if they would go. Lady Clara looked on the ground for her bracelet, which she dropped on purpose, in order that she might not seem too much pleased with the proposal; whilst Zoe, with becoming composure and courtesy, assented to the arrangement. Soon afterwards he rose to take leave. Zoe invited him to dine with them the next day; for independent of wishing to please Clara, she had not met so agreeable a man for some time.

"That I cannot," said he. "I am engaged to dinner at my friend Lord Seaborne's, but if you will let me come in the evening, I will try to get away in good time, and if I am prevented doing that, I will call before I leave on Monday. An invitation from you is too great a privilege to let it lightly escape; I wish to hope that I am laying the foundation of an acquaintance that will not soon pass away."

"Well, what do you think of him?" asked Clara, as soon as the hall-door closed upon him.

"Why, I must confess, I don't much wonder at your being *éprise*, but, for Heaven's sake, mind what you are about; with all his soft, bland, susceptible manner, he will be wary how he commits himself. I can understand him now better than I did, and make allowances for him; he is quite sincere whilst he is with you, means all he says, and is quite in earnest in all the interest he seems to take; in fact, it is the vivid way in which he feels every thing that makes him so dangerously agreeable. But, my dear, those who are with him, have him, and if you want to hold him, you must not let him go from under your immediate influence;—he is too indolent, and too fond of pleasurable emotions, to fight against the stream he is in. He has the quality (which will not tell in your favour) of finding something pleasant, or at least very tolerable, in every person and every circumstance that comes in his way."

"Zoe, you are a perfect witch for understanding men!" cried Lady Clara, laughing, "but now tell me, do you think he cares for me?"

"Yes; I call his coming this morning a very good sign, but it will require good management on your part, to make it end as you wish; there is no depending on him when he is out of your way; and, besides, I can see he hates trouble. We shall not see him again this time; he will cool down about us when he gets out of our meridian into that of Lord Seaborne. However, we shall be sure to see him next Wednesday at the festival, for he will be only too proud to appear in public with two women such as we are. We must go and hear him preach to-morrow."

"I never heard him," said Clara, "and I am very curious to know whether he is as eloquent in the pulpit as out of it; I have heard he is a very fine orator."

"I don't fancy that it will be oratory that will take much hold on me," said Zoe, "there will be more words than thoughts. I never yet heard any thing that came up to my idea of eloquence in public speaking."

Zoe was quite right in her calculations. Horace O'Brian did not come again; instead, there came an elegant *billet* with tickets for reserved seats for the ensuing festival, and a promise to be in waiting for them at the private entrance.

Clara was piqued, but said nothing. On the day appointed, Zoe dressed to go with the most profound indifference to the whole affair, the only point of interest being to watch the progress of her friend Clara's flirtation.

"I do wish", said Clara, "there were likely to be any one there, in whom you could take an interest; these things are so insipid when they stand on their own charms, unless it be to some half a score critics and amateurs, and you are neither one nor the other. I wish you had a Horace O'Brian of your own, but you have been so good-natured to me, that I feel sure you will have something by way of compensation. You know that is my favourite doctrine."

"The only compensation I want, is to see Horace O'Brian behave himself conformably to what a true lover ought to be," replied Zoe, "but make haste, for we have no time to lose; your very reverend admirer will not stand in the cold to wait for us."

They arrived in due time. Horace was there to receive them, they were soon seated, and every thing went to Lady Clara's entire satisfaction.

The oratorio began; it was a ponderous, scientific, cold-blooded affair, which has long since been drowned in the Lethe which posterity provides for the greater number of the "works destined for immortality" confided to her by unappreciated genius. Posterity is a very Mrs Brownrigg in her way of treating the foundlings committed to her tender mercies.

Zoe gazed round on the crowd of well-dressed people, sighing in weariness to think that amongst the multitude of amiable looking faces, there was not one who cared a straw about her, or to whom she was of the least importance; to be sure she could not have pointed out one person in whom she took the smallest interest herself, or who excited her benevolent sensibilities in the least; but every body likes occasionally to take refuge in a gentle shade of misanthropy, and to feel ill-used when there is nothing to amuse them. So Zoe sat in a dignified abstraction to all that was going on, comforting herself with the thought, that if Everhard had been there she would not have been so completely an object of indifference.

There was a slight disturbance near her, caused by a person making his way to one of the reserved seats a little on her left; she turned her head to see what was the matter, and she neither thought of the new singer who just then began his first recitative, nor did she relapse into her abstraction the whole evening; her attention was occupied with the new comer, who certainly was a sufficiently remarkable man. He was very large, and intensely ugly, much marked with the small pox, he had a look of *rouéism*, that was by no means charming to the eye of respectability, but it was mingled with a genial *bonhomie* and kind-heartedness that attracted the beholder to him with an irresistible instinct. A radiant intelligence that glanced from his large brown eyes, gleamed like lightning over his face, giving it an appearance far beyond beauty. A forest of shaggy brown hair, not confined in a queue as was the fashion of the day, fell like a lion's mane about his head and neck. His limbs were cast in the mould of a giant, and looked strong in proportion; but he seemed withal somewhat worn and broken with struggle and excess. Altogether he was as different from the surrounding multitude, as if he had belonged to a different race of men, or had come from another planet. Zoe soon found that the stranger on his part seemed to have his attention quite as much attracted by her; she felt that he took no notice of any thing or any body else, and that he was watching her slightest movements. Women have a wonderful instinct for knowing when they are admired.

"Who was that remarkable looking man?" said she to Horace O'Brian, as they were passing to their carriage.

"What remarkable looking man?" asked Horace. "I saw no one near us of any importance, except Lord M——."

"No, no, it was that striking looking man who came with Lord M——'s party."

"Ah, a very singular character indeed; it was the Comte de Mirabeau, a French adventurer of very doubtful character, but who has nevertheless contrived to obtain currency in very good circles here. They say he is clever, but there are strange tales about him; and I confess I wonder at so correct a man as his lordship, being intimate with him."

Zoe raised her eyes, and saw the stranger standing close beside her; he must have heard all that Horace had said. Zoe coloured with confusion and vexation. The stranger did not seem in the least disconcerted. He stood with immovable gravity till the carriage drove off, and then rejoined Lord M——'s party, handed her ladyship into her carriage, got in after her, and was driven away, doubtless to the still further astonishment of the Very Reverend Horace O'Brian, who would have been very glad to be intimate with his lordship, for he was an influential member of the administration of that day.

"My dear Zoe, what a stupid evening you must have had; you looked quite absent and *ennuyée* all the evening. What did you think of the oratorio?"

"It is so long since I was in public before, that I found the light and heat almost intolerable; one must get used to the hard labour of fashionable life, before one can find the pleasure of it. I confess, just now, I would (barring the disgrace) quite as soon be committed for six months to Bridewell, as be condemned to go through a 'London season'!"

"So you are going to turn a fair recluse, *à la bonne heure*," said Clara, laughing. "We shall see. Who was that ugly man who never took his eyes from us?"

"Did Horace say when he should be coming again?" said Zoe, without noticing the question.

"He brings the children on Friday, when he will remain with them till the beginning of the week."

"Good night," said Zoe, yawning, and taking up her candle.

Was Zoe quite as much tired as she appeared? We really cannot settle the question to our satisfaction; we appeal to the reader, telling him, at the same time, that she sat in a deep reverie for full half an hour after she had dismissed her maid, at the end of which she extinguished her lamp, saying, "Doubtful or not doubtful, I wish any body would bring him here and introduce him. I have heard so much of Mirabeau."

CHAPTER VI

– · –

The morning after the oratorio the old Duchess of N—— was sitting in her pleasant summer-house, reading a volume of Massillon's sermons; she had a most imperious notion of her own dignity and always dressed up to it. Her stiff black silk dress and point lace ruffles and apron, her hair powdered and combed back from her high forehead, the searching half sarcastic expression of her face which still bore traces of its former beauty, her erect carriage, and the gracious dignity of her whole bearing, formed a charming picture of a thoroughbred English lady of the old school. In truth, the duchess was a very remarkable old lady in many ways, and for nothing more, than that whilst she was a great stickler for all the conventional etiquettes of society, she had a singular charity for all eccentricities that had any thing genuine to extenuate them, and her intolerance of even innocent affectations was extreme. She was a strong-minded woman, though somewhat warped and prejudiced. We have mentioned her to the reader several times as Zoe's great friend and upholder in society against all gainsayers. She had been a widow many years, and constantly wore a large miniature of her husband, who had been killed at the siege of Quebec. She was sitting on this particular morning, reading according to her custom before she was visible to any callers, or even to visitors staying in the house. Her missal with silver clasps lay beside an ivory crucifix on a table before her. A small ebony writing-case clamped with silver was within reach, and a pretty gentle-looking girl sat engaged in needlework at a table in a corner of the room.

"Sophia, child!" cried the old duchess, in a clear quick voice, "can you not see that the sun is shining through that window and

338

nearly blinding me? must I get up myself to put the blind down? I like to see young people attentive; they should never wait to be told what to do, but always keep their eyes open."

Sophia rose quietly to do what was required—"A gentleman is coming this way," said she.

"Who can it be?" said her grace; "I never admit gentlemen here, and Stratham knows I never receive any visitors in this place. How can he have been so inattentive; do you see who it is?"

"It is the Comte de Mirabeau, I think," said Sophia, blushing.

"Well," said the old lady, looking keenly at her, "and what have you to do with blushing about the Count Mirabeau? He has done more mischief to women than he is ever likely to repair; you are never to believe a word you hear Count Mirabeau say, do you hear? You have nothing in you to attract him in the way of conversation, so if he talks to you it is for no good; now remember you have been warned."

"Yes, madam," replied the girl, submissively.

Further admonition was cut short by the entrance of the count. The old duchess looked at him with a surprised and stately air, enough to have abashed the self-possession of any mortal man; but the Count Mirabeau was something more than mortal. He approached the duchess without appearing to notice her stateliness, and kneeling on one knee, he kissed the hem of her lace apron. "Pardon, most gracious lady," said he, in a deep mellow voice: "pardon for two culprits, but whose faults are both united in me; Stratham did all that usher could, to keep me from your presence; he protested against my coming here so long as I was in hearing, indeed, he refused to tell me where I should find you; so, in fact, he is innocent, and I being doubly guilty, you must stretch out your ebony sceptre and show me grace. I must be forgiven before I can speak my errand. Your grace must be aware that nothing but a strong motive would have enabled me to run the risk of your displeasure."

The earnest look and tone of the count, made the duchess believe something urgent was the matter; and, besides, incomprehensible as it may seem, he was a great favourite with her, a puzzle only to be explained by the strange influence he obtained over every one he came near;—none but those at a distance from his fascination, could be severe in their judgment on him.

"Well," said she, lightly touching him with her wand; "and what brings you here in this madcap way, against all my rules? What are you come for? People don't sin prepense for nothing."

"I want your most serene graciousness to order your carriage, and take me out with you this very morning to pay a visit."

"You do! and where may it please your modesty to wish me to take you?"

"I saw Mrs Gifford at the oratorio last night; she is the most wonderful-looking woman I ever beheld—she has penetrated my soul—I cannot live without being presented to her. I know some other friends of hers, but it will be more to my credit to go under your grace's auspices. I want her to think well of me. Your grace has been so indulgent to my follies, that you surely will not refuse the first wise thing I have desired for many months," continued he, pleadingly.

"You know, Count Mirabeau," said the duchess, gravely, "that you are not a fit person to be introduced into a quiet orderly family. You are not a fit companion for a young woman. I have a great regard for Mrs Gifford—too much to take you to see her. I will have nothing at all to do with it, and I shall warn her against having any thing to do with you."

"Mrs Gifford is not a woman like other women; she is strong and wise. If such a woman had fallen to my lot, I should not have become the reckless outcast I am; it is a desire to unite myself with what is good and excellent, that now impels me; does your grace see nothing in me worth redeeming? Oh, if your grace will but take me, it will at once introduce me to a pure world, where I may become worthy of a place. If I intended aught wrong, it is not to your grace I should have applied for a passport. I hope", continued he, proudly, "your grace does not think so meanly of me, as to believe I would disgrace your recommendation."

Much more was said on both sides; but the submissive earnestness of the count, and the consciousness that as she could not actually prevent the acquaintance, it would, in many respects, be better to come through her, and also the impossibility she shared, along with every body else who came in contact with him, of

340

refusing any thing he chose to set himself to obtain, vanquished the old lady's resistance; and, though blaming herself for her facility, she ordered her carriage, and proceeded with Count Mirabeau to visit Zoe.

The ladies were in the garden when the carriage drove to the door, and the old lady and her companion followed them there.

Before they appeared in sight Zoe felt a conviction who was coming; the blood rushed from her heart; she felt choked, and when the duchess and her companion appeared she almost sank to the ground.

"Well, my dear child! how do you after your first appearance in the world after so long an absence? You look but pale this morning; I have brought a young man whose head you completely turned with your bright glances:—will you allow me to present him to you, in the hope that he may recover his senses on a nearer view. Count Honoré Gabriel de Mirabeau—Mrs Gifford."

Zoe made the requisite curtsey, and the count made a profound bow, as all well-bred gentlemen ought to do; but he could not utter a single phrase; he only went very red, and dropped first his cane and then his snuff-box, the contents of which flew over Lady Clara, who just then unfortunately came up. This occurrence, however, seemed to break the spell that lay on the count, and the witty, graceful manner in which he extricated himself from his *gaucherie*, only rendered his awkwardness the more inexplicable.

"His father", said the duchess to Zoe, as they walked a little in advance of the other two, "was a great friend of my father's, and though the son is a sad dog, and has committed more sins than he will ever be absolved for, and he will want more masses when he dies than I fear his poor soul will ever get said for it; yet I cannot help liking him. He is on a large scale, both morally and physically, and we little people cannot always judge wisely of such men; any way he is a man of genius, and they have always the seeds of redemption in them; now, though I have brought him (he gave me no peace till I came), yet don't you, my dear, go and be very intimate with him; remember you are a young woman, and he is in England under a cloud as it were; you must not let him have the *entrée*; but I know you are prudent, still it is as well to put you on your guard against him, for he has the tongue of the old serpent himself. I don't feel as if I had done a wise thing; to be sure he would have found other means of coming if I had refused to bring him; but, remember now, you have been warned."

Zoe smiled; this "remember now, you have been warned", was her grace's way of throwing up all responsibility; after she had once uttered her warning, she knew not what self-reproach meant.

The duchess now gave the signal to depart; the count apparently took no notice whatever of Zoe, beyond a formal and hurried bow; Zoe and Lady Clara accompanied them to the gate. Zoe politely expressed a hope to see the count again; he raised his eyes quickly to her face for an instant, and a flush suffused his whole countenance. He did not speak, however, and the carriage drove off.

A fortnight elapsed, and Zoe neither saw nor heard any more of him; she was angry at herself for the hold he had taken on her imagination; she was troubled at the blind stirring of passion she felt in the depths of her heart—she was ashamed and abased at the consciousness that she was giving herself to another, she who had vowed to live in cold and stern fidelity to the memory of Everhard. She had not forgotten him, she had not become indifferent to him, she loved and revered him still, as an angel from Heaven: never, for a moment, did she place the image of Mirabeau in the pure shrine she had dedicated to him; her love to Everhard was a thing apart; she loved him now, as men worship beings of a superior nature, she felt that she could go to him in all her troubles; if the world were cold or harsh she would have gone to him for refuge and comfort, but the hot passionate feelings which he had given back to her own keeping were without occupation, lying latent in her heart; passionate emotions which till then had never been thoroughly awakened, never satisfied, were roused at the approach of this strange new object. His ungovernable impetuosity had a charm for her, after the calm self-government of Everhard. Mirabeau had taken possession of her imagination, and all the strong passion of her nature. He overbore her love for Everhard in the same way that an earthly affection obscures the sense of religion in the soul; not obliterating it, for it still lives there, but burying it under the burning lava of excited earthly emotion. She blamed herself, and strove by every means to repress the thoughts that more and more absorbed her; she once thought of writing to

Everhard, to tell him to assert his possession of her heart, and not leave her longer to the cold abstraction of her own strength and constancy, to beg him to save her from herself;—but she involuntarily shrank from this; she dreaded lest she should be taken at her word, and the new idol broken and taken from her. Everhard was too pure and self-controlled to sympathise with her passionate weakness; besides (and it was an intense relief when she recollected it), she did not actually know where he was, nor could she with the most honest endeavour have ascertained. The question was thus set at rest for her, and she tried to shut her eyes on her growing indifference to Everhard. In fact, a strong genuine emotion asserts its supremacy over all the reflections, and resolutions, and theories, with which we may endeavour to blank it out. One emotion may always be conquered by another; so it is not very wonderful that poor Zoe, in spite of all her struggles, found herself sinking every day deeper and deeper in dreamy reveries about—Mirabeau! Then began the restless, aching sense of absence. The hours became intolerable to her, Lady Clara's dissertations on Horace O'Brian altogether insufferable, she could not bear to be alone, and if in company, she was abrupt, restless, absent; the sameness of her life was insupportable, and yet nothing she could devise improved it. The duchess had gone to Hastings, so she could hear no intelligence from her: if she drove out, she was restless till she returned; when in the house, she fancied going abroad might bring some good; she always involuntarily assumed the attitude of watching or listening.

If Lady Clara had not been the most easy tempered of women, she must infallibly have quarrelled with Zoe, and left her house; but fortunately she was a good deal engrossed with her own affairs; she dragged Zoe to visit the cihldren, who had been established in a farm-house about two miles off, and persuaded her to invite them to spend a long day; the Rev. Horace O'Brian happening to come over from town that very day to see them, brought them himself; so that, on the whole, Lady Clara did not pay much attention to her friend's distractions.

About a fortnight after the duchess had brought Mirabeau to call (it was the longest and most weary period Zoe had ever known), on descending to breakfast one morning, she found cards of invitation for a grand dinner-party which the duchess intended to give in honour of her son's birthday, with a note, telling Zoe that she had returned the day before from Hastings, and intended to go to see Garrick in "King Lear" to-morrow, if Zoe and Clara would accompany her. This restored all Zoe's animation; she resolved to drive over after breakfast with Lady Clara, and take their reply themselves.

The old lady was sitting in her summer-house, and received them most graciously. She had much to tell them about what she had seen and done during her absence, and was remarkably full of news and good-humour; but Zoe listened in vain for the name she wished to hear, it was not mentioned; at length, in very desperation, she took courage and said, "Have you heard or seen any thing of Count Mirabeau since the day he emptied his snuff-box over poor Clara?"

The old lady looked keenly at her, and replied, "Count Mirabeau is gone away, no one knows where; he disappeared the day after his visit to you, so probably you had the last of him—for, before he comes back, he will no doubt have got into some scrape that will banish him out of good society."

Zoe's consciousness would not allow her to say more, but all her desire for the dinner-party and theatre had vanished. She shortly afterwards took her leave, and had hardly patience to listen to the parting arrangements for the next evening.

Arrived at home, she flung herself on the sofa, and hiding her face in the crimson pillow, endeavoured to crush out the consciousness of what was passing within or without, holding herself stretched and still, in the stiff rigid tension of endurance. Lady Clara went to her own room to write letters.

At length Zoe heard the door open without any announcement from the domestic, and a step noiselessly approached the couch; but it was a step that sent all the blood like boiling lead through her veins. She started up—Count Mirabeau stood before her!

The life she had lived in her own heart, since she last saw him, completely obliterated the recollection that they were almost actual strangers to each other. She was confused and oppressed with the consciousness that the secret of her heart was laid bare to him, and that he could not but see it. She could not utter a word of common greeting. He looked gloomy and moody; there was a determined and almost savage expression in his countenance.

"You are ill; something has happened," said Zoe, forcing herself to speak.

"Yes, madam, I am ill—ill at ease. I have this day done a cruel action; how would you have me feel after it? Women can gloss over every thing with the varnish of sentiment or duty; and of course, madam, you, with your smiles and roses, never knew what remorse meant; but I tell you, that remorse is the only hell a noble-minded man can dread. Women feel nothing, but the hell of consequences; understand nothing, beyond the blame of the world, and the loss of reputation."

"Nay," said Zoe, gently, "some women can fear the reality of doing wrong, more than the blame attached to it; and for remorse, there are none who have not a chamber of bitter regret, into which they dread to look."

"Then you know what it is to feel that you do not justify your actions to yourself; there is a point of sympathy between us. And yet I should be grieved for you to have your heart wrung as mine is."

"What is it?" said Zoe. "Can I—may I—"

"Yes," rejoined he, "I will tell you—I came to tell you.

"I have this morning sent away a young creature to encounter all the evil there is in the world, for women who have placed themselves under the world's ban. She had loved me, sacrificed every thing to follow me into this country; women have no perception of virtue or excellence in one who has committed all her sins from love; so you may think I have only performed an act of morality in casting her away from me—but I know I have behaved damnably. Any way," continued he, after a pause, "we must always approach our deities with sacrifice; and the more innocent, the more excellent is the victim. I have done this for you, Zoe; because, since I looked on you, there has existed no other woman in the world for me: I wished to put away every thing that could stand between us. I did not dare to approach you till all that could offend you had been put away. Zoe, I am come to give myself up to you. I only ask you to let me come to you. I have known no rest since I saw you last, and now that I have committed this cruelty to be free to love you, do not cast me away from you; say you accept my sacrifice—no, not sacrifice, for I would freely give everything, life itself, to be beloved by you. Say that I may come and worship you, and find peace. Do not send me away to be alone."

Zoe trembled violently, but she did not speak.

"I know", continued he, still more passionately, "the world does not speak well of me—I am no credit to you, my fortunes are broken, and I am an outcast both from my country and my father's house;—but I ask nothing from you till you freely give it. I only ask you to let me remain near you—let me live in your presence. Oh, Zoe! if you had crossed my path earlier, I should not have been the battered, sullied wretch I am. Heaven has rained all its curses on me; but it has sent me to you to be purified and calmed. Speak one word, Zoe, and say that you accept the office, that you will be all to me, that you will be my angel."

Zoe breathed thick and heavily—but she did not utter a word.

"Zoe! is all I have done of no avail? Why will you not speak? What do you see in me to trifle with?"

She made an effort, but no sound came from her lips.

"I thought you were superior to womanish weakness," said he, contemptuously; "but perhaps you do not consider me worth deciding about; in that case, I can relieve you from your embarassment." He rose as if to leave the room.

"I may not—I dare not," burst from Zoe's lips in suffocating accents.

"How dare not?"

"I belong to another," said she, in a sharp, quick tone, as if the utterance gave her physical pain.

"Do not deceive yourself, Zoe," said Mirabeau, in a calm, cold voice; "your heart does not belong wholly to him at this moment;—do not sacrifice my happiness and your own to the fashion of a word which no longer has a meaning for you. What is the good of calling yourself constant, when you know you are so no longer?—do you fancy you can hide yourself from me? Zoe, you will never find one who can love you as I do. I only ask you to allow me to be near you—to let me pour out my whole soul before you. I only ask not to be forbidden to give myself to you. Is that requiring so much from you?"

346

If he would only have interpreted her emotion, she would have been thankful; but that did not suit him.

"Nay," said he, "I cannot be satisfied without a reply from you; tell me only that you accept me, I ask nothing from you in return. I do not wish to distress you;—I will depart now, if you desire it;—but if I go, I do not return. Now speak,— shall I go?" He fixed his eyes steadily upon her—there was a pause.

"No," said she, at last, in a tone so choked, that it was scarcely audible.

He folded his strong arms round her, pressing her to his bosom, on which she lay like a child, and he whispered, "Zoe, you must let me love you always."

A footstep was heard approaching the door; Mirabeau placed Zoe on the sofa, and sprang back some paces, so as to be leaning against the chimney-piece, when Lady Clara entered.

Zoe was too much agitated to attempt a word; but Mirabeau began a conversation full of brilliant nonsense with Lady Clara, which so engaged her attention, that she never noticed Zoe. Shortly afterwards, she went towards a table at the window to fetch her netting. Whilst her back was towards them, Mirabeau darted forwards, stooped down and kissed Zoe's feet, which were on a footstool; then, without moving a muscle of his countenance, said in a quiet voice, "It is time for me to go. Farewell, madam," and bowing profoundly to Zoe, he approached Lady Clara, of whom he took a laughing leave, in order, as he said, "to escape being entangled in her net", and quitted the room.

CHAPTER VII

– · –

A profound calm always follows gratified passion, of what nature soever the passion may be, which is in exact proportion to the previous tumult. Desire sleeps, and we wonder at our own eagerness; of course it awakens again and again, the refluent wave flows foward bearing down every thing in its progress, until the tide is at its height, and then—!

The first fullness of satisfaction is, however, widely different from the exhausted calm of that "sad satiety", which comes when we know the whole length and breadth of that which we have been struggling to obtain; when there is no more mystery remaining in it, and it yields no hope or sensation that we do not recognise afar off.

When Zoe came to reflect on the occurrences of the morning, she was terrified at what she had done. She could not reconcile the solecism of loving two men at once; and though her feelings had been as spontaneous as Nature itself, she was self-reproached with unfaithfulness and wrong. The more her heart refused to feel unhappy (for there was a secret joy that welled up from its depths), the more strenuously she felt that she ought to be ashamed of herself. Perhaps after all there might have been a little genuine shame in the matter, when she saw the calm radiant edifice of her high platonic constancy disappearing before the presence of a much more earthly emotion; undoubtedly she did not feel self-complacent on the subject; but there is no wrestling against facts, and it was an undoubted fact that she did love Mirabeau, though with a sort of dread she had never experienced before.

This is all we can say to pacify the reader's indignation at Zoe's dereliction from her allegiance to Everhard. "FOR EVER", can only be a mortal's word, so long as the PRESENT, that gave it birth, retains its influence.

The next day, Zoe did not feel at all inclined to join the party to the theatre; she was not well for one thing, and she had a strong disinclination to leave the house. She made an excuse, and much to the annoyance of the old duchess, who could never bear any one to break an engagement, remained at home.

She was sitting plunged in a confused reverie, of which it would have puzzled her to give an account, when she was roused by the sound of wheels; a hurried parley was held at the door, and Mirabeau, with his dress somewhat disordered, and his eyes flashing, entered the room.

"I am come, madam," said he, in his deep voice, "to know why you did not keep your word and accompany your friends to the theatre. Do you know that I went there to meet you; why were you so childish as to stay away? Perhaps you wished to avoid me, but you see that is impossible when I choose to see you. Do you think I am a man like your other lovers, to tremble at your caprices or to bend to them? I am your master;—do not set up a petty opposition to my desires, it offends me; give yourself up to me;—who is there to come between us? Does any one care for you as I do? Are you not more precious in my eyes than all the world contains besides? Why then do you keep up this childish pretence of independence? Do not I love you more than you can possibly love yourself?"

This appeal was uttered with a passionate rapidity, that prevented all possibility of reply. Zoe was stunned and astonished—she had never been addressed in her life before by any man, except with most perfect deference.

"Why, I ask," said he, after a slight pause, "did you not go to the theatre to-night?"

"I was not well, and I did not feel disposed," said Zoe, with some haughtiness.

"Not disposed!—I believe it," replied he, contemptuously. "You repented the word you said yesterday, and, like a woman, wished to draw back.—Zoe! Why do you rebel against me, and try to put these ridiculous formalities between us?—Will all the struggles in the world unsay what you have already said?—Will they break the bond that binds you to me?—It is in vain you attempt to withdraw yourself—your being is swallowed up in mine, and this womanish vacillation makes me angry; it is unworthy of you. It will not alter the fact, that you are unfaithful to that other, that you have given yourself to me, and that I will keep you mine for ever. This weak opposition irritates me, displeases me. It lessens the respect I have for you—and you cannot set yourself free."

Zoe sighed.—"I am come", continued he, "to fetch you to the theatre. Your dress, no doubt, was got ready, before you made up your mind to stay away. Go, and put it on—or, come as you are. I can stay but ten minutes, and why should you deprive me even of ten minutes, you cannot recall them;—come as you are," said he, changing to a look and tone of tenderness singularly different from the harshness with which he had at first addressed her.

"There is no one there you wish to dress for—tell me, is there?" said he, impatiently, observing that Zoe hesitated.

"You know there is not," said she, in a low voice.

"That is well—come along.—Bah! the night is stormy, you will catch cold, your poor tender frame will suffer, you must have a mantle." He rang the bell impetuously. "Your mistress's cloak;—quick."

The wondering Abigail brought her mistress's head-dress and fan also; for, with the instinct of a waiting-woman, she divined that they were needful.

"Bah! what need of these details?" said he, impatiently. "You women fritter yourselves away, body and soul—you could think of a set of ribbons in the day of judgment; there is nothing large or grand in your natures." He wrapped the cloak round her as he said this, with the most scrupulous care, and, almost carrying her to the carriage, bade the postilion drive for his life.

Exclamations of wonder, and a whole storm of questions, greeted the entrance of Zoe and Mirabeau into the duchess's box. Zoe was horribly afraid of the old duchess; but Mirabeau interposed, to divert attention from her.

"Your ladyship has lost your wager," said he, smiling, to Lady Clara; "you said your friend would not come, that nothing would bring her. I love to conquer difficulties better than to listen to a five act tragedy. You excited my spirit of enterprise. I went in your name, and conquered!—Will you not, after this, entrust me with

350

some mission for yourself? I will do any thing; tell me any thing you desire," said he, with emphasis, "and I will bring it to pass, especially if it be impossible.—Let me be your providence. Ah! then you will ask nothing, you leave yourself in my hands, like a true believer. Well, then, I will make the heart of an insincere man earnest!" He darted a meaning glance at her, and she cast down her eyes beneath it.

"Well," said the old duchess to Zoe, "I don't understand all this, it is very extraordinary; how did you come?—or why did you come at all, if not with us? Really it is too eccentric."

"My dear duchess," said Mirabeau, reverentially, "Mrs Gifford is a victim to circumstances. Visit me with your displeasure. Mrs Gifford always tells the truth, and fancies it impossible for any one else to do otherwise; and, when I made use of your name, she came with me as unsuspectingly as a lamb with its butcher. Your personal influence must indeed be terrible, when the mere utterance of your name in a request was sufficient to bring a fair lady in dishabille to the theatre on a night like this. I must appeal, not only for your forgiveness, but also intreat your intercession with Mrs Gifford for hers. But indeed, your grace owes me some thanks for the proof I have elicited of your influence over Mrs Gifford. The influence of some women is not a world's wonder, but a world's miracle, an enchantment producing effects without visible means."

He spoke in such a respectful truthful tone, there was such fascination in his manner, that the duchess was not proof against it. She tapped him with her fan, shook her head, and said, "I think you are an acquaintance who will do Mrs Gifford no good, and the less she has to say to you the better. Only consider how seriously you might have compromised the dear unsuspecting creature, had I not fortunately been here to receive her, after your wild-goose errand."

"And does your grace really believe me so mad as to have run the risk, had I not been perfectly certain that joining you would effectually check all surprise or surmise at our entrance together? Believe me, I well knew the value of your grace's presence, or I should not have ventured on such an escapade. I had heard of your influence, and I wished to try it. Mrs Gifford is one worth influencing."

351

"Indeed she is a charming creature," said the duchess, quite mollified; "but don't do any thing imprudent to get her talked about, or I shall never forgive myself for introducing you to her. I don't believe half the ill that is said of you, or rather I believe in all the good that is in you; but you are not a proper companion for a young and lovely woman."

"But then there is your grace to counteract my ill effects," said Mirabeau, in a mocking tone.

He only once approached Zoe, and that was as they left the theatre. He whispered in her ear, "Foolish and faithless one! will you not now trust me to carry you scatheless of blame through the conventionality of life? Trust yourself to me."

When he handed the duchess to her carriage, he said "I must make haste or I shall be late; I am engaged to supper with Mr Wilberforce. I like to study the respectable virtues first in my friends, and then, if they seem worth any thing, I can set them up for myself."

"Well, now Mrs Gifford," said the old duchess, when they were seated, as she drew up the glasses, "how came you to trust yourself with that wild man? What did he say to induce you to come with him?"

"Really, your grace, I hardly know; he ordered the post-boys to drive furiously, and I was at the theatre before I had ceased to wonder why I left home."

"Take care," said the duchess, "he does not persuade you into worse mischief some of these days, for he has the tongue of the old serpent himself."

"How did you and Horace get on, to-night?" asked Zoe, when they were once more seated in the drawing-room.

"What on earth!" exclaimed Clara, who had not spoken a word since they left the theatre; "what on earth possessed you to come in that wild way? Why could you not come quietly with us? Horace was wondering about you all the evening. I never saw such a person as you are—never easy but when all the men are taken up with you." There was a slight pique in Lady Clara's manner that appeared through the tone of badinage she attempted to assume, and it did not escape Zoe's notice.

"Clara," said she, kindly, "you do me great injustice if you think

352

I want to attract Horace, even if he were to my taste (which he is not); after what you told me, I should consider myself the most heartless and dishonest of human beings, were I to wish to attract him. I will do any thing in my power to serve you, though you cannot need my assistance, for Horace certainly cares more for you than any one else; but do not, even in thought, accuse me of trifling with your feelings, for the pitiful gratification of my own vanity."

"It is all very fine," said Clara, "you think yourself above all female weakness, but if it were not to attract Horace, what other motive could bring you? Did you not stay away, as you told me yourself, in order that he might not be obliged to pay attention to any one else? did you not insist on staying at home, in spite of all our persuasions? and then to come after all!—If you really cared for him, I would say nothing; we should be on equal terms, and might each do our best; but it is because I know you despise him, and care nothing about him, that I am so indignant at your trifling. But you seem to think me altogether a fool!"

Lady Clara had worked herself up into a passion, and here burst into a fit of hysterical weeping. Zoe was altogether bewildered by this sudden tempest, and fancied that Lady Clara must have gone deranged. She had been so engrossed by her own feelings of late, that she had never noticed the fact that Horace had really seemed more occupied with her, than Lady Clara was at all likely to approve; and, in utter absence of mind, indeed, with her heart, as the reader knows, distracted by hopes and wishes infinitely removed from the Reverend Horace, she had smiled on him and talked to him without any sort of calculation as to the appearance it might bear; and Lady Clara had not unnaturally interpreted her abstraction and frequent abruptness of manner, and all the inequalities of temper she exhibited, to her struggles to repress a growing partiality for the said Reverend Horace O'Brian. Nothing of this, however, dawned on Zoe's comprehension; but she saw that her friend was suffering, and she was much distressed at the turn her fancy had taken. She did not speak to her, but placing a large goblet of water beside her, retired out of sight till her agitation should subside, which at length it did. Then, taking her hand and sitting down on an ottoman at her feet, she said in the kindest tone she could assume,

"My dear Clara, what frenzy possesses you? Horace O'Brian

353

does not care for me, does not even admire me. Do you not see that he fears I shall prejudice you against him, on account of his affair with Clotilde, and that he is endeavouring to propitiate me? He is attached to you, but he cannot make up his mind to propose; he is too full of the mitre he is hoping for, and that is your rival, not me. You will have some trouble to bring him to the point, but love, or even admiration of me, will not be one of the hindrances. Horace O'Brian's great aim and object is now to be made a bishop, and to obtain that, he would marry his grandmother if it were needed. All sorts of people come here, and he may fancy I have some influence, for when men are intriguing for place or power, they make a lever of the veriest straw. Somebody told me that the old Bishop of Lichfield was dangerously ill;—if you can serve him, he will make court to you, and you may have as much of his love as ever you want. It is not sufficient that you are charming, and that you love him, you must be able to help him on in the world. Think over all your friends and acquaintances, and let him feel you have some influence. Why, Clara! love seems to have obscured, instead of brightening your faculties."

"Zoe, you are very good to be so patient with me, and I am very childish; but I am very unhapppy," and she put her arms round Zoe's neck and hid her face in her bosom.

Zoe soothed and caressed her, and at last restored her to something like cheerfulness.

"You really are the best comforter I ever knew," said Lady Clara, smiling, as she took up her candle.

"I wish I had any body to comfort me," said Zoe to herself, when she was alone. "I am losing my nature, I think; God knows what is to become of me!"

CHAPTER VIII

– · –

When Zoe came to reflect calmly on the occurrences of the theatre night, she was piqued at the tameness with which she had allowed herself to be domineered over by a man whom she had as yet hardly accepted for a lover; she determined that the next time he came, she would assert her own dignity, and act up to her old maxim, that "no man can stand being treated too well".

She had ample time to nurse her anger, and mature her plans, for Mirabeau did not make his appearance either the next day, as she confidently expected, nor the next after that;—nor did he send her note or message, or in any way testify of his existence. From being angry, Zoe became anxious. She fancied that he must be ill, or that he had met with some untoward event, for she knew his reckless and impetuous character. She conjured up visions of all sorts of evils, to which it ought to have been her privilege to minister; finally, humbled, as her proud mind had never been humbled before, she began to speculate on what offence she might have given him. She tasked her memory with every look and word during the last evening they were together; the result was—deep perplexity. That her present lover was not a man to be trifled with, she clearly saw; and bitterly resolved that when he returned to her, she would run no risk of again ruffling the plumes of her "tasselled gentle".

At length, quite wearied out of all remains of her dignity, she determined to discover his abode, and send an embassy to him. Accordingly one fine morning, she proposed to Lady Clara that they should go to town for a "day's shopping". Lady Clara joyfully assented, and they set out to celebrate that truly feminine mystery.

After they had turned over silks and seen ribbons and feathers enough to have apparelled half the houris in Mahomet's Paradise, she and Clara each selected a magnificent dress, in honour of the duchess's dinner, and bought a quantity of those elegant nothings, which women contrive to manufacture into irresistible attractions. It is an odd fact, that whenever a woman sets up a lover, she should set up a great deal of finery at the same time; but whenever a woman falls in love, she shows it by dressing and adorning herself after the most elaborate fashion. To do them justice, women do not love dress for its own sake so much as is supposed; there are few who would dress for dinner if they were thrown on a desert island, with no lover in company. Zoe was not at all insensible to the charms of becoming attire, and in the care of assorting the shades of trimmings, and the inspection of a box of exquisite French lace that had just been smuggled over, her late anxiety was, we are ashamed to say, suspended for the moment; be it remembered, all this care was to look well in the eyes of another. There is some pleasure in wearing pretty things, when one we love is to behold them.

At length, when all was bought and ordered, and the footman paused for his direction, and the real object of her journey to town was to be transacted, Zoe feared that Clara, that the footman, that the very coach-horses, would divine her secret; she coloured, hesitated, and at length summoned courage to order them to drive to a bookseller whom she named; then, turning with a sort of apology to Lady Clara, she said, "We may as well get that French novel, or some new books at any rate, for they have sent us nothing worth reading lately." Her heart beat violently, and she talked on rapidly, till the carriage arrived at the door of the shop. Clara would not alight, and Zoe entered alone.

She asked for several things, and bought half-a-dozen books she did not want to read, before she could summon confidence to ask for a pamphlet by Count Mirabeau, which just at that time was making a sensation.

She knew it was Mirabeau's publisher who was speaking to her so blandly—she asked a question about him.

"Count Mirabeau?—Ah! a wonderful genius, pity he should be so eccentric and irregular; a man of great powers—very—much cleverer when you come to talk to him, than you would fancy from his writings: he was here, only a few minutes ago; it is a pity you missed him, as you might have liked to see him."

Zoe thought it a great pity too. "Does Count Mirabeau often come here?" continued she.

"Oh yes, several times a week. He generally calls about this time, but to-day he was earlier."

"Can you give me his address?" said Zoe, with a desperate effort at indifference.

"Certainly," replied he, "or, if you like to leave a note, I will forward it immediately."

This, however, Zoe refused, and taking the precious scrap on which the address was written, she left the place.

Anything so beautiful or graceful had never before entered those dingy precincts, and when Mirabeau returned later in the day, he did not fail to hear of the lovely apparition who had been inquiring for him. He had no difficulty in divining who it was: he had now reduced her to the state he wished, and the next morning, whilst Lady Clara in her dressing-room was solacing herself with the new books, and Zoe in her little morning-room was sitting writing, and destroying the paper as fast as she wrote, Mirabeau stood beside her! He entered, according to his custom, unannounced;—Zoe's pique, offended womanhood, fears, anxiety were all forgotten in the deep throb of joy that seeing him caused. "My own Zoe!" was all that was said, for many minutes. No word of explanation was given or asked—he was there, she required no more. He persuaded her to walk out into the grounds, where there would be less fear of interruption; there, in those walks, which had so won the admiration of Lady Clara—in those shaded seats, which she had declared wasted without a lover—sat Mirabeau and Zoe in a happy trance. He had placed himself on the ground, sometimes covering her hands with kisses, sometimes gazing into those glorious eyes, which were cast down on him, dimmed with ineffable love. The sun-light glanced in upon them through the boughs which though autumn had already begun to thin, still a pleasant chequered shade came through the green leaves. A few expressions of passionate tenderness, broke forth at intervals, but the time of words had not yet come.

They were together, and required nothing beyond. There was no "before or after" for them yet; the present moment absorbed all their being.

"Oh, Zoe!" said Mirabeau at last, "is not this worth an eternity?"

"It is," replied Zoe, in a tone not louder than a sigh. "I am so happy, that it begins to be like pain."

How the hours flew, neither of them could have told; when at length Mirabeau quitted her, Zoe remained dreaming and entranced on the same spot, not thinking, not remembering, but wrapped round in happiness; it seemed as if it were needful for Mirabeau to go away, before she could become conscious of the extent of it.

She went all that day in her blessedness; and then began the thought, "when will he return?" and she began to think of the next meeting, and to live in the hope of it;—for it is true of all things, but of happiness more emphatically, that it "holds in perfection but a little moment".

CHAPTER IX

— · —

Before Zoe left her room the next morning, a note was handed to her, with information that her grace's own page waited for an answer.

> "My dear Mrs Gifford," (so ran the note)
> "Will you and your friend, Lady Clara, come and spend a long day with me? I want to consult you about arrangements for my *fête*; you have both of you a genius for such things. I wish either of you could tell me whether the day will be fine to accommodate me! Come early, and oblige your affectionate friend,
>
> "MARGARET N."

Zoe wrote an answer in the affirmative, though she did not feel much tempted at the prospect it opened. Lady Clara insisted upon finishing the last volume of her novel before she stirred, and Zoe, seeing her so much engrossed, mentally resolved that she should never lack a good supply, so long as she remained her guest.

They found the old duchess in a most gracious mood, and as much occupied in arranging the details of her *fête*, as if she were still asserting her claim to be at the head of the fashionable world.

It was finally settled that as a fine day was highly doubtful, it should be a natural dinner in the dining-room, and that whatever rurality might seem advisable, should be improvised when the time actually came. "I shall not live to give many more *fêtes*," said the old lady, "and I have quite set up my heart upon every body enjoying this one very much indeed. Now, children, is there any one either of you would like to have invited? If there is, sit down and write a card."

"Has your grace any objection to ask the Reverend Horace O'Brian, the Dean of——?" said Zoe. "You have seen him, he was of the party to the theatre the other night."

"Write by all means," said the old lady, "that is if he be not already invited; look over the list of guests, here it is. Whilst you have the pen in your hand, you may write a card to Count Mirabeau; he has reappeared since the invitations were issued; and add a note in my name, to beg he will make a point of coming, as some of the parties he will meet here, may be serviceable to him. His father, the crabbed old 'Friend of Man', was an admirer of mine some forty years ago, and although he has since become so wild and eccentric, he was in those days a man of whose admiration any woman might feel proud; and I take great interest in his son, though he both does and says things to make the hair of one's head stand on end; still it is more the fault of his bringing up, than any vice of his nature; and I have a great deal more regard for him, than for many of those who pass for being more respectable; he has some tenacity and substance in his character, and I do honour that whenever I see it;—still you must recollect, children, that though it may be all very well for me, who am besides an old woman, to be friendly with him, I do not recommend him as a companion to either of you; so remember, you have been warned."

Zoe wrote the note with a beating heart. It certainly would have surprised any one not in the secret, to see the reverence with which, after this, she listened to the old duchess, and the zeal with which she arranged stands of flowers, legislated about lustres and chandeliers, and finally showed the resources of a whole "committee of amusement", in her own unassisted genius!

Zoe did not again see Mirabeau till the day of the *fête*; he was obliged to go into the country, and had, besides, to work day and night to have a work he had promised ready for the printers by a certain day. But this absence was not painful and heavy like the last; he found time to write her passionate, if hurried letters, and she had to reply to them. They were the first love letters she had ever written in her life.

At length the grand day arrived, and Zoe dressed for the occasion, with a feeling of delight and buoyancy she had never known in her life before. She could hardly help smiling at herself, as she gazed on her reflection in the mirror, it looked so bright and happy.

"Youth is a movable feast, after all," thought she, "I never felt so youthful as I do to-day. Pray Heaven!" she sighed a moment after, "that it may not be the forerunner of some ill; if I were a heathen, I should forthwith offer a sacrifice to avert the omen of too much happiness."

"Really, Zoe!" cried Lady Clara, when they met in the drawing-room, "I never saw you look so well; when I left my room I was pretty well satisfied with myself, but I am more than half out of conceit, now that I see you."

"If Horace O'Brian's heart be not burnt to a cinder to-day, he must be an insensible brute," said Zoe, laughing.

When they entered the drawing-room at——Castle, it was about half full. They paid their respects to the duchess, who was dressed in great state, and then found seats at a little distance, where they were soon surrounded by some of the most distinguished-looking men in the room. Zoe looked round for Mirabeau, and as she caught his eye, her glance said to him, "All this is for you." He made his way towards the spot where she sat—as he passed her chair no ear but her own, caught the low passionate exclamation, "My Zoe!" He did not attempt to enter into conversation with her, he talked to those around him; but almost every sentence he uttered had a secret meaning for her.

She kept her eyes fixed on the figures of her Indian fan; but she felt his looks upon her, and knew every change that passed over that wild countenance; and no one in all the vast apartment suspected the secret communication that was going on between them.

The fashionable men and young *élégants* round her, flattered themselves that her air of gentle preoccupation was the effect of their individual fascinations, for it seemed utterly impossible that any thing so precious as was each one of them in his own eyes, could be altogether indifferent in hers; and Zoe was so happy, that she really thought them, one and all, very amiable, and not at all bores.

We may as well mention here, in order not to interrupt the course of this history, that, in consequence of her very charming behaviour on this day, poor Zoe incurred the necessity of having to refuse three separate offers of most respectable hands, with the hearts thereunto appertaining, and all at the imminent peril, as the owners averred, of "blighting them irrevocably"! This may serve to warn women that they cannot be charming with impunity.

A movement was at length made towards the dining-room. A wizened, diminutive, changeling-looking man, offered his arm to Zoe, and handed her down stairs. He set himself seriously to entertain her, and little as she was disposed to care who became her neighbour, she soon found her interest excited by her strange-looking companion. Indeed, as Zoe was not destined to fall to the lot of her lover, she could not well have been more fortunate, for this peculiar individual was Wilberforce, one of the most remarkably agreeable men of the day. Mirabeau, however, was on the opposite side of the table, and within both sight and hearing. Horace O'Brian and Lady Clara sat together near Zoe, and he allowed all his attention to be engrossed by his fair companion, except just the portion he contrived to bestow on Wilberforce, who was the friend of influential men.

The guests had all been selected for either distinguished talent or social reputation. These quintessential *réunions* are often failures; when people are obliged to go into company, armed *de pied en cap* in their reputation, to meet others cased in equally brilliant sheen, a metaphysical influence seems to pervade all, and impede the natural use of their faculties. But the good duchess was destined to succeed; the dinner went on pleasantly, and the guests talked in their natural manner.

Zoe said to her companion, who had been telling her some amusing anecdotes about the king and queen, "How happens it, that though power is always imposing, yet the kings and ministers, and all parties invested with it, seem insignificant?—They do so little, compared with the means they have at their command."

"Persons at a distance may fancy they achieve little, because they see nothing of the difficulties of their position," replied he; "invisible hindrances impede the simplest action—placing a man at the head of affairs, is like setting him to walk on a rock of load-stone in iron-bound shoes; no one merely looking on, can see why it is he makes so little progress. Having to set a cumbrous machinery in motion, and to act with it, absorbs much strength and enthusiasm, for which there is nothing to show!"

"Kings and nobles", said Mirabeau, who had been listening to what Zoe was saying; "seem insignificant, because their position is an exaggerated one, and their capacities are not magnified in proportion;—to make the most of the means at their disposal, would require them to be a race of heroes and demigods, like the first founders of their order. The doings of average men look small and poor beside the amount of power placed at their disposal—generally speaking, they really achieve as much as nine out of ten men ever accomplish, but they seem to do less, because they have had larger characters cast to them in the world's drama than they can fill."

"I should like to see a real hero," said Zoe.

"He would not be at all like what you probably expect," replied Mirabeau; "heroes, whilst they are living and struggling through their labours, do not appear the trim well-polished characters you find in romances; they are not finished in the Sir Charles Grandison fashion. Life is not a stage representation, with every incident placed in its most effective light; there is blood, and sweat, and fatigue, and much failure, before aught heroic can be achieved. Your heroes are washed and trimmed, before they are put in history, and the greater number of their deeds buried in silence. A hero would shock all your notions of respectability; he would be on so much larger a scale than you have been accustomed to see, that you would only find him probably full of inequalities, rough, cruel, unjust; you would see the details were not finished according to the bland conventionalities of polite society—and you would be unable to take in the design of his character as a whole. A hero requires to be removed from the present time and placed on a pedestal of at least a century of the past, before the eyes of men can take in his greatness. Heroes are not gods, or they might work like Nature, silently, majestically, and without visible effort;—but they are men, only of a larger soul; and they have to do their work like men, with all the impediments of an imperfect will, fiery passions, and the sense of an illimitable task spreading itself out before them, with the consciousness that all their toil and effort produces only shortcomings, and that their aim is so high they cannot attain to it;—thus they who are constantly grappling with a task not to be done easily, but which takes all their strength, have none to spare in making themselves amiable, and in conciliating approbation. They who are despatched into 'dark regions to slay monsters for us', do not return without bearing marks of the fray. The world would soon come to dissolution if heroes were not sent into it from time to time; but heroes would not be convenient drawing-room acquaintances."

"Yet," replied Wilberforce, "we have the Model, in whom no short-comings or imperfections are to be discerned."

"And what was said of Him during life?" rejoined Mirabeau.

"I wish you could give me a receipt how to conquer difficulties," said Lady Clara, "I am not a hero nor even a heroine, still there are many things I wish to accomplish and cannot compass."

"Difficulties cannot be artificially overcome," said Mirabeau, "nor is there any invention whereby a man may be spared the trouble of conquering them; they must be grasped firmly, strangled, crushed, trampled down in manful fight. The savages are not far wrong, when they believe, that the strength of their conquered enemy passes into their own body."

"Yes," said Lady Clara, slightly shrugging her white shoulders, "but we so soon get not to care about things—the inclination for them so soon passes away, that it is hardly worth while to weary ourselves; even annoyances are not worth so much trouble to avoid. It is better to resign ourselves, and take things as easily as possible."

"I have often felt a painful sympathy", said Zoe, "for men who might have been heroes had they lived in another age—they are great men *manqué*—they succeed in nothing."

"And success", said Wilberforce, "is the only point of which the world takes cognisance; it is never grateful for intentions or efforts, nor even for imperfect success."

"And that", said Mirabeau, "is not so unjust as it may seem, for failure is an evidence that there is a flaw somewhere. If there is a want of facility to conform themselves to the actual circumstances in which they are placed, men will break down on all occasions, will succeed in nothing; why should we pride ourselves in being men, unless we actually achieve all that we have to do, whether it be small or great, the minutest domestic arrangement, or the government of an empire? A man ought never to say anything that requires to be done, that is beneath me, nor feel any thing that comes in his way beyond his power; for nothing is impossible to the man who can keep his will erect and firm."

"Ay," said Zoe, "but our firmness of will depends so much on the accidental variations of our inclination. We forget the point of view in which we but yesterday beheld the object; and, as Lady Clara says, except in the heat of the moment, it does not seem worth while to make a strong effort."

"In general," said Wilberforce, "men are strong in habit, and weak in will. Habits give us no trouble, there is no friction; the obstacles to the little exertion required by a habit are worn smooth and almost obliterated, like the head of an old sixpence."

"Yes," said Mirabeau, "our vices are oftener habits than passions; habits wear men into uncouth shapes, as water models stones. All mechanical contrivance is habit materialised; it is continued action without any effort of will, except in the beginning."

"It is a great consolation", said Wilberforce, "to take refuge from our unstable noisy efforts, and the vain show in which we delight ourselves, in the knowledge that there is a Wisdom higher than our own, wherein is 'no variableness, neither shadow of turning'. Indeed, that seems the only knowledge that brings no sorrow with it."

The conversation then merged into the general topics of the day; and the duchess soon after giving the signal, the ladies left the dining-room, and proceeded to the grounds, which had been ornamented for their reception. Most of the gentlemen joined them shortly after, out of compliment to the duchess, whose guests they were. Her son, however, was obliged to remain to keep a knot of veterans company, who would have deemed an early rising from table as a perilous innovation on the principles of the British constitution.

"You will see me to-morrow," said Mirabeau, in a low voice, to Zoe, as they were drinking coffee in the drawing-room.

"Will you not come to see the children to-morrow?" whispered Horace O'Brian to Lady Clara. "Your presence is as great a blessing to them as it is to me; they do not rejoice in it as much as I do."

Never was oracle of old more pondered upon than these vague words.

Soon afterwards, the party broke up, for the duchess, like a loyal lady, followed Queen Charlotte's example, and did not patronise late hours.

"What a delicious dinner-party!" exclaimed Lady Clara, as they drove off.

"Yes, it really has been very agreeable, I have seldom enjoyed one more," replied Zoe.

"What a stupid affair!—I declare I never met such a set of shallow conceited men, and how absurdly over-dressed both Mrs Gifford and her friend Lady Clara were."

"Mrs Gifford is a dreadful flirt, and very much gone off in her looks.—As to that Lady Clara, her manners are sadly against her, poor thing. I am glad we have got away early, for it began to be very heavy."

Such was the conversation that passed in the carriage immediately behind Zoe and Lady Clara—for,

> "This vain world is all a dream
> Where nothing is, but all things seem."

CHAPTER X

— · —

If any one ever expected that "to love", would render them happy, they might as reasonably lie down on burning coals, in the hope of taking rest.

The next day, Mirabeau arrived almost before Zoe had dared to hope for him, but the gleam of sunshine had already passed from his features; he looked ill and moody.

"What ails you?" said she, anxiously.

"Nothing more than usual; you are deceived if you expect me to be always wooing you with smiles and gentle words—there is something deeper than those; it is childish love that expects to be fed on smiles and honeyed words. Zoe," said he, abruptly, after a pause, "I am ill—I am mad—I am come to you to be exorcised. Let me sit here beside you, and lay your soft hand on my shaggy mane—there—all sorts of gentle and healing influences distil from your touch." He laid his rough head upon her knee, and she bent over him uttering broken words of gentle tendency. "Ay," said he, after a little while, "had I earlier met with you, I should have been a different man; why did we never meet till now, when it is all but too late? You, too, have you ever met with a mate who could rouse all the noble faculties of your soul? Are not you too, cramped and perverted from what you might have been? Zoe, you must be mine. Why cannot we always be together?—and yet, to belong to each other now, it will require to break down all the conventionalities in which you have been bricked up. You would have to stand amid the ruins of your worldly position;—but, Zoe, I can bear you up through all; you may lean securely on me; ruined and broken in my fortunes as I may appear, still I can bear you up above the scorn of the world. You may love me, Zoe, love me with your whole heart—I can bear the weight of it;—intense passionate love embarrasses most men, and they throw it back upon the being who offers it;—but, if you love me, Zoe, you must give me your whole being—you must abandon yourself to me. Strong as you are, I am stronger still, and can give you in return love such as you never dreamed of. Tell me you love me, Zoe!—let me hear you say so—the words do me good."

"You know I do," said Zoe, in a low voice.

"Ay, but I cannot hear it too often. Tell me so again and again."

"I do love you, with all my whole soul," said Zoe, firmly; "does that satisfy you?" she added, with a slight smile.

"Zoe," said he, after a pause, "my energies have never yet been called forth for any thing but to struggle with oppression—pitiful inflictions that brought no glory in either conquering or enduring them; but I will yet do that which shall make me worthy of your love. Oh, you cannot know the strength and healing that lies in your words. I have long wished to talk to you about myself, you will interpret me with a loving heart.

"Oh, Zoe! when I think of all the good that was in me—how it has been broken, perverted, crushed out, till I am so soiled and defaced by evil passions, so scarred and thunder-riven, that no glory I can ever achieve, will make me bright and whole again. Zoe, I am not given to indulging in vain regrets, but when I think of these things, my heart seems as if it must burst.

"My father! how would I not have loved him! but he too arrayed himself against me to break me. We were both strong, and if I have not been crushed, I have been broken. All natural affection has been turned to poison and gall; I would have loved all whom nature has given me, father, sisters, wife, but they all bent under me and failed me in my need. Zoe, all the love I have ever known has been illicit. I was driven into the wilderness to perish, and I have become as rough and barren of all good as itself. Zoe, you have not sought your own happiness in loving me, but you have made mine. I have it in me to overcome the world. I have already mastered, in loathsome persecutions and ignoble misfortunes, what would have killed most men; but there has been no dignity; no glory; I have only succeeded in avoiding being stifled and swallowed up in stinking mire. Aught of employment for the energy I have in me, is further off than ever. I am consumed by my activity, and the candle lighted at both ends is fast disappearing—it has given a bright light on a worthless game. Those men whom we saw yesterday, are babies to me;—I feel I hold them all in my hand;—I grasp them and can turn them as it pleases me. I am their born master, and yet they, one and all, value themselves above me, because they have been able to keep in the trim garden of respectability. They regard me as an Ishmaelite, an outcast, and fancy they stretch out a hand to aid ME! Me they pity! me they apologise for knowing! and speak of me as one they must give an account of! No sympathy, no work!—all my strength must be consumed in battling with the world for my daily bread, in avoiding my creditors;—pursued by debts, dragged down and steeped in poverty to the very lips, unable even by my labour to supply the degrading wants of life;—and knowing what I ought to have been, what I have it in me to be;—oh! Zoe, is it not maddening? is it not enough to burn the heart that is in one to ashes?"

The giant-like man wept, his great chest heaved and his whole frame shook with the strength of his emotion. Zoe, inexpressibly affected, threw her arms round him, and clung to him, striving with passionate caresses to soothe him. There is always something dreadful to a woman in the sight of a strong man's emotion. For some time she spoke no words; at length, burying her face in his thick black locks, she whispered:

"Dear Gabriel, remember that the same Providence which has permitted all these trials and obstacles to befall you, has also ordained that you should not be overwhelmed by them. An object worthy of your energies will yet, fear not, be disclosed to you; and who knows for what great things you have all this while been fashioned and fitted? Slight difficulties would not have trained you—you required to be disciplined by what was harder and stronger than yourself; so that must needs seem beyond all credence rough and savage which has befallen you. Your great heart", said she, smiling sadly, and passing her hand over his rough brow, "would have disdained petty schooling; you have tried your strength with destiny herself, and are come alive and instructed out of her school. You have it in you to be great, and some great task is yet appointed you to fulfil. Let not your faith in yourself fail; remember the words you spoke only yesterday, about difficulties conquered."

"Ay," said he, bitterly; "but the reality of things comes upon us at times stronger than the wise theories and aphorisms, which we have framed when at ease. Today, I am weary and broken, and all philosophy sounds like mockery. Zoe, it is you who have brought this black fit of despondency upon me. It is seeing you, so bright and radiant, that has shown me the wretch I am—it is like looking up to Heaven, and seeing the miserable depth at which I lie beneath!"

"Dear Gabriel!" said Zoe, softly, "all the value of my radiance, as you call it, is, that it may give me power to soothe and brighten up your darkness a little. I never cared much about my position in life before, but now I feel glad that I am one of the world's 'respectable people', that I may give you the benefit of it all. All that I have is yours!"

"Thanks, Zoe. I will be content with knowing that is so. Oh! if I had you always to stand by me in my hours of darkness—they would be dark hours no longer," added he, gaily; "but come, the evil spirit is again off me, let us go into the garden.—Where is your friend?"

"She is gone to see the children of a friend," said Zoe.

"Ah! that Horace O'Brian's, I dare say; he is a plausible clever fellow, and might be bought body and soul for a mitre; but unless your friend can give him something else besides her heart, he will hardly value it. I had much conversation with him yesterday."

"He has a good deal of feeling," said Zoe, "and yet it is odd, that those men of feeling, do the cruellest things."

"Because", said Mirabeau, "their feelings are the lazy spontaneous growth of pleasurable emotions; they have no deeper root than inclination; all their energy has been choked out of them by ease; and, to save their own soul, they would shrink from doing any thing that was disagreeable at the moment. When people systematically try to spare themselves trouble, they are sure in the end, to act either like fools or villains."

"And yet," said she, "perhaps none would feel more shocked than they, were they told beforehand what they will do. 'Is thy servant a dog that he should do this thing?'"

"Yes," replied Mirabeau, "it seems at a little distance that there must always lie some great gulf between ourselves and an evil deed, and we fancy that having to leap it, will bring us to our senses when we stand upon the brink;—but you may believe me (for I have had experience)," he added, with a laugh, "that those deeds which are the very worst to look back upon come step by step so naturally, when you are once in the way, that the climax which gives the deed its name, is a result as little strained, and gives no more of a shock, than coming out of yonder door into this garden. 'What a little thing to fuss about!' is the involuntary comment of every one, who has been unfortunate enough to become criminal. It is the *first* declension from the level line of what is right that must be jealously regarded, for the inclined plane is so gentle, that it is easy to fancy we are going straight along. Nobody ever sees an action as very wrong when under the excitement of doing it."

"Then I suppose that explains the mystery of the Reverend Horace O'Brian's coldblooded conduct to poor Clotilde," said Zoe—"I wonder whether he will ever suffer for it."

"I believe", said Mirabeau, "the good and the bad that is in man, is compensated beyond its actual worth; and, though nothing is ever to its full extent, either so bad or so good as it logically ought to be from the elements called into action to produce it, yet no action can be committed without a consequence ensuing. But now tell me what is this about O'Brian. What has he done?"

"It is a story so common, that it seems almost childish to waste any indignation upon it;—and yet whatever befalls ourselves, has quite an original and emphatic air in our eyes." And then she related what is already known to the reader.

"Poor little girl!" said Mirabeau, when she ceased. "She must have been a sweet creature, but it is a law of Nature that the weakest must go to the wall—there is no evading it; the weak must break when they come in contact with aught harder than themselves—but, on the other hand, the same qualities that impelled him to behave so cruelly, will work to his own hindrance, and incidentally Clotilde will be avenged."

"Dear little soul, she does not dream of such a thing!" exclaimed Zoe; "but how do you think matters will end with Clara?"

"Does your friend know the history you have just told me?"

"Yes."

"What is that line of your English poet?

'And men think all men mortal but themselves.'

We shall see, I cannot pretend to prophesy the effects of your friend's fascination; but now my time is expired, and I must go."

"Oh, no, no, not yet!" cried Zoe.

"How gladly would I be always with you, and that you know, but there is no option for me just now;—it is a great blessing to be under the law of necessity, it saves much useless struggling. I am to dine with Sir Gilbert Elliot at five o'clock, and it is now past two; so you have nearly reduced me already to an impossibility. My own Zoe, you send me back a better man than I came; I cannot believe in the black thoughts that then oppressed me."

"When will you come again?"

"Soon, sooner than you expect. Commend me to your friend— and do not forget that you have undertaken to cover me with the mantle of your respectability! I fear", said he, as he lifted her in his arms like a child, "it will be Gulliver clothed by the Lilliputian—no offence to your serene highness—but I think I shall require more than you can supply; so farewell, my own darling." He was gone before Zoe could look round, and when she found herself really alone, she felt very much inclined to cry. She did not like the way in which he had departed at all:—restless and dissatisfied, though she would have been puzzled to say at what, she returned to the house.

Lady Clara shortly afterwards returned, bringing the two children with her. "My dear Zoe," she exclaimed, "the poor things begged so much to come and see you and the gold fish, I could not find in my heart to refuse."

"I am just delighted you have brought them. I intended to tell you, and then I forgot until too late." And in playing with the children Zoe recovered her composure. The boys had a holiday given them for the remainder of the day, and a very merry day it was for all parties.

"Did you see Horace this morning?" asked Zoe, when they sat down together at night, after quietness had been restored in the house.

"Oh, yes, and we had a long and most delightful conversation;—he said and looked every thing that could be desired. It was more like our old intercourse than we have had yet; and he said more than he ever ventured to say before."

"What was it?" asked Zoe, seeing that she hesitated.

"He said, that if his daughters resembled me, all his wishes for them would be more than gratified—that I was his ideal of what a woman ought to be; and then he seemed embarrassed, as if he had said more than he ought, and began to talk hurriedly of something quite different."

"Well, I call that the best thing you have told me yet," said Zoe; "but he gets on very slowly—it is quite provoking."

"And what did you do all the time of my absence? It was very rude in me to leave you."

"Oh," said Zoe, "I was in the garden part of the time;—one must make the most of these fine warm days, they are the last we shall have this year."

It would have brushed the bloom of Zoe's happiness, to have made it a subject of conversation, even to her friend. We do not want to tell of it when we are very happy.

CHAPTER XI

— · —

Many changes had come over the Rectory since the reader last visited it. Uncle Oliver was becoming very infirm, and had long employed a curate. Aunt Martha was still living, but she was very feeble and scarcely able to move across the room, even with the assistance of her ebony staff and the stout arm of the country girl engaged to wait upon her. She still kept her little spider-legged table beside her easy chair, and knitted indefatigably; though somehow her knitting now never achieved any shape.

Cousin Sarah Anne, who married the "young squire", had by the death of the old man, progressed into the style and title of Mrs Copley the squire's lady. Sarah Anne had proved herself worthy to face Rhadamanthus, for though she had not achieved the full complement of "bringing her husband seven daughters, and making eleven thousand cheeses", yet she had done a great deal towards it.

She was famous for her cheese, butter, and poultry, and had obtained celebrity for her method of fattening calves. Her children were brought up to be notable; she had four, two boys and two girls; the eldest, a girl of about thirteen, was herself in miniature, and followed her about in thick black worsted stockings, a stuff frock, and blue pinafore, into the dairy and over the house, visiting on the younger children all the cuffs and scoldings she herself received from her mother.

Every body has some pet virtue, and Sarah Anne especially prided herself on her economy; she boasted that she had once dined thirteen people for one shilling. It was her pleasure, however, to appear at church on Sundays, with her husband and four children in the Grange pew, dressed in the most wonderful array of

374

silks and many-coloured ribbons; whilst all her household were arranged in a pew at some distance, but within view; and woe to the luckless dairy-maid who ventured to cast a look on any of the plough boys, for Sarah Anne was the very dragon of propriety.

The "young squire" was scolded and henpecked, till by dint of hearing so constantly of his wife's virtues from her own lips, he ended at last by believing as he was told;—he smoked his pipe in the porch and drank his tankard of ale, and fell asleep in his three-cornered arm-chair every evening over his county newspaper, as his father had done before him; he took all his wife's crossness very peaceably, indeed it may be questioned whether he would have believed her to be the sensible woman he did, unless he had heard her sharp objurgatory voice ringing through the house all day long; he took it for the natural sign of her energy and thriftiness.

One evening Sarah Anne was knitting a stout worsted stocking, and her husband the squire was sitting opposite to her, smoking his evening pipe in their warm cosy parlour, when one of the female servants rushing across the red tile paved hall, burst into the room, exclaiming:

"I say, missus, here's one come from the Rectory, to say the parson's took with a fit."

The boy, who brought the intelligence, thrust his head into the door-way, confirming the intelligence, and begged her to go down to the Rectory directly.

Sarah Anne did not lose her presence of mind; she sharply reprimanded the servant who stood by with open mouth, desiring her to go back to her work, for a lazy, good-for-nothing hussy as she was, and then, clothing herself in an old pelisse, and a battered beaver bonnet, she bade her husband find his hat, and putting on her pattens, gave the lanthorn to the boy, took hold of her husband's arm, and set off to the Rectory.

When they arrived, they found all in confusion, the servants crying and running hither and thither; the poor old lady, querulously demanding what was the matter, and on the point of falling into a fit herself, from fright and agitation.

The surgeon had arrived a few moments previously, and was now attempting to bleed the rector in another apartment. Sarah Anne first administered a few sharp words, by way of bringing every body to their senses, and then inquired how it had happened. Half-a-dozen tongues were set going at once, and she contrived to ascertain that her uncle had assembled the household for family worship at the usual hour, when nothing remarkable was perceived; but, on the servant entering a short time afterwards with his basin of boiled milk, she found him lying senseless on the hearth-rug.— "I thought how it would be, ma'am, when I heard the death-watch last night: it all comes from Sally upsetting the salt, and breaking the salt-cellar, last Thursday;—I was certain sure something was going to happen, for the looking-glass in my room fell down without hands, and was all broken to pieces this blessed day!—Something could not help but come of it," added she, sententiously, almost satisfied that her master ought to die, to pay due honour to her auguries.

The surgeon here entered the kitchen, to say, that the rector had recovered his speech, and that she had better see him.

Sarah Anne was so shocked for a few moments at the change in her uncle, that she forgot every thing else. His mouth was drawn to one side, and he had entirely lost all sensation down one side of his body. When she drew near, he intimated, in scarcely intelligible accents, that he wished Zoe should be sent for express.—"A postchaise," articulated the poor old man, with difficulty.

This restored Sarah Anne's sensibility to its usual composure;— she could not refuse, and, as she turned away, with a scarcely repressed toss of her head, to execute the unwelcome command, her mother hobbled into the room, supported by her stout country girl, whose broad face was blistered and swollen with crying. "Brother, brother," cried the old lady, in her sharp querulous tones, "what is all this? Well-a-day!—But you shall not leave me, we will both go together, we have lived together nigh forty years and we'll not be parted now. Give me a chair, child," said she to the servant; and, seating herself close beside the bed, took hold of her brother's hand, and tried to rub it between her own, scarcely less useless and palsied.

Sarah Anne in the meanwhile retired to the tea-room, to indite such a letter to her cousin Zoe as should do credit to her own dignity and sensibility, whilst it should keep up the tone of superiority which she still imagined she had a right to maintain over her cousin. She was not much in the habit of letter-writing, so, as the reader may imagine, she had a task of some difficulty to encounter; but Sarah Anne was one of those singularly fortunate persons who come up to their own ideal in every thing. She went to work, whilst a man was despatched to the inn for a chaise, and wrote the following epistle.

"Dear Cousin Zoe,

"It has pleased the Dispenser of all mercies to strike my dear uncle and yours with a fit, which promises to cut short his valuable life, which afflicting event (that tries the courage of the boldest) he is prepared (having mercifully recovered his senses) to meet as becomes a minister and a Christian, and the way in which he has spent his long and (I may add) innocent life.

"He has asked for you, and begged that a chaise might be sent for you; I hope that you will not allow any of your fashionable engagements to prevent you complying with his request, as it would not be a reflection that would console you on your own death-bed, which sooner or later will overtake us all.

"As I am placed in a leading station here, you will, I know, attribute my request to the proper motive—but I shall feel glad if you will not bring with you any assortment of fashionable apparel. I do not wish the simplicity of the inhabitants of this parish to be corrupted by the sight of vanities, which would make them discontented with the 'station into which they have been called', as the catechism teaches them every Sunday afternoon. We who are placed in a superior station ought to be careful what example we set to those below us.

"I am, in haste, dear Cousin Zoe,

"Your humble Servant,

"SARAH ANNE COPLEY."

Sarah Anne did not seal up this letter without first reading it over to her husband, who was quite astonished at the performance. "Why, Sally," said he, "thou art quite a scholar, girl; it is as pretty a letter as ever I heard. I did not think thou couldst have written like it."

"Oh," said Sarah Anne, with a toss, "I would write quite as well as another, if I had time to give to such things; but I consider that a woman ought to be a good wife first and foremost; and I shall teach my girls not to be bookworms. I think, Will, you ought to be very thankful. If you had had your own way, you might at this moment have had Zoe Gifford for your wife instead of me, and been the husband of one who is neither fish nor flesh, instead of a father of as fine a family as any in England: and where would you have been then, I should like to know?"

Zoe could not arrive before the following evening, and Sarah Anne made use of the time to order a most imposing new hat and feathers, though her husband remonstrated against it as extravagant, seeing "she was so soon going into mourning" but she sharply retorted, that though it became all people to be humble and affable, she was not going to be disparaged beside her cousin Zoe; and that she had saved enough of his money to buy a new hat when she chose, without being accused of extravagance.

When the chaise drove up to the Rectory door, Sarah Anne was ready to receive her cousin, in a new hat and feathers, and the very stiffest and most radiant-coloured brocade dress her wardrobe afforded. Zoe, anxious as she felt about her uncle, could scarcely help smiling at the figure which presented itself; however, she greeted her cousin very cordially, who was much consoled to find that Zoe was attired merely in a white wrapper and plain black silk mantle, and that her bonnet was a coarse straw, "without any trimming to signify, and not at all tasty", as she afterwards said to her husband.

Poor Uncle Oliver remained still in the same state—there had been no change in him since the night before. He rallied a little for a few moments when Zoe entered, and told her it was a great comfort to him to see her; but he soon fell off into a doze, with her hand in his.

Zoe felt very mournful; he was the last relation left, except her aunt and cousin; and whatever other friends we may have, we care for relations as we care for nobody else.

Zoe was in due time summoned down to supper. Sarah Anne had determined that her supper should be as imposing as her head-dress: there was a hot round of boiled beef at the top, a roast goose at the bottom, with all sorts of vegetables at the sides, and a large plum-pudding in the centre. The silver branch candlestick—that never saw light but on very grand occasions—had been brought down, all the glass that could by any means be displayed was set out, and Sarah Anne flattered herself that Zoe would be quite as much impressed with the magnificent display as she was herself. Zoe, the doctor, Sarah Anne, and her husband, sat down to table: the supper passed off without any incident, except that Sarah Anne ruined the front breadth of her best gown in carving the goose.

Zoe declared her intention of watching beside her uncle all night, in spite of Sarah Anne's assurances that the best room had been got ready, and a fire lighted in it, on purpose for her.

There is something almost appalling in watching all night beside the couch of sickness. The chill night air, the heavy stillness, the tall flickering shadows cast from the rushlight, all produce a sensation as of being in the presence of an unearthly being; the very sleeper, though our most familiar friend, seems transformed into something awful and mysterious.

The old man did not speak during the whole night; Zoe raised him up to give him his medicine, but he seemed quite unconscious of who was beside him. Towards morning he opened his eyes, and said, "You are very good to me, Zoe," and then relapsed into his former insensible state. At five o'clock she was relieved from her watch by the nurse, and retired to take the repose of which she stood in so much need. She did not again see poor Uncle Oliver alive; the nurse knocked at her door about eight o'clock, to tell her that all was over: "He went off like a bird, poor old gentleman. He just muttered a few words I could not understand, and then he was gone. He was always a good man, and a real gentleman, if ever there was one," said the nurse, wiping her eyes. "Well, we must all be took some time, and it's well for them as can make as good an end as he did. I ask your pardon, ma'am, for disturbing of you, but I thought it would be a comfort to you to know. Now, if you will excuse me, I will go, as I've many things to see about."

The whole of the day the house was in a state of bustle and confusion that was quite painful to Zoe, who established herself in her aunt's apartment, that she might see and hear as little of it as possible. The old lady took very little notice of Zoe, and when informed of her brother's death, seemed much less affected than they expected; she only said, "Ah, well-a-day, we shall not be long parted." When the girl brought her knitting, as usual, she put it on one side, saying, "I shall not want it again; but you have been a good girl to me, and I give you these needles, and the silver sheath too, for a keepsake"; on which the girl went crying into the kitchen, and said she was "sure missis was going to die, she was so mild and strangelike".

Her fears were realised. The old lady took to her bed that day; the doctor declared nothing was the matter, but that unless she were roused, she would die from the conceit of it. From whatever cause it came, the old lady sank rapidly; and when the coffin was brought home for Uncle Oliver the undertaker had to receive orders for another for Aunt Martha. They were both buried on the same day, amid the sincere tears of the whole parish; and they were long regretted by old and young.

Zoe, who had become uneasy at receiving no letters, had two put into her hands on the day of the funeral; they were both from Lady Clara, but owing to the mysteries of a cross post, she received them together; they were to entreat her to hasten her return, as the eldest boy had been attacked with something which they feared was scarlet fever. There was a postcript to one of the letters, saying, that Count Mirabeau called a few hours after she left, and seemed singularly annoyed at finding her absent, and that the note she left for him did not seem to please him. This intimation Zoe scarcely heeded, so entirely were her thoughts engrossed by her child's illness. She signified her intention of departing so soon as a chaise could be procured. Sarah Anne, having secured the pattern of as many caps and sleeves as she desired, had no further wish to detain her, though she suggested she had better stay till after dinner.

Zoe went over the house and garden for the last time, and lingered in all the spots associated with childish recollections. She could never hope to behold them again, as the place was about to pass into the hands of strangers. Her uncle's study was the last place she visited; she sat down in his old black leathern chair quite overpowered. Sarah Anne, who was with her, exhorted her "not to take on so, as it could do no good, and would not bring back those who were gone".

Zoe begged her uncle's writing-desk, and an old copy of Virgil, in which she used to construe with him. As they were of no value, Sarah Anne made no objection.

The chaise having now arrived, she accompanied her cousin to the door. Zoe left proper messages for the squire, and drove away.

"I wonder", said Sarah Anne to her husband, "whether she will ever invite any of us to see her in London. I am sure she cannot say but what we have given her of the best, and showed her every respect whilst she has been here. I wonder what she gave the servants; I shall ask. I saw her give the gown she came in, to Nancy, who waited on her; but I shan't let her wear it. I really cannot see what beauty there is in her, can you?"

"Eh, what did you say, missis?" cried the squire, rousing from his nap as her voice ceased.

"I ask you whether you think Zoe Gifford a beauty?" said she, sharply.

"She would be well enough, if she was not so proud—keeping one at a distance like; and yet I have known the day, when she might have been thankful for an honest man to look at her."

"I warrant she has forgotten all that," replied Sarah Anne. "But I must go and look what those servants are doing at home; I declare we shall never be straight again."

Leaving her husband to finish his after dinner sleep, Sarah Anne proceeded to soothe herself by looking into her mother's hoards, to see what valuables had fallen into her possession, and to pack them up for transportation to the Grange.

CHAPTER XII

— : —

It was late at night when Zoe arrived at home. Lady Clara met her on the doorsteps. "I am so thankful you are returned!" was all that she could utter.

"For God's sake tell me the worst.—He is not dead?"

"No, oh no;—but the doctor has been here three times to-day. I was on the point of sending an express for you."

Zoe did not say another word, but went instantly into the room where the child lay. It was the third day of his illness;—he was delirious, and did not recognise his mother. He seemed to be suffering under a degree of terror and anxiety that was most painful to behold. When Zoe entered, he fancied she had come to carry him away to some place where all sorts of mysterious evil was to be practised against him, and he screamed so violently, that Zoe was obliged to conceal herself behind the bed-curtains.

On inquiring for the youngest boy, she found that he had been removed to the farmhouse where the little O'Brians were staying; in fact, he had not been in the house since his brother had begun to feel unwell. "On the very morning when Frederick first complained," said Lady Clara, "I offered to take them both with me for a walk; Frederick refused, but Charles was delighted; the children were so pleased with their playfellow, that they entreated me to leave him till night. I complied, but at night Frederick was so much worse, that, with a sort of instinct I cannot understand (for I suspected nothing really dangerous), I determined he should remain all night; it was a damp wet evening, and that I think decided me—and most providential it has proved; the next morning the doctor pronounced it scarlet fever. How he has caught it, I cannot imagine—he has not been out of the grounds since you went."

"But Charles?" said Zoe anxiously. "Charles is well? when did you hear of him?"

"He is quite well; I heard this evening at six o'clock."

"Thank God for that!" said Zoe; "but now, dear Clara, you are exhausted. I shall not go to bed to-night, I could rest nowhere but by his bedside. Do you retire—believe me, I am most grateful for all you have done, but you must keep yourself well for the sake of us all."

Lady Clara at length consented to go to bed, on condition that Zoe would yield her place to the nurse at daybreak, and that she should take some refreshment now. Zoe changed her heavy dress for a loose wrapper, and then, after hastily swallowing some coffee which Lady Clara brought, she returned to her son's bedside, and dismissing the attendant to sleep, remained alone to watch. She had always been tremblingly alive to the slightest ailments of her children, and had often needlessly tormented herself and every body round her. But now that sickness was indeed come, and in a shape that threatened to be mortal, her energies were roused, and all her anxieties merged into a stern breathless composure. Towards morning, the child fell into a doze; but it was troubled and restless, he seemed haunted with muttering dreams. It was a chill autumn night; the light had been removed into the adjoining dressing-room, as it had seemed to distress the patient. A thick white mist, like smoke, covered the ground, and the beams of the waning moon made every thing look ghastly and fantastic. There is something unearthly in this dim, white light; it is the light by which one would expect to see a supernatural manifestation. Zoe's thoughts had of late been familiarised with scenes of sickness and death. A mother's heart is always foreboding, and as she sat there listening to the tossings and mutterings of her darling child, occasionally raising his head to give him drink and medicine, smoothing his rumpled pillow, and bathing his brow with cooling applications, she felt as if standing on the threshold of the two worlds of life and death; her very fears seemed turned to stone, in the presence of the great stern inevitable Necessity which crushed all thoughts of prayer or hope out of her heart. A prayer is the natural speech of humanity in times of trouble and distress; but prayer seems so feeble when we stand in the presence of a great reality like death, that utter dumbness and stupefaction seizes upon us.

Early the next morning the doctor arrived; he declined giving any decided opinion, said it was a very severe case; that he was glad—very glad, Mrs Gifford had come back; that he would return toward the middle of the day, and that he would be able to speak more decidedly when he saw the child again in the evening. With this vague response, the wretched Zoe was obliged to be content. Lady Clara, with much difficulty, persuaded her to lie down for a few hours, but she refused to remove further than the dressing-room, and there, on a sofa, chilled, and utterly exhausted, she fell into a sleep, that scarcely veiled the consciousness of her misery from her.

When she awoke, she found it was near noon, and sprang up with a start of self-reproach, at having been away from her child so long. Lady Clara entered with some breakfast, and the intelligence that the child had fallen into a quiet sleep. She prevailed on Zoe to change her dress, and to go for a short time into the open air before she returned to the sick chamber, promising to take her place meanwhile.

Before Zoe had completed her toilet, a servant came to the door, to say that Count Mirabeau was below. Zoe felt absolutely indifferent, at that moment, whether she ever saw him again or not—but she went down to him nevertheless.

Mirabeau had come with the intention of spending several hours with Zoe, and had been pleasing himself all the way with anticipating her joy at seeing him; he had also many things to tell her, in which he knew she would rejoice.

He had not seen her since the day after the dinner-party, and as that had arisen not from his own will, but from Zoe's unexpected departure to her uncle's, he was infinitely more anxious and impatient to see her now, than he had ever felt before.

He sprang to meet her as the door opened, but started at the sight of her pale face, and sunk, discoloured eyes—"Good Heavens! Zoe.—What is the matter?—You in sorrow, and I here! Tell me what it is?"

Zoe sank on the sofa, and burst into tears, "Oh, Gabriel, my child is dying!"

"Nay," replied he, sitting down beside her, "you are tormenting yourself without need; other children have been as ill, and have recovered."

"No," said Zoe, sobbing, "it is the worst kind of fever, and the doctor gives me no hope."

"I am more afraid for you than the child; have you had it yourself?"

"No," said Zoe.

"Then you shall not go into the room again; you are of more worth than a hundred children, and I cannot run the risk of losing you; what is to become of me if you fall ill and die! Promise me", continued he, vehemently, "that you will not go near him again, but be content with the doctor's report:—why cannot he remain constantly with him? and Lady Clara—she may nurse him, but you, you shall not stay in this infected place. Come away with me now, and let me see you in safety!"

"Oh, Gabriel! how can you talk so?—I cannot even remain longer with you here. I must go back to his room; it is very mournful for you to come and find me thus, when you expected a happy meeting. I cannot think even of you now, except to feel you are my friend, and will not weary of me in my sorrow. I will write every day and tell you how he goes on; but do not come again to see me till I tell you. I shall know the worst to-night:—now farewell, dear love," said she, rising and preparing to leave the room.

"I will certainly neither remain nor return to embarrass you, madam," said Mirabeau, in a sarcastic tone, "I perceive I do not stand in your regard so high as I had flattered myself. I came, anticipating a happy meeting all the way as I came along; but it is only fools who are sanguine, and this will teach me never to feel too sure of a good reception. However, it may be some relief to you to learn, that I shall go to Scotland to-night for some time;—I shall hope to find you restored to something like composure when I return, and willing to see me if I should chance to come. I have the honour of wishing you good day, madam," added he, bowing profoundly, and retreating towards the door.

"Oh! do not leave me in that mocking way!" cried Zoe; "you are the only comfort I looked to in my trouble, I thought you would feel for me, for I am very wretched!"

"That is unfortunate," returned Mirabeau, coldly, "I have an unhappy temper, and should be a bad comforter. I am a brute, I dare say;—but", said he, shrugging his shoulders, "what would you have? Caprice and coldness always act unpleasantly upon me. I had prepared myself for a different reception, and I am disappointed; it is better I should be so, than you; however, if we meet again, I trust it may be in a more congenial mood, when there will be neither uncle, nor child, nor sick puppy-dog, to prefer their claims before me. Again I have the honour to wish you good day, till it be more convenient to you to receive me." He bowed again when he reached the door, and departed.

Zoe, stupefied with surprise at the bitter tone in which he had spoken, could not believe he really intended to quit her in such a manner; but, on lifting her eyes to the window, she saw him proceeding with hasty steps down the garden, and he disappeared almost immediately behind the holly fence. At another time she would have been almost distracted at this occurrence, but her one great sorrow absorbed all her feelings, and she felt little beyond surprise. She returned to her child's room and found him still asleep, but it was heavy and he moaned in it.

For several days longer he hovered between life and death; at last, however, he was pronounced "out of danger", and in Zoe's rapture of thankfulness, she became conscious of the depth of misery out of which she was raised. Still the doctor prohibited any interview between her and her youngest son, and it was near a month before it was judged prudent for him to return home.

Zoe and Lady Clara were both ill from fatigue and anxiety; sea air was prescribed for all; accordingly, the fifth week after Zoe's return from the Rectory, saw them established at Hastings.

All this time she had been scarcely sensible of Mirabeau's absence. She more than once felt astonished at her own insensibility; but now that her pressing anxiety was removed the reaction came. Her health and spirits were weakened by long confinement, and she had less strength to stand against the deferred hope, the wearying suspense, that every day became more intolerable.

Mirabeau had now been gone near two months, and she had received no tidings from him. She walked every day to meet the post, and her heart sickened at the smiling shake of the head, and "no letters for you to-day, ma'am", which constantly greeted her. Before leaving home she had written a few lines to him, telling him of their departure from Richmond, and had sent it to his bookseller to forward; but it was doubtful whether even his bookseller knew his address.

The last thought that enters a woman's heart is to blame him whom she loves. Men are much more magnanimous, and show their superior nature in nothing more than in that they never suffer their judgment to be impaired by any misgivings; however bitterly they may quarrel with their mistress, they are always equal to the effort of self-defence and justification. A true woman always blames herself, and it is a point on which her lover, to do him justice, never contradicts her.

Zoe wandered alone amongst the cliffs every day, sinking deeper and deeper into despondency. On the most minute self-examination she could not discover any thing in what she had done, but what, under the circumstances, she should do again;—still she could not bear to blame Mirabeau; she made all sorts of excuses for him, and laid the blame on something in her own manners, of which she was not conscious at the time.

Women are generally very perverse about their lovers; it has been sarcastically said, that "they never believe themselves loved, unless they are ill-used". We fear it is true, that most women prefer violent, selfish, even cruel, demonstrations of love, to the most generous, self-denying, silent renunciation;—any way it is certain that a selfish, imperious lover, gets much better treated than a generous one. Women like to make sacrifices to those they love, and they like to have them exacted. Zoe was infinitely more gentle, loving, and tractable with Mirabeau, than she ever would have been, under any circumstances, with Everhard. Her very nature seemed changed. Mirabeau was of a larger and stronger character than even Zoe. His genius mastered hers, and she felt it. He held her proud imperious nature in subjection, he kept her in a constant ferment. She was never quite sure of him, never at rest; and it was delightful to be so tormented!

A woman often loves a man who is her inferior in all things, but she never finds any comfort in it; she is constantly endeavouring to make him her master, but never succeeds; it is all obedience on the voluntary principle, and never compelled by the "right divine" of a monarch.

CHAPTER XIII

— · —

The boys grew and thrived at Hastings like young giants; but Zoe became every day more pale, thin, and unhappy. Lady Clara, with all her gaiety of temper and goodness of heart, began to find matters too *triste* and *ennuyeux* to be endured much longer. She tried to persuade Zoe to return home, and it was settled they should do so at the end of ten days, and in the meanwhile, Zoe continued her solitary strolls.

One dull-looking afternoon, such as autumn often assumes to prepare us for November and winter, Zoe put on her bonnet, and merely leaving word that she should not be absent long, turned her steps in her accustomed direction.

To people who are not happy, there is a soothing influence in the leaden hue of the sky, which seems one entire cloud;—the mild air which scarcely a breeze stirs, and the many tinted leaves that lie on the moist ground, giving an earthy and not unpleasing odour as they rustle and crush beneath the foot. An afternoon like this, is far more congenial to a state of mind like Zoe's, than a bright sunny season. However dull a day may have been, there is generally an attempt at brightness towards the close; if one were superstitious, it might comfort one's heart to see the bright streaks that break the sky to the west a little before sunset, when the sun shines forth between his prison bars, after one has given up all hopes of seeing him that day.

Zoe walked along listlessly watching the sun sink lazily behind a bank of cloud;—she had gone further than she intended, it was beginning to grow dusk, and in some haste she turned to retrace her steps homeward. Her attention was drawn to a figure on the cliffs above her;—it was that of a man, wrapped in a large loose riding coat. Zoe, though not a coward, instinctively quickened her pace, but by this time the individual had descended to the level ground, and was standing in the path immediately before her, apparently with the intention of stopping her way. There was no other passer by in sight, and she was at some distance from any dwelling. In the desperation of her fear, Zoe raised her eyes to the stranger, intending to make an appeal to be allowed to pass on, but she well nigh sank to the ground at the apparition she beheld, for it was Mirabeau himself who stood before her.

"Nay, madam, if I alarm you so much, I had better go away again," said he, in a mocking tone; "but it is late for you to be out alone. Allow me to escort you home."

They walked for some paces in silence. He was watching her intently.

"Zoe," said he again with more tenderness, "you are ill, you are sadly changed, you can hardly support yourself. Tell me what it is."

"Oh, how could you leave me as you have done for so long without a word.—Is it any wonder I am ill?"

A few drops of rain began to fall; he did not speak, but taking off his large cloak, he wrapped it round her, and seeing from her agitation she could scarcely walk, he passed his arm round her waist and almost carried her along.

"I have been a wretch," said he, at last, "but you shall be well again now that I am come back to you. Zoe, I never intended to make you suffer thus; tell me you forgive me, or I shall never forgive myself. Zoe, you are more to me than the whole world beside: I have been mad, angry, but that very bitterness showed how much I cared for you. But it is forgotten now, and we are again to each other all we ever were? Tell me, is it not so?"

Zoe did not reply in words, but Mirabeau felt her press the arm that was round her.

"Zoe, now that we have found each other again, we will never separate more; there is nothing for me in this world beside you: I will never grieve you again."

Zoe entered the house in a very different frame of mind to that in which she had quitted it. She made an excuse to Lady Clara for passing at once into her own room. She required to be alone, to think over the happiness so unexpectedly restored to her, and which she still almost feared was a dream.

Early the next morning, after breakfast, Mirabeau made his appearance, and remained some time, making himself as gentle and charming as mortal man could be. By daylight he was even more shocked at the change the last few weeks had produced in Zoe's appearance; but he quieted his conscience by thinking, "It is only nervous; and she will soon get better now."

A servant was once engaging herself to a "place of all work". "Pray have you any followers, young woman?" asked the mistress, "for I do not allow them." "Then I fear, ma'am, we shall not suit," replied the poor girl, "for there is a young man I have kept company with nearly seven years, and I should not like to give him up."

"You are going to be soon married to him then, of course?"

"Married!" said the servant, indignantly. "Oh dear, no, ma'am; such a thought never entered my head."

"Then what is it all to end in?" asked the lady, very pertinently.

Now if any one has asked Zoe what *her* "keeping company" with Count Mirabeau "was to end in" she would have been much puzzled to answer. In fact, she had never once thought about the matter; and it was with astonishment only to be equalled by the extreme naturalness of the inquiry, that she heard Lady Clara, as soon as the departure of Mirabeau left them alone together, say, "I had no idea you were so intimate with the count, Zoe. You never told me you were engaged to him; and considering that I have always told you every thing, I do not feel myself well treated; but I suspected something that day I came into the room and found him leaning against the chimney-piece—I don't know why. It has so happened I have never been in the way when he has called since. I began to think he had vanished, it is so long since we saw any thing of him. When did he come back?"

"He has been in Scotland," said Zoe, "and he startled me by his sudden appearance last night;—he met me in my walk, and brought me home."

"Oh-h," replied Lady Clara, "I see now why you went to bed without supper! But, my dear creature, will he be a good match for you?"

"Upon my word, Clara, he has never made me an offer yet."

"No! Then what does he mean?"

"I don't know; but really I have never thought about the matter."

"Then the sooner you begin the better. You are not a person to be trifled with.—But what do you intend?"

"Well," said Zoe, "to tell the truth, I have had a vague idea of being friends all our lives, but I have never thought of any thing beyond the present, and if you had not spoken, there is no saying how long it might have been before I had done any thing so prosaic."

"My dear Zoe," said Clara, very gravely, "you take me for a thoughtless, giddy creature; but, after all, I think I have more practical sense than you have. Unless you intend to become Madame la Comtesse de Mirabeau, he must not go on visiting you as he has done. Remember you do not stand alone: you are the guardian of your children. Count Mirabeau is a most wonderful man, but he is a more than questionable character; even if you marry him, your discretion may very reasonably be called in question, but terms of intimacy, except with that view, cannot for a moment be tolerated;—to talk of friendship for such a man is nonsense, unless, like the good old duchess, you had had a *tendresse* for the father, which made you patronising for the son. You love him, and now I have the clue to all that has perplexed me in you since we came here; and before Frederick's illness; in fact, ever since the night of the oratorio. You have been playing a most hazardous game, and it must go on no longer, either for your own sake, or the children's. Zoe, you know I care for you more than any other woman under the sun, and therefore it is, that I speak thus plainly;—you are not angry with me?"

"No," said Zoe, "not at all—but I never once thought about any thing, except seeing him."

"Would you marry him, if he asked you?"

"Certainly I would," replied Zoe, distinctly.

"You have, decidedly, every right to please yourself," said Lady Clara, "but it will not be a wise match for you—for him, of course, it will be every thing that is fortunate;—but whatever you do, you must not compromise yourself by going on any longer in this ambiguous style."

This conversation left Zoe uneasy and anxious, the shadowy romance of her connexion with Mirabeau was over. After being lapped in an Elysian dream, she had suddenly jarred against earth with a rude shock.

She felt the good sense of Lady Clara's observations. With persons of Zoe's character to perceive what is right, gives them strength to perform it. She suddenly was roused as from slumber, and saw whereabouts she was standing. She perceived there was a real world to be considered, of which she had been too long forgetful.

Matters came to crisis sooner than she anticipated. Two days after the foregoing conversation, Zoe, Lady Clara, and the two boys, were sitting over the breakfast-table on a morning of storm and rain. They were far from expecting a visitor, but the door bell rang. "That is Count Mirabeau if it is any one," said Frederick, "he always rings furiously, and he always comes when no body else would be admitted; he likes to make people do what they don't want."

Lady Clara laughed, but had no time to reply, for at that moment Mirabeau actually entered. He was restless and absent, and he had evidently something on his mind; he seemed impatient at finding the room full of people;—at the end of five minutes it seemed as if he could endure it no longer, he said abruptly to Zoe:

"My God! madam, do you intend to remain in the house all this fine day?"

The boys both laughed at this joke, as they thought it; but Lady Clara giving a malicious glance at Zoe, said to the boys, "Come, I want you to help me to pack some books, and if you will find my keys, I will give you the paints and brushes you were wishing for before breakfast."

"Oh! that is capital," said they both together, "you will spare us our lessons this morning, won't you, mamma, and let us be useful to Lady Clara?"

"Yes, yes," said Lady Clara, "you shall have a holiday, for I shall want you all the morning, so come along."

CHAPTER XIV

— · —

After the door closed, Mirabeau remained a few moments silent, gazing earnestly on Zoe, as he stood before her. "Zoe," said he, at length, "the time is come when you must prove whether your love for me is real. Last night I received news from France: I must return thither immediately; a career at last is opened, even for me. True prophetess that you are, you foretold this to me when I would have despaired. Now I come to ask you to share my destinies. I feel, I know, there are great things before me; with you to be my angel, my support, my counsellor, I feel strong to govern the world; with you by my side, I go forth to conquer and to rule. I am not speaking vain words of boasting—you know I am not. Zoe, till this moment I never knew how much I loved you, I never knew the hold you have upon me: without you, power and honour would be insipid and worthless. It is you who give all meaning and value to my life. Tell me you are mine, that you will go forth with me."

Zoe felt that the crisis of her fate was come. For the first time she had listened to Mirabeau in the hope of hearing something beside words of love. She was one of those who dare to look their fate into the very eyes:—it is only weak souls who trifle and seek delay. She crimsoned over face, neck, and arms; but she spoke in a steady voice as she said, "If it is to become your wife, Gabriel, that you are asking me, I am willing to do so: there can be no discomfort or danger to me where you are."

Mirabeau smiled bitterly, and tossed back his long shaggy locks. "Why," said he, sternly, "do you name Wife to me? Why do you speak to me of that cursed one? She has been one of those who have made me what I am, who have made my life the mad guilty course it has been. Yes, my wife was a fool, but she spoiled and ruined my existence. We are divorced, it is true; but divorce with us does not allow either party to contract new ties: till that woman dies, you cannot be my wife. You see that even to gain you I will not tell you a lie. But what! does your courage fail at the *first* sacrifice required? Does your love, after all, prove only lip deep? It is only great souls that have it in them to make sacrifices.—I thought you were one."

Zoe looked at Mirabeau for a moment, as if she doubted whether she heard him aright; then, when there was no doubt under which she might find refuge, when his meaning stood in all its audacity before her, then all her womanly scorn and indignation at the outrage broke forth, bearing down like a lava torrent all sentiments of love and gentleness; her lip quivered, and her nostril dilated, and all the pride of her nature flashed from her eyes.

"This, then," said she, "is the goodly fruit of the love you profess for me. You have known your position from the beginning, and now, when you believe me fluttering in your toils, when you believe that I love you as a weak woman, you come, and dare to propose that I should disgrace my children, stand forth to the world as an abandoned woman, and take my place in the ranks of the hundred other women you have loved and abandoned! If that be all the return—"

"Nay, madam," interrupted Mirabeau, "if you begin to talk of gratitude I must own myself a bankrupt; I was not aware you wished to drive a bargain. I can repay your sacrifices with nothing but my love; and that, it seems, counts for nothing when weighed against the loss of worldly consideration. I was a fool to believe you different to other women, to believe that you would have greatness of soul enough to *give* yourself to me. Women let themselves be taken, and then, pretty dears, think they avoid the sin and scandal by acting under compulsion. A woman's love is no compliment, she is the prey to whoever will take her; she feels no pride in belonging to you, she would have got up the same pride in belonging to another, the same love for any other who had courted her. No, you are made of the same stuff as all the other women I have known; but I love you, Zoe, with all the force of my soul; you possess me like a demon, and you shall be mine. You shall not drive me mad, and remain yourself in your cold and selfish safety; your whole being shall be molten into mine. You are worthy to be a portion of me, Zoe. I do not love with soft honeyed words; I love you like hatred—and hatred it will be if you oppose me. If you let me leave your presence now, I shall not go forth a despairing lover, I shall hate you, I shall despise you.—I shall never forget you, but I shall remember you with bitterness and curses, as one of those who have made my life a howling wilderness, as one who had the power to save me, and would not stretch out a hand, preferring to dwell in worldly respectability without me. And Zoe, you will never be able to forget me; you will think of this hour, but you will think of it with bitter and vain regret—and shame that, in this hour, when I had put my future fate into your hands to mould it as you would, you sat quietly calculating, and in cold blood could prefer yourself to me."

"Monsieur de Mirabeau," said Zoe, haughtily, "threats and taunts take no effect upon me. You are unjust, and you know it."

"Zoe!" said Mirabeau, in a voice of pity, "when I am no longer here the false strength that enables you to set yourself against me will fail:—who is there can supply my place to you? When I am gone, what comfort will you find in the consciousness that you have saved yourself and lost me? For if you fail me now, all hope of good is over for me. You have power to do with me what you will, to make of me what you will: you know not the extent of your power over me.—I never knew it till this moment, when my fate is trembling in the balance. Oh, Zoe, do not cast me out for ever. Think, what can supply your place to me? My place to you? For we love each other, Zoe. Think, when I was away from you lately, did your children fill up your heart? Did you find that the congregation of people, about whom you were perfectly indifferent, and who form what you call society and the world, could comfort you? Does their opinion weigh with you in such an earnest matter as this, when they would not, any one of them, have influence to determine the colour of your ribbons? Is it to the fear of what these might say that you sacrifice me and yourself? Oh, Zoe! I can supply the place of all these things to you; but pile up together all the small things in the universe, and will they outweigh me? Zoe, I do not taunt you,

I do not threaten you. You see I am gentle and humble; I can kneel to you, most humbly and reverently, as to an angel from heaven, and entreat you not to leave me, not to withdraw your presence from me. Oh, Zoe! no man ever loved a woman as I love you:—will you save your reputation at the cost of my happiness? Will you sacrifice me at the shrine of a word that has no substance—for a formula? Can noble self-sacrifice be a dishonour?"

Zoe sat all this time pale and motionless, only the convulsive grasp of her fingers round each other showed the struggle that went on within. "Gabriel," said she, when he had ceased to speak, "you can break my heart, and it is hardly worth while to put forth so much strength only to do that. You know, I love you;—if it were only myself at stake, I could not contend against you; I would sacrifice myself to you, though with my eyes open to the consequence; for when I had become a thing of no account, a woman dishonoured and cast out by the world, I should lose my power over you; I should become a degrading burden to you:—but, no matter, I would rejoice to become an outcast, if by so doing I could give you one moment's pleasure. You may beat down all my self-defences. I am your captive, helpless and submissive before you. I do not set myself up against you. If I did, I was wrong. But you see I am humble now, I own your power. But oh! in mercy try me no further.—I cannot be yours.—I cannot dishonour my children. I cannot leave them. I am not my own. I cannot give myself to you. You may kill me. I am dying now with this agony;—but I will not yield. I am theirs, I am their mother, and they shall not lose me. For the love of God! Mirabeau, be merciful and deliver me."

Mirabeau smiled scornfully.

"Certainly, madam," said he, ironically, "I will pain you no further by my presence; but I cannot deliver you from the consequences of what you do. If you love your children more than me, you are prepared to abide by the loss of my love. I have offered myself to you, and you reject me; you insult me, by preferring other objects before me. I will leave you with what you have chosen; but", said he, breaking out into a terrible and savage voice, "do you think I am one of those small creatures who swarm round you, who pretend to love, and, if rejected, can, with a look of folly, pretend to wish you well, and to become that neutral platitude—a friend!

Do you think that I—I, ever can, or ever will be, your friend! No; when I cease to love you, I shall hate you. Do not trifle with me. Choose, Zoe."

Zoe did not speak, she felt all turned to stone.

"Zoe! my Zoe!" said he, melting into a tone of unutterable tenderness; "pause one moment before you decide, before you throw me off for ever. I love you; oh, Zoe, you know not the world of meaning rounded into that word.—Oh, come along with me.— Make but a sign.—Look at me only, and I will stay."

Zoe sat with her head averted, and neither spoke nor moved. He retreated some steps towards the door, keeping his eyes still fixed upon her. Zoe felt every step fall upon her heart. Still she sat motionless, frozen with grief and terror. Suddenly he returned, knelt at her feet—cold tears fell from his eyes over her hands, his voice was choked and husky; "Zoe, for the last time, I implore you to speak."

Zoe shivered with agony, but she gave no sign.

"Then all is over," said he, rising, "and your love is a vain thing." He left the room; and, when Lady Clara returned some time afterwards, she found Zoe lying stiff and senseless on the floor.

CHAPTER XV

— · —

Zoe remained so long in this rigid deathlike state, in spite of all means used to restore her, that Lady Clara, in great terror, sent for medical assistance. The doctor, when he arrived, pronounced it a species of catalepsy, the effect of some great shock, and under that stilled exterior, the powers of life were working to destruction; he seemed apprehensive of a fatal result—or, at least, that the crisis would be attended with some terrible struggle. After lying many hours in this life-in-death state, the chains that held her seemed gradually to relax; she did not become, at once, conscious of what was around her, but tears streamed from her still-closed eyes. Her breathing became regular, and her senses were unlocked from the strange torpor that had enthralled them. She was, however, as weak as an infant. She recognised Lady Clara, who had never for a moment quitted her; but she was unable to speak above a whisper; at length, she fell into a gentle sleep, which continued for some hours. In a few days, she was apparently in her usual health, but so unnaturally still and quiet, that Lady Clara was far from feeling easy on her account.

They left Hastings, and returned home, so soon as Zoe could bear the journey. She went about as usual, and engaged in her accustomed occupations; but she never made the most distant allusion to what had passed between herself and Mirabeau at their last interview. Once Lady Clara said something about her recent illness, but Zoe shrank in evident pain; "Not yet, not yet," she said, "sometime you shall know every thing; but there are some wounds we do not look at, even to dress them;—let me alone a little while longer.—I am not insensible of your true friendship, though I seem so cold."

Thus the winter passed. Lady Clara gave up all her own plans, that she might remain beside her friend, and seemed to have forgotten all her own private store of hopes and fears. All that was frivolous or thoughtless in her character disappeared before this appeal to her better nature.

The little O'Brians had left Richmond whilst they were at Hastings. A letter from the father, containing grateful thanks, most gracefully expressed, for all the attention they had received from Zoe and her friend, seemed to have closed their intercourse with the family.

Early in February, the old Duchess of N——, who had taken a great fancy to Lady Clara, insisted upon her coming to stay a short time with her, to assist her in doing the honours to a large party of visitors she was expecting. Zoe would not suffer her to refuse, and she went.

The weather had been stormy, and for more than a week past no visitors had been near Zoe; but the very day after Lady Clara's departure, a carriage drove to the door to Zoe's great annoyance. She, however, with the nervous vacillation induced by her state of health, could not resolve to deny herself till the moment for doing so was past, and the visitor, whoever he might be, had been admitted. The Reverend Horace O'Brian was announced by the servant. For Clara's sake Zoe exerted herself to receive him cordially; she inquired after the children, and expressed her regret that Lady Clara should be absent. His manners were abrupt, and he was in evident agitation which deprived him of his usual graceful urbanity. The conversation on ordinary topics soon flagged, for Zoe was too weary to sustain it. At length, by an evident effort he roused himself. "I am on the point of departing for Italy," said he, "on account of my daughter Susan, who has been ill, and is ordered to a warmer climate. I come to you—I am come to ask—Mrs Gifford I know you think me a heartless scoundrel—and no wonder, for I have been one. Men make excuses to themselves for that sort of thing, and pass them lightly over with a jest; but no man ever acted as I have done, and felt his heart at ease after. You know too well to what I allude. Till I became free again, I knew not how I had cherished the image of that gentle angel. I know she is lost to me for ever; but I can think of no one else; all other women seem coarse and trifling beside the memory of her.—I shall never marry again.—I wish you at least to know the sincerity of my regret for the past. You mentioned Lady Clara—she is all a woman should be, gentle, and good, and fascinating in every way; but I am now expiating a fault committed long ago.

"I might have been happy with Clotilde, but my cursed vanity, my selfish worldliness, made me mad and blind—and now that another woman, every way too good for me, is within my reach, I cannot take the blessing offered. Mrs Gifford, we can never escape from the evil of our own faults. It pursues us years after they are committed. I have not trifled with your friend—do me that justice at least; but you do not know how hard it is for a man to check himself, to measure his words, to refrain from the society of a fascinating woman. I could not leave England without some explanation to you. I must have seemed inconsistent. I never have dared to let your friend see how much I valued and admired her; my words would have borne a meaning to her that they did not to me. Therefore it is that I seemed so cold and contradictory. Now that I am going to Italy, I must see Clotilde once more. Do not gainsay me, for it will be in vain. Tell me in what convent she is buried."

He spoke rapidly, his words were broken and unconnected. Zoe in vain tried to discourage him from his project of seeing Clotilde again;—she was fearful of unsettling her, and she felt by no means sure that her religion would prevent a relapse into an earthly sentiment;—it certainly was a very hazardous experiment, and she was, besides, terribly disappointed at poor Clara's prospects. But Horace O'Brian was too impetuous to listen to her reasons, he was too earnest, and she was too weak, to contend with him. She gave him the name of the convent of which Clotilde was now the abbess, and asked whether she should write and prepare Clotilde for seeing him.

"No," said he, "things always arrange themselves better than we can scheme them. I have already intruded too long upon you; I must now go. If you mention this visit to your friend, I wish you also to tell her the high respect I entertain for her. I am fully aware of all her worth. Now, madam, farewell! I am deeply grateful for the patience and consideration you have shown for me."

He bowed and left the room.

Zoe mused for some time, considering whether it would be better to tell Lady Clara all that had passed. On the whole she decided merely to mention his visit in general terms. His departure for Italy would prevent her nourishing any vain hopes; and, moreover, if Clotilde went through the ordeal preparing for her, in the way Zoe anticipated, then in the ordinary course of things, the Reverend Horace O'Brian would take the good yet within his reach and be much happier than he deserved with Lady Clara, who, as he truly said, was a great deal too good for him;—and, in the meanwhile, there was no use in vexing her with an account of his revived love for Clotilde. Horace might make the confession himself, if ever she were destined to hear of it.

CHAPTER XVI

— · —

It was the hour of recreation in the convent of Santa———. The sisters were all assembled in the garden; but the reverend mother (such was now the style and title of the gentle, unassuming Clotilde) sat in her pleasant parlour alone. The few years that have passed since last she appeared before the reader, have made a great change in her appearance. She is no longer the timid, unformed girl; her form has developed and matured to a fullness of womanly beauty; a self-possession and gentle dignity have taken the place of her former shrinking manner: the habit of directing the proceedings of others gave this, for though her sway was gentle, she was too conscientious not to be firm. No unruly passions struggled within her bosom to disturb its holy serenity—all earthly thoughts were dead, she lived in her religion; earthly hopes and fears had ceased to touch her sympathies. There was nothing austere or ascetic about her; but her thoughts constantly fixed on the mysteries of the unseen world, the communion of saints, gave a holy imaginativeness to her daily life. Love of the infinitely holy and true, as embodied in the doctrines and devotions of the Church, satisfied all the yearnings of affection, without the alloy of trouble and unrest that attends those who invest their love in earthly objects. She thought of the one great trial of her young life, her dream of passion for Horace O'Brian, as of a temptation from which she had been delivered, through no power or merit of her own, and she looked with feelings of humility and gratitude on the happy tranquil lot appointed for her in its stead. On this day she was sitting at her open casement, looking into the garden where the nuns and novices were walking. She was interrupted by a lay sister, who came to say that an English gentleman and two little girls were in the reception room, and wished to see her, for that he brought her tidings from home. Clotilde rose immediately, and proceeded to the convent parlour. The Catholic Church thoroughly understands all that is graceful in costume, and the robes for both the clergy and the religious orders are the perfection of arrangement in drapery.

The black flowing robe, falling in ample folds to the feet, the veil floating over the head and shoulders, and the fair young face of Clotilde peering out of the white plaited wimple, made a beautiful picture. If she had studied for a century, she could not have devised a more becoming costume than the one in which she now made her appearance to Horace O'Brian. She recognised him at once. A slight tinge passed across her cheek at the unexpected sight of him who had been so much to her, but it was a blush at the recollection of her former weakness. It passed instantly; and with her own sweet voice she said, "This is very kind, Mr O'Brian, to take so much trouble to bring me news of my dear friends at home. When did you see my mother? How are my brothers? You cannot tell me too much about them."

Horace O'Brian was abashed and confused; he had not settled in his own mind what he expected to see, and he felt something very like awe, before the sweet, grave, tranquil face that now appeared to him. The two children had shrunk behind their father, and peeped at her with timid, wondering eyes;—she was Miss Gifford still, and yet not Miss Gifford; they did not dare to approach her in that strange black dress;—and then of late, they had been accustomed to the quick lively manners of Lady Clara.

"Ah, you have brought me the dear children once more! You do not know how glad you have made me feel. But have you forgotten me, my darlings? and will you not come and play with me again? I have a beautiful garden here, and we will build another castle for the doll."

The little ones ventured from their hiding-place. She took them on her knee, and they soon became as friendly as ever.

"We have got another doll since we saw you, a very large one with wax hands and feet—and we have learned to read, and to say hymns too; may we say some to you?"

"You will tire Miss Gifford," said their father.

"Tire me!" cried Clotilde. "Oh! if you only knew the joy it gives me to see them once more. They are grown like little angels."

Horace thought this a very good sign in his favour, and he said, "Perhaps you will let them go and see the garden, for I have many things to say to you."

Clotilde gently inclined her head in token of assent, and turning to the children, she said, "Will you come along with me, my darlings?" At first they did not like leaving their papa, but on his promising to wait till they came back, they took courage and went with "Miss Gifford", as they still called her.

"See what I have brought you!" cried she to the nuns who gathered round, themselves like so many children. The little O'Brians were handed from one to another, caressed, feasted with all the most delicious *confitures* of the convent, and showed so many beautiful things, that they soon became quite at home, and were contented that Clotilde should leave them for a while, to return to their father.

"Now," said she, with a smile, "let me hear all your English news; the dear children will be very happy where they are for a short time."

Horace O'Brian told her of Zoe's illness, about her brothers, and about a visit he had recently paid to his Rectory at Sutton—but he was *distrait* and troubled, as he gazed on the gentle creature before him. His narrative was by no means consecutive or lucid; Clotilde had to gain her intelligence by many questions.—Horace was reminded of his singular behaviour, only on perceiving the mild surprise that appeared in Clotilde's blue eyes, at his contradictory statements about the age and number of Marian's children. "Clotilde," said he, in an agitated voice, "it is in vain for me to attempt to converse on other matters, till I have eased my conscience by asking your forgiveness. I am come to Italy for no other purpose. Tell me are you happy;—then, at least, I may be once more at peace with myself."

Every thing that was passionate and tender beamed in the eyes of Horace;—the tones of his voice were soft and earnest—but what once had power to move her whole soul, now failed in its magic. She looked at him steadily and calmly, whilst she said,

"For what have you to ask my forgiveness? You never did any

404

thing to need forgiveness from me. And why do you ask whether I am happy?—Can you not see yourself that it is well with me?"

"Then, Clotilde, have you altogether forgotten me? I confess with bitter shame, that I deserve it at your hands, but I had still dared to hope differently. I am free—my wife is dead—or I would not have dared to appear before you; and those children are once more motherless."

Clotilde looked perplexed and slightly troubled. "Oh, Clotilde!" cried he, "if I had formerly listened to your voice, I should have been wise and happy now. Clotilde, do the angels interpose in our behalf when we have once rejected them? At least, my children have not sinned against you. Take them, bring them up in your own presence, make them good and pure like yourself. Clotilde, will you grant my request?—Will you take my children and educate them?"

A mild pleasure beamed from Clotilde's eyes, as she said, "Oh! this is beyond all my hopes! but are you indeed in earnest? You have not embraced our holy faith?"

"No," said Horace, "I have lost Heaven, it is no matter now what comes to me; but take my children, and make them like yourself."

"And did you indeed come to Italy to have these precious children brought up in the only true way? Then indeed have my unworthy prayers been granted! Do you know, I have said prayers constantly for you and these darlings to the Blessed Virgin, and Father Bernard, our holy confessor, he also has prayed for you; his heart will rejoice to hear these tidings!"

"I care for no prayers and no rejoicings save your own, Clotilde," said Horace.

"But I am not Clotilde now," said she, "I am called the Mother Angelique."

"Then you are an angel now, both by name and nature," said he, warmly.

"When will the children come? I feel impatient till we have them."

"To-day, to-morrow, when you will," said Horace, "but you will let me visit them."

"Whenever you please," replied Clotilde, "at the visiting hours."

"And you will promise that I shall always see you?"

Horace received no reply to this request. Possibly Clotilde did not hear it, for her attention was drawn to the children, who at that moment reappeared laden with treasures, and wild with spirits; they both began talking at once to their papa of all they had seen. "And we are to come again, papa, to hear the nuns sing in the beautiful chapel! Oh, how I should like to stay here always!"

"Yes," said the other, "if papa might come too.—Will you ask him, Miss Gifford?"

"Miss Gifford has invited you to come to-morrow to stay with her, and she says I may come and see you. Will that do, my queens?"

And so it was settled. The children with their father departed, and Clotilde was left once more alone:—And what were her meditations? Was her tranquil bosom agitated with the blind tumult of earthly feeling? Had the sight of the only one she had ever loved, rendered her unfit for the discharge of her sacred duties? No. Clotilde had passed once for all, into a higher, purer region— where the storm of passion cannot come nigh. She went into her oratory, where she returned thanks for the miraculous answer to her prayer in these children being once more placed in her care.

CHAPTER XVII

— · —

The little O'Brians came according to arrangement, and were installed in the convent as boarders, all the inmates vying with each other which should do the most towards spoiling them. Clotilde, however, took care that a certain portion of lessons should be gone through every day. And certainly, whatever might be Horace O'Brian's motive in consigning his children to the convent, he could hardly have done a wiser thing; for the practical example of the subdued temper, the meekness and gentleness, of the daily life of Clotilde and her nuns, did not fail to have a most beneficial influence upon them, which lasted all their life. When they were fairly settled, their father—whether he really felt inclined to go the journey, or whether he wished to try the salutary effect of a little critical absence in re-awakening the tenderness of Clotilde—certain it is, that he left Rome with a party of friends to make a tour through the southern parts of Italy, intending also to cross over into Sicily.

It seemed as if Clotilde's tranquil life was destined about this time to suffer nothing but invasions. Scarcely had Horace departed, when she received a letter from Zoe, not written in her usual bold, decided characters, but faint, uneven, and almost illegible; it was to say that she was ill, and that she and the boys were on the point of starting for Italy, and would take up their abode with Clotilde, if she could receive them. "A dear and most kind friend will accompany me," said the letter in conclusion, "one who has been more than a sister to me; you must take her in also. I have suffered much, dear Clotilde, and it may only be a sick fancy, but it seems as though with you I should find peace and healing. I am restless and oppressed till I find myself once more with you." Clotilde's tears fell over this letter; she knew how utterly bowed down the heart of her mother must have been before she could have written thus. She lifted her eyes to the image of the Virgin: "Oh, Holy Mother," cried she, "intercede for her, that her heart may be open to receive the only true consolation provided for us. Amen."

The nuns, who dearly loved a little gentle bustle and excitement, were delighted to hear of the expected visitors, and every hand in the convent was busily employed in decorating and preparing the rooms for their reception. The little O'Brians were scarcely less enchanted at the prospect of so soon seeing again their two playfellows, and longed for their father's return, that they might tell him all about it.

At length, after various delays, Zoe and her party arrived. The passage had been stormy and tedious, and Zoe was so weak on her arrival, that she had to be carried from the carriage into the parlour. Clotilde was much shocked at the change in her proud and beautiful mother; she was obliged to leave the room abruptly, in order that Zoe might not be agitated with seeing her emotion.

The little O'Brians carried off the boys, to show them all the wonders of the place; Lady Clara, who had ever been unremitting in her attention to Zoe, assisted her to undress; and when she was laid on her bed, in the bright picturesque-looking room, taking a hand of Clotilde and Clara, she said with a smile, "I am come to get well here, and I must do that before I can repay your kindness." It was the strange gentleness and submissiveness of Zoe's manner that affected Clotilde more than even the change in her appearance.

Total change of scene, however, soon wrought a beneficial influence on Zoe's health and spirits. So long as she remained at home, where every object reminded her of what had been, where the very trees seemed to nod their heads and mock her as she passed along, it was hardly to be expected that, with her best efforts, she could avoid sinking deeper and deeper in despondency. But we are creatures of time, which wears down all our sorrows; example, too, has a strange magnetic influence over us, almost like sorcery; and the regular occupations, the tranquil habits of all who surrounded her, after the lapse of some weeks, wrought Zoe into a more healthy frame of mind, and the apathy in which she had been wrapped melted away.

Zoe looked on Clotilde with wonder, and something not unlike envy.

"Oh that I were altogether such as you are!" exclaimed she one afternoon, as she lay on the couch in Clotilde's parlour, watching her employed in preparing linen and bandages for the hospital. "What good has my life done to myself or any one else? What profit has there been in all the intellect and beauty on which I so foolishly and vainly prided myself? When I was a child I used to fancy I would do great things, and now my life has nearly passed away, and I am thus."

"Dearest mother," said Clotilde, laying down her work, "all these gifts must seem wasted unless they are dedicated to the highest uses, not to our own glory. He who bestowed them, He alone can find due employment for them; He is the only being whom we may securely love, whom we may venture to serve with all our soul and strength. In Him alone can we safely put our whole trust. Do not think me presumptuous in speaking to you; they are not words of my own wisdom. You know how once I suffered when I was in the world. Well, I found no consolation until I submitted myself to Him, made my will and wishes His—believing them, feeling them to be the best, though I had suffered so cruelly from them. And oh!" said she, raising her eyes, "believe me, no happiness from gratified wishes can be half so sweet as that which follows the submitting of ourselves to Him who is the Highest. They are not mere words I am speaking, as you would know if you would only once sacrifice your hopes and fears to Him, and wait in peace." The tears streamed down her cheeks as she spoke thus, but they were not tears of unhappiness. She came up to Zoe, and putting her arms round her neck, said, "I seem to love you so much more than ever I did, since you were in sorrow."

Zoe kissed her fair forehead, but she made no reply.

The little O'Brians came running in, to say that their papa was come home, and was waiting in the parlour. Lady Clara, who just then entered with a vase of flowers, hit it against the table, the vase was broken, and the flowers fell all around. She was looking at Clotilde, and so was Zoe. Clotilde quietly began to gather up the fragments and the fallen flowers, saying, "Perhaps, Lady Clara, you will go and receive Mr O'Brian, ask him to come here and take an English tea with us; but are you well enough to see him, mamma?" continued she, turning to Zoe.

Nothing but the most perfect unconsciousness was to be discerned in Clotilde's manner.

"I should like to see him of all things," said Zoe.

Lady Clara departed on her errand with a heightened colour, whilst Clotilde quietly repaired the confusion occasioned by Lady Clara's accident.

Horace O'Brian's temper had apparently been ruffled by some untoward occurrence, for though he followed Lady Clara into Clotilde's parlour, he looked sulky and discomposed; he scarcely paid any attention to Zoe, merely making a few slight inquiries after her health, and her journey, and showed some anxiety to know how long she intended to remain. To Lady Clara he was almost rude, and to Clotilde, from whom, however, he hardly removed his eyes, following her slightest movement, he was cross and abrupt; he made no attempt to keep up conversation, but seemed all along to labour under the idea, that he was a singularly ill-used person. After sitting for about a quarter of an hour, he rose to depart, declaring that he had an engagement.

"When will you come again?" asked Clotilde, kindly.

"Whenever you will ask me."

"Well, then, come to-morrow."

These few words seemed to restore his good-humour as if by magic. He spoke quite affectionately to Zoe, and entreated that she would allow him to take her eldest boy to ride with him the next day, on a beautiful English pony he had brought over for his own daughter; and promised to fetch him. He departed without noticing Lady Clara—till he reached the door, when seeming suddenly to recollect himself, he turned round, and said negligently, "Oh, good night, Lady Clara, I beg your pardon."

Zoe saw Clara go to the window, trying to repress the tears that started to her eyes.

"Do you like your children to have any thing to do with horses?" asked Clotilde, when Horace was gone.

"Oh, yes," said Zoe, "I wish them to become good horsemen."

"I am very nervous about horses," said Clotilde, "and I do not like the idea of his going out."

The next morning Horace O'Brian was at the convent early, and brought with him, not only the pony for Frederick, but another horse with a lady's saddle for Zoe. After a little persuasion, Zoe consented to accompany him, and they set off. Lady Clara watched them depart, and then sat down, burying her face in her hands, and cried bitterly. Clotilde looked at her with compassion. She saw exactly how matters stood; she could almost have smiled, to think that it had fallen to her lot to comfort another, under the same trial that had once been almost heavier than she could bear. She wondered how it was she had become so indifferent to one who had once been so dear; and then she sighed, to think of all poor Lady Clara must be suffering. On passing to the table where she usually sat, she was startled to find a letter addressed to herself; and her surprise gave way to indignation and horror, as she perused the contents. It was nothing less than a mad declaration of love from Horace O'Brian! who, driven to desperation at finding no chance of a private interview, had taken that method of making known his passion. It was the letter of a man perfectly beside himself; every thing that regret, despair, and mad wild passion could dictate, was uttered with an eloquence that might have won admiration, had it not excited shame and horror in the bosom of her to whom it was addressed. It seemed to Clotilde that she was committing a sin even to read it; all her ideas of purity and sanctity were cruelly outraged. Our dearest wishes often seem like judgments when they are granted to us after the first heat of desire has passed over. So it was with Clotilde: she sat for some time undecided what course to pursue; then, passing into her oratory, she despatched a message requesting Father Bernard to come to her directly. The old man speedily obeyed her summons, for he expected to hear nothing less than that all the English party staying within the convent walls had suddenly got converted, in answer to the "Novena" he had caused to be put up for them. His celestial castles in the air were destined to be rudely overthrown. His horror on receiving Clotilde's communication was scarcely inferior to her own. He first gave her the absolution she earnestly craved for becoming acquainted, however involuntarily, with such a sacrilegious proposal—for we omitted to say, that Horace proposed that Clotilde should abandon her convent, and fly with him to England, and there become his wife!

"We must be careful how we deal with this wild, bad man," said the old priest; "if we drive him beyond bounds, he will remove the dear children out of our hands, and then who will save their precious souls? We must pray that this mad passion may be overruled to good. You have influence over him, and you must use it."

"I, Father!" exclaimed Clotilde. "I can never see him again."

"You must constrain yourself, my daughter; remember, it is in a good cause you are working; you must overlook your own feelings, when it is a question of saving souls to the glory of the Church. I will be with you, and stand beside you, whilst you speak."

"And that poor Lady Clara," cried Clotilde, "who loves him so much; why cannot he love her, and marry her, as he ought to do?"

"The Devil is the author of confusion and every evil work," rejoined Father Bernard; "but we may yet baffle his malice, if you are earnest and faithful."

Clotilde remained for some time longer in her oratory, endeavouring to calm and prepare her mind for the task before her.

She was disturbed by a confused noise, very different from the stillness that usually pervaded the place, mingled with shrieks, and the trampling of hurried feet coming towards her room. Immediately afterwards, a violent knocking came to the door; on opening it, a crowd of nuns, pale, agitated, and breathless, told her, in phrases hardly intelligible, that the pony, on which Frederick Gifford had that morning gone out to ride, had just galloped into the yard, covered with blood and foam, without its rider! Sick with horror, Clotilde hastily descended, and there found all as she had been told. Half-an-hour of the most agonising suspense followed. Vain hopes and useless conjectures wearied every heart. Father Bernard went forth to see if he could obtain intelligence, but every moment seemed to increase the agony of fear. At length, a group arrived at the gate. Clotilde hardly dared to look—suspense seemed at that instant more tolerable than certainty. When she ventured to raise her eyes, she saw Horace on foot leading his horse by the bridle and supporting Frederick. At length all were assembled in the parlour, and Frederick deposited on the sofa. Horace O'Brian clasped his two little ones to his bosom, in a transport of thankfulness; Zoe knelt beside Frederick, with her arms round her other son, looking with intense anxiety, as Clotilde and Lady Clara examined him to see what injury he had sustained. Beyond a few bruises, he was unhurt; no bones were broken, nor was there any serious contusion. The doctor just then came in, and confirmed their report. The revulsion of feeling was almost too much for Zoe—she burst into tears. The doctor administered some medicine to the boy, and he was removed to bed, with orders to be kept quiet for the remainder of the day, and then there was leisure to give an account of all that had happened.

This accident prevented every one from thinking of their own private embarrassments. Lady Clara was too busy about the child to think of Horace; Horace was, for the moment, too much engrossed by his own children, to think of Clotilde; and Clotilde was too much engaged in thinking about every body else, to have any thought to spare for her own situation.

"Oh, Clotilde," said Zoe, "till I saw my child lying, as I fancied, dead before me, I never knew how much more wretched I might be. Oh! how thankless and selfish I have been, to feel unhappy, when both my children are left to me! I feel now as if I never could be sufficiently thankful!" She followed Lady Clara out of the room to go to Frederick—for she could not bear to have him out of her sight. The other children would not remain quiet, unless they might see all that was going on, and they soon crept out of the room. Horace and Clotilde were left alone.

If Horace had ever dared to hope, one glance at the severe and majestic gravity of her countenance undeceived him. He was dismayed to recollect his reckless audacity, and stood silent and confused before her. Clotilde was the first to speak;—"Mr O'Brian," said she, "I have seen the letter you wrote to me, and placed upon my table. It is not an outrage upon me alone, that you have committed;—you have been guilty of an act of sacrilege; and you have caused me to be guilty of sin, in becoming cognisant of it, though, thank Heaven, it inspired me with nothing but horror. You must never come within these precincts again—depart at once. I would not wish to hate any one, but the very sight of you is painful."

"Oh, Clotilde, Clotilde!" cried he, "pass any sentence upon me but that; I was mad, frantic, to dream that you would stoop from your purity to such a wretch as I; but do not bid me depart; you have all power over me, I submit myself to you. I will do any thing, so you do not utterly banish me. Pardon, pardon, on any terms, if not for my own sake, for the children's."

"It is not fitting that a worm like me, should arrogate a power that belongs alone to your Maker!" said Clotilde, austerely. "To please me, is not the motive from which you ought to act. Oh, bethink you of your high calling, and rouse yourself to more worthy actions! If I could speak one word that might be the means of enkindling in your heart, thoughts and feelngs such as behove a man, who will one day have to give an account, not of himself alone, but of those committed to his care. Oh, for very shame, rouse yourself and consider, whether it is fitting for a man who has the care of souls upon him; who look to him for their guidance in this world, and their knowledge of the next; to be giving loose to unruly desires and effeminate emotions!—Is it a light thing to have the blood of all these souls upon your head?"

Horace O'Brian actually trembled before her rebukes. "Tell me," said he, submissively, "what you would have me do?"

"I would have you", replied she, "return to your own land, and fulfil the duties imposed upon you by your station. I would have you consider something higher in life than self-pleasing; study something more noble than self-indulgence."

"Oh, I will do this, and more than this; there is no penance I would not thankfully perform to appease you;—but tell me that you do not utterly despise me."

"What am I," rejoined Clotilde, "that I should dare to despise any one? But I can think of you with no complacency during your present course."

"Oh, tell me—may I hope to become worthy to have a place in your thoughts? Will penance and amendment avail?"

"Become what you ought to be, and you will attain something far better than any approval I can give."

"But will you keep the children till I can worthily claim them?—

Till you yourself believe they will be as well with me as with yourself?"

"I will do so, if you wish it," replied Clotilde, hardly able to repress the joy this proposal gave her. "But now, you must depart, and return no more."

There was an air of majesty in her command, that Horace did not dare to disobey;—he retired from her presence as from before a queen. Clotilde fell on her knees before the image of the Virgin, and returned thanks that the heart of Horace had been moved to let the children remain with her.

Horace, without taking leave of his children, or seeing any of his friends, departed the next day for England. Clotilde's words seemed to have struck some hidden chord in his heart. His eyes were suddenly opened to a sense of his own worthlessness—a feeling of humility sprang up in his heart for the first time;—he became alive to a sense of the requirements of his position in life, all slothfulness and love of ease, were burned out of his heart. From the day on which he left Clotilde's presence, he became a different man. The image of Clotilde became to him that of a saint, and stimulated him onwards in his course of well-doing.

A renovating moral influence seemed to distil on all within the sphere of Clotilde; her gentle example told on all around her.

Zoe roused herself from her torpor of sorrow, and felt that life still retained claims upon her; a desire to exert herself, to work at something, no matter what, arose within her breast. Her boys had already lost much time, and she now became impatient to return home, to the occupations and duties that lay for her there. After a sojourn of three months the whole party prepared to depart. The little O'Brians, however, still remained with Clotilde, as they had not been claimed by their father.

CHAPTER XVIII

— · —

When they arrived in England, Lady Clara proposed to leave Zoe, and go to her own home; but Zoe entreated her so earnestly to remain with her, to make up her mind to live with her, that Lady Clara, albeit very doubtful of the abstract wisdom of taking up her permanent abode with any dear friend, suffered herself to be persuaded. In fact, when it came to the point, she could not bear the thought of leaving Zoe, between whom and herself many points of union had arisen; sickness and sorrow knit the hearts of friends together as no communion of happiness ever does.

It was determined that the boys should be sent to Eton till it was time for them to go to college.

Zoe received no tidings either of Mirabeau or Everhard. A fatality seemed to hang over her lovers, whereby they were, at what threatened to be the very crisis and climax of fate, spirited away from her into silence and space. Clotilde would have said it was her guardian angel who interposed, but we doubt whether Zoe would have been of the same opinion.

The memory of Mirabeau, however, faded like a dream, or like the passing away of a fierce tropical storm; he retained no practical influence over her, he did not modify her character. He had roused her strong passionate nature, but as the storm sank to rest, so did the recollection pass away. It was singular, that the more she occupied herself with her boys, the more the memory of Everhard was reawakened in her bosom; he had always associated himself with her in all her interests, in all her occupations, and she now found herself constantly referring to his opinion, to his judgment, to things that he had once said, to counsels that he had formerly given; so long as the boys remained, they formed a bond between him and her. Mirabeau, who had impetuously refused to divide his interest in her with any other object, who had sought to concentrate every one of her thoughts and feelings in himself, had left no trace of himself now that he had passed away. There remained no community of interest between them. He had never given her his confidence about his own affairs; he and his doings had always been shrouded in mystery, which perhaps had not been without its effect at the time; but it was not the basis to build on, to endure absence.

Zoe found herself constantly referring to Everhard, to his opinions, to his works. It was not love she felt for him, she was too wearied and exhausted now for passionate emotions; besides, Everhard had long since ceased to excite them: it was a tranquil affection, a firm and trusting friendship, that strengthened day by day. She felt as sure of him and of his love for her, as if she had never parted from him. She felt sure that he would not only forgive her passion for Mirabeau, but that he would have allowed her to talk of it to him, as to her most indulgent friend; for she knew that Everhard loved her, and not himself in disguise. After all, either a man or a woman might be very proud of inspiring such an affection, though it says a great deal for their strength that they can endure it, for they must love without the hope of being beloved again. Some people have the faculty of enduring the rack with more fortitude than others.

One day, towards the latter end of July, the old duchess (who was now very infirm, and scarcely ever stirred from her home) came to see Zoe, and spend the day with her. After she had been placed in the most comfortable place in the sunny morning-room, seated in the large easy chair (for which Clotilde had embroidered a cover), with a table beside her, and a cushion under her feet, the old lady found herself quite at her ease, and proceeded to take her tatting out of her work-bag: at the same time she handed a letter over to Zoe, and lifting up her spectacles said, "There, my dear, I have brought this letter because I want to know what it is about, and I cannot read those cramp foreign handwritings; it is from our old friend Count Mirabeau; he always writes as if he were in a rage with his pen and ink, and had not patience to form his words. Just make it out to yourself first, and then read it to me, will you? It came several days ago, but I have not been able to get to see you before, and now I am become quite impatient to hear it."

Zoe started as if a serpent had stung her. All her recent tranquillity vanished, and left a sensation of hurried pain and baffled desire: she did not attempt to speak, but taking the letter, went to another part of the room. There was not much in the letter beyond an account of his election, and the flood of triumphant success which poured in upon him. She had to read it every word, and to listen to the old lady's commentaries, and her own personal experience of elections, and wherein English elections differed from French ones, till she was almost mad with the irritation. Her own name occurred in a postscript: "I hear Mrs Gifford has been ill, but no doubt she is recovered by this time, for she is one of those strong, cold souls who will hold both death and hell at bay, and make terms with them (*parlementer avec eux*); such women are more wonderful than lovable." In another part he said, "It is not triumph alone that I seek; there are a thousand revenges in all I am achieving." A few words immediately following the sentence were effaced. Zoe's senses were in a tumult; all her old feelings for Mirabeau once more broke their bounds: she was overpowered by the bitter, sarcastic tone in which he named her; she saw how cruelly, how unjustly he judged her; and she was almost mad with agitation. How the remainder of the day passed she knew not, but it seemed as if it would never end. She at length was free to taste the luxury of being alone in her chamber, where she might weep as long and bitterly as she pleased.

It was many days before she recovered from the effect of the letter; but time never was faithless to a sufferer yet: there never yet was one whom he did not console.

An unexpected event turned Zoe's interest into another channel.

One fine morning the Reverend Horace O'Brian made his appearance. He was shown into the drawing-room, where Zoe was sitting alone. After a few very awkward attempts at conversation, he blushed, and inquired whether Lady Clara were within, and whether he might have a few moments' conversation with her. "So it is coming at last," thought Zoe, "now that poor dear Clara has schooled herself to be resigned without him. But whenever one's wishes are granted, it is always just when we have become indifferent whether we obtain them or no." She did not say this aloud, of course; she only gravely answered, that she "would go and look for Lady Clara". She had too much feminine sympathy to allow her friend to come in until she had made herself look as well as possible.

When Lady Clara entered, Horace O'Brian was seized with a very edifying and becoming sense of diffidence, as to whether, in spite of all favourable symptoms, he might not have been making himself rather too sure of her.

It was with manly and unaffected candour that he entered into a statement of his bygone errors, he did not in the least attempt to extenuate his former behaviour to Clotilde, nor did he disguise his madness and rashness when in Italy; but he told Clara, how long he had known her worth, and how sensible he had become of her attractions, and concluded by declaring that she held his happiness in her hands, and he said the most charming things in the most irresistible way. He assured Lady Clara, that she was without a rival in his breast, for that he loved her as entirely and devotedly as her perfections deserved, and then he made an appeal to her on behalf of the children; in short, he was perfectly in earnest, and very anxious about the result, so of course the reader may conclude, that he left nothing unsaid, or unlooked—for looks in these cases are more effective than words. Some people may think that Lady Clara was sadly deficient in "proper womanly spirit", as it is called; we are very sorry if such was the case, but we cannot falsify truth. Lady Clara had long loved Horace O'Brian, of late it had been very hopelessly, and now that he came to her with a declaration of his own attachment, and a candid avowal of all his former errors, it was not in her nature to stand out for a punctilio; she never once thought about either her "spirit" or her "dignity". What she said, never exactly reached us, but Horace O'Brian was grateful and happy. Zoe sent the dinner away three times, before any one appeared to eat it—and yet Lady Clara was ungrateful enough to complain that it had been sadly hastened that day! Zoe sympathised warmly and thoroughly in her friend's happiness, and quite forgot her own affairs. There was no necessity for any delay. Six weeks from the day on which Horace O'Brian had declared his love, Lady

Clara became his wife; and never was that magical ceremony performed over two people, who more confidently believed it would bestow the most perfect ideal of human happiness.—If happiness be the natural result of logical premises, Horace and Lady Clara had no reason to fear disappointment.

Horace could now boldly claim his children. He wrote to Clotilde a history of all that had befallen him: in conclusion, he said, "If I am become in any wise a better man; if I am at all deserving of the happiness that has fallen to my lot, it is to you, to your precepts, to your example, to your influence, that I owe every thing."

The joy of Clotilde's heart may be imagined, but it was a terrible trial to part with the dear girls; however, she had the satisfaction of hoping she had grounded them in the principles of her own religion; but her loving soul was torn to lose them, many tears were shed on both sides, and the promise of "coming again very soon", consoled neither party.

Both Horace and Lady Clara were surprised at the great improvement visible in the children. They were much grown and developed in every way; Lady Clara said they reminded her so much of Clotilde in their manner, that it was like being in her company; and perhaps she never had said any thing for which Horace felt so pleased and grateful.

After this, events flowed on in an even, continuous course. Zoe always spent some weeks in every year with the O'Brians.

After the usual time spent at Eton, her eldest son proceeded to Cambridge, where he distinguished himself highly. The youngest boy showed a decided predilection for the sea, and nothing else would satisfy him but entering the navy.

CHAPTER XIX

— · —

One day in early spring of the year 17——, a stranger was seen passing up the steep ascent that led to Gifford Castle; his dress and appearance had something ecclesiastical about them. He did not seem old; but he had the look of an athletic man, worn down by ill health. His hair was nearly white. There was a look of calm, stern composure on his countenance, which would have amounted to austerity, had it not been for a pair of large lustrous eyes, that seemed like wells of soul and feeling.

He passed along, and turned into a private path, with which he seemed well acquainted. It was overgrown with grass and briars, so as to be almost impassable; but it led at length to the castle door. He walked on like one in a dream, seeing nothing, yet conscious of every thing. He rang at the hall bell, which sounded with a shrill and startling echo, as of a place where no one dwells.

The door was opened after a short time; the servant started back in joyful astonishment, mingled with doubt.

"Can it be you, Father Everhard, come back to us?"

Everhard, for it was he, was startled in his turn. "I did not expect", said he, "to find any one here who would remember me. I understood that all the family were from home."

"So they are, sir, only me and my wife, we live here, and keep things in order a little. The garden must seem to you a sad wilderness; nobody has been here since they came back from Italy. But won't you walk in, sir, and perhaps you will condescend to sit down in our room, it is the only place that has a fire in it; and my wife will be overproud to set her eyes on you again. You may remember her, sir; she was a young slip of a girl when you were

421

here, whom my lady took from the hamlet, and brought up and taught herself."

The room into which the loquacious servant ushered Everhard had formerly been Gifford's study. Everhard would have given the world to be alone. A chill suffocation, as from a tomb, struck on his heart. He seemed to be farther from Zoe, standing there in that desolate room, than he had been during all the years of his separation from her.

"Maybe Father Everhard would like to be by himself, as he goes through the rooms," said the woman to her husband, hardly knowing why she said so. Everhard bowed his head in assent; he could not trust himself to speak.

"The doors are all unlocked, sir; I open the windows myself every day when it is at all sunny."

Everhard went first into those rooms which had been common to the whole family—the chill, deserted aspect was not in them so intolerable.

At the door of Zoe's boudoir he stood trembling and agitated, as if it were her actual presence into which he was about to enter. The light blue hangings had not been removed, but they hung faded and moth-eaten; nothing that he could identify with Zoe remained, except the actual chairs and tables, which stood stiff and tarnished against the walls. The whole room, which had formerly been so redolent of beauty and grace, was now like a corpse that has been embalmed: the actual lineaments indeed preserved, but all that made the beauty and the soul departed. The singing of the birds, and the rustling of the trees, contrasted strangely with the stillness of the deserted room. The window was open, and he looked forth: the view from it was the same in all the great outlines, but all that had endeared it to him had passed away.

Zoe's flower-beds were so overgrown with weeds and grass, that scarcely a trace of them remained: rank, luxuriant vegetation, giving the idea of waste, not fertility, had obliterated all marks of the "trim gardens" that had once bloomed there. Several lilac and laburnum trees grew almost into the window, and were heavy with their luxurious flowers. The trees were everywhere bursting into leaf, the air was laden with spring odours, the sea was shining and glittering in the distance, and small fishing-boats, with their white sails, were sailing about in all directions.

It was on such another day, that he last walked in those gardens with Zoe. He stood as in an oppressive dream; the minutest incidents of that day came fresh into his mind, as if they were written in a book; the weight of memory was intolerable. A groan that burst from the very depths of his soul, was the only utterance of his dumb anguish.

He had been standing for he knew not how long, when he was roused by the voice of the housekeeper, and he perceived that the shadows were beginning to lengthen.

"Dear heart, sir, I feared you were taken ill, you were so long by yourself, and I made bold to come to you; it's a weary thing to come back and see the place so changed; the house though is in pretty good repair—the ceilings are all water tight, except just one of the attics; to be sure, the grand drawing-room has got sadly mildewed, and every day I expect to see the damp begin to show itself, on the fine painted ceiling; the gold of it is all blackened as it is. Maybe, if you are going up to London, you would just tell my lady, that it is a pity to let such a fine property go to a wilderness, and all for want of a little paint and whitewash; I am sure I have done my part, and slaved night and day to keep things decent, and I hope you will say so, sir, to my lady, if she asks any questions. I do my duty, sir, for I wish nobody to be wronged.—But, sir," she continued, seeing that Everhard did not look as if he knew what she was saying; "my husband and I thought it would be a shame to let you go to the village, you that used to belong here, as I may say, so we have done up what used to be the library, and made it more comfortable like, and I have made bold to get a bit of dinner, and it is quite ready, if you will please to come and eat it. These rooms are all damp, and I doubt but you will have been staying in them too long."

Obeying her gesture rather than her words, Everhard followed the chattering housekeeper into the library, where a good fire had been lighted—an arm-chair, and a small table, spread for dinner, had been drawn close beside it.

Everhard had not yet been into this room.—The books had all been removed, but the pictures that Everhard well recollected, still hung in their old places; and much of the heavy furniture had been

423

brought in from the other apartments, so that its appearance was much more comfortable than might have been expected.

The bustling housekeeper soon returned bearing in a fowl, that had been killed and roasted whilst Everhard was indulging in his meditations; her husband followed with a bottle of old port wine (for he had fallen legitimate heir to all that had been left in the cellar at the breaking up of the establishment).

"I hope, sir," said he, respectfully, "you will take the will for the deed; if we had had more notice, we might have managed better."

Everhard roused himself to thank the good people for their attention, and to please them put something on his plate.

They left him to finish his meal alone; but as soon as the door closed behind them, the woman said to her husband, "He is not long for this world, poor gentleman; there's death in his face."

"He seems changed since he came in, to my thinking," said the man; "where was he when you went to him?"

"In madam's sitting-room—her *boudoir*."

"Ay, I thought it would be so; he was always fond of missis; we all knew he came to see her, and worshipped the very ground under her feet."

"Lor! I always thought he was such a good man," replied his wife.

"And do I say he was not? you fool!" said the husband, angrily; "he was fond of missis sure enough, but he never said or thought any thing that all the world might not know, that I'll stake my life on."

"Why, how do you know?"

"Because I watched them when they little thought of it."

"Poor gentleman!" said the sympathetic housekeeper, "no wonder he should be so cut up at seeing the old place look so like a wilderness, as if nobody cared about it."

Everhard remained plunged in the chaos of his own sensations, the events of that day had utterly overwhelmed him. His head ached and throbbed—his veins seemed filled with fire;—he felt as if he were going mad. The housekeeper entered to remove the things.

"Why, dear heart, sir!" she exclaimed, "you have neither eaten nor drank; is there any thing else you could fancy better?"

"No, no, my good woman, I am sorry to have been so much trouble; bring me some water if you will, for I have a burning thirst. Have you any writing materials in the house?"

"My husband has some white paper, I know; but whether it is such as the like of you can write upon, I can't say."

She presently returned with some pens and coarse paper. "I did not think", said she, "that cold water would be so good for you, so I just made you something that will be better for you, if you have the fever on you."

Everhard thanked the good woman for her attention, though he felt it somewhat oppressive, and again he was left alone.

The desire to approach Zoe, to commune with her, was a necessity if he were to live. He could not rest: he paced up and down the room. At length, taking up one of the candles, by a sudden impulse he went towards the chapel. Some of the pictures still hung against the walls; and the altar-piece that Zoe was putting up the first time he saw her, was still in its place. A ladder, that had been brought for some accidental purpose, and some workmen's tools, stood so as to remind him forcibly of the aspect the place bore on that evening. There are certain superstitious feelings to which all those whose emotions are excited are liable; they seem worse than childish when repeated, but they are phantoms that the heart alone can raise. Everhard's agitation was calmed;—he felt a strange certainty that Zoe must soon be in that very spot again. That chapel was the only place that seemed to speak to him of the past, without desolation. When he returned to the library, he wrote to Zoe. Words and tears were equally intended for the relief of man: both have healing in them.

"Zoe,

"I am in England, I am here, why are you not here? I am farther from you in these your accustomed places, than I have felt during all the time we have been separated. There is no need to tell you that you have been my thought day and night;—you know it. You know that you have been the life of my life:—that you have kept me from all sense of ill. I have walked overshadowed by your presence;—but now—now, that I am come back to your accustomed places, and find you no longer where I always found you before, I sink under the sense of your absence. I cannot endure again what I have endured to-day;—Zoe, I must see you. Come to me. Come here. You know that I have endured, you know that I would have died before I would have caused you one perplexed thought, but now, I can struggle no longer. I must see you again. Oh! you know not, you cannot know the fierce unslaked thirst of absence. Come to me, my one beloved, and do not delay. The hand of death is on me; I am only come to England to die. This is no vague presentiment; the sentence of death is within my heart, and I have a very short time before me. My unutterable yearning to behold you, to hear once more the sound of your voice, is mightier than death. I cannot, I shall not, die till you come. The end, which has shown me the worthlessness of every thing else in this world, has made you more unutterably precious. Zoe, I have not spoken to you for long years. You do not know all you have been, all you are, to me. I could not have spoken and lived apart from you. I durst not break the silence in which I had frozen myself up. Do not, my beloved, think me cold; there are no words into which my love can form itself. My love has been life itself; and only now, that I am dying, can I speak of it at all. But it will not depart with life—I take it out of this world with me. Zoe, my beloved, when I am no more here, let it console you to know that you have never given me one moment's pain; you have never said or done one thing I would wish recalled. You do not need that I should say this; but let it remain for you on record, that when I can no more tell you how much I have worshipped, no thought of doubt or remorse may come near you; for I know the terrible light that death casts on our past deeds to the most tenderly treated friend, and I would spare you that anguish. In no one respect would I have wished you to be other than you have been. I have never had a shadow of doubt or distrust of you—not for one second. I *do* indeed 'know all that is in your heart'. Your last and sweetest assurance has never failed me!

"So long as you could by any possibility be compromised, I have refrained from even wishing you to be near me—but death swallows up all things except love. Come to me then, and let me die here. The shadow from Death's presence has already fallen upon me. When we are called to die, it is the most solemn act of all we have to transact under the sun—it gives a tragic dignity to the pitiful details of life. It is to no joyful and tumultuous reunion that I am bidding you. I call for you to stand beside me on the brink of the unknown darkness into which I am about to plunge. I ask you to come with me to the threshold of the Infinite. When I enter, I must loose your hand, but come with me so far;—it is the only desire I have; for dwelling near to death, quenches all vain wishes. You are the life that I must resign. You are the secret of all that has been worth any thing in me, and I would have you visibly present when I resign you; be the *last* object on which my eyes rest.

"Zoe, I shall seem cold to you, and yet it is my very soul that speaks; but all meaning seems to have gone away from words; there are none that will tell you all I want you to know. Zoe, I love you; my whole being is rounded in that one word;—my heart thirsts with an overwhelming longing to hear once more the sound of your voice. I fear I must depart without it;—the dark depths open to receive me,—the weight of eternity is upon me,—I stand at the juncture of the mysteries of life and death. Oh! come to me before I depart hence!"

Everhard did not seal this letter; he left it intending to add something more definite about himself the next day before post-time. The next day, however, he was unable to leave his bed, being delirious with fever. The surgeon from Minehead was sent for; he was the son of the surgeon who had practised there when Everhard lived at the college. He was a skilful man, and the housekeeper was a careful nurse, but the fever increased in spite of both.

Everhard's strength had previously been so completely under-mined, that he had no chance of recovery from the first. Indeed, the surgeon said that even if this attack of fever had not come on, he could not have lasted many weeks. The man and his wife took counsel together on hearing this, and with much pain and care, the man wrote what he considered a very proper letter to his lady—for he had, as we have seen, the idea that his mistress and Father Everhard were more to each other than appeared to the world—and he would on no account permit the surgeon to write.

CHAPTER XX

— · —

Zoe was dressing to go with her eldest son to a large dinner party at the Duke of L——'s when a letter was brought in to her that contrasted strangely with the silver salver on which it was handed. It was very dirty, and had been folded and refolded many times before it had been finally reduced to shape, and the red wafer came half over the back.

"Dear my lady, that is not fit for you to touch, it is some petition I suppose; I should not wonder if we all got some disease some of these days from those nasty things; there is no other lady who would meddle with them as you do."

The torrent of the Abigail's eloquence was suddenly stopped by perceiving that her mistress had fallen back into her chair, pale and rigid, her eyes fixed on the crumpled and dirty letter which had so much excited her wrath.

"Oh! dear, my lady, do not look in that dreadful way. What is the matter; no bad news I hope?" She deluged Zoe with Hungary water and essences, looking all the while with curious eyes hoping to discover the mystery.

In a few moments Zoe regained her self-control, and telling the woman that she would be obliged to go from home immediately, she ordered her to make the needful preparations. She then sat down and wrote a few lines to her son, enclosing the letter she had received to account for her hasty departure, and in less than an hour she was on her way to Gifford Castle. She travelled without delaying a moment, except to change horses. One thought absorbed her, one feeling swallowed up all others—the devouring anxiety lest she should be too late.

It was the evening of the next day before she arrived. "Am I in time?" was all she could articulate to the old servant who came to the door.

"The doctor is with him, ma'am.—This way please." Zoe was hurrying up stairs hardly knowing where she went. "I will go and tell the doctor you are here."

He left, and Zoe paced up and down in uncontrollable agitation. The doctor entered after a few moments, which to her had seemed hours; he started at her pale and agitated appearance.

"Is Father Everhard still alive? Can I see him?" she asked, in a voice scarcely articulate.

"Alive, certainly, but in a state of stupor that will only terminate in death. Your seeing him would do no good, he would not be sensible of your presence; if he should recover his senses for a few moments, which is just possible, you shall know. I will watch beside him, and if there is a change I will send for you."

"Then there is no hope? He is dying!" cried Zoe in an accent of despair. The doctor shook his head sadly, and turned away.

After he was gone, all Zoe's hopes and thoughts centred on the chance of being summoned to see him, for she felt if she could only hear his voice once more, she could bear the shock of losing him; the hope of seeing him kept the other evil in the back ground.

She listened to each noise with an intensity of anxiety as if every sense was absorbed in that of hearing. She sat with a strange unnatural patience, expecting every instant a summons. At length a step approached the door—the doctor entered—one glance at his face was enough, she saw that all was over, and fell insensible on the floor.

It was long before she recovered her consciousness, and then it was only to relapse into a succession of fainting fits. The agitation and fatigue of the last two days had exhausted her frame, and she was for several weeks unable to rise from her bed.

Her son, who arrived two days after her, was indefatigable in his attentions, but as he did not know the secret of her interest in Everhard, he was utterly unable to account for the passionate burst of emotion with which she received the account he gave of all he had done to show respect to the memory of his father's old friend;—neither could he make out why the death of a man whom she had not seen for years, should afflict her so much more than the loss of her husband had done; but members of the same family are generally the last people in the world who draw inferences, so Zoe had neither question nor surmise to annoy her.

The first day she was able to leave her room, the old servant man sent a request to be allowed to speak to her. He entered somewhat embarrassed by the sense of his consciousness of his mistress's secret.

"I have made bold to bring you, ma'am," said he, in the most respectful manner he could assume, "what few things were about poor Father Everhard.—I sealed them up myself, and nobody has seen or meddled with them but me. He was writing nearly all the night before he was taken ill. I have kept the portfolio safe too; you will judge best, ma'am, what you think right to be done." He placed the portfolio on the table, and retired.

To Zoe it seemed as if the dead had risen from the tomb to say farewell. Hitherto she had shed few tears, but now she wept long and uninterruptedly.

On opening the packet, she found the miniature and broken chain, which had so long been Everhard's companions. In the portfolio was the unfinished letter, addressed to her; with which the reader is already acquainted.

Zoe reappeared in the world, for life subdues us back to its occupations and even to its amusements; they who live cannot dedicate themselves to grief. Zoe's position in society was a conspicuous one: her eldest son was not married, and Zoe was at the head of his establishment. If worldly prosperity could nourish the heart, Zoe was prosperous beyond the lot of women. Her eldest son had entered Parliament, where he distinguished himself; his house was the resort of all the distinguished men of the day. The radiance of Zoe's beauty had faded, yet she commanded more homage now in the decline of her life, than she had done when she first appeared as a young beauty.

Her youngest son rose in his profession, and was several times mentioned in the "Gazette" with honour.

Some time after Everhard's death, Frederick Gifford (the

Member) married his old playfellow, Susan O'Brian, now a lovely young woman;—her sister went to Italy after the marriage, and became a nun in Clotilde's convent. It certainly caused some scandal that the daughter of the Dean of——should be a Catholic and a nun; but that did not hinder the Rev. Horace O'Brian from being made a bishop after all. As he grew older, his character matured and improved, and Lady Clara had no reason to repent her love and constancy to him. They had a large family, but Horace brought none of them up to the Church, which, considering all the patronage he had, spoke highly for his unworldliness. The friendship between Zoe and Clara continued without any break during their lifetime.

Zoe was neither insensible nor unthankful for all the blessings of her lot—she went through life with a composed and chastened spirit. But life is no holiday game; they who live earnestly are weary enough at their journey's end—they rejoice when the time comes to rest from their labours.

> "The mildest herald by your fate allotted
> Beckons, and with inverted torch doth stand,
> To lead us with a gentle hand
> Into the land of the great departed,
> Into the Silent Land!"